Cam & Beau

Cam & Beau

A Novel

Maria Cichosz

NON
CANADA

Copyright © 2020 by Maria Cichosz

All rights reserved. No part of this book may be used or reproduced
in any manner whatsoever without the prior written permission of the publisher,
except in the case of brief quotations embodied in reviews.

*Publisher's note: This book is a work of fiction. Names, characters, places and
incidents are either the product of the author's imagination or are used
fictitiously, and any resemblance to actual persons living or dead
is entirely coincidental.*

Library and Archives Canada Cataloguing in Publication

Title: Cam & Beau : a novel / Maria Cichosz.

Other titles: Cam and Beau

Names: Cichosz, Maria, author.

Identifiers: Canadiana 20200255967 | ISBN 9781989689073 (softcover)

Classification: LCC PS8605.I217 C36 2020 | DDC C813/.6—dc23

Printed and bound in Canada on 100% recycled paper.

Now Or Never Publishing
901, 163 Street
Surrey, British Columbia
Canada V4A 9T8

nonpublishing.com
Fighting Words.

We gratefully acknowledge the support of the Canada Council for the Arts
and the British Columbia Arts Council for our publishing program.

For my friends in the city of Toronto, as it was in that crazy golden time. I'll never feel that way again.

I want to change systems: no longer to unmask, no longer to interpret, but to make consciousness itself a drug, and thereby to accede to the perfect vision of reality, to the great bright dream, to prophetic love.

Roland Barthes, *A Lover's Discourse*

1. Cam

Silence itself—the things one declines to say, or is forbidden to name, the discretion that is required between different speakers—is less the absolute limit of discourse, the other side from which it is separated by a strict boundary, than an element that functions alongside the things said, with them and in relation to them within over-all strategies. There is no binary division to be made between what one says and what one does not say; we must try to determine the different ways of not saying such things, how those who can and those who cannot speak of them are distributed, which type of discourse is authorized, or which form of discretion is required in either case.

Michel Foucault

One

It was in the lobby, its oppressive bright expanse opening before me, that I began to feel a sudden and powerful need to get fucked up. I wanted to get away from this hospital, from Beau. I wanted a drink. I wanted fifty drinks of the strongest, nastiest, most toxic alcohol available. I wanted to drink them all and then drink some more until my body screamed at me to stop, please stop. I wanted drugs, the bad ones from the Health Canada subway posters that made the girl in the triptych progressively more scraggly, scab-faced and punk-haired, the ones inspiring the tantalizing question passed off as ad copy: *Drugs, do you know where they'll take you?* Some chemicals that would core out my brain, yeah. I wanted these inside me and I wanted them quick, wanted them working before my mind had the opportunity to fully register anything else. I wanted to be fucked up, outside of myself, unconscious. I wanted everything—cigarettes, booze, whatever it was Cliff took when I wasn't around. Oh, I wanted it.

"Do you want me to take the streetcar back with you?" I asked.

"No, I'll be okay," he said. "I'm gonna walk. I have to think."

I have to get fucked up, I thought. I have to put chemicals in my brain.

Beau must have seen some part of this unsuppressed desire in me. I imagined it was reshaping my face. I imagined I looked hungry. "Are you okay, Cam? Will you be okay?"

"Yeah, I will. I'll catch up with you later." Except I won't, because I'll be fucked up.

"Don't do anything stupid."

"What?"

"Like your hand. Don't do anything like that."

"Okay."

In a sudden and uncharacteristic move he took my recently healed hand in his. "Promise you won't."

It was hard to speak because my throat was thick with something wet. "No, no, I promise."

He squeezed my hand and let it go. "I'll see you," he said, smiling just a little, "later, okay?"

"See you, Beau." I wanted him to know I'd be fine. Even though I was going to get fucked up. I took a few steps back and we kept watching each other until he finally turned around and started walking down University. I stood and watched him get lost in the throng of people at College, clutching at the delicious electricity pooling in my right hand. It almost made me follow him, its charge licking away at my fingertips. He was tired, he needed to rest. He needed to shore up his resources for the coming hardship, lull his body into acceptance. I needed to get fucked up. There was no good that would come of me following him now. Give him space, take your space. But that spark in his fingers, oh.

I stood for a moment in the grey noonday light, breathing in the dry air, coating my lungs with frost. My hand, tingling, had found my phone in the pocket of my pants. Now I was texting Cliff saying, *hey are you around?*

He got back to me immediately, the phone buzzing in my hand, warm with potential.

yeah what are you saying?

you wanna chill for a bit? My hands shaking as I typed in the message.

Buzz.

yeah for sure.

It wasn't hard to get a hold of Cliff, or to end up on his couch with my fifth (maybe sixth?) beer in my hand, clearing away the desperate copper tinge that had settled near my tonsils as he asked me what I wanted to *do*.

"I don't know," I said. "What have you got?" Everything was beginning to feel far away, unimportant. Numbness pooled in my face, my feet. I closed my eyes with the pleasure of it.

"You wanna do some coke?"

"No, better than coke."

Cliff pulled out a cigarette and lit it, sucking down a third of the clean white stick in one drag. He offered me the pack and I took one, lighting it from the burning end of his. I didn't think, just put it to my lips and pulled pulled pulled. The smoke flooded my lungs, thick and nauseous, and I coughed it all out, hacking away at a bunch of phlegm in what felt like the deepest recess of my chest. It only took the nicotine a second to hit my brain and I felt woozy but tense.

"You never smoke," he said.

"Never," I agreed, and took another drag. It was horrible and burned all the way down and I made myself hold it for a moment. This disgusting government-regulated chemical depositing illness in the back of my throat, yeah, that was what I needed. I smoked it down to the filter, stubbing it in Cliff's ashtray with a flick of my wrist. I felt that this act, this smoking of my only cigarette since the first one in the concrete yard of my high school, this breach of my bodily integrity, was just the right thing. Let it burn, let it poison. Smoke it all down, yeah.

Cliff stared at me, amazed. "Whoa, easy there, bud. How do you like that?"

"It's awful," I said, and he laughed. The desire for more poison coloured my vision.

"They grow on you."

"Yeah, it's called addiction," I said, at which he laughed long and hard and lit another. He held out the pack again and I took a second though the buzz in my head from the first was overwhelming, sickening. I smoked weed every day and never imagined my lungs blackening, but I imagined it now—nice and crispy and charred, yeah. I dragged deep and coughed again. It was what I wanted, to feel sick like this, poisoned like this. I needed more more more.

"You know what we could do?" His eyes lit up like a showroom. "You would like this, Cam. We could have some emm."

Emm. I knew he meant M, MDMA, but to me it sounded like an intimate murmur, an affectionate name for a well-loved girl, Emily. He could have offered me smack and I would have taken it, arm out and ready. Shoot me up, bud.

"Oh, yeah?" I finished my beer and then it was time for number seven. I thought. I couldn't believe how sober Cliff looked. I realized Cliff must drink tons, more than I could fathom. He must drink legitimately toxic amounts.

"Yeah, you'd love it. It's like the best weed you've ever had but a million times better."

"How would I feel?"

"Happy, really happy. Excited, ready to do shit."

"Yeah, okay, let's do it. What is it, a pill?"

"Usually." Cliff stood up, shuffling around in the kitchen, and came back with a big Ziploc bag. He threw it on the table. It was full of off-white powder, powder that was almost brown. Like brown sugar, really. "I just have it loose though. It's really pure, eh, this stuff. My friend from Western, he's in pharmacology, he just dropped it off for me. What do you think?"

I laughed, coughed. Somehow I was holding a third cigarette. Or was it my second? It must have been my third because there was no way one could have burned for so long. I was drunk, wasn't about to get less drunk. Yeah, emm. Let's have this fucking fabled emm that everyone always goes on about. "I think yeah, yeah let's do it."

Cliff clapped his hand on my back, hard, obviously pleased. All right Cam, yeah. He brought out a little square mirror and laid down four short lines of the brown sugar, the *emm*, two for him and two for me. I looked at them the way you look at a big roller coaster, a drop from a tree, a precarious gap between stepping stones in a river.

"You know how to snort? Eh, don't worry, watch me. We'll roll up a bill," he said, producing a twenty from his wallet and rolling it into a tube between his palms, "and just cover up one nostril and breathe in through the other. Once you feel it in your nose it'll burn a bit, eh, but suck it in deeper until you feel it in your throat, okay?"

I nodded, watched Cliff lower his head to the mirror and expertly suck up both of his fat lines, sniffing in profoundly and wiping his sleeve across his nose. "Ah," he said, sniffling up something watery, "just do it like that."

I took the bill from him and brought it to my nose, testing out the feel of it against my skin. My heart was beating fast but not too fast thanks to the seven (eight?) beers glowing in my stomach.

"Don't sneeze or snort it out if it feels weird because you'll scatter it everywhere," Cliff said. Wise counsel.

Somehow, incredibly, I was leaning over the mirror, index finger over one nostril while breathing in as hard as I could through the other, dollar bill pressed too tight against my face. It hit my flesh hard, exploding beneath my eyes, making them water, itching madly while I struggled to suck up the other line.

"Snort it back, snort it back," Cliff said, and I did, feeling the chemical hit the back of my throat. It tasted like baking powder and pharmacy, crumbled travel-sized Tylenols. I immediately felt and understood the drip—like the cavity in my head was a cave full of stalactites, little drops of water dribbling down to form spectacular geological formations.

"Whoa," I said. I felt it immediately, vast rushes of something (*euphoria?*) taking over my head.

"Crazy, right?" Cliff was still sniffling and I saw that I was too, that the amount of mucous that had suddenly formed in my nose was disgusting.

"*Yeah*, but *fuck* that burned."

He laughed, pounding his hand on my back. "It'll pass in a bit, but whoa, look at you, eh? Snorting it all up like a pro."

"*Yeah*," I said, suddenly in a fantastic mood, suddenly in a mood to agree with absolutely everything Cliff might say.

"Look at that *snow*. We should go outside and enjoy the snow, hey?"

I looked outside where it was definitely snowing, big soft flakes tumbling leisurely past Cliff's window. It looked magical, like the Coke holiday commercials with polar bears and penguins. I couldn't believe it was suddenly snowing. I checked the clock on the wall and it told me it was three-fifty—no, four-ten.

I felt I had lived a hundred thousand years since morning and expected it to be dark, expected it to be late night and dead. The alcohol, the drug, made time stretch out into long shining pools. I felt timeless, out of time. The time on the clock was obviously wrong. It was obviously arbitrary.

"Eh, Cam?"

"Wow, this emm." A great wave of pleasure lifted me from my seat and took me to the window, where I peered out to find the entire world frosted with what could have been vanilla ice cream. "It's like the fucking *North Pole* out here," I said. "Let's hurry up and get some shoes on."

We forced on our shoes and coats and ran down the stairs, taking two at a time. Cliff missed a step near the bottom and jumped down to the door, steadying himself against the entrance glass. We laughed wildly, and then he pushed it open in a burst of cold air that led us, finally, outside. The drug was coming on very strong.

"This snow is *fantastic*," I said, taking in the dizzying sky and the cold cold air that clouded just *delightfully* from our mouths. I thought of nothing but the snow coming down, the feeling of it on my face. "Wow, this *emm*." I knew it was the thousandth time I'd said it but couldn't believe that little bit of powder had put me into this sprawling headspace.

"I know, it's good right?"

"I just wanna fucking, *move*," I said, jigging across the sidewalk, back and forth.

Cliff grabbed hold of my arm and busted a move and then we were fully dancing it out, our limbs moving in uncoordinated, intuited ways that felt so *good* with this bubble of pleasure in my brain.

"Fucking, dance it out!" Cliff said.

I thought of how ridiculous we must look to people passing by on their way home for the day and laughed. "Do you want to—"

"Go fucking, dancing?"

"*Yeah.*" It was the best idea in the history of the world. Going *dancing*. A great wave coming from within me and behind me all at once buoyed me forward, propelled my feet down the sidewalk. The feeling of the bottoms of my soles on the pavement, cold rubber treading, mediating between my suddenly lively feet and the ground, was incredible. I could have walked a hundred thousand miles.

The trees were lovely, all cushioned with falling snow, the world insulated. Sounds fell short in the muffle and the sky was turning that big city orange. With the bite of crisp air in my lungs I almost couldn't stand the beauty of it. A great yearning built in my chest and I breathed deep. It was like the city had decided to unravel around me in its stretched potentiality and cradle me at the same time with all its edges so soft. Cliff lit a smoke and asked me if I wanted one and I said *yeah*, the sharpness of the tobacco *delicious* in the cold.

"I feel," I said, the wave rising right to the top of my skull, "like seven million *dollars*."

"I'm loving your energy right now."

"Wow, this emm is something *else*." In the sudden radical clarity bringing the world into focus I understood I could never do this drug with Beau, because the sight of his small solid frame or his sure stance or his delighted, self-satisfied laugh would send my heart spilling out of my mouth. Beau *Larky*, ah. The thought of him with his big winter hair and the angle of his neck as he shook it out from under his toque sent bursts of warmth through me, set off fireworks in my head. I am so in *love*, I thought, then looked at Cliff to make sure I hadn't said it out loud. I am just brimming with it, sloshing all over the place. I was fantastically sloppy and this made me laugh.

My phone buzzed in my pocket, all warm potential. Reaching into my pants I felt the exaggerated excitement of receiving an unexpected text—who could it *be?* It filled up my skull and of course the text was from Beau, his strange perfect name in an envelope on the screen, so neat. The buttons were slow with cold, the display frozen with digitized afterimages that couldn't clear away fast enough. *hope youre okay*, he said.

"Beau *Larky*," I said, this time out loud, coming to rest against a big maple. I was debilitated.

Cliff stopped beside me, rocking back and forth in his shoes, toe to heel, heel to toe. "Beau Larky?"

"Just texted me." I slipped the cold phone back into my pocket, undone by the thought of him smoking on the couch in his pajamas, worrying. About *me*.

Starbursts.

"Is he coming dancing?"

"No! But I am."

Cliff slapped my back really hard and we collapsed into a fit of laughter, holding onto each other's shoulders. "You're such a good friend, Cliff!" I said, the thought working in reverse, formed as I said it instead of the other way around. "Even though you're my dealer." Horrified at the way I'd said it, the way it must sound, but not really. I laughed again. "I don't mean it like that! You know what I mean."

He caught me in a headlock and ruffled my hair hard. I was surprised my toque managed to stay on, and this too was impossibly delightful. "I know, I know," he said. "You're not bad yourself, eh."

It was seven on a Wednesday, so there weren't really a ton of places we could go, but Cliff usefully remembered that it was Bluegrass night at the Silver Dollar Room, where we took advantage of their bathroom to snort back two very liberal lines of emm each that made my nose drip and itch and my head swell with generous good will. "Whoa," I said, as Beau did when he was extremely impressed. I imagined Cliff must have vast mental lists of every possible place one could go to get wasted in the city on any given night. Why didn't I go out with Cliff more often? "Here's to us getting wasted more often," I said, sloshing back one of the various shots and glasses Cliff kept setting down in front of me. Somehow my sleeve was wet, the vast wooden table we'd seated ourselves at was wet.

"Let's *dance*," Cliff said, standing up as he downed a shot of something clear.

"Okay!" I said, now remembering why we'd come here—because we'd had the greatest idea ever. My sober self would have never, in a hundred million years, gotten up to dance with

Cliff at the Silver Dollar Room when the band was just only warming up and everyone else in the place was seated with a drink in their hand. But my drink was in my *system* already, blending fantastically with this incredible *emm*. I saw why they called it your *system*, the electric energy flowing out of my head and into my limbs making this abundantly clear.

We were definitely the only ones dancing, our bodies liquid with the emm, though I didn't realize this until much later. I was pretty sure I was doing my weird trance-grunge thing, feet glued to the floor while my body moved in a way that was absolutely *correct*. It was wonderful. Cliff had long hair, almost down to his shoulders, and it stuck to his forehead in strands as he headbanged with relish, eyes closed. I didn't think about anything except the beat, now of the band starting up, and the warmth radiating through me, like I had an oven at my core. A couple of girls in shiny dresses joined us at some point, reservedly dancing near us and then with us, which I thought was fucking *great* because absolutely everyone should really get out here and feel this music.

Cliff was like a box of gears, shifting from one mode to another with little warning. He was dancing with one of the girls, inching closer and looking involved, and then he was grabbing my wrist and pulling me to the bar for *shots, man!* I reached into my pocket and then into my jacket and all my pockets again to find that I'd lost my wallet somewhere, probably while we had been running and kicking through the falling snow, laughing madly. "I lost my wallet," I told Cliff, and he laughed and then I laughed and then we were laughing again and it was irrelevant where the worn leather thing might be. Tomorrow I would be sober and I would cancel my credit card and whatever else, get a new student card, a new driver's license. Tomorrow in the sober daylight, yeah. For now it could sit under piles of snow and get wet, get found, get used, whatever. It could all freeze and that was okay.

That was when things started to get really hazy. I had small, ecstatically clear moments of awareness, like Cliff offering me another (another!) hit of emm and me saying, yeah, yeah definitely, but when I snorted it from the driest part of the bathroom sink I could find my nose bled and I felt sick. I wiped away at the blood, just a thick little drip, really, with the brown paper towels that felt like unprocessed wood pulp on my skin. I filled my palm with some lukewarm water from the tap and brought it to my dry mouth, swallowed. The water felt good and I had another couple swallows before heading back unsteadily, bumping into people's chairs and ignoring their calls to hey watch it, watch where you're going.

Another recollection: dancing crazily, not afraid to pick up my feet from the floor, one of the two shiny dress girls shimmying up to me to yell something into my ear to which I could only, inevitably but with great joy, respond to with, *what?*

It wasn't until I threw up beside our table and we got kicked out of the bar by a big guy in a black muscle shirt that I realized I was wasted. Waste. Ed. Cliff and I stumbled outside, slipping around on the unsalted pavement and holding onto each other's jackets, shoulders. He was wasted too, I saw. He was fucking *slammed*.

"You okay there, bud?" he asked, slurring the words around, his smile sloppy and gathered at one corner of his mouth.

"I'm *great*," I said, and burst out laughing, the acid remnants of throwing up nothing but alcohol burning at the back of my throat in a way that was surprisingly easy to ignore. I slipped and grabbed a handful of Cliff's coat in time to recover. "Whoa," I said, sounding like Beau all over again, "they really oughtta salt the fucken sidewalk."

"I know, *right*. Oh shit, oh shit there's the streetcar."

We saw it coming up the track, its lights weak through the dry blowing snow that cut at our faces like sand. We ran for it and the driver honked at us for cutting in front of him but let us on because it was late and freezing, and because we were obviously wasted. I collapsed in the first empty seat I registered and Cliff sat beside me, still laughing under his breath. "Oh man," he said, "that was a mission and a half."

"Truly."

"What are you saying right now?"

"What am I saying? I think I'm gonna crash somewhere."

He took off his hat and pressed his hands to his cheeks to warm them. "Are you going home?"

I felt glacial, immovable, but no longer even a little nauseous. I couldn't conceptualize the amount of alcohol I'd just downed except in very vague, abstract terms. I thought about Beau and how he'd be sleeping, probably, sleeping off whatever grief he had in him, and about my wastedness and how it would be loud and obvious in the deep silence of the apartment. I imagined Beau in one of his many white t-shirts, could very clearly see all the dark hairs on his arms, the way he'd be curled up, knees almost to his chest. "No," I said. "I don't think so."

"Do you want to crash at my place?"

"Oh, yeah. Oh, that'd be so great, yeah. Is it okay?"

Cliff laughed. "Of course, yeah. You can sleep on the couch."

Gratitude flooded my body and eased my mind. The thought of seeing Beau, smelling Beau—it was too much. I knew that if I saw him tonight I would tell him. I would tell him everything, and *fuck* whatever he had to say.

The knowledge, so long felt but never spoken, welled within me, sloshing around in my chest. How had I managed to keep it for so long? It was dangerous, raw, pushing so close to my throat that anything, the smallest bump or kink in the streetcar tracks, might send it all spilling out. Yeah, Beau Larky. I had to stay away from him.

Cliff kept laughing and jostling and proclaiming but I grew silent, feeling the snorted emm draining out of me like water.

"Are you coming down?" Cliff asked. He was sitting up very straight, maybe to keep his alcohol firmly inside his body.

"I guess so," I said, surprised.

"Yeah, it doesn't last as long when you snort it. Too bad, eh. But look at *you* dancing up a storm in there, huh?"

"I couldn't even stop my feet from moving, man." I was beginning to remember the morning, which was bad, but not as bad as I expected it to be yet, with some of this magical, fantastic *emm* still mixing with liquor in my blood. I didn't talk much and lowered my eyes and by the time we got on the subway Cliff left me alone, letting me gaze out the window into the perfect black glass of my own reflection. The heaviness was back and I felt it as I walked beside him, drunk and tired and acutely aware of how fucking wet and cold my feet had become, how useless my sneakers were. I wanted nothing more than to take off my shoes and peel off my frozen socks and stick my feet under a blanket, rub the clammy flesh until some semblance of feeling returned.

The compounded hours I'd moved through so effortlessly now settled themselves on my shoulders. Heavy, heavy. My body was a repository of heaviness. How had I lived through this day? I felt I had lived a thousand lifetimes.

Cliff's apartment was warm, damp with the living musk of growing weed. I kicked off my shoes and sat on the couch to work at my socks. They were soggy and stuck to my skin, reluctant to come away.

"Fuck," Cliff said, doing the same, "I didn't even feel how cold my feet were until right now."

"I know, right? Fuck."

We sat in the near-dark rubbing our feet, illuminated by the weak green glow of a kitchen nightlight. Before we left Cliff had raised the blinds over the window and now I stared through it, watching the snow still falling, white and pure against the orange of the big city winter sky. Something about the light pollution made me think of the hospital and of Beau's fear, so briefly exposed before he could pull it back and contain himself, be self-contained. And he should be scared, why shouldn't he, because the nausea was coming for him and probably worse, probably other things too that were much worse. He should be scared because he was young as fuck and his blood was filled with sickness, and soon with poison. He should be scared because this was the worst time of his life, and other than a handful of friends, he had no one. And most of all, he should be scared because the chemo, the secondary round of more intense, more serious, more adult chemo, would certainly destroy him.

I stood, my cold feet sticking to the hardwood but relishing the warmth and cushioning of the deep red shag. I found the window and leaned on the sill, its chill cutting into my bare arm. I watched the snow falling so softly now that the wind had stilled and thought: Soon I will know my own fear. Soon I will be afraid in ways all my own.

"Cam, what's *wrong*?" Cliff had come up beside me and wasn't smiling, for once. "You look like someone died."

His last word stuck and wouldn't let go, squeezing at my throat.

"Dude, don't get mad," he said. "Don't get mad, but is it Beau? It's that you're—it's that you're in love with Beau."

Hearing him say it out loud like that took the breath out of me, like someone had punched me in the gut. So blatant and glaring, this fact I'd tried to conceal so dearly, dragged out into the dark room and lying between us like a fresh corpse, open and steaming. I surprised myself by not flinching. I must have been too drunk to blush. Staring out into the soft frozen night with its great orange sky I thought about this carefully, about what it meant to have this incantation spoken into being, this desire vocalized: *You're in love with Beau.*

"Yeah," I said, not looking at him, not looking down, staring only at the sky. "I love him."

Such truth. I felt heavy and light, very very light. I'd said it and there, I'd said it, so.

And suddenly it mattered very much to ask: "Do you think he knows?"

"No. I don't know." He leaned on the wall across from me, arms crossed, my confidante now. How strange that I should put such trust in this stoned man with no commitments or schedules who fed me drugs like they were vitamins and had asked me, so many times, whether I'd broken my hand jerking off over Beau. Then, finally: "No."

I don't know if this hurt or relieved me. I was drunk, numb from the sill, dizzy from standing, unsteady with the last of the emm. "Cliff, you can't tell him. Ever."

"No, no."

"You've always thought that."

"Always, yeah."

"How did you know?"

"I don't know, I just did."

"Oh, come on."

Cliff sighed. "I don't know. The way you look at him. The way you talk about him. The way you are, sometimes."

Now I blushed, deep and furious. Of course.

"How do you stand it?"

"I don't know."

Cliff sat down, his back against the wall, and I did too, facing him. Maybe it was the emm in our bodies that made this surreal conversation possible, but I didn't care. I wanted to speak, wanted to ask. I was hungry for it.

"You're not gonna tell him?" he asked.

"No," I said. "I don't know." It's too much, it's too much. "You don't think he knows?"

"Maybe. I don't think so."

I tilted my head back. "How can you know and he not know?"

"I don't know. But he obviously thinks the world of you."

"Oh yeah?" My voice cracked.

"And listen," he said, putting his hand on my knee, "I don't really know a lot, but I know that it's not good to keep things like that, really intense things, all bottled up in yourself. Because one way or the other you'll regret it."

And in all his sincerity, the emotion so poorly fitted to his features, he was right. I would regret it. I had put myself in a situation in which I couldn't win and there could be only, inevitably, regret.

I slept long and hard and awoke on Cliff's couch, jagged shards of light coming in through the exposed window to attack my eyes beneath their lids. I shifted slightly and immediately regretted this small move that sent a thousand sharp pins into the front of my skull. The cotton in my throat and needles in my eyes explained to me, impatiently, that this was a hangover. I shrunk from the light, hiding my face in the crook of my arm, rolling over and thinking; what the *fuck*.

My lungs ached in a deep, cored out way I didn't understand until I remembered all the cigarettes outside the bar, the—the fucking Silver Dollar Room. I must have had a dozen to myself, pulling in smoke like it was nothing, my body lacking the capacity to complain. I lifted my fingers to my face to find they reeked of nicotine, the smell seeping from them to turn my stomach. My jaw ached profoundly, like it might come off its hinges if I wasn't careful, the insides of my mouth all mangled. I swallowed and tasted blood in the back of my throat.

And then I remembered a series of things that made me want to die: Beau, the hospital, Cliff, the alcohol, the emm, Beau's text, the bar, the dancing, the lost wallet, more emm, throwing up at the bar, the sloppy TTC ride to Cliff's apartment, and worst of all, worse than anything else that could have happened, was the part where I *told Cliff I was in love with Beau*.

I pressed my face into the couch and made a strangled sound. Why the *fuck* did I do that? What was I thinking? (I don't know; I wasn't). It was the emm and my exhaustion and Cliff's sincerity and the heaviness in me, the heaviness and my desire to rid my body of it, if only for a moment. Fuck, oh fuck. I wondered what Cliff thought now, his prodding suspicions confirmed. Why he cared to know. What he might do now that he knew, now that he'd voiced this thing, brought it into being with his words, my words. Ultimately they were my words.

But is it Beau? It's that you're in love with Beau.

I wanted to die, to disappear from the earth. Curl into this couch and sink into it until I was nothing, no one, until all feeling and consciousness had drained from my body, left it inanimate, invulnerable.

Cliff you can't tell him ever.

I sat up and the broken glass in my head was pulled by gravity, tumbling to shift position. Everything swam.

Do you think he knows?

Two

When Beau first got sick I put my hand through the bathroom mirror, knuckles crashing through silver glass to send it raining into the sink with surprising slowness. The crisp sound of long shards meeting porcelain was not violent but loud and bright and melodic, or nearly so.

Though I could see my knuckles were crisscrossed with ugly red lines my hand registered pain only distantly, in a disinterested way. My stupid, twisted face and throbbing hand and the surreal, posing headline: Was that really me? Did I really do that? Dizzy with the thrill of all the shining broken glass.

I tried to clean it up with my other hand, my undamaged one, scraping all the shards into a pile so I could sweep them into a dustpan or something, but the floor in our bathroom was tiled and all the little grooves made the job hard. My bad hand dripped blood on everything, big fat drops smudged by my arm making crimson arcs on the washed-out blue. Wrapping my oozing hand in toilet paper, I knew that no matter how well I cleaned up the mirror would still be missing, and it wouldn't take much imagination to see what I'd done.

When Beau came home and saw my hand, the mirror, the floor, he lost it, throwing me into my jacket. "Why did you *do* that? What were you *thinking*? What the *fuck*. What the *fuck!*" Shaking me by the shoulders, saying, "Are you gonna be all fucked up by this? Huh, Cam? Are you gonna be losing it on me?"

He was so mad I thought he might hit me. "What are you fucking, *doing?*" Yelling it out down the hallway as we made for the stairs, running a hand back through his hair. "What are you fucking, *doing*, fucking up your hand over this?"

I recalled the bite of a hard surface, the horrible impact of it, and felt nothing but shock at how angry Beau was as I tried to remember the last time I'd seen him this way. Seething, scared.

In the Jeep he collapsed in the driver's seat and leaned hard on the wheel, face resting against his crossed arms. "I'm sorry, Cam," he said, breathing. "I'm sorry, man, I know. Let me see your hand. I think you seriously broke it."

I held it out and he took it between his own, cradling my wrist. "Can you bend it?"

"No," I said. It was stiff and swollen. All at once I saw it had grown large.

He swallowed, and then the cold front was gone from his eyes. He looked at me cautiously, pre-emptively, as if I might do something reckless and unexpected, like set myself on fire.

Later, after we'd sat for three hours in the stale air of the overcrowded ER, after the doctor had pulled my bones back into place without the aid of local anaesthetic, after I'd been given a prescription for pathetically weak painkillers and a cast that would be an impediment and make me think of this hateful, awful thing every time I struggled to wash my hands or tie my shoelaces or do up my coat for the next two months, Beau turned to me and asked if I was going to be okay.

"Well yeah," I said. "It's just my hand, it's not the end of the world, so."

"I mean, are you going to be okay in general, about all this." He swung his hands, gesturing to the room, himself. I was constantly surprised anew at how much complex, finely grained feeling Beau could transmit when he wasn't careful. I would see more of it in the next couple months than I had in the whole time I'd known Beau, in the whole time since we'd met.

"Hey," I said. "Of course I will."

How we lied to each other back then, Beau and I. The blatant way we lie to the people we love.

I felt that if I stood by Beau and weathered this for him it would be okay. As if the sheer force of my desire could will it so.

The things we tell ourselves when we know we're in over our heads. The groping way we reach for justifications, explanations that might somehow iron it all out. Sitting at the kitchen table late into the night annotating my Bourdieu and thinking: but this is something different, something *else*. Something I don't understand. It's like Beau and I were playing chess and passing the bong on the living room carpet and then I was here, picking him up from chemo with my hands in my pockets to hide my nails all chewed down to the quick.

Like that first great confusion—I was myself, contained and deliberate, and then I was not.

Some critical theory is more critical than other critical theory. Bourdieu takes his time, tries to get at what symbolic violence might be, but Foucault cuts down to the heart of it with all his usual certainty.

It is not only illusion, *but vanity as well*, he says, *to go questing after a desire that is beyond the reach of power.*

Three

That winter when the treatment started Beau got really sick, sicker than I've ever seen anyone get. He stopped talking about going back to his job and hid under his blankets, shivering with the year's first real cold seeping into the apartment through the windowpanes. He stopped eating almost everything and threw up a lot, less with the weed but still a lot, all the time. The amount of weight he lost was radical, frightening. I watched a line of bony knobs emerge down Beau's back, pressing the presence of his spine through his shirt. His wrists became angular, sharpened. I was scared, very scared all the time, my throat all cotton as I coerced him into having toast, having some oatmeal, having a protein shake.

I didn't know how to do this, how to compromise between Beau's agonizing, primal thinness and his sincere, exhausted conviction that he couldn't eat. *Please, Cam.* My calls to the clinic increased exponentially.

Beau loved to sleep. He slept all the time—under the heap of heavy blankets in his darkened room with the door shut tight, on the living room couch under that ratty grey blanket we had out there, curled into a corner with only the tip of his mess of hair showing, dozing in a kitchen chair to be jolted awake by the clattering lid of a pot boiling over. I wondered if he slept because he was afraid of how sick he'd gotten, or to escape the profusion of light that came with waking hours. Outside he squinted, bracing himself against the glare even as his mouth worked into a smirk. Beau had so much humour about everything. *My fucking, eyes*, he'd say, dramatizing the aversion, while I started to feel like my insides were made of gelatin.

So much sickness in so small a person—surely it would kill him. Surely it would ooze from his eyes, all black and viscous and glistening—the sickness. It was all I could think.

But then suddenly I was the one who was sick, waking in my darkened room with Beau sitting on the edge of my bed near my pillow, pressing a wet cloth to my forehead and telling me not to worry and to relax, Cam, please, Cam, take it easy. I struggled to sit up, forced back into my sheets by a combination of hot nauseous vertigo and Beau's hands (relentlessly) on my shoulders. I didn't understand how I'd gotten there, so tangled in so many sheets and soaked through the shirt clinging to my skin like a film.

"You need to rest," Beau told me even as my mind worked overtime, struggling to piece together the sequence of events that had put me in bed with this throbbing heaviness in my skull. "You've had the craziest fever for the past two days."

How was that possible? Beau was the one who was sick. I immediately felt the need to sit up again and make sure everything was in place—had he eaten anything? How did he get to yesterday's appointment? How did he get *back?* And oh my god, had I not been to the university? "What day—"

Beau eased me back down. "It's Thursday," he said. He was gentle, firm. It was all the things I wished I could be. I sometimes wondered if my inability to stop thinking about Beau was actually a profound desire to be like him, contained and deliberate.

I tried to think back to Monday. "Fuck," I said. And then, feeling the fever more strongly, "fuuuuuuuck."

"I called—"

"I missed—I missed my seminar and I missed my fucking—my fucking meeting with my *advisor*, and I missed teaching my fucking *class*." The hot squeeze in my parched throat made me feel childish, ready to sob.

"Cam, listen, I called your department and told them you were really sick. For real."

"You what?"

"I called them and just said you were down and out."

I tried to sit up for the third time, elbows flying out to support me. Beau pressed me down. "Seriously Cam, will you just fucking, chill for a minute?"

I let him place the blessedly cool cloth on my face again, my skin sighing under his touch. "Who did you talk to?"

"The secretary, ah, I don't know her name. Mary? Marian? And to your advisor."

"You talked to Johnson?"

"Yeah."

"What did he say?"

"He said he was sorry to hear that and not to worry about it. He said he'll talk to you next week."

Beau stood, taking the cloth with him. The air in the room, smelling pretty much the way I did when I didn't shower for three days, stirred against my wet skin.

"Can you please, Cam, just stay in the bed for a sec while I go wet this?" He backed toward the door, watching me the way he had when I broke my hand—like I might do something radical. Like I might set myself on fire. "Just wait."

I lay back and studied the irregularities in the ceiling, which was hard because the room, with the shades of the single window drawn against the white diluted December light, was very dim. I could hear Beau shuffling around in the kitchen, running the tap and opening the fridge, slamming it. In my confusion it was extraordinary to have him in the background in this way. The predictable sound of his footfalls on the wooden flooring was ordinary, solid, so different than him stumbling around the apartment in a daze, moving from his bed to the couch and back, shuffling sleeping sites, leaving trails of weed, tissues, NyQuil, or the gagging heave and lurid wet plop from the bathroom followed by his dismal cough.

Beau came back with a very cold, very wet cloth and a glass of water tinkling with ice cubes. "Here," he said, letting me sit up a bit so I could drink. "How do you feel?"

"Okay," I said. "Really hot." I saw through my haze that he wore two big hoodies one on top of the other, the hoods piling up at his neck, and endured a wave of debilitating tenderness.

"Don't even worry about your department, Cam, they seemed fine on the phone."

I closed my eyes as he held the cool cloth to my skin. "How did you get to your appointment?"

"I just took the streetcar."

I pushed myself up. "Jesus, Beau. You must have felt awful. I'm so sorry."

He eased me down, shaking his head. "I was okay," he said. "It was my last one."

"Really?"

"Yeah, that's it." He knocked on the wood of my nightstand and we sat in silence for a moment, absorbing the room's stale dark warmth and the full import of this statement. Somehow, while I had slept through my fever and sweated through my sheets, this horrible thing had ended with a final transfusion of poison (medicine, I told myself, medicine) into Beau's system. I had not even been there, warming a pleather chair and drawing upon the receptionist's vast reserve of disapproval. Now I searched Beau for signs of recovery, though I wasn't sure what they might be. Less pale? Less eye bags? More weight? Maybe less cynicism in the upturned corners of his lips. I couldn't find any of these. He looked to me as he always had since early September—tired but collected.

"When will you know for sure?"

Beau shifted so he was sitting all the way on the bed, his back against the wall and legs stretched out beside my body. "Like late this month, maybe January."

"Not sooner?"

"Lynch said my body has to readjust first and then they can do some tests to see."

I wished passionately that it was now.

"Listen, Cam, I know why you came down with this fever." He shifted the cloth on my forehead, where it was becoming warm. "I see you every day just . . ."

(and here I didn't breathe)

". . . *mourning*, man, you're just fucking, mourning over me and you break your back driving me and working overtime and trying to get me to eat and worrying, and you just wear yourself out, you know? You make yourself sick. Like with the mirror."

I clenched my right hand, liberated from its cumbersome cast just last week. It felt new, vulnerable. Not quite solid in the way it used to be. "It's true," I said.

"But listen, I'm gonna be okay, I feel it in me. In myself. Lynch said chances are really, really good that this treatment will work. Really good. And I need you to be okay, to not make yourself sick like this. To take care of yourself, Cam, not just me. Okay?"

"I know, I know," I said, suddenly tired. He was so right—I'd been making myself sick for him since I was a fucking kid.

After this final appointment was over and done with Beau became frighteningly *happy*, his upbeat sarcasm saturating the apartment, helping me out of bed and back into the daily up-at-six-AM grind of knowing that soon I would have to speak with Johnson and explain to him my lateness, my radical impatience, the edge I added to everything, the vacancy inscribed all over my display window face. Did I not take anything seriously? Was I not aware of the generous university funding I was wasting? What did I expect when I put in so little effort, and should he not speak to my committee about my increasingly poor performance? It was imperative that I find a good explanation, because removal from my very prestigious grad program meant separation from the forty thousand dollar funding package paid to me in quarterly instalments, funding very necessary for things like rent now that Beau hadn't worked in three months.

Beau wasn't worried—he squeezed my neck and joked about all his favourite people to rag on, a list headed by such promising names as Linda the chemo clinic receptionist and Cliff, and roughed up my hair, and drank an astonishing amount of coffee, and talked me into marathon Scrabble sessions punctuated by fat sticky joints made with blunt paper wraps. He started spending a lot of time in his closet darkroom, the acid-vinegar smell of stopper and developer wafting from beneath the door, walking around with clipped sections of negatives, holding them up to the light, singing along to Paul Simon in his off-key way that drove me nuts (kodachro-*woah*-ome), the lyrics something I'd picked up from him rather than the actual songs, second hand. Photo trays and discoloured rags piled up around the kitchen sink, crowding the counter in the mornings.

He started getting excited about *Christmas*, of all things, about visiting my mom and helping her with her tree and having dinner together, because did I think that she would maybe make that fucking, unreal cheesecake again this year, and didn't she want some help shovelling her driveway? Not that it had even snowed yet, or that Beau could shovel much of anything. Coming home from class I watched TV from the couch while Beau sat cross-legged on the floor, untangling vast piles of Christmas lights. "How about *this* shit," he asked, wrapping them around our little tree in a loose symmetry. "How about *that*."

"That's great, Beau," though I wasn't really looking, though reruns of *Iron Chef* appeared all-consuming. Because it didn't really matter what he had done with the lights—it was more about this feeling of sudden intensity between us that came from—I don't know. Having avoided something awful. Having not stepped in the street just a moment too early. Beau didn't say so, but I knew he was relieved we'd managed to get through it without telling anyone. He made me believe in incantations, the power of words.

Driving up to my mom's house in Ajax, the old Cherokee's all-season tires slipping around in snow drifts every few meters as I coaxed the car up the 401, Beau invoked this power. "Cam," he said, "you absolutely can't tell your mom that I'm—that I was sick."

"What?"

"You can't tell her, okay?"

"Beau."

"Seriously, you can't."

"She's going to know."

"No, she's not. How would she know?" He had his feet up on the dash but was angled toward me, hands loose in his lap.

"You don't look well, Beau."

"Well she can't know, okay? Please, Cam. I feel like it would just be so fucking, bad. She would worry like—ugh."

I moved the wheel back, jerking the Jeep out of an exceptionally sticky drift. "She would worry, yeah. She would worry a lot."

Beau sighed and pulled his toque further down over his hair, which stuck out in a panic of static. Beau's big winter hair, crackling with dryness. At least he hadn't lost the hair. "I know you know, Cam."

"I do."

"It's bad luck, I feel, to talk about it now that the chemo is done." He looked around for wood, and, not finding any, knocked on his head instead. The newly superstitious Beau Larky.

"I won't tell her, don't worry."

"You've always got my back, huh."

"Yeah, yeah."

My mother met us at the door, already standing on the porch and waving as we pulled into her freshly white driveway. She was wrapped up in a big thick-knit sweater, its wool folding around her form. I wondered what my mom did out here, how she spent all her time. Working on the house, for sure. Watching reruns of *CSI* and *Criminal Minds*. I hoped she had her friends over a lot. I hoped she wasn't feeling super observant today.

We got out of the Jeep, slipping around on the driveway, and my mom was already halfway across the yard, her boots leaving big, sure prints in the snow. She hugged us both in turn, first me and then Beau, her all-enveloping self smelling like *home*—kitchen spice and laundry and that old perfume she's been wearing since I can remember.

"It's good to see you, mom," I said.

"It's good to see you too, baby," but she was looking at Beau, searching him, her face shifting not on the surface but structurally, somewhere far below.

"Beau, honey. You look a little worse for wear."

Beau smiled. "Yeah, I know, I know. Flu season hit hard."

She turned to me, searching my face, and then back to Beau, unable to look away. "Are you guys eating? You really need to take care of yourselves."

"Of course we're eating, mom," I said, but she was already talking over me, saying, "here, what am I even saying, come on, come on and hurry inside."

She ushered us in, eager to get us out of the cold, and we stood in the hall, shaking snow from our hair. Beau thumped his shoes on the rug, leaving rings of slush.

The house looked like a two-page spread from one of those lifestyle magazines I was so familiar with from the blue pleather waiting room, built of the kind of attention to seasonal festivity people my age couldn't conceptualize or afford. A big holly wreath on the door, Christmas lights on the roof, a Yankee Candle (Cinnamon Bayberry) lit in the hallway. My mom had pulled all the stops and put little bundles of greenery and dishes filled with candy canes all over the house. The tree in the living room was unreal, its tip scraping the ceiling. I saw, coming closer, that all the ornaments hanging from it were handmade—little wooden balls and angels glued together from lace and ribbon. I felt like a little kid.

"Whoa, Cathy, this is amazing," Beau said. "How did you have time to do all this?"

My mom laughed. "All this?"

"All these decorations. And the tree! It looks amazing."

She waved off the compliment, but I could tell she was pleased. "Sit, sit! I had the girls over a couple nights and we just decided to do some crafting. Brenda had a magazine, you know, one of those craft catalogues, and we just thought we'd give it a go. You wouldn't believe how easy it was."

Good, this was good. My mother having people over and not just *working on the house*, adding endless series of improvements to this big home she shared with no one. *Working on the house* was something my mom had been doing forever—planting and replanting the garden, re-painting rooms, adding siding, refurnishing the living room, adding an island to the kitchen, paving the driveway, digging a pond in the backyard, building birdfeeders, turning unused bedrooms into workshops, reading rooms, studies, sitting rooms. She was good at it, though. She could have gone into business. I knew that if I went into the garage it would be full of paint cans, used brushes, bits of wood, caulking, dozens of tools, buckets of nails, screws, and washers of various sizes, ladders, books on how to fix stuff up. Such direction—I sometimes couldn't believe she was my mother at all.

"Do you guys want something to drink? I have beer."

"Yeah, that'd be great," Beau said.

My mom started to get up, smoothing down her large faded jeans.

"Mom, don't even worry!" I said. "I'll grab it for you, you should just sit down and relax for a bit, huh?"

"Thanks, Cam, that's so nice of you. Are you sure?"

"Yeah, yeah." I waved her away. "It's no big deal. Wine for you?"

"Oh, yes, there's some on the counter I think."

The kitchen was quiet and very warm. I leaned on the counter and breathed in the smell coming from the oven—turkey, and homemade stuffing for sure. My mother had changed up all the kitchen towels and oven gloves to match the house, red and white and plaid and Santas hanging from every available surface. The new island glared at me, solid and imposing.

From the living room I could hear her laughing, cracking up though trying not to over something Beau was saying, his voice low and conspiratory. It threw me back to being a teenager, Beau sitting around my kitchen and chatting up my mom while she cooked, coaxing explosive laughter from her in exchange for dinners, cookies, inquiries about school. Beau was fascinated with parents, family. With what it meant to have these things.

On the fridge were at least a dozen photos, most of me, some that Beau had taken and sent to my mom. There I was as a kid, a really little but already lanky kid sprawled out on an absurdly lush lawn in bright red shorts and a blue jersey and big hair too long for the summer heat. Looking at this picture I always thought it must have been my Jays jersey, though you couldn't see the front because I was lying stomach down, and this must have been from before, when my dad was still around and taking me to games, wanting me to play catch. Which I sucked at, still suck at.

Others: me in a maple, hanging precariously from a branch; reading, incessantly reading, slumped into a series of chairs, counters, couches, and floors with books held lovingly close to my near-sighted face; a picture from Blue Mountain that we had someone take for us, my mother and I in old ski gear smiling hard, red-faced. And this one from high school, the first picture with Beau that had made the fridge: Beau and I sitting on the back porch, the old back porch from the old Scarborough house, our bodies twisted around to smile for the camera at my mom's sudden request. We both turn inward as we look over our shoulders, our angles giving the shot a nice symmetry.

Our heads almost touch.

Feeling a pang of something (nostalgia, love) deep in my gut, I almost unpinned the picture from the fridge and shoved it in my pocket. My mom would notice its absence—she noticed everything. We are so *young* in that picture, Beau and I, traces of sunburn smudged on our smooth faces like eye black. So young it hurts. Beau is wearing a plain white t-shirt, faint outlines of his shoulder blades barely visible through the fabric. The shape of his back made me feel like a puddle of water.

Whenever I looked at this picture I tried to read my younger self's face. I remembered the day, its dry heat and the dizzy pleasure of having Beau Larky hanging out with me in my backyard. How did I look? Did I look like someone sick with love? Dazed, I thought. Squinting a little under the crushing noon sun. Surprised at the suddenness of the photo, eyebrows tilting up even as I squint. And happy—most of all I thought I looked happy.

And this one from prom, Beau and I fresh-faced in suits, young and handsome with our equally young and polished dates by our sides in shiny dresses. I didn't remember our dates. I only remembered Beau, his excellent compact body a lesson in symmetry.

Here I'm at convocation in my gown, holding up my diploma, my mom at my side with her arm around me and her smile wide. She is puffed out, ecstatic because her only son is graduating at the top of his class. Beau had taken the picture, motioning for us to move closer together, directing us with his hands. During the ceremony, as I walked to the stage to receive my degree, nervous and proud, I looked up to scan the crowd for Beau and his camera and cracked up when I saw him giving me a thumbs up over the lens. "Fucking, Master of Philosophy," he said later, lighting up the congratulatory blunt he'd rolled. "No big deal."

And this final one, a new addition that I hadn't yet seen, encased in its own plaster frame: Beau and I sitting together in my mom's backyard just this past summer, big smiles all around, unshaven and stoned. We'd shared a joint in the Jeep on the way over and were squint-eyed, lazy and pleased with ourselves. I thought I looked remarkably put together. What did my mom think, pinning this photo up among the others in its own frame? Seeing her only son move in with his best friend?

She must know. I didn't know. I didn't think about it.

What I wanted to know most when I looked at these photos, bending down to grab a lemon or a couple bottles of beer in the summer, was if I looked different. I felt there must be something fundamentally different about the Cam that showed up in pictures after Beau, something that the younger Cam lacked, or still had. Whatever it was, I couldn't find it. By next Christmas there would be a new photo on the fridge, another image for me to mine as if all the information it could offer wasn't already there, laid out in its celluloid surface simplicity.

All my smiling dazed selves looking back at me, and all I drew was a blank.

Bringing in two bottles of Heineken and the wine for my mom, hands wet from condensation beading on the glass, I was blindsided by my mother's request that I tell her more about Foucault.

"Foucault?"

"Beau was telling me about your dissertation."

"Oh yeah?" I looked at Beau. We had never once discussed this. I worked long involved hours and was secretive about my work, labouring under the impression that he couldn't care less. And I couldn't have shown him, anyway—it was too transparent, too much of my bleeding heart woven into its pages. He would certainly know.

"Yeah, I was just telling your mom about some of that stuff you've been writing about."

"Yeah? Like what stuff?"

"Like how silence structures discourse, how what's not said can be just as important as what is. The relationship between silence and power."

"Silence and power," I repeated, stunned.

"It's amazing, when you really sit down to think about how many codes are structuring what can and can't be said. It's such a simple thing, but so fundamental. Like how words can only mean because there are spaces between them. There's a system, a grammar to it all." Sounding a little stoned, though he wasn't: "Just wild."

My mom was digging it. "Beau, you sound like you're the one getting the Ph.D."

He laughed and took a swig of his beer. "Not likely. I'm just quoting the professor here."

I flushed, flustered. How had he known? Had he looked through my notes? Read my annotations? Imagining Beau poring over these, decoding them, trying to decide what I was about, filled me with panic, and I swallowed my beer faster than necessary.

Before we ate, Beau and I stepped out onto the back porch for a smoke, which my mom must have assumed meant a cigarette but Beau and I knew meant the generous joint in the tin in my back pocket. It was already dark, the last of the evening sun barely colouring the sky in the west—purple and black, and then the winter night. I cleared a spot for myself on the steps, brushing away fresh snow with my glove. The wood was cold, and a little wet. I pulled out the joint and clicked at it with my lighter, slowly turning its tip in the flame. Beau stood over me, hands jammed deep in his pockets.

"What are you so mad about?" he said.

"Since when do you go through my stuff?" It came out all stiff and I saw that yeah, I was mad, more angry than I'd been with him in months.

"Cam, you just left some of your papers on the table and I read through them, I'm sorry, man."

"Silence and power—I can't believe you. Do you just go through my notes and shit when I'm not around?"

"Cam, I really didn't mean anything by it, I didn't think you'd get upset like that." He kicked his feet through the snow, shivered, looked up at the sky.

I held the lit joint, too mad to toke. I wanted to break it in two, smother it in the snow, stomp on it. "That was my *stuff*. When you leave your stuff around, I don't go shuffling through it, regurgitating it to my fucking mom. Jesus."

"Honestly, Cam. I just wanted to see what you were studying. You never talk about anything you're doing. You're writing a fucking, dissertation and you don't even talk about it."

"I don't want to," I said, hurt because he should know. Of all people, he should be the one to understand. I killed the joint on the railing, smushing it a little too hard but careful anyway, because Beau wouldn't be able to eat if he wasn't high. "I'm fucking exhausted, I don't want to talk about what I'm doing in school, what I'm *theorizing*," I said. "You should respect that. Especially you, after everything. What do I have to do, walk around hiding shit from you? Jesus."

I bit the inside of my lip, hard, and stared across the frozen yard, its lines softened with pillows of snow. My ass was cold. I felt that if I didn't stop myself I would burst, screaming at Beau with all the words I knew, the anger sloshing up against my sternum like water.

What was this? This was something else.

Beau looked at me like he was seeing me for the first time. I shoved the joint at him, pressing the mangled thing into his gloved hand. I felt bad that it was so beyond saving. Our breath made clouds in the still frozen air.

He sat down beside me and patiently rerolled the smoke, his fingers shaping it into some semblance of what it had been, tearing away at the paper a bit before licking it back, securing it. I could see from the hunch of his shoulders that he was done talking. He relit it unevenly, on an angle, severely canoeing the joint into a sad thing I couldn't stand to see, and dragged once, deep and hungry like Cliff, before hacking into a series of coughs. Sweet thick smoke hung over his head. His coughing annoyed me, brought shades of illness with it. Reminded me of desperate hurried high school pot smoking, of Visine, cologne, but also of post-chemo Beau throwing up in the kitchen sink, back heaving as he clung to the counter, knuckles white.

Beau passed me the joint and I took one hit before going inside, slamming the sliding door behind me. He didn't turn around.

"Is it cold out?" My mom stood at the kitchen counter spooning sweet potatoes into a serving dish.

"Yeah," I said, pulling my gloves off. The warmth of the kitchen was a wall against my body. "Can I help?"

"Sure! Can you put out plates and stuff?"

"For sure."

"Beau's not coming in?"

"He's just finishing his smoke."

My mother handed me the potato dish and pulled the turkey from the oven. It was huge and brown. "Beau looks *horrible*."

"Does he?"

"He's so *thin*."

"Yeah, well. You know." I set the potatoes down and laid out plates, keeping my back to her.

"Cam, don't tell me you don't notice."

I shrugged, searching the drawers for cutlery. She'd rearranged everything since I'd last been here and there were strange wooden kitchen utensils where I'd once found forks.

"What's wrong with him?"

"Nothing, mom. He's been sick. Antibiotics and stuff for the past few weeks."

"Has he been to a doctor?"

"Oh yeah." My appetite was gone.

"And?"

"He's got a flu. He's had a hard time getting over it. Don't be offended if he doesn't eat much, he's not a hundred percent."

"Poor Beau."

"Yeah."

My mom turned, wiping her hands on a red Santa-themed dish towel. "Cam, make sure you take good care of him," she said. "He's so *thin*."

What am I? His keeper? Am I Beau's keeper? I wanted to yell it at her, the roar in my chest returning once more. I felt that if I had to tell my mom any more lies I'd be sick. I wished I'd smoked more.

"I—"

The slam of the sliding door cut me off, Beau coming in stamping his feet and peeling off his gloves. He shot me a smile, sheepish from under his toque. It was pulled too far over his ears and made him look clownish, young. "Smells good," he said.

"Beau! Come in here and don't stay out in the cold so long." My mom urged him inside, all but sat him down. He pulled off his hat, brushing a hand through his hair. It was all static.

The toque, the lopsided smile, the winter hair—they made me desire him profoundly.

She insisted on taking his jacket, easily defeating his slow movements of protest. I couldn't remember the last time I'd seen Beau stoned and not been stoned myself.

It was debilitating.

"I hope you're feeling hungry," she said. "I was just telling Cam how *thin* you've gotten."

"Oh yeah?" he said, clearly to her, but he was looking at me, his eyes half meeting mine from the floor.

"If you feel that flu coming on again you need to get different antibiotics, okay? Don't let Cam let you out of the house when you're sick."

Beau smiled, shy and stoned. "Oh, Cam definitely wouldn't let me go out without fourteen different layers on," he said.

Watching Beau's sleepy movements, his thoroughness with his plate, his goofy smile, all the anger leaked from my body. I felt tired and couldn't remember why I'd been so upset. It was something about boundaries and what they meant, about why certain ones could be breached so much more easily than others. But that sloshing anger—that was something else.

When we said bye to my mom, leftovers wrapped up in Tupperware and aluminum foil crushed against our bodies as she hugged us on the porch, it was late. We drove in silence in the dark, Beau leaning against the passenger window, his knees up against the dash. I watched the headlights of oncoming cars sweep across the windshield, blinding, momentarily illuminating the inside of the Jeep before passing out of sight. It was cold and I kept my gloves on, enjoying the stiffness of the tendons in my recently healed hand. If I tilted my wrist just right they creaked like freshly compressed snow and ached.

I didn't know why Beau would go through my Bourdieu and Foucault—I doubted he cared about the theory. Checking up on me, maybe, trying to see where my head was at. As if he could access me secondhand like that, feel me out through traces left in what I'd read. Beau taking stock, seeing where I focused my energy, deposited my thoughts—trying to understand, I imagined, in the same way I did when I scanned his plate to see if he'd eaten anything, or listened by his door to check if he was coughing a whole ton in his sleep. All this feeling out, and why he couldn't just ask me? If he wanted to know.

He could just ask—if he wanted.

The road calmed me, the quiet rush of pavement smoothing down my thoughts. Would I lie to my mom about long flu seasons and antibiotics? Absolutely, though it made me sick. Beau was right, anything was better than talking about the blue pleather clinic, receiving the weight of her worry. It was too difficult to use words, so concrete and definite, to make people understand, and it was even worse to think of what they might say in exchange as they fumbled for the correct response.

Nothing, let's say nothing. Let's not talk about it.

"Cam."

"Yeah." I sat up straight, startled. With his slumped body and his head back like that, lips slightly open, I'd thought Beau was asleep.

"I hope you know I'm actually so sorry for looking through your stuff," he said.

"It's okay. I overreacted."

"But I get why you're mad. I shouldn't have done that."

"You know, if you want to know what's going on with me you can just ask."

"I don't know, man, sometimes I feel like you're so caught up in your head. You get so distant and I just feel like, how can I even—*approach* you. When you're far away like that."

We sat in silence, Beau staring out the passenger window and me watching the road lines flash by and thinking, do I get like that? Far away.

"You're a really private guy, Cam."

I laughed.

"No really, and I don't want to intrude on your space. The last couple months have been not the greatest, and I'm sorry for that too."

I shook my head. "I hope it'll be gone. I hope you'll be better—for the new year."

Beau knocked on his head like he had on the drive up, but didn't smile. "Amen, man."

And then: "You know, you weren't always so private."

"No?"

"Well, in a way you were, but it's different now. Since I got—sick." He hesitated over the last word, like it might pain him to say it aloud.

"How do you figure?"

Beau adjusted the heating knob, cranking up the volume of lukewarm air blowing from the vents, and held both gloved hands over the one closest to him. "Like sometimes I'll just look at you when you don't think I am and you just look *consumed*. Like whatever you're thinking is going to swallow you whole."

Oh, come on, Beau. Come on and let me off easy this one time. You must know. Can you not feel it on me? It drips from me like sap.

It was what I wanted to say, but instead I didn't answer and drove, staring at the road because that was safest, because not answering was far safer than shit like Beau going through my annotated readings, telling me I looked consumed. He rolled a joint in his lap and lit it for me, passing it over without comment.

The weed was sticky sweet, soothing in my throat and so fragrant in the Jeep's closed space in which I felt I might die from the unbearable weight of restraining myself from touching him, from fixing his toque and oh. I let him pass another and then we were home and hitting the bong, our feet up on the coffee table as we watched snow falling through the living room windows.

When I woke up it was late afternoon, my body heavy and my head filled with what felt like cotton. Beau was in the kitchen frying bacon, salty and sharp, and I thought, I couldn't move if I wanted to. But I did, flowing like molasses from the couch and into my jacket at his urging that we needed to *get more weed*. Out the door and precariously down the stairs and out into the bright winter sun, dazzling on snow and the bodies of passing cars. Easy, easy, though I felt distanced from the world around me by about four layers of soundproof insulation lining the inside of my skull. I moved in slow motion toward Wellesley, stopping for coffee that might somehow wipe away this thickness. I imagined gargantuan amounts of THC blocking receptors in my brain.

The cup was warm through my gloves and I held it between them, inhaling the bitter burnt morning smell as I sat on a half-snowed bench watching the cars go by, everything leisurely and blinding. Squinting through the impossible afternoon glare of sun on snow and metal hurt my eyes but was somehow pleasing in the same way as being outside in the crisp air and burning my tongue on the too-hot coffee. I felt that nothing could touch me. The lateness of the day was a fact, distant and irrelevant as silence and discourse and all my other Foucault-isms.

When I got to Cliff's I leaned hard on the buzzer, putting my whole body into it. I stood in the warm lobby for a couple minutes, watching slush pooling around my sneakers until I realized I'd gotten no answer. I buzzed again, this time longer, and was cut off by Cliff crackling across the intercom.

"Yeah?"

"It's Cam."

Static jumped at me. "Oh shit, come on up!"

He buzzed me in and I did, taking the stairs slowly and growing excited at the prospect of sitting down.

Cliff opened the door in a tee and a pair of sweatpants. "Shit, look at you, Professor Pothead." He laughed his way into a cough.

"What?"

"Dude, you are stoned as shit, hey."

I laughed. "I've come for some—" pausing for dramatic effect "—*marijuana*."

"I don't know why you'd come here for *that*."

"Crazy idea I had."

Cliff moved aside and let me in. His shades were open, and bars of brilliant winter light flooded the apartment. The place smelled good, like it had been doused with Pinesol and Febreze. I threw myself onto a beanbag and stretched out. "What, are you having your mom over or something?"

He settled onto the couch across from me. "No, your mom," he said. He tried to keep a straight face but couldn't. "Nah, sometimes I just like to clean up. Feels good."

I nodded. "I know what you mean."

"And look at you, hey, bringing in all the fucking holiday cheer."

"Holiday cheer?"

"You're all smiles for once."

"Yeah, I guess so, huh."

Cliff slid down from the couch to his carpet, a big, beautiful, deep shag the colour of red wine, reaching for a joint from the table and leaning in toward me, close. For the first time I saw that he, too, was stoned. "Things going well with—everything?"

He kinked one eyebrow so hard I almost laughed. I could see that he'd meant to say *Beau*, are things going well with *Beau*, and what was *that* supposed to mean?

"Things are all right," I said. It occurred to me that probably everyone in the whole world who had met me for even a second could see what I was all about, as in, yeah, that guy's hopelessly in love with Beau Larky. Maybe this was okay. My body felt like syrup.

Cliff lit the joint and passed it to me, undeterred. "You do anything sappy for Christmas?"

"Yeah, we went up to my mom's place. She put on a huge spread."

"Tree, lights, turkey, mood music, booze, softly falling snow? The full suburbs special?"

"Pretty much."

"You know, I've been thinking a lot lately about you and Beau."

"What?"

"Yeah, weird, huh, but I've just been thinking about all the different people I know and how they are. Seasonal inventory, you know? And I've been thinking, *man*, you guys are *so lucky*."

"What? How do you mean?"

He laughed. "I know, you're all like, what's all this about? But I mean, you do *everything* together. There's not even a question about it. Bong rips and Christmas at mom's house, hardcore family shit, you know? Everything. You get such obvious pleasure from each other's company. I can't imagine seeing that much of anyone, hey. *Anyone*. But you guys thrive on it. You're lucky, to be so close. It's a rare thing.'"

I smiled, flushed and moved despite myself. "It's not all bong rips and Christmas all the time."

"But it's great, man. No, really. I find it very moving. Hey—don't laugh, I mean it. Remember a couple weeks back you guys were here with Jared and Scott and that girl, uhh, Stacey?"

I did—Beau and I had gone together to do a weed run and catch a movie, but ended up hanging out for a couple hours at Cliff's instead. The guys were friends of Cliff's, big dudes in Yankees jerseys and flashy Nikes and hair shaved down close to their heads. The girl must have been someone Cliff was seeing, maybe—I saw women leaving Cliff's apartment all the time and had stopped paying attention.

"You were telling some story, or maybe explaining—yeah, that's it, explaining something complicated—I don't remember what, because I was looking at Beau, who must have been *baked* and was just sitting there in like, total and complete awe, paying total attention, and I thought, man, he really respects you. I would love to have someone look at me that way when I talked—or ever, hey."

I don't think I could have answered if I wanted to. He drifted out of his storytelling demeanor, so practiced from hours of stoned yarn spinning, and focused on me.

"You and Beau have been friends a long time," he said.

"A long time," I agreed.

"It's good," he said, "to have a friend like that."

I didn't know what he meant, and didn't care. Accepting a new ounce from Cliff and tucking it into my coat, I tried to imagine how it could be that Beau really paid attention when I talked and somehow, miraculously, sat in *total and complete awe*. I didn't understand this, but knew I would turn it over in my mind on the way home the way one examines a rare coin, a surprising lump on one's body, a newly returned essay all marked up in red ink, reading it closely for signs and meanings. I would put it away for later and then come back to it, again and again, until I wore it thin by handling it too much.

I saw this was a Christmas present in Cliff's own way, better than the weed he insisted I not pay for but maybe not better than the brand-new volume of Bourdieu folded in shiny gift wrap left for me on the kitchen table, identifiable only by my name dented into the foil with black ink in Beau's steady hand.

Four

In his "Postscript on domination and love," odd and sentimental for so rigorous and sociologically inclined a man, Bourdieu wonders if love might not be *an exception, the only one, but of the first order of magnitude, to the law of masculine domination, a suspension of symbolic violence.* Or is it, he goes on, *the supreme—because the most subtle, the most invisible—form of that violence?* He sticks with the first possibility, which isn't the best move and leaves him just about scalped by the feminist theorists, who say, basically, and what would a man know about it? What would a man know about domination and love, since he, unlike the woman, can have both.

Foucault, on the other hand, would say that we are never outside of power, that everything is tainted with it—even love. The realist in me knows this to be true, but the romantic chafes at it, wants Bourdieu to be right against all reason. My confusion dots the pages, annotated carefully in pencil in the margins of this brand new copy of *Masculine Domination*, given to me so recently by Beau Larky himself. Leave it to Beau, with his non-academic imagination, to pop by Chapters and pick up this particular book, overlooked by me in favour of more obvious volumes like *Distinction* and *Language and Symbolic Power*. This was good, and I'd better have something good to tell Johnson, whose most recent and aggressive email didn't ask if there was a time that might work for me to meet but instead explained that he *expected to see me* on the fourteenth during his office hours. This was apparently what happened when you didn't answer your advisor's emails, ever. My recent dreams had been not of Beau, but of letters notifying me of severed university funding.

But of course I thought of Beau, still. Feeling better after three weeks without chemo, the colour returning to his face and some of the thinness disappearing from his wrists, Beau had managed to get a job at a Starbucks near campus where I passed by at least twice a day between classes. His old location, after a string of unexplained absences, would not take him back. From the street I could see him at the bar, shaking ridiculous oblong containers of caffeine and soy milk in his (absurdly handsome) green apron, flashing smiles at women waiting for drinks that must have made them half in love before the cup had passed from his hand to theirs. At home he imitated this manner with me, thunking down too-full cups of coffee on the table beside my stack of texts and announcing, as the liquid sloshed onto my notes, that my fucking, double soy caramel non-fat macchiato, extra shot of bullshit, had arrived. If I had time I stopped in to see him and have a free drink, but most days it was enough for me to stand outside the window, breath fogging in front of me, and see him being okay and self-contained and so essentially himself.

One day in January, it must have been the second week of the spring semester, Beau saw me peering in through the window and waved me inside, his face brightening at the sight of me. It was one of the things I never tired of, seeing the pleasure in Beau's body spilling over the counter to greet me.

"Cam!" he said. "Do you have some time? Sit down and I'll get you a drink, huh? Can you stay?"

"Yeah," I said, shuffling onto one of the tall stools set out near the baristas' end of the counter. "I have lots of time." There was no way PHIL4007: Theorizing Limits could compete with Beau Larky and his energy in this warm, fragrant space.

"My shift ends in half an hour," he said over his shoulder, busy with a pitcher of something sugary. "Can you wait that long? You look cold. I'll make you something legit."

"Yeah for sure." I took off my gloves and laid them out on the counter, warmth flooding back into numbed fingertips.

Beau set a tall, frothy cup in front of me. It smelled of spice. "This is our fucking," he looked over his shoulder to make sure his manager was out of earshot, "feature *eggnog* drink, okay. It's pretty fucking," checking again, "legit."

I laughed and thanked him and pulled out a course reader to look at, taking off my hat and jacket. I settled down with my elbows on the counter and my face over the steaming cup, fully intending to read, but somehow ended up watching Beau instead as he moved from the counter to the blenders to the cash register and back. His apron was tied at the small of his back and had managed to pull his shirt partly out of his jeans where it had been neatly tucked that morning. His brow furrowed in concentration as he worked, shirtsleeves rolled to his elbows in a careless way that made me weak. I couldn't let myself come in here every day or I would just watch him, just drop out of life and watch Beau Larky making coffee with that clean white shirt and green apron on.

When he was finished Beau wiped his hands on the apron and came to sit beside me, absently fixing an unravelling sleeve. "How's the eggnog?"

"It's good," I said.

"You look good," he said.

"What?"

"You look calm, for once." He regarded me with sudden gravity. "You had a good day? Talk to Johnson?"

"Not yet."

"It'll be fine. Trust me."

"Yeah."

"Listen," he said, playing with the corner of one of my gloves, "this morning I went to Princess Margaret for some blood tests and other stuff."

"Today?"

"Yeah, earlier, and tomorrow afternoon I'm going to see Lynch so she can tell me what's going on, like how the—how everything went."

"That's scary," I said, out loud, and almost put my hand over my mouth.

"Yeah," he said, surprised. "It is." He began to flip through my reader, pages whirring under his thumb. "I was gonna ask if you want to come with me, maybe. If it's not too much for you. I know you take this stuff really hard."

"No, I won't take it hard. I mean, Beau. Of course I'll come."

He nodded and put his hand on the back of my neck. "I knew you would. Thank you." The gratitude seeped through his touch.

The doctor was incredibly tall, her hands bony and enormous, and had long hair cut all the same length, no layering, like she'd done it herself with a pair of scissors, gathering the frizzing brown mass in a fist and snipping away. Looking down I saw her shoes were flat and round-toed, closed, the kind with the single strap across the top; something a schoolgirl would wear. A totally unpretentious woman.

"Beau," she said, holding the door, ushering us into her office. She motioned to the couch opposite her desk. "How are you feeling?"

"Great, I'm feeling awesome. I hope." He laughed, but not with any real conviction, and sat forward, hunching over his knees.

The office was smaller than I'd imagined and had only one long window facing due south into the brick of an adjacent building. Lynch sat across from us at the desk, folding her hands into a pile of knuckle. She didn't wear glasses but looked like she would, her mannerisms arranged around the absence—a hand always coming up to touch her face, skim her brow, check her lipstick. She radiated immense warmth.

"Cam," she said to me, "it's so good to see you here," and I had a panicky moment of wondering if maybe I'd met her before and couldn't remember. In my exhaustion I'd forgotten all the names of the chemo nurses, but they sure knew me.

"I've heard so much about you," she clarified. "It's good to finally meet you."

"Oh," I said, dissolved by the idea that Beau talked about me enough for her to know my name. "It's good to meet you too."

"I've been telling Beau to bring you along for months," she said. "He's incredibly stubborn."

"Shh," he said, like she was his lover. "I am not."

She opened his file and in the way she scanned it I saw everything. "Beau," she said. The level of intimacy in her intonation surprised me. "I'm so sorry about this."

"Oh," he said. "Fuck."

"It wasn't as successful as we'd hoped, unfortunately. Your white blood cell counts are still extremely high."

He hung his head in this awful pathetic way from which I saw, all at once, that he'd expected only good news or else he would never have brought me here. "But I feel so much better."

"It's the contrast of not having chemo that makes you feel better, but on a cellular level things have not really improved."

He shook his head, hair hanging in his eyes. I wanted desperately to touch his knee.

"Do you need a minute? I can leave you alone for a moment, if you want."

"No," he said, "it's fine," except it wasn't.

She looked at me instead, like I might answer for him. She thinks I'm his boyfriend, I thought, absurdly. I shook my head.

"So now what?"

"We were thinking another session of chemotherapy, different drugs. A little more intense, with some new side effects."

"What kind of side effects?" I said, because Beau wasn't looking at anyone anymore.

Lynch sighed and made a motion with her hands. "Spinal pain, dizziness, nausea, vertigo, weakness, chills—your immune system is worn down, Beau, and will get more so. You'll find that you might get infections more easily. It's really important that if you're running a fever over thirty-eight you go straight to the ER."

"Okay," Beau said.

"And that you have someone drive you to and from treatments. That's really important." She looked at me, and I saw it was a question.

"I've been driving him," I said. "I'll drive him."

She nodded.

"How long?" Beau said.

"Three, four months. I want to get you started on this treatment right away to minimize the chances of the cancer spreading to other organs, or to your bone marrow, which can happen in cases like this."

He groaned, a sound like *oh-ho*, but drawn out and cracked.

"Beau," she said. "I know it sounds discouraging, but this is really your best option, at this point. I'll prescribe you some anti-emetics and some really good pain medication, to make it easier for you."

"Okay. If that's what has to happen then okay."

"You can maybe reconsider the counselling. I know you don't think so, but it can be very helpful."

"Can we not talk about that, please." There was a momentary tension that dissipated when she closed his file, looking down at the desk. I felt her putting the issue aside tangibly, as if it were a folder or pen.

Counselling for what? I touched his shoulder and he let me, looking up to meet my eyes. His were wet and red. He's not okay, I thought, and maybe it's not just this, maybe he hasn't been okay ever and it's just another thing we don't talk about. I saw, with visceral immediacy, Beau's room in the group home, its single window and thin grey carpet worn through near the door, unravelling to expose the concrete floor beneath, the narrow mattress and scratchy institutional sheets on which I'd spent so much time, craning my neck to exhale smoke through the screen we'd been unable, despite repeated attempts, to pop out.

The scuffed white walls and his stuff all over the floor, piles of clothing and dirty socks, the damp basement smell of the whole place and the cheap standard-issue bedside table with the wood veneer on which he kept dog-eared photography magazines and Zig-Zags and deodorant and a series of small plastic pill bottles, clear and orange and blue. It was from their labels that I'd first learned his name was Beauregard, silently forming the strange regal word to try it out, see how it felt on my tongue.

"My anti-depressants," he explained. "To regulate my 'behaviour.'" He finger-quoted the last word, making a face.

"I'm supposed to take one of each now," he said, popping open the bottles, "and one of each later. Twice a fucking, day, man."

"But you don't take them," I said.

"No. Well, officially I do. On paper." He laughed. "Mostly they go down the toilet."

I watched him collect a palmful of pills and shake them around in his fist like a maraca. With their chalky texture and pastel colours they looked like candies. "How do they make you feel?"

"Hazy," he said. "Like someone else."

Lynch was talking about treatment details, naming off a list of drugs and handing Beau printouts that he folded in half, and then into quarters and eighths. I saw his hands were sweating, leaving wet prints on the creased sheets.

"What are the odds that it will work?" I said, suddenly desperate.

She looked at me and touched her temple, brushing back a loose strand of hair. "With the second time around we usually expect decreased success rates."

"What kind of rates?"

She sighed. "Forty, maybe fifty percent success, in cases like this."

Beau made a motion like he might stand but sat back, wavering. A small tremor went through him, obvious in his stiffened shoulders even through sweater he wore.

Lynch looked at him kindly, with what must have been affection, though how she could manage this I couldn't say. "Beau," she said. "I know those numbers don't sound good, but they are ultimately just numbers. Low odds are better than no odds, and you shouldn't get discouraged. Often different drugs work in unexpected ways. I wouldn't recommend this if I didn't feel it came with a good chance of remission."

I said nothing, humbled by the hard authority of compiled statistics from hundreds, possibly thousands of people like Beau, one-half of them no longer breathing, freed from carrying the sickness diffused in their blood. I saw, with clarity grown in the clean winter light of Lynch's office, that it had been absurd of me to think I could somehow mediate this experience for him.

As we were leaving, folded papers and pamphlets stuffed into coat pockets, Lynch stood and squeezed Beau's shoulder. "You should come see me next week," she said, everything about her softening. "You should bring Cam."

"Okay," he said.

"If you're having a hard time you can call. It's not an imposition."

"Okay."

He stepped out and I made to follow him, but she stopped me with her big angular hand on my arm. "Cam," she said. "He's going to feel very bad, today. He would really benefit from talking to someone professionally, in my opinion, but I don't think he's willing. If you feel overwhelmed there are people you can call." She pressed an orange pamphlet into my hand, unlikely smiling faces evidently meant to represent *Support Networks*. "It's a lot of work for one person, a situation like this. Do you understand?"

"Yeah," I said, "of course," but knew she'd meant something else, something that could not be said without the breach of an implicit boundary.

Make sure you take good care of him. He's so thin.

I caught up with Beau in the hallway, walking behind him and respecting his space, the space he demanded with his stiff hunched shoulders and fast pace. We waited for an elevator on the empty floor, just the two of us in the big polished lobby. I felt nothing but knew that inside me structures were shifting to better accommodate the coming pain. I could not pull any mirror stunts this time. I would have to be solid.

Forty, maybe fifty percent success.

Oh, please let me be ready for this hurt, I thought. Please let me be ready.

An elevator arrived and opened, but Beau didn't get in. He stood by the wall as its door closed, head down. I watched the red floor numbers begin to descend.

"Beau?" I had an insane urge to kneel down before him.

"I don't know," he said, "how I'm going to do it. How am I going to do it? The chemo is so bad, Cam, it's *so bad*."

"Hey, hey, come here, come here." I folded myself around him and he let me, leaning into my body with his. I felt his hands on my back.

"Cam."

"I know."

"Oh."

"It will be okay, it will be okay."

We stood still and breathing. "I think," Beau said, "I need to go home and lie down. I think I need to go to bed, man." I felt his exhaustion as a physical force, an emanation of sick energy. He was done, that was it. He would sleep for days now, blocking out the world. I felt everything blacken and thought, frightened: I don't know how long I can keep it together. I don't know if I can do this for him right now. Already my throat was tight, my head beginning to ache. Please don't let it be worse than the mirror. Please don't let it be like that.

Five

Do you think he knows?

I stood up, woozy, regarding the toppled cans and streaked mirror and cigarette butts on the table. Disgusting, it was all disgusting. I needed some coffee and water, definitely a tall drink of the coldest water around to rinse away this cotton colonizing my throat and tongue.

The apartment was quiet and smelled like weed, tobacco, spilt beer. Down the hall I could hear Cliff snoring, sleeping so soundly. The weak golden light filtering in through the window told me it must be late morning, and the clock on the far wall, regarded through a haze of growing unease, confirmed it was just past noon. I found my shoes and squeezed into them, which was hard because my feet were bare and the shoes were still soaked, wet and cold on my skin. It was in this twisted position of leaning down to jam a thumb into the heel of a sneaker to force it onto my resisting foot that I realized it was the fourteenth, definitely the fourteenth of January, and that today was the day Johnson *expected to see me at twelve-thirty to talk about my progress.*

Feeling the dregs of the emm, the bad chemical remnants of the drug eating away at my brain, I almost cried. How could it be that things always worked out this way? Fuck, fuck.

I threw on my jacket and edged out the door as quietly as I could—if Cliff came to say bye, I'd slam the door on him—and then I ran. Ran hard, and fast, not like I had yesterday coming from the hospital, all measured and aching. I slipped on new ice and startled a group of people at the corner of Yonge, again at Charles. I knew I should think of excuses, but in the rush of traffic and the glare of afternoon sun against my tender eyes it was impossible. *My funding, my funding.* I chanted this as I ran, allowing my brain to process some of the consequences of not moving fast enough. My funding, fuck.

Cutting through Vic campus I crashed into a girl carrying a load of books that fell to the wet pavement and didn't stop, didn't stop as she called after me saying *asshole, watch where you're going.* I danced through the traffic roaring up Queen's Park Circle, splashed through slush and mud in the park, not caring that my pants were soaked, my shoes were soaked. People turned to look and stare. What's that guy's deal? I don't know, I don't know. I tore down Hoskin and then up Spadina, tasting metal in the back of my throat. I weighed a thousand pounds and it was hard, but I ran, springing over the sidewalk, my long legs so suddenly useful to me. When I got to the department it was twelve forty and I was late, ten minutes late but that wasn't so bad, better than an hour, better than forgetting altogether.

I stopped running when I hit the soft blue carpeting at the top of the stairs. The office-lined hallway was quiet and I leaned against the wall, telling myself to breathe, breathe. Take a minute to at least not be so winded and sweaty, so obviously late, reeking of incompetence. I took off my toque and smoothed down my wet hair and unzipped my jacket and then, collecting my body from the wall, allowed myself to knock on Johnson's sturdy oak door, that's what tenure is for, yeah.

"Come in," he called, and I did, edging into his messy sunlit office. Stacks of periodicals, unmoved since I'd met him, lined the room's baseboards.

"Cam," he said. "I don't know what you think it says about your level of commitment to this department and your study when you show up at only one of the several meetings I make with you and are so blatantly late."

Not good, not good. I stood near the door and jammed my hands into my pockets, aware that my sneakers were pooling mud and slush and salt on Johnson's plush rug.

He regarded me from across his desk, leaned back, sighed. The look he gave me was knowing, hard. We were still for a few moments during which I didn't breathe. "Sit down, Cameron," he said finally, and with some pity. "And close the door."

I did, taking the chair across from him. This was it, this was it. My heart hammered away in my chest, my throat. I felt it might come out of my mouth if I didn't keep it shut.

"I want you," he said, "to give me one good reason why I shouldn't ask the department to put you under academic probation, or better yet, terminate your time here, since it's so obviously what you desire."

I bit the inside of my cheek and balled up handfuls of my pants, pressing them tight to my thighs. So it had gone that far then, so then I was fucked.

Johnson sighed again, a long sigh pregnant with exasperation, boredom. "It's really in your best interest to do so. I've never, in my fifteen years here, had this problem with any student. You don't show up to classes, you miss your own teaching commitments, you skip my meetings, you don't answer my emails. You must misunderstand the nature of your time here, in this coveted spot that over *three hundred* applicants compete for, and for which a mere *three* are chosen."

He leaned closer, hands folded on the desk, and for a moment I was afraid he would smell last night's liquor on me, my clothes. I felt the weight of his gaze on my muddy cords.

"Nothing you say can hinder you, at this point."

I swallowed, and the spit got stuck in the cotton clogging up my aching throat. I wished passionately for water. "It's just that someone very close to me," I said, slowly, "the most important person to me, that I know, is very sick, and it's been very hard for me to deal with. Very hard. If it makes any difference, I've been doing my readings for orals, all of them, and I've worked through the first chapter, or as much of it as I could. It's not that I don't care about the work, I really do, it's just that now is a bad time for me, in my life. The worst ever, I think."

Johnson leaned back in his chair, unfolding his hands. He lowered his glasses so he could see me better, a gesture I knew well from class. I saw he was re-evaluating.

"It was my personal guess," he said, "if you don't mind me saying so, that you had a substance abuse problem."

I laughed in that sudden wild Cliff way, a single stray laugh left over from last night, and stifled it with my hand, horrified. I shook my head. "No, no."

"What is the illness, if you don't mind me asking?"

"Cancer. Leukemia."

Johnson paused, regarding me again. He was unflinching. "My wife died of cancer, cancer of the breast. Many years ago, now."

"I'm really sorry."

"I know you are."

We sat in silence, Johnson leaning back precariously in his chair while I sat rigid in mine, still gripping handfuls of my pants. I watched the dust caught up in the golden air behind his greying head and thought that whatever happened wouldn't be so bad, not nearly as bad as seeing the bones in Beau's wrists sharpen and reassert themselves.

"If what you say is true, and this program is something you care about, I won't get the department involved yet. I mean *yet*. I need to see some work from you, something concrete, a full proposal and an annotated bibliography for the second chapter, before the end of next week. Does that seem fair to you?"

"Yes, yes, that's more than fair, thank you, thank you so much."

"If you don't get it to me then we'll be looking at academic probation, given that you aren't making satisfactory progress toward completion of your degree. Am I understood?"

"Yes, absolutely." I stood up before he could change his mind, take back this miraculous statement. The corduroy on my thighs where my hands had been was mashed up, crumpled, dirty. Johnson looked at it discreetly, indifferently, as if it were of no more significance than the rich carpet or leaning periodicals.

"Cameron."

"Yes?"

"Give your someone my warmest wishes. I understand that it can be very hard."

I nodded, dumb with gratitude, encumbered with great blinding luck, and, closing Johnson's door very softly, collapsed against the wall outside his office. I wasn't a religious person but now suddenly I prayed, saying thank you, thank you that at least this one thing is still salvageable and that not everything is completely fucked.

And now to face Beau Larky once more, sober and straight-faced and carrying nothing but my sincerity and this impossible lie.

When I came through the door Beau was sitting on the couch in a worn old university shirt that might have been his or mine, his feet up on the coffee table and a book he hadn't been reading open in his lap. He looked wasted tired, everything about him wan and blurry. He smiled wide at the sight of me though I was so obviously dishevelled, but his eyes were cloudy and far away.

"Don't take this the wrong way," he said, "but I was starting to get scared you wouldn't come back."

2. Beau Larky

So that is how I must name the attraction which makes it exist: an animation. The photograph is in no way animated (I do not believe in "lifelike" photographs), but it animates me: this is what creates every adventure.

Roland Barthes, *Camera Lucida*

One

Beau Larky wakes each day thinking: If this doesn't work out, I could fucking, die. The *could* is a prop that keeps everything as a matter of contingency in a way *will* does not. There are things he finds more manageable as contingencies, and in this he is not so different from the man who loves him.

There are things he, too, does not think about.

Like that he can't eat, finding the sight of food strange, alien, as when he'd been on mushrooms and stared at a handful of candy, thinking, you want me to put this in my mouth and eat it? No fucking, *way*, man. That food all tastes the same, poorly textured and metallic, difficult to chew with his sore, swollen gums. That he is constantly on the verge of throwing up, a great physical unease forming the background of his days. It is impossible to know when the nausea might peak, leaving him soaked, taken over.

Having never felt anything but ease with his movements, Beau finds it hard to take orders from his body: slow down, breathe, take a seat, go to bed. He is clumsy and slow and loses his balance, the world tipping on him uncannily, vertigo circumscribing his walk into a strange pitching motion. I'm fucking, twenty-four years old, he thinks. I'm twenty-four years old, and what the fuck is this?

He wants to take the stairs, carry groceries, walk places. He wants to stay awake through movies and look forward to breakfast and smoke weed to get high instead of to keep from getting sick. To think about sex like he used to, like he hasn't in months. He wants to feel at home in his body, in control of its desires. Sometimes he stands in front of the mirror and looks at his prominent collarbone and thinning face and tells himself he has to eat, has to at least fucking, try. On the surface he looks pale, unrested, angular. It's difficult to imagine that somewhere inside him there is a grave cellular misunderstanding, a full-blown war. How can there be, in the ordered, contained interior of Beau Larky, a force with its own volition? A thing so fundamentally at odds with his wellbeing.

There are days he wants to tear at his skin, strip it away as if the pain of this act could justify the uselessness, the impotence of months and months of sitting through chemo while his cells destroy each other. He thinks he understands Cam and the mirror, almost.

It has something to do with wanting and not being able to. Something about the gap between those two things and the static it creates. In Cam this energy is not localized but diffuse, a hum of energy adhering to his body and clothes.

These short cold days Cam is silent and intense, spending long hours sitting in the kitchen powering through texts with a gravity of focus. Beau sees him without seeing him, the blue pencil held between lips and restless foot and blank absorption fixtures in his mind. He feels he can see Cam through the wall, his long body and all its positions embedded in him with a physical weight, like an imprint through some sort of second sight. Sometimes Beau looks up and is surprised to find, more and more often now, that Cam isn't actually looking at the book at all, but sitting up and staring somewhere far away, his concentration not broken but forgotten, set aside, sloughed off like a skin. Cam spends a lot of time gazing off at things that can't be seen, and at times like these Beau thinks he looks desolate, unreachable, an island unto himself.

What are you thinking, Cam, he wants to say. Staring so far away. There are huge chasms between them that can't be bridged with any words, or at least any Beau knows.

Beau takes long showers during which he stands and thinks, the scalding water pattering dull pressure against his back. In the shower he is removed from all things. The drumming of the water against the tub calms him and he empties his mind, reading the copy from shampoo bottles, in wonder at the aggressive brand names and lurid adjectives. He scans lists of ingredients and wonders which of them has given him cancer, as if the culprit might be highlighted or printed in bold, before squeezing a bunch of the product into his palm.

Sometimes he stands there, bottle in hand and mind blank, long enough for to Cam knock on the door and ask if he's okay. "Yeah, I'm good," he says, snapping back as if drawing away from a precipice.

Beau Larky has never once thought there is, or was, anything between him and Cam. Well, maybe sometimes he's thought it, sometimes when they sit close together or when he looks up to catch Cam watching him and sees him flush, heat flooding his face, but he writes these off as the ordinary undertones that crop up in any good friendship when people care for each other and are in close physical proximity a lot of the time.

There are tensions between all kinds of people. Beau knows this because he's been in six different foster homes during his short life. Tensions between fathers and daughters, mothers and teachers and neighbours, between siblings, between all kinds of people at school, between coworkers. Not usually between parents, but often between parents and other people's parents. There are tensions, especially, between young men, young men placed together in a group home, their cooped-up energy, their need to show off. The way the guys looked at each other's bodies, trying to figure out whose looked the least boyish. The way they all looked at Mike Mescini, his prodigious broad body parceled out in little adjacent packages of pure muscle. Wow, they thought. Whoa.

People over the years have suggested to him, both jokingly and not, that there might be something more going on between him and Cam than the two of them are willing to admit, and sometimes he isn't so sure they're wrong. Because why else would Cam do it, he thinks. Why else would he fucking, forget to sleep and drive me around and listen at the door and rub my back and cook and clean and pay my half of the rent? And smooth away my fucking, hair like that when I'm sick, when I can't even get out of bed. It's the gentleness that gets him. He can hardly stand it.

Because he loves you, he thinks, in a way you don't understand. The way people love their family, no questions asked.

And he's developed, over time, a gauge he sometimes uses when he feels unsure in this regard—he puts his hand, his entire warm palm, over the back of Cam's neck and feels him, each time and with consistency, shiver.

And what does that mean?

Because he loves Cam intensely, with a singularity that sometimes frightens him, Beau chooses to disregard these thoughts. There are times Cam looks at him like he wants to tell him something, his face open and full of great shifting things, and Beau's heart quickens because he isn't sure what it could be, or if he wants to hear it (but maybe he does, he sometimes thinks maybe he does).

And he says, *hey* or *what* or *do you wanna fucking, smoke a joint*, and the moment is broken, put away, forgotten, not something that has ever happened or could have happened between these two people, Cam and Beau.

Two

When Beau wakes up he knows it's going to be a really fucking, bad day. He sits up and perches on the edge of his bed, bent over himself, dizzy heat pressing into his skull. It's already light out, sun filtering dimly through the window where he's forgotten, again, to draw the shades. Increasingly he does things to their bare minimum degree, unable to apply himself in anything but brief flickers of splintered energy.

His head throbs and he smooths back his hair, as if counter-pressure on his skull might somehow subdue the dull pulse between his ears. Exhaling slowly, he stares at the floor, amazed at the clean winter light spilling across it. Feeling beneath his jaw he finds his glands are swollen, tender to the touch. He's getting an infection, or something. He thinks that if he takes a little more time before standing he might be able to keep from throwing up.

The apartment is quiet, and very cold. Cam has already gone for the day, leaving a shallow cup of stale coffee and a stack of readings on the kitchen table. Beau puts on the kettle and eases into a chair, back aching. He crosses his legs and rubs his feet, frozen even through two pairs of socks. He feels eighty years old.

When the water has boiled he pours himself tea and sits hunched over the steaming mug, warming his palms on the hot ceramic as he slowly, reverently, leafs through Cam's xeroxed stapled theory. The words look beautiful to him, a poetry in a language he doesn't understand, can't read. *Intensity, incipience, virtual, actual, potential.* He traces Cam's underlinings and circlings, follows his penciled traces through the columns of text, reads his annotations in the margins where individual letters bleed into each other. Cam's writing is not like his own—it leans and melts where his stands solid, legible even when rushed.

Intentionality, Cam has written, with no other explanation, as if it should be obvious what this says about the text. Squeezed in further down the page: *thought / expression, the gap*. Beau turns these words over, lips moving to form their shape as he reads. It is a trace of Cam, an external representation of something complex and inner and cryptic, because Cam is like that, full of things that mean something other and more than what he says.

Calmed by the natural flow of multi-syllabled words strung together, he forces himself to eat a piece of dry toast, working it past his tender gums and raw tongue, moistening it with tea to help it slip down his sore throat. He needs to settle his stomach before he can think about pulling on clothes, shoes, wrapping himself in layers to shelter his body against the February chill. Extended movement seems impossible.

He told Cam he'd pick up groceries, at least some basic stuff like bread, but the new chemo leaves him sledgehammered, physically bruised. He calculates the distance to the store and multiplies it by his exhaustion and finds that this sum still has to be divided by the staggering, disproportionate amount of time Cam spends doing shit for him, hours and hours and days of unspoken, freely given time that he does not understand but cannot not refuse. He needs this from Cam, or someone.

There is only Cam.

At the store the fluorescents are bright and the aisles cold. His sensitivity to the grocery freezer chill unnerves him, and he curls into his jacket's protective shell. He feels permeable, as if his skin were not an adequate barrier between the world and his insides. Outside it's snowing hard, big wet flakes accumulating in a heavy slush on the sidewalk, his face, his clothes. The bags cut into his hands through his gloves, leaving his fingers numb. Though it's only early afternoon the light is already fading into that grey blankness that accompanies big snowfalls on short days.

Six blocks from the apartment Beau stops to lean against a wall, putting down the bags to slide his hands into his pockets. He's out of breath, dizzy, head hollow and chest pained, somehow cored out. He stares up at the swirl of white, emptied, and thinks that he fucking, hates his body. He hates everything. He feels vague and distant and knows he's running a fever, which is bad, which is something that shouldn't happen with his cell counts so low on those weekly printouts, small grave numbers circled by Lynch like an ultimatum. He needs Advil and a few of those anti-inflammatories to dull the ache in his vertebrae.

I need to go to fucking, bed, he thinks. I need to sleep it off.

The streetcar rattles by, appearing to float through the blowing snow rather than physically travel along any sort of track. He considers taking it. His heartbeat is faint and sickly, tied to the dull throb in his head. How can he do anything? He doesn't know. He wants to be indoors and stoned. To rid himself of the desperate feeling in his throat, like the waves of illness rolling through him might make him cry, less from pain than frustration.

Forcing himself to walk the remaining distance, Beau closes his eyes and counts steps as his shoes soak through. He feels warm and knows he's ill, too ill to be out and doing this shit like everything's okay when it's not, when it emphatically just isn't all right.

The apartment is a fourth-floor walk-up, dividing him from his bed with four flights of stairs, eighteen steps per flight, each flight divided into two stretches of nine. Seventy-two fucking, steps. He stands in the lobby, snow melting from his clothes, bags set down by the wall in a halo of slush as heat floods back into his fingers and cheeks. He imagines he looks wet and flushed as he sags in the corner, surveying the stairs and taking deep slow breaths. Come on, he thinks, picking up the bags, it's not so bad, come on, urging his uncooperative diminished body into action.

At the top of the first flight he's overtaken by a coughing fit and a dizzy spell, hacking up a glistening wad of mucous from his thick throat. He leans hard on the railing and considers that it might be better to leave the groceries there and wait till Cam gets home, or at least ask someone for help, like the big bearded hipster on the second floor, or the Jamaican couple downstairs.

Cupping his phone through the fabric of his coat, Beau is overcome by a strong desire to call Cam, who will be sleeping in lecture now—he has Epistemology in Postmodernity on Tuesdays, which Beau knows from reading the titles scrawled on course readers. Just to ask when he's coming home and hear him speak in his low reserved way strained with worry. It'll be okay, Cam often says, and Beau believes him. Totally, completely, his words an authoritative text.

But calling is impossible, because Cam would drop the lecture without thought, arriving at the apartment in a shroud of intensity. Beau's careful with these things. It secretly horrifies him how willingly Cam lets his commitments go, releasing them like stringed balloons as if there wasn't a life's worth of work invested in getting this final, weighty degree. He suspects that Cam, who had broken his own hand in a single moment of what—grief? Panic? Anger? Beau doesn't know—has somewhere within him a serious self-injurious streak, a radical recklessness manifest in his total disregard of self.

Two times nine is eighteen, he thinks, breathing raggedly up the second flight. Eighteen times four is seventy-two. Eight times nine is also seventy-two. He counts thirty-six (six times six) steps, the rhythm syncing up with the throbbing beat of his heart in his skull. He has Paul Simon stuck in his head, the ridiculous one about the fifty ways, and chants the song silently, stupidly, in the blank way one punctuates rhymes with pauses when trying to ignore physical strain, each word marking his progress and the movement of his feet on the stairs.

It's then that his vision narrows to a single point. He tries to sit down but gets caught in the thick of the vertigo overtaking him in a great sudden wave, his shins hitting linoleum among the confusion of cans rolling down stairs with their dull rhythmic ka-thunk ka-thunk ka-thunk. He thinks immediately of the bread (it'll get fucking, crushed) and tries to sit up only to find that the cool floor has its own gravity, one intimately tied to the heaviness of his head. He presses his cheek to the tile and closes his eyes, a thing that should stop the room from tilting in on itself but only amplifies the freewheeling feeling, like being too drunk to fall asleep without throwing up first.

He can't remember passing out.

Cam's arrival is seamless, bleeding into Beau's consciousness with familiar hands on his face, his shoulders, his neck. Cam's saying, oh my god, oh my god, moving his lips in this barely spoken litany. Breathlessly, rhythmically, like a prayer.

"Beau, hey. Hey, Beau, come on. Are you okay? Oh my god."

I'm okay, he wants to say, I'm fine, but what comes out is a groan. The stairwell's fluorescent light is painfully bright and he squints, squeezing his eyes shut.

"Jesus, Beau. Are you hurt?" He presses his palm to Beau's forehead, cool and wet against the hot skin. "Oh my god, you're burning up. Did you fall?"

"I passed out," he manages, body stiff and bruised.

"Hey, stay still, stay still," Cam says, gently lifting Beau's head just enough to get his hands beneath it. Fingers probe his cranium, dipping into the tender spot where his neck meets his skull, Cam furrowed in his extreme focus. It's only when he checks his hand that Beau realizes he's been looking for blood.

"Oh, Beau. Are you hurt? Do you think you broke anything?" His palm back on Beau's forehead, smoothing away wet tangled hair. "You feel so hot."

Beau flexes his fingers and toes and they obey, reluctantly. Everything is enormously heavy. "I think I'm okay," he says.

"Can you stand?"

"I think so." But standing seems physically rigorous, unthinkable. Like, can you run a marathon? Yeah, I think so. He wants to ask Cam if it's a theoretical question, give him a hard time, but knows it wouldn't come out right. He tries to prop himself up with a decided lack of success.

"Hey, hey, hold on," Cam says, getting an arm beneath his shoulders, slowly pulling him into a sitting position. Beau slouches against the wall, tipping his throbbing head back and closing his eyes. He weighs a hundred million pounds.

"Beau, you're really not well," Cam says. "I think we should go to the hospital." He sits down across from his friend, pushing a dented can of tomato sauce out of the way. Beau thinks he looks sick in his own way, with worry or want, or both.

"No fucking, way," he says, withering at the thought, the hours upon hours of fluorescent lights and antiseptic floor cleaner sedimented in his body boiling up like bile. The revulsion curls deep in his gut, the feeling of his alarm going off at four in the morning for Starbucks opening shifts. "I'm fine, Cam, I'll be fine."

Cam is demolishing the inside of his cheek in a way he must think is subtle. "You have a really bad fever, man. Remember what Lynch said? She said fever over thirty-eight means ER."

Beau groans, pressing his palm to his forehead, trying to gauge the heat radiating from his skin. "You think it's that bad?"

"I think it's bad, yeah. I think you're passing out all over the stairs and it's fucking bad, Beau."

"It'll go down, it'll go down. I'll take some pills and go to bed. I'll fucking, sleep it off."

"Are you kidding," Cam says, and Beau sees the recklessness in him, its vastness and strength. "Sleep it off, are you kidding! This is like in the summer, when I fucking told you to go to the doctor and you said it was fine! You said—" he stops himself, looking away. "You're *sick*, Beau, you're really sick. I don't think you can sleep it off."

Beau lowers his head, bending it to his knees. Keeping it upright is painful and makes the world swim. "I just can't go there right now, I'm there all the time, it's like, *fuck*. They're gonna keep me there so long if I go. We're gonna wait around for *hours*, man, *hours*. You have to understand, Cam. I know you know."

"I know, I know," he says, "but what the *fuck!* What are you even *doing*, carrying up all these fucking groceries?" He swings his arm, gesturing at the litter of cans and boxes and eggs, their yolks pooling around their carton, bleeding through its sides. "What are you even doing, going outside today?"

"You asked me to!"

"Are you fucking stupid! If you were feeling well! If you were feeling okay and there wasn't a fucking blizzard outside! I could have gotten this stuff, Beau."

"It's not your fault, it's not your fault," he says, fighting down a wave of nausea. "But please, Cam, let's just wait a bit and it'll go down. Please, man." He sounds desperate even to himself, and knows this betrays the gravity of his unwellness more than anything else.

"Can you stand?"

"I don't know."

"Come on, I'll help you up, okay? Ready?" Cam pulls him up and Beau feels very faint, worse than he'd feared, collapsing against Cam's body. Cam is surprisingly, unexpectedly strong, holding him up firmly and with ease, like he's been prepared for this all along. Beau wonders if Cam's sudden strength is a result of his comparative weakness or of Cam's adrenaline, signified by the beat of his heart sounding through his jacket like a hammer.

Beau presses his head to Cam's chest and closes his eyes against the fever in his skull, now its own thing with agency and desires that are well-articulated and separate from his own. They lean together for a moment, Beau on Cam and Cam on the wall, feeling each other breathe.

"Beau, I know you don't want to," Cam finally says, "but we have to go to the hospital. I'm sorry, man."

"Cam," he says, the name muffled by the fabric of its owner's coat.

"You know I wouldn't make you if it wasn't serious."

"I know, I know I have to go, okay? Just give me a minute, fuck."

"Okay, okay," Cam says, his hand cool on the back of Beau's neck. From its tender weight Beau understands Cam is afraid.

"Beau?"

"Uh huh."

"You can't pass out, okay? You have to stay awake until we get there."

Somehow they make it down the stairs, Beau's arm looped across Cam's shoulders where Cam holds his wrist, his other arm tight around Beau's waist. They move slowly, Beau slipping every couple steps to be brought up with a jerk as Cam braces himself against the sudden weight.

In the Jeep Beau collapses into the seat and presses his cheek against the window, the glass wonderfully cold and laced with intricate patterns etched in frost. Heat pounds behind his aching eyes. "Not feeling good, man," he says.

"Hey, I know." Cam gets in and shuts the door before realizing the windshield is already covered with a fresh layer of wet snow, newly accumulated since he'd parked. He makes a small frustrated sound and gets out, wiping at the glass with the sleeve of his jacket.

"Fuck," he says, getting back in, packed deposits of snow sitting in the folds of his clothes. His breath clouds in the closed space. He cranks the heater and backs out without really looking, swinging the Jeep onto the slick road. It takes Beau a moment to figure out that the Cherokee's uncanny orientation (markedly different than the seventeen million other times they've pulled away from this curb) is a result of Cam taking the wrong way up their one-way street, cutting directly to College instead of driving around the block.

"Road safety first, huh," he says, and closes his eyes with the hope this might dispel some of the rising nausea sloshing around behind his lids with each bump.

"Yeah, you're gonna get the not-entirely-legal route today," Cam says. He stares straight ahead, fingers tapping out his impatience on the wheel. There's a lot of end-of-day traffic and Beau can see it's driving him nuts, changing the way he sits, hunched forward because of his height and checking the mirror obsessively, like he'd rather get out and push the car than sit in it moving a couple feet at a time. Some things, like driving (and reading, Beau thinks), lay bare the incredible energy he carries, exposing its full intensity inadvertently, as an afterthought.

Cam swings down a side street and Beau listens to the Jeep's tires crunching on snow, spinning at the maximum acceptable speed for a residential area. Sheltered from the wind, the snowfall is reduced to big wet lazy flakes softened by coloured lights strung from wide Victorian porches. He thinks of Christmas and how excited he'd been, how good he'd felt the second the chemo was done, how fucking, *hopeful*. He hates this in himself, the eager weakness with which he'd tempted it, the thing inside him. As if, as if.

But he knows it's true.

Putting lights on the tree while Cam watched TV like he wasn't interested though Beau could see he was pleased to death, floored with relief pressing his long loose body into the couch. He thinks of Cathy hugging him so tight, pulling him to her breasts, trying to gauge his thinness from the weight and shape of his body against hers. Cathy, who he'd lied to, who he'd insisted Cam lie to. It was a horrible thing, and a cowardly one. He didn't want to face her worry, couldn't do it when there was the hope of being maybe, possibly (please, please) better.

He knows he hasn't handled it well, this thing. He's been stubborn and willful, as if this could somehow beat out the indifferent force of his illness. There is a new, deeply superstitious turn in him he can't shake (though he's tried, telling himself he's twenty-four years old) through which he involuntarily assigns meaning to all things. Omens, he thinks, unable to put the idea down. Fucking, signs.

"It's natural to find things more meaningful when you're in a dire situation," Lynch said when he told her about this, arms folded on her desk. "Many people find that when confronted with the possibility of their own death, it's helpful for them to imagine there is logic and sense in the world beyond what we can see."

He looked at her seriously, desperately. It didn't matter how he looked at her, because she wasn't going to sit up with him on the cold bathroom tile at two in the morning.

"Are you saying I'm turning all religious or something?"

"Are you?"

"No."

"Well then, no. I'm saying if you're finding meaning in things that you wouldn't have thought twice about before, it's not unheard of in your situation." She paused, studying him across the desk, thinking he looked young and earnest and afraid. "Do you find it helps you?"

"Sometimes. Sometimes I just feel like I'm jinxing everything by feeling hopeful, or acting too confident, or . . ." he trailed off.

"You feel like what you think or do will have an impact on your condition, but it's important not to ascribe that kind of causality. It's very important that you don't blame yourself."

Do I blame myself? he thought, hanging his head for a moment, and decided no, that's not it. It was that he increasingly saw things as competing agencies, volitional forces that met and pushed on each other, applying pressure until one or the other had won out. That he saw, suddenly, how everything had its own energy, from the static clinging to Cam's clothes to the dread pooling in the clinic waiting room to the two of them sitting here now, her enormous professional calm vast and cool like an ocean, lapping up against his—what? His insides felt like a field of white noise.

"Do you ever talk to Cam about it?"

He shook his head. "No—I can't."

"Because you care about him."

He nodded.

"You should consider," she said, "that he's already as worried as he's going to be, so you might as well. I imagine that with a background in philosophy he'd have quite a few things to say about finding meaning."

Epistemology, Beau thought. Cam had explained this to him as, what can we know and how can we know it? Theory of knowledge, he said. Like, why make meaning one way and not another? Standing at the kitchen counter sipping coffee, gesturing in the abstract way Beau imagined he used when teaching.

"There are also support groups, and classes you could go to, if you wanted. You can bring a friend, it's not as isolating as you think. Take Cam with you—I'm sure he'd really like that. He just wants to help you the best he can. Or you could see a counselor, a psychologist. You might be surprised how much it helps to talk to someone you don't have a personal relationship with."

"I'm not doing that," he said, having had enough social workers and psychiatrists and prescription drugs to last him a lifetime.

Lynch touched the corner of her mouth with her finger, checking for lipstick. She leaned closer, stretching across the desk, and when she spoke it was soft and deliberate. "Have you ever considered, Beau, that you might be depressed?"

He had, in fact, considered it all the way home from her office after that awful appointment just two weeks before, the wind pulling the breath out of him and pushing it back into his lungs as he walked with his head down and his hands deep in his pockets. He'd stood with Cam on the sidewalk and felt the force of their negotiation taking place beyond anything that was said, the angles of their shoulders communicating their mutual desire to be alone.

He needed to go, and Cam had let him. He needed to be by himself because he felt full and shaky and knew he would cry as he almost had in the elevator, wiping his sleeve across his eyes because he could not, would not do this thing in front of Cam.

He walked home in the clean noon light and everything seemed new to him, starkly outlined in its plain beauty though January had succeeded in washing the world varying shades of grey. The road was the colour of chalk, bleached with salt and frost, and something about this filled him with extraordinary sadness of an irrevocable kind he hadn't known for years, now, the kind that bit into his bones and somewhere deeper, too. Like the pang of understanding that the priority of foster parents was their own children, and that he was nobody's child, and thus nobody's priority.

He felt static and desperate, like he wanted to run but couldn't, or worse, like the running wouldn't even begin to loosen the hot dark thing pushing on his throat. He kept his head down because his vision blurred and his eyes felt warm and he knew he looked wrecked, distraught, unwell. Forty percent (or so), though he hadn't wanted to know the number, though he was sick of numbers running his life and it was Cam who'd asked. There were numbers for shit he didn't even know could be counted, like three different kinds of platelets and all the white blood cell stats (especially crucial) and his fucking, blood protein, all stacked up in columns like a tally, his body's fluctuating wellness quantified by machines.

Got cancer in your blood, man, he thought, and felt ill all over. Cancer in your blood and that's the worst kind, because once it gets in your blood it's everywhere. He didn't understand how they could somehow extract it if it was spread all over, circulating through his ailing body with each pump of his heart, searching out soft vital zones to settle down in. He knew how these things went: it would be chemo now for a while, until it got more dire, and then they would recommend some kind of surgery, something serious and painful and useless—can't think that shit, can't think that, he told himself. Cam says I can't think that shit, and he's right.

The stairs exhausted him. In the apartment he shut the door and sagged against the wall, hot and beaten and sorry and hateful of everything, overtaken by great wailing sobs. Thinking: Do I really sound like that? Is that really me?

He felt weak and stumbled to the couch, crying harder than he could stand, suddenly brimming with sorrow that was heavy and thick and couldn't be set aside, blackening the edges of his vision. This is what happens when you walk around acting like everything is no big deal, he thought, distantly, shocked at the coolness of the idea.

Beau's throat seized up and he pressed his face into the cushions, trying to curl himself against them as tightly as he could. Oh why why why, he thought, eyes wet and raw. How will I fucking, stand it? His chest heaving as if it might eviscerate itself without warning, sending his lungs spilling from his body and into his lap.

It occurred to him that Cam could come home at any moment—that he was being so loud he wouldn't even hear him coming through the door and would be caught like that, naked in his despair. He made himself stand but couldn't stay upright, sorrow pulling him down to the floor. He crawled to the bathroom, howling and hating himself for it, wanting to dig his nails into his skin until he drew blood. In the bathroom he did, keeled over and pressing angry red crescents into the soft underside of his arm. The tile was freezing cold and he hated it, this place where he spent so much time on his knees.

Cut it out, he thought. Fucking, stop it, stop it right now.

The strength of his sobs scared him. They gave no sign of abating, coming one after another, waves unvaried in either frequency or force. What did he want? He couldn't have said. There was an enormous, splitting sadness in him, a fundamental loneliness that nothing could ease. For the first time in his life he thought he understood what was meant by *wretched*.

He blew his nose and wiped at his face and thought he would feel better if he showered, but when he got into the tub he found he couldn't stand. Instead he ran the water as hot as he could take and sat bent over himself, shivering because their bathtub was shallow. When it had filled he lay down and bent his knees, submerging himself as much as he could. The water flooded into his ears with a soft pop and he lay still, listening to all the sounds of an old apartment building in the early afternoon: water rushing in pipes and voices downstairs and someone's music from farther away, a fast careless beat, everything muffled and distinct all at the same time, carrying distorted through the amplifying medium.

Beau Larky closed his eyes and tried to even out his breathing. A visceral memory of chemo and all its intricacies, its IVs and waiting for them to put in the IVs and the poking around (because sometimes there were medical students, and sometimes they needed to practice) prior to the pop of punctured skin and the cold dripping fluid numbing his arm and then the band-aids and bruising and the way the light got afterward, sharp and indifferent, and how hard it was to walk straight, and the nausea catching up to him at night, and his knees against the cold tile, heaving up all the nothing he'd eaten, and Cam's fucking, face, like he was the one who was sick, like just watching it all caused him pain—this set him off again, triggering deep seismic heaving in his chest. Oh oh oh, he thought, oh fuck, and wanted to be dead.

After a while the sobs dwindled into deep shaky breaths and he felt a little better, the hot water drawing the blackness out of him like a poison, its urgency seeping away. It'll be okay, he told himself, but what he really wanted was to hear it from Cam, who made it sound like a statement instead of a wish, and who would add: You'll see.

He was overtaken by a surge of love.

Later he sat on the couch staring into the January gloom, watching the light change through the windows and feeling hollow, emptied of all emotion. His insides felt like they'd been scraped down, the remainder of the sorrow, now manageable, clinging to them like a film. He sat and waited and for Cam to come home, but Cam didn't return, not then, not until the next afternoon when he let himself in so quietly, as if this could distract from the mud on his pants and stains on his shirt. He let Cam shower and they didn't talk about it, or about how Beau had sat bent over himself in the bathtub and lost his grip on the world.

"Beau, hey. Are you passing out?"

He opens his eyes and looks around, groggy and warm. His throat is tight and dry. "No, I'm good."

"You can't pass out, okay?"

"I'm trying, Cam."

"I know man. Just . . . you have such a high fever."

Beau can see Cam's afraid, but thinks he'll black out no matter what Cam says, because the window just isn't fucking, cold enough to keep him awake and the motion of the Jeep sways him and—

"Beau, come on. Please. We're almost there."

"Okay," he says.

"What are you thinking, huh."

"Fucking, miserable shit." He presses his face to the window, fighting down another wave. He thinks, distantly, that under other circumstances it would have been intolerably beautiful out, with the snow so soft and the streetlamps and the deepening dusk.

Whether Cam, who spends a great deal of time beating worn trails in his mind concerning his roommate's thoughts, would guess any of them, is hard to say. What he intuits is more of a feeling, a vague shift in mood he picks up through extended proximity, and something stronger, too. "I know man," he says.

And then: "Listen, they're definitely gonna want you to stay overnight, and probably a couple nights."

Beau groans, and it's almost a sob.

"I know, I know. But I'll stay with you, okay?"

"Cam."

"Yeah, I'll bring Scrabble and chess. And joints."

"You don't have to do that. You have class and shit."

"Is this really a conversation we're having? I'm not going to *class* when you're in the fucking *hospital*."

Beau laughs, floored with warmth. "Okay, okay," he says, and bends over himself, suddenly vertiginous, telling himself he won't be sick, not here in the Jeep.

"Beau?"

He shakes his head. "It's fine, it's fine. Ugh."

"Listen," Cam says, and Beau sees that he's pulling up to the curb, that they've somehow made it all the way to Toronto General and its impressive ER drop-off area where Cam has found *street parking*, of all things. He can already see the yellow ticket tucked under the Jeep's wipers when Cam comes back out to move the car. "Don't get out, okay? Just wait and let me come around and get you. Okay?"

"Okay," he says, closing his eyes, and then there's Cam opening the passenger door and checking his forehead and pulling on his toque for him, the toque that must have fallen off in the Jeep or maybe earlier, Beau can't say. Cam making executive decisions is good.

"Here." Cam helps him out and holds him up.

Beau leans on him, their breath making clouds that mingle above their heads in the frosty air. "I can walk it," he says.

"No, come on. I'll help you."

"Let me walk it, man. I'm fine, it's right there." He gestures vaguely in the direction of the ER's sliding doors, just visible beneath the awning across the street.

Cam lets him go and Beau can tell it's reluctant, that Cam doesn't agree but can't argue. If it were up to Cam he'd be waiting in the Jeep while a wheelchair was found for him, and what kind of shit is *that*, having fucking, cancer and needing wheelchairs and being too dizzy to walk by yourself? What kind of shit is that when you're twenty-four years old? It's unfair and awful and just another insult, he thinks, added to his pile of worldly misfortunes that had begun when someone with the last name of Larky received several firmly worded letters and then finally a surprise visit from child protective services requesting they give up a kid with the unfortunate name of Beauregard for government care. Life is a fucking, sick joke, he thinks. A crackling dark cloud passes over his mind.

Cam locks the car and they start out across the street, slipping around on the soft couple inches of almost-slush lining the road, already turning brown in spots. Cam hovers by him, watching his movements like he's going to write an essay on them, cite them. Nobody loves you like he does, he thinks, and knows it's true.

The body-heaviness is unbearable, lodging in his back and shoulders as a powerful need to be horizontal and unconscious. He often wonders if the cancer is really in his blood and not in his bones, where such profound unease settles with such regularity. He slips on the hospital driveway and Cam catches his elbow, grabbing a handful of jacket. They look at each other and Beau says *I'm fine*, because they're only a few meters from the sliding doors and whatever, he can do it, it's not like he can't fucking, walk.

The driveway has a slight slope that for some reason having to do with hospital administration remains egregiously unsalted, and so the second time Beau slips it's fast and sudden and leaves Cam holding a fistful of nothing while Beau Larky hits the pavement, legs going out from under him. His head meets it first with a crack that is shocking, like nothing he's ever felt before. It reverberates in his teeth, flooding the inside of his skull with bright blinding pain that lights up behind his eyes and fills his vision with starbursts of many colours—red, green, white—before rendering the world black and void of all things.

And if anybody wants to know what desperation looks like they should see Cam now, on his knees in the slush touching his roommate's face as he watches the spot beneath his head turn a deep regal red. It is both nauseous and strangely beautiful in the way blood on snow can be, as those who have seen it know.

Three

When Beau comes to he immediately knows he's in the hospital, the sounds of heels squeaking on polished linoleum and nurses chatting and someone crying over the soft wheeze of a respirator down the hall seeping into his consciousness even before he opens his eyes. Gentle industrial sounds, like a factory on near-mute. Someone is being paged to radiology over the grainy intercom. He opens his eyes and sees the inevitable green curtain, IV stand and stiff sheets, a small dose of empiricism confirming knowledge more felt than understood.

He tries to move his head and wishes he hadn't, the single motion lighting up a map of pain behind his eyes. There's an icepick lodged between his skull and spine, sharp and stabbing and intimate with all his nerve endings, right down to the tips of his fingers. Fuck, he thinks, scared now, because he can't recall how such pain has come to originate from his skull, or what it means. He reaches up to gently probe the back of his head, finding it tender and thickly bandaged. This profusion of gauze where there had been none is uncanny and makes him deeply nauseous. He closes his eyes against the sensation.

His mouth is impossibly dry, the flesh of his tongue dead and swollen like he's just spent a week wandering around in the desert with the fucking, worst pasties of life. He wants to sit up but can't. There's an IV taped into his arm and another into his hand, and he guesses he must be on many serious hospital-grade drugs that will explain, as soon as he finds out what they are, the grogginess clouding his mind. His thoughts move slowly, like the last bit of glue trying to make its way out of a bottle.

Head injury, he thinks. Head injury because—(what?) The profundity of blankness rising to meet him in trying to complete this thought is terrifying and total. (What), he thinks again, and stares out over the resulting inner static as over a waste, vast and empty like the surface of the moon.

A brief moment of panic flares up before he can damp it down, becoming once more self-contained. No, no, he thinks. There's no fucking, way. This isn't a fucking, movie and it will come, all of it will come back and you're on a lot of drugs, man. He strains his mind and sees that yeah, there are many things indeed, pieces of information just beyond his reach, vague shadow shapes beyond a dimly lit room. The ka-thunk of something (cans?) on stairs, and—riding in the Jeep, and the coolness of linoleum, and of the frost-painted window.

The green curtain rustles and a man in blue scrubs comes in, pulling it closed behind him. He is young and unshaven and obviously an intern sticking out the night shift. There are no windows or clocks, but Beau feels the lateness of the night keenly, deep in his gut. "Hello, Beau," he says. "How are you feeling?"

"Okay," Beau says, forcing the word through his uncooperative parched mouth. Something in it is bleeding, maybe his tongue.

The intern pulls up a chair to Beau's bed and sits down, crossing one leg over the other, ankle on knee. "I'm Dr. Rajma," he says, scanning his clipboard. "Do you know why you're here?"

Beau shrugs, touching the back of his head like he's asking a question. Not an intern after all, though he must be no older than thirty. He would kill for a glass of water. "I'm on a lot of drugs," he says, motioning at the IV.

The doctor laughs. "Yes," he says. "We've got you on morphine and some antibiotics, and you were given antipyretics earlier."

Fucking, morphine, he thinks, relieved. *Yeah.*

"Are you feeling any pain at all?"

"Only when I move my head."

"Okay, that's good. If you had to rate your pain on a scale of one to ten?"

Beau laughs, finding the question surreal. He wonders if maybe his head isn't just totally fucked. "I would say like, a five, maybe?" He moves his head experimentally, wincing. "A five point five."

"Okay, good. We can up that morphine for you if you feel it gets worse."

"It's fine," he says, frightened at the prospect of more mind-loosening drugs.

The doctor checks his clipboard, flipping back a page. From Beau's low vantage point on the bed it looks like a chart. "Do you know why you're here?" he asks again.

"Obviously I fu—injured my head, somehow."

"Do you remember what happened?"

Beau reaches, extending his psychic energy into a single point of focus, and comes back with nothing but a handful of isolated sensations, all temporally disjointed in his mind like a puzzle put together by someone who is blind, or not all there. "No. I mean, I must have fallen, but I don't know."

"The original reason for your ER visit is listed here as a high fever, of particular concern due to low white blood cell counts from ongoing chemotherapy," Rajma says, tapping his pen against the clipboard's edge.

Beau groans, the physical memory of months and months of chemo hitting him like a great weight. Like a ton of bricks, an expression he doesn't find at all clichéd. He'd nearly forgotten, since waking, that he is sick, and now feels weak and unsettled, dizzy with the remembrance.

Rajma looks at him curiously, eyebrows raised. "Does that sound at all familiar to you?"

"Yeah, yeah. Too familiar." He recalls the heat, the contrasting coolness of the Jeep's window keeping him awake. The returning details slip into place, filling in parts of a vague whole.

"And then," Rajma flips the page again, "you slipped coming up our driveway here, in the ER drop-off, and sustained a concussion."

Beau looks at him, eyes widening. Like, are you fucking, kidding me. Are you fucking, pulling my leg, or what.

"Nothing too serious," the doctor clarifies, quickly. "Although your scalp split and bled quite a bit, as your lanky friend with the blood all over his pants can testify."

"Cam," he says. "Shit. Is he here?"

"He's out in the waiting area."

Beau is weakened by an image of Cam in the waiting room with dried blood on his cords, bent over himself and staring down between his feet, elbows resting on knees with hands hanging motionless between. With his hands stilled, willed to stillness, possibly cradling the bad wrist that gives him trouble even now. In Beau's image Cam hasn't bothered to remove his coat and sits with it zipped up, curling into the fabric forming a thin shield between himself and the room, the garish lighting, the situation. "Is he okay?"

"Oh, he's fine. He's been waiting for a quite a while. He doesn't take 'no' very well for an answer."

"Yeah, that's Cam," Beau says, and melts into the sheets, relieved to the bone not to be alone in this green-curtained room with his mind so fogged, whether with drugs or bruising on his brain, he can't say. "Can I see him?"

"As soon as we're done here. You've got eight stitches on your scalp, where the bandaging is, which should take no more than two or three weeks to heal up. Also," looking at Beau directly, "with this type of concussion it's possible that you may not remember events leading up to your injury."

"Yeah, I don't, I—" he presses the heels of his hands to his forehead, squeezing his eyes shut. "There are small details but they seem disconnected, and there's stuff that's—not even there. Is that normal? That there's stuff totally gone?"

Rajma nods. "Completely normal. Sometimes with this kind of head injury we see a very low-grade form of retrograde amnesia, in which patients can't recall events directly before the injury took place. It's very short-term and should clear up completely within a few days, weeks at most. Nothing permanent," he says.

What the fuck, Beau thinks. What the fuck is this Twilight Zone shit.

"We've done some scans and determined there's no serious damage, only some bruising that's being controlled for swelling."

"So I don't have some kind of permanent memory loss shit going on."

"No, nothing like that."

Beau nods even as a new feeling comes over him, unfurling like a sheet or wing over his hazy mind—the cold unease that comes with the unmistakable certainty that one has forgotten something important, misplaced or lost some vital thing. Something vital, like—(what)?

"I'm going to ask you some questions, Beau, if that's okay with you." More clipboard tapping, some harsh scribbling of ballpoint pen against corkboard.

"Okay," Beau says, and is asked a series of questions about his full name, age and address, his job and housing situation, his education, where he grew up and what his parents were like, a question he answers by saying he has no idea, except that they gave him an exceptionally inconvenient name to have while being thrown around between group homes brimming with hard scrappy adolescent boys. Through this, they taught him how to appear unfazed by jeers, taunts, pain, loneliness. To appear unfazed by anything at all.

Dr. Rajma, who turns out to be a neurologist, tells Beau his recall seems fine, and that he'll be back to talk with him later, potentially running some further scans.

"How long do I have to stay here?" Beau asks. The psychic static that overtook him on the walk back from the clinic is coming on strong.

"At least overnight, and likely another night, I would say. You've got an infection and a bit of a fever still, and combined with the concussion it would be best to play it safe and see how you do."

Beau groans without meaning to. The static is horrible, fusing into a physical dread penetrating everything at a near-cellular level. His pulse throbs in the stitches.

"Beau, you need to understand this kind of injury can make you feel disoriented, tired, foggy, nauseous. Generally unwell.

You might get dizzy or feel sensitive to light, noise. All of these things are normal symptoms and you shouldn't feel too concerned—they'll go away with time." The doctor has short, dark bristly hair that makes a rasping sound when he runs his hand through it. "Do you want to see your friend? Before he paces a hole through the floor out there."

Pacing, of course. Beau can see this clearly: Cam channeling his intensity, head far away while his body works off anxiety on its own, without consultation, his incredible energy laid bare. He nods, drained.

Rajma leaves and Beau closes his eyes and then Cam comes in alone, pushing through the curtain. He doesn't look like he's been pacing, but stands by the bed with his hands in his pockets and his jacket over his arm, all great quiet intensity. "Beau," he says. There are, as the doctor promised, large splotches the colour of rust dried onto his cords just above the knees.

Beau isn't sure if he's been so happy to see anyone, ever. "Cam," he says, "hey. Are you driving them nuts pacing out there?"

Cam shakes his head and takes Rajma's chair, letting its legs scrape over the tile as he brings it closer. "I was, earlier. I think I ran out of steam." He glances at his watch with a practiced motion from which Beau knows he's been doing it about once a minute since arriving in the waiting room. "I mean, it's been eight hours."

"Shit, Cam. I'm so sorry, I had no idea. I've been totally out until like, half an hour ago."

"Yeah, they stitched up your head, huh." He leans closer, brimming with a tenderness beyond his ability to contain. "Beau, the neurologist said you have a concussion. Are you okay?"

Cam's sincerity hits him in a way he doesn't expect, tightening his throat. "I think so," he says. "My head is killing me. I just feel like—Cam, I feel like there's shit I can't remember."

"Hey, hey. It's okay. What kind of stuff?" He shakes his head. "Wait, wait, I almost forgot," he says, pulling a bottle of Perrier from inside his folded coat. "I brought you some water. You must be so thirsty, huh."

Beau's eyes grow hot and he tells himself he won't cry, not over this, not in front of Cam. He isn't in control of himself, and this frightens him. It's like he hadn't even realized how fucking, shaken up he felt until he saw Cam and this bottle that of course he would bring. Dazed and jarred, like he's been dumped out of a bucket onto a hard surface with no warning.

"Yeah," he says, holding the bottle to his chest. Cam opens it for him without comment and raises the bed so he can sit up. He watches Beau drink and wipe awkwardly at his mouth with his IV-laden arm.

"Beau," Cam says. "What's your head looking like, huh?" His intensity is like a whole other person in the room.

Beau can't read his mood. He turns his head to let Cam see the bandaging, moving slowly because everything aches. The tape over the gauze crinkles.

Cam draws an audible breath. "Eight stitches, eh. Is it a big cut? It looks like they shaved away some of your hair." He traces the edge of the bandage with his fingers.

"I don't know. I can feel it though." He imagines his brain shifting away from the point of impact and crashing into the front of his skull, bulbous and swollen, straining against the bone. "Cam, what if it's fucked up my head?"

"No, the doctor said there was no damage. They ran scans."

"I just feel so hazy. And I can't remember shit all about what happened."

"He said that's common, with this kind of injury. He said you wouldn't be able to remember events just before. He said maybe even the whole day of."

"Well, I definitely can't."

"You had a really bad fever. You passed out coming up the stairs with groceries, which I don't even know why—which I can't fucking *believe* you were even doing."

"Yeah, me neither," Beau says, and Cam laughs, running a hand back through his hair.

"And then I drove you here, and the fucking pavement wasn't salted and you slipped and cracked your head so hard I thought you were dead, man." He looks down between his thighs where his hands are twined together, fingers interlaced. "And you bled so much. You should have seen my face."

"Cam, that's so awful."

Cam shrugs. "It wasn't the best time I've ever had. You don't remember any of that?"

"No. I mean, there are little details I can recall, but they're all disjointed, it's hard to even place where they're from." Cans on stairs, he thinks.

"You'll remember, Beau."

"But what if there's other stuff?" he says, propping himself up on an elbow in an ambitious move that sends a wave of pain through his head and neck, forcing his eyes shut.

"Hey, Beau. You've gotta relax. The tests said it was okay." Cam eases him down. "You're on a lot of drugs right now. You're in pain, you know?"

Beau imagines the inside of Cam's cheek is raw and bloody from eight hours of him going to town on it. Cam gets a distracted look when he chews it, mouth closed and pulled up on one side like a smirk that doesn't quite match the distance in his eyes, focused miles and miles inward. "I know, but I can just *feel* it," he says. "I just fucking, *know* there's shit I can't remember beyond that. Stuff I've forgotten. Blanks, man."

"Like what?" Cam says. He's pulled his chair close enough to lean on the bed, arms crossed.

"I don't know, I've just got this feeling like—" he shifts to take pressure off the back of his skull "—like when you're walking around the house and you go into a room and you're like, what the fuck did I come in here for? And it feels like it's right there but just out of reach."

"Beau," Cam says. He speaks quietly. "You know what the doctor told me? He said you would be disoriented. He warned me about it."

"I really am. I feel totally messed up."

"Beau, I know. But he said it would go away."

"Don't you ever feel a gap between what someone tells you is true and what you feel?" Beau says, and Cam looks away so quickly he has to add, "what?"

"Nothing." And then: "Yeah, all the time. A discrepancy."

"So it's like that." He turns the academic word over in his mind. *Discrepancy*. This is the word for the shadow of the wing.

"But he asked you questions, right? To see if you're remembering okay."

"Yeah, he asked me about like, where I live, what I do. Stuff like that."

"And you were fine."

"Yeah, totally. Except I don't think it's that kind of thing."

Cam leans in. "What do you mean?"

"I mean it feels more fundamental, important, but can't be summed up in that way. It's not like a single fact or something. He asked me if I remembered bits of information, and I do. This other thing is more of a feeling that something is there, was there. Something I should know." He sees a room in which things have been shifted around or removed, their absence betrayed only by discoloured outlines on walls where paint has not been exposed to sun. Ghost shapes. "I don't know, Cam," he says. "I hate this whole thing."

"You've been so sick," Cam says, and all of a sudden he's so *sad*, like he can't even look at Beau, has to look at the floor instead. The sadness reshapes his body and the way he sits, like he's been holding a weight and only now allows himself to sag beneath it, exhausted. Beau tries to remember if Cam has always been this way and he just hadn't noticed until now, and finds that he doesn't know. In this sadness, more than anything, he sees there are entire continents of things he's not understanding.

"Cam, you need to get some sleep, man. You should go have a shower at least, and come back in the morning." It's already morning, his internal clock tells him. Outside people coming off the night shift are stepping into the first rays of sickening sunlight, heading home to their beds, but not before sending their children off to school, as one of his foster mothers had done, coming in at seven AM bleary-eyed and smelling of janitorial chemicals. He would kill to see a window.

Cam zips up his coat and rests his hand on Beau's head, shy. "I'll come back, okay," he says, and the look on his face dries out Beau's mouth all over again. He thinks: What? Cam, what?

As soon as Cam leaves he feels horrible, like starting to think the wrong thing for even a few moments might leave him lost, somehow off balance. The hypnotic names of prescription antidepressants (fluoxetine, sertraline) and their jarring disyllabic trade names (Prozac, Zoloft) surface in his mind unbidden, and he recalls the bitter tang of holding these beneath his tongue for too long. The shapes of the pills, the fluoxetine in its white and mint gel capsules, 20mg, and the blue sertraline, pressed tabs that left powder on his fingertips when pushed out of their bubble packaging into his waiting hand. He wonders if maybe there is something fundamentally unstable within him that had settled, burrowed deep for many years, and now this fall has dislodged, rattled loose.

Beau thinks: If there's a drawer of shit that's been arranged just so, and then you fucking, upend that drawer all over the floor and the shit goes everywhere, how can you guarantee it'll all get put back just the way it was? Further (another academic word Cam is always dropping in his papers), how can you be sure that everything's been put back in the first place? That nothing's been lost? He thinks of film canisters he'd dumped out of his pockets by accident and tried to find for weeks, one day lying flat on the floor to pull his phone from under his bed and seeing them all there, half a dozen lost at different times, the little plastic containers choked with strings of dust. And developing the film, amazed at its contents as he held the newly dry celluloid strips of negatives up to the light.

It occurs to him that you can't know what you're looking for if you don't even know what you've lost.

Four

March is long, wet and grey. Beau doesn't see this firsthand but feels it out from the slush trailing in with Cam's sneakers to leave salt stains on the green hospital tile, the weak light flooding through tall windows opening onto brick walls and white skies. He is in the hospital a lot, spending overnights breathing his way through big squeezing liquid pressure in what must be the very core of his bones but Lynch says are just nerve endings, inflamed tissues responding to bad drugs. Something has gone wrong somewhere, either in Beau's reaction to his newly upped chemo dose or in the aftermath of the concussion and its cognitive haze that makes it impossible to walk without sudden spells of vertigo, dizziness, nausea. And the scans look fine, and the chemo has to run its course, so what can he do? He lies around feeling feverish and displaced, head light with assorted painkillers.

Beau has been at Toronto General for the better part of two weeks, and he doesn't feel good. He doesn't feel like he has a handle on things anymore, whatever that means. As if this was ever something he had, a grip on these colossal shifts within his body. He knows things have been forgotten, irrevocably lost no matter what anyone says. He can see it in the moments of emotional static that fill him for no apparent reason, yawning out of ordinary conversations, opening up a pit of (what)?

He lies in his stiff starched bed in the fucking, awful blue open-backed hospital gown he hates, hospital robe and hoodie over top, and longs for weed. The drugs make him slow and stupid and he dreams of joints, big RAW paper wraps, blunts rolled from grape cigarillos, bongs, pipes, vapes, hot knives and their white ghost smoke so thick you could cut it. There is a single clear memory he can't stop rerunning, Cam turning from the stove with scalding hot butter knives held in oven-gloved hands, pressing them together just right so they make that *tsss* hiss and smoke just plumes, fucking, *piles* into the two litre pop bottle Beau's holding and they both laugh so it's hard to hold everything still, saying, as if it were the obvious thing: *diiirty*. He thinks of their cutlery drawer, black scorch marks left on so many of their butter knives. Beau knows this was a good time in his life, and misses it.

Cam is there a lot, pretty much all the time Beau isn't lobotomized by painkillers that make him feel like he's moving underwater, but internally so. He comes in wearing things that make it obvious he's having a hard time, old plaid shirts that are definitely Beau's, cross-hatched black and navy and red sleeves too short for his arms, leaving his wrists exposed and somehow naked-seeming, vulnerable. Beau thinks he doesn't look good, unshaven and unrested and moving like he weighs a ton. He pushes Beau around in the blue canvas hospital wheelchairs, down the halls, to the lobby, upstairs to see Lynch. Out into the parking lot for joints where Beau huddles in the chair in a jacket that is definitely his but feels big on his suddenly small body. He doesn't have to turn around to know Cam has his shoulders hunched protectively, like he wants to hug himself.

Cam crouches down in front of him in the endless slush of the back lot and cups his hands over the lighter, shielding its flame from wind. With everything icy and wet and Beau's haze of a hundred different drugs he looks, in his great intensity, like he's about to propose. Instead he stands and nods, satisfied with the size of the cherry they've managed to spark despite all the wind.

Like he's about to propose—this is how Beau puts it to himself, and later can't get the words out of his mind, or the image of Cam down in front of him like that. There's something romantic about it, though he couldn't have said what. He thinks of upset drawers and missing objects.

Cam removes him from things. Watching the brilliant orange end-of-day light bleeding onto the far wall, he's pulled back from vast interior ledges by Cam coming in breathless, gloved hands still hidden in his pockets against the cold, telling him to come on, get dressed, get your coat on, you have to see this sunset, man. Beau dresses painstakingly, with as much haste as he can manage given that he's hooked up to not one but two separate IVs and full of drugs that fuck with his general sense of balance. Cam helps him into his coat and kneels to tie up his shoes.

Outside the light taints everything, colouring the white rectangles of snow topping clean-edged roofs and refracting in the panelled glass of surrounding buildings. It's been a day of cold distant sun, the kind of sun that seems remote but can soften snow, its glare causing hungover walkers to lower their heads and shield their eyes, bring out their sunglasses. The snow is already shining, hardening into the ice-topped sheen it will develop as dusk creeps in and the temperature drops.

Cam wheels him up the hill to the legislative buildings where they sit together, Cam on a bench and him in the chair, watching the last of the sun catching the steel of buildings on either side of the canyon that is University Avenue, hospital alley. In the narrow park forming an island among six lanes of traffic, the trees are bare and strung with white lights.

It was intended to be the city's main commercial stretch, Cam tells him, shopping and restaurants and multi-level malls, but now houses the University Health Network's various institutions facing each other across the street. They're connected by fluorescent-lit institutional tunnels running beneath the busy avenue, constructed during the Cold War in case of fallout, now used to move patients unobtrusively between hospitals.

How do you know that, he asks, and Cam says that a lot of geography and urban planning students like to take theory courses. He wants Cam to tell him more about this, the strange history of this city that exceeds its own blueprints, tunnels echoing with the muffled rumble of traffic somewhere above, but doesn't know how to ask. Cam goes on anyway, telling him that Toronto General started as military hospital shed during the War of 1812, and Mount Sinai went up in the twenties as an institution for Jewish doctors, who were not welcome to practice in other hospitals then. Sick Kids is modeled on the Great Ormond Street Hospital in London and runs first screenings of Disney-Pixar films for little bald-headed children with rare terminal conditions, and Princess Margaret is a world-class cancer treatment facility with seventeen radiation machines housed in lead-lined basement bunkers, but they don't talk about that.

When Cam leaves in the evenings Beau is overtaken by enormous physical heaviness and thinks: Nothing, I feel *nothing*. What's worse is that he knows the feeling, has felt it before, sometimes for months at a time, and fears it. Seeing people as if from a giant distance, feeling tired in a way that extends beyond drugs and chemo and head injury grogginess into something marrow deep, a weight in his blood and each of its cellular components. Lynch's suggested reading material calls it apathy, a clear symptom of depression, but to Beau it's *nothing*, a hum of white static with no knowable beginning or foreseeable end.

He doesn't bother checking which other symptoms on this protracted printout he might find familiar. He wants to sleep all the time.

He drifts in and out of dreams that feel so real he's sure they must have taken place, but can't tell whether these are fictions, or memories, or a bit of both mixed up in some way he can't disentangle. They contain details too exact, too minute, too specific to have been made up. Like getting lost in Quebec City on the way to some east coast conference Cam had been invited to, driving the wide one-way boulevards that seemed always to slope suddenly up, the whole thing built on a hill in the old style, a relic of a time when cities were made to be fortresses, places that could be defended if necessary. It had been raining hard, a steady grey drizzle melting the last of the clinging snow. The Jeep's windshield kept fogging up as Cam leaned forward, peering out ahead and alternating between running the wipers and the defogger. It changes direction, Cam said as they drove past the St. Lawrence for the fourth time, the wide river covered in dirty crumpled ice sheets moving glacially downstream. Depending on whether the tide is coming in or out. From the ocean.

Really? Beau asked, and he said yeah, it's contingent, and Beau, amazed at this idea, that a body of water so ancient and massive could be subject to something so ordinary, forgot to consult the unfolded roadmap in his lap at the crucial juncture, and Cam, seeing that they would have to make this circuit once more to get back on the freeway, said, quietly: You know, the least you could do is look at the map for me.

And it seemed to Beau then that what was meant was not what was said, but something greater and something more.

His questions leave Cam looking distracted, caught off guard, and Beau wonders if there isn't something inadvertently cruel about them. He sets up two different piles in his mind: fact and fiction, memory and dream. He's beginning to feel, more and more now, that some things are not either, or are otherwise beyond his ability to separate. Or maybe I'm just remembering differently, he thinks. Maybe things look different after they've been put back in ways that make them catch the sun and throw shadows at new angles. When familiar things are made strange.

And he watches Cam, sometimes, as he sleeps in that hard plastic chair by the hospital bed, and there develops in his mind an idea: there is something between them that cannot be said, that is not spoken about, that he doesn't know. Maybe he had known, at some time, but not any longer. He feels certain that Cam knows, but to ask him about this is impossible.

Cam brings Scrabble and chess and they play for hours, nurses peering in to shush them for their uncontainable laughter. Cam lays out ADMIRING and Beau retorts with CATS, Cam spells out INTONATION and Beau slaps a NOD on the end of that fucker, so by the end of the game the board is crisscrossed with really impressive words hinging on really fucking, short ones. He finds chess challenging, hesitating over each move as its potential implications unfold on the board before him, the squares lighting up in Ls and diagonals in his mind. The game has gained a complexity he doesn't remember it having, before. It had all seemed so straightforward, requiring little thought, its sequences occurring to him naturally and with ease, like mixing photo chemicals: nine parts water plus one part D-76 equals five hundred mills of developer, period.

Now he makes moves reluctantly, recoiling in advance at the certainty that there is some possibility he's left unconsidered and will be blindsided by. There are so many factors he hadn't taken into account.

But Cam isn't a very good chess player, and these fears seem unfounded. Sometimes Cam gets him into check and they both stop in a moment of superstitious hesitation (like, *how?*), Cam looking like he's tripped some kind of wire, and Beau wants to ask: What? But the question is explosive and out of place, and also, what? He isn't as good at chess anymore? He finds things newly strange? It all sounds so banal. Some switch in his mind has been flipped and now he can't unsee what he's seen, and what he's seen is different than what he saw before. He sits still and patient, unnerved by the new jerky quality of his movements, not wanting to get caught off guard. Thinking, take it in. Take it in and let it go.

Though the pain is bad he begins refusing the morphine, frightened by how freely it's given, upped, doubled. Already his system feels empty without it, nerve endings stretching toward the drug and its haze of bodily distance. He settles for Percocets, powdery round pills that leave his mouth dry and his mind blank. In this state it's easy to put on headphones and dissolve into the soothing tropical riffs of "I Am a Rock," a song that after thirty or so consecutive listens develops a surprising lush island quality. He floats, an astronaut pushing softly away from the station, and thinks: None of this is happening to me. This is all temporary, unimportant, and sometime soon I'll look back on this and be astonished by how I lived through it. Things said to him make it into his brain and get lost there, ricochet and die as vibrations disappearing into flesh, becoming dumb.

More than anything he wants to go home. He smells it on Cam and his clothes (fucking, *street clothes*) carrying in the wet afternoon air from slick grey sidewalks that breathe cold into everything porous. Leaning over the hospital bed or taking off his coat Cam exudes pot and cooked pasta and sleep, deep sleep.

Beau imagines he must go home and sit in the kitchen, smoking a bowl in the dark before passing out on the couch or his never-made bed. He sees Cam sitting in the rusting folding chair closest to the fridge, leaning forward in the warm dark space, resting his face in his hands to watch smoke curl away from him and disappear.

More and more he tries to imagine Cam, to feel him out because he's realized, as Cam sits by the bed hunched over his big blue course readers the thickness of bricks, that there's something about him he doesn't get. It's in his exhaustion, his intensity and his face, so open, always changing with something happening just underneath.

Like, what is he *thinking* in there?

Cam is new, different than he remembers, and Beau wonders who, between the two of them, has actually changed. These distinctions seem increasingly difficult to make.

He begins to long for mundane things: the view from the balcony, the threadbare couch, weak light slanting through the kitchen early in the day. Real showers in his own bathroom. His bed, made neat each morning, sheets crisp and fresh and not washed in fucking, Javex. Smoking weed whenever. To see these things fixed, still, as they appear in his mind, and not somehow altered, would be a balm for his thoughts. A bit of solidity.

His longing drives him each day to see Lynch, at first with Cam and then alone, pushing himself down the halls, to the elevators and up to hematology, into her open white office with its rasping carpet where he asks, each time, to be discharged. I just need to be home for a bit, he tells her, and she says, as always, Beau, your cell counts have been weak and you don't react well to the drugs.

So let me take the painkillers home! What difference does it make?

And she apologizes and shows him his charts, as if the details of these weren't already fixtures in his mind.

But he returns each day, out of breath and hot from pushing the chair on his own, maneuvering awkwardly into elevators and around corners, stitches wearing into his sides. It's a negotiation between himself and Lynch and he doesn't want Cam there, looking like he's been shot in the leg and told to play it off like it's no big deal. He feels Cam becoming his arbiter, mediating matters, applying pressure as best he can. He can't let Cam do that for him.

One of the things he feared most, upon learning of this cancer thing and then gradually seeing the way it wore him down, was the collapse of boundaries between himself and Cam, in terms of dependency. And now it's happening, quickly, with it being so much easier to let Cam push his chair, get his shoes, roll his smoke, even read to him, than it is to do these things for himself. There is a creeping change in his own attitude, waiting for this lanky man to arrive each day after lecture, holding his phone to his chest but refusing to text when Cam is late, never going so far as texting. Feeling the minute rise and fall of the device against the sluggish beat of his heart.

Need, that desperate thing he's managed to avoid his entire life, has caught up with him. It's like nothing he's ever felt, Cam coming to this awful bare room every single day to sit with him for hours, bringing all his favourite munchies, Coffee Crisp and chocolate milk and clementines as shiny as pumpkins but a thousand times sweeter. No one has ever cared for him like that before. It's—what? Unconditional. He sometimes feels that if Cam stopped coming, he would be devastated, inconsolable. If Cam stopped coming, he doesn't know what he would do. In this there is the forced understanding that he has no one, that Cam is *it*, and that he's let it get this way between them.

Thinking about it flips his stomach.

But that's the limit, and there have to be some limits. With Lynch he will negotiate alone, no middlemen. He's begun to feel, strongly, that Cam might be a middleman. That Cam is most comfortable not leading or following, but mediating. That Cam has no problem acting as a buffer between opposing forces, and no sense of self-preservation.

Beau knows Lynch has seen his file, the entirety of it dutifully filled out by the federal government since he was two years old. He sees strategic value in this, and makes a daily point of emphasizing that he's really *not feeling well*. Not feeling well overall, he clarifies, in general. She nods and jots this down, giving no indication one way or the other.

Then one day, as he rolls in for his midmorning appointment, the muscles in his arms screaming, she says, "it can be lonely being in a hospital all the time."

He nods, out of breath.

"It can make you feel out of sorts, psychologically unwell." She taps the spine of his file against the desk. It is big, full of papers in many different colours with tabs and stickers dividing them. "It can trigger periods of depression."

"That's pretty much how I feel about it," he says.

"I think your counts have levelled off enough that it would be better for you to go home, at least for the weekend. What do you think? You could come back for your session on Tuesday."

He tries not to look too excited. "Would I have to check back in again?"

"No, not unless there are further complications. And your head is fine, based on the neurologist's report."

Except it isn't, it's all out of order and he can't get anyone to agree with him on this point. They don't have the right scan for it, whatever it is. Their instruments can't register it.

"Why don't you call Cam to come get you? You can go this afternoon, if you want."

He watches her sign the forms, flipping back and forth between translucent pink and yellow sheets. "I will," he says. "I'm going to text him right now."

"Beau," she says, lining up the documents and tapping them on the desk to bring them flush, "you have to be careful with him."

He looks up from his phone. "What? With Cam?"

"I don't want to give you advice about your personal life," (though she did, all the time), "but you need to understand it's a lot of work to take care of someone getting treatment, and I see a lot of people become overwhelmed by it, especially when they don't have any help."

"I wouldn't let Cam do that," he says, thinking of that recklessness. The middleman tendency.

"He probably wouldn't tell you if he was exhausted, but he is. I ran into him in the atrium yesterday, and he looked very tired. You should consider the support group, at the very least. You don't want him to get burnt out." She hands him the yellow part of the form, keeping the pink for herself. "He obviously loves you very much."

He mulls this over on the way down in the elevator, watching the floors light up, interns and nurses in solid pink and blue scrubs getting on and off with their plastic badges, ready for lunch. A pure bright thing expands in his chest.

The nurse comes to pull his IV, leaving his hand so stiff and sore he can hardly make a fist, and then Cam arrives with *street clothes*, his favourite Levi's and tee and grey hoodie, their weight surprising after so much time spent in the papery blue gown. The clothes feel big, like they aren't his, but also solid and substantial, a shield against external things. They smell like home. He stands gingerly, experimentally, keeping a hand on the bed.

"I can push you," Cam says.

"No, let me walk. I want to walk. You know?"

Cam has gathered up his things, headphones and books and a stack of finished newspaper crosswords and the old burgundy duffel containing his clothes, and now stands by the door, waiting. There is no camera because fluorescent light has a harsh exposure in black and white that Beau can't stand, the one-dimensional finality of a sharp-edged cardboard pop-up. "Okay," he says, but when Beau moves across the floor like it might shift on him Cam offers his arm, and they leave the hospital together.

In the Jeep Beau leans back and puts his feet on the dash, closing his eyes. He's sat here so many times, pressing the shape of his body into the seat, that to do so now hurts him with gladness. He exhales slowly.

"Hey, you okay?" Cam asks. He drives with one hand loose on the bottom of the wheel, arm resting against the window.

"Yeah, I'm fine. It's so good to be coming back." Back home, he almost says, but knows the word will get twisted in his throat.

"Yeah," Cam says, "it's so good," and all at once Beau notices how long his hair has grown, how he's forgotten to shave.

"You miss me?"

"What do you think?"

"I think yeah. I think you missed me big time." He puts his hand on Cam's neck to feel him shiver.

"Saved a ton of money on hydro," Cam says, "not having you around turning on all the lights in the place. We should do this more often."

"Yeah, you get sick too and we'll chill on the government's dollar."

He shakes his head. "Beau, that's awful."

Outside everything is newly white, the world dusted with a thick layer of wet late-season snow. Bits of shimmer still hang in the crystal air. I'll never take anything for granted again, he thinks. In the Jeep it's warm and he feels safe, like when he first started coming over to Cam's, hanging around the kitchen and having long lazy talks on the back porch, dazed with sticky summer heat and Slurpees from the 7-11 on the corner.

Telling himself, just don't get too attached. Thinking, *you can't let yourself get all fucked up again* even as he watched Cam skateboard in the parking lot, their shadows growing long together. Walking back in the cooling evening he chewed gum while Cam carried the board under his arm, casually, as if this were the most natural thing in the world, and knew he'd never loved someone so much in his life.

The prospect frightened him.

The apartment is clean and smells of Pinesol, coffee table clear of weed crumbs and DVDs all in their cases. Cam has obviously vacuumed. The pile of shoes constantly blocking the door is gone, matching pairs of sneakers and loafers lined up by the floorboards. He kicks off his shoes and leans on the wall, taking everything in. He's unsteady all over again.

A place for everything, he thinks, absurdly, and everything in its place.

Cam helps him out of his coat, quiet. "You wanna nap?" he says. "I'm just finishing an essay for Monday. I'm pretty behind on everything."

"I'm just gonna shower," he says, wanting the heat on his skin. He isn't nauseous and this is good.

In the bathroom he runs the water as hot as he can take and stands in front of the mirror, undressing. He is angular, thin. He needs to eat more. The time for pills is coming but he doesn't want to take them, needing clarity and remove from cloudy remembrances. Beau tries to see the bandaged spot from the concussion but can't, it's too far back on his skull, and when he turns his head in the mirror he catches only a glimpse of white in the sunken place where his hair has been cut away. It hurts, still.

I look like death, he thinks. No wonder Cam looks at me like that when I look like fucking, death. The mirror is different than he remembers, bigger and with a thin silver frame where the other had none. This change in the ordinary jars him, and he thinks: *why?* It's something he should know, another missing piece of information that has been dislodged beyond his reach. The term *memory lapse* occurs to him clinically, as a description in his ever-expanding file.

You're okay, you're okay, he tells himself, suddenly desperate, and steps into the shower where he is too weak to stand and must sit beneath the hot stream. He tilts his face up into the spray, letting it soak through his hair. The heat disables him, loosening some core thing necessary for thought and function. He's all dizzy, though whether from the effort of moving around all day for the first time in two weeks or from the relief of being home, he couldn't say. He bends over himself, curling over his bony knees, wrapping them up and pressing them close to his chest. He can't look at his ankles and wrists where the bones assert themselves against his skin most urgently. Considering the amount of weight he's lost and the period of time he's lost it in is enough to send him into a panic attack, and he doesn't have the energy for that.

His skin flushes red from the heat and he imagines the sickness leaking from him, black and viscous, diluting in the flow and disappearing down the drain. Be well, he wills himself. Get better. As if it were a matter of personal will and not of discontented white blood cells moving through him with their own logic and volition.

Curled up in the steam he feels good, breathing the humidity in deep. His hospital bracelet, laminated white plastic encircling his wrist, is still on, and he reads it for the thousandth time:

```
LARKY, BEAUREGARD
DB 12/04/198–   24   SX: M   CHEM
ID 1347741   ADM/REG DT: 25/02/201–
UNIVERSITY HEALTH NETWORK
```

It amazes him, his life summarized in four abbreviated lines, the big name he's never really gotten used to, the birthday he knows nothing about. It's like I don't even know who I am, he thinks. It's like I don't even know myself. He wants to pull the strip of plastic off but it won't fucking, go, pressing hard into his skin when he tugs. He extends one arm out of the tub and searches for his jeans, wincing, digging through their pockets for the little plastic bottle. He finds it and pops four pills, tipping his head back to wait for the pain to ebb. Ten minutes on an empty stomach and the oxy does its thing, loosening his limbs and slowing his mind, everything taking on a cinematic quality. He closes his eyes and breathes. Put on *Bridge Over Troubled Water* and go to bed, he thinks. Yeah.

"Beau? You okay?" Cam's knocking drags him into the stubborn solidity of material things.

"I'm okay," he calls, drawn back to himself as through a spell from the fog of some psychic abyss. Water streams from his upper lip and over his nose, flowing from its tip in rivulets.

He turns off the shower and emerges into the steam, drops of vapour condensing on the ceiling and clouding the jarring new mirror he doesn't look at. When he opens the door and steps into the wall of cold air rushing to meet him Cam is on the phone with his mom, his voice carrying in muffled syllables down the hall. Beau puts on pajama pants and a hoodie and lies on his bed, listening to Cam talk softly, with a tenderness he must not be aware of. Occasional varied snatches of *yeah mom* and *I was thinking* and his sad laugh that somehow always tightens Beau's throat make their way past his door.

Like, when did that sadness seep into his voice?

Beau imagines Cam sitting cross-legged on his bed, bent over himself and tracing vague lines on the covers with his fingers as he talks. Far away somewhere in his head. He can see that Cam loves her—Cathy—in his own way, though he never talks about it. Worrying that she'll worry, calling her to check in, making halfhearted admittances of being overworked while claiming it's fine, he's fine. Cam is both like her and not—they share a resourcefulness, a warmth that comes through in their inability to be stern, an energy that is productive in her, well channeled to specific, thoughtfully planned ends, while in him it fuses wrong somewhere within, short-circuiting into a saturating nervousness. Beau has always loved this in them, the clear relation of difference.

Meeting Cathy, he was immediately drawn to her generous energy and inability to keep from laughing at his kitchen banter and willingness to always have him around like he was her family, too. He had trouble leaving the place because he'd never felt that kind of welcome, like he could walk into their house at any time of day and it was more than okay, it was an event. She was the kindest woman he'd ever know, feeding him real food and asking his advice on her many domestic projects and getting him that amazing big-lensed Nikon FM2 one Christmas, a real SLR with its film reel and different exposure speeds and little black canisters full of golden Kodak, the most expensive thing he'd ever owned. His first camera ever that he felt his lip quiver as he unwrapped, saying, no way can I accept this from you, and her shaking her head and smiling, asking if he liked it even as he felt overwhelming, enormous, frightening love for her. For this woman and her son, the sight of whose lanky frame approaching the group house made his heart beat fast as he took the stairs down two at a time to throw open the door. Flips and Trev yelling, *Larky, your boyfriend is here.*

Always thinking, if they move me away from these people I'll die.

He falls asleep, lulled by distant conversation, and then Cam is in the doorway, no longer on the phone, leaning hard against the frame. "Hey," he says. "You wanna sleep? I made you some tea and toast."

Beau yawns, sitting up. "Aw. Cam."

"I was gonna roll a joint. Should I let you sleep?" He crosses his arms and something about the motion is protective, like he's trying to hold a part of himself in.

"No, I could eat. I mean, I haven't eaten in fucking, ages." He puts on socks like he's never done it before, moving at half speed.

"You all stoned?"

"Yeah, percs. My spine was killing me." He stands, testing his balance, and finds it's good. He can't get over how soft his clothes are. In the kitchen he gets scissors and stands by the counter, trying to get at the hospital bracelet with his left hand until Cam wordlessly takes them from him and snips it off.

On the couch he tucks his socked feet beneath himself, curling into the cushions and their familiar feel, all give, nothing like the firm adjustable hospital mattress. The physical layout of the apartment soothes his mind, stroking it into submission: the ancient gas stove, piles of books stacked on the coffee table, leaning precariously by the couch and stuffed into the armchair, a lazy series of hoodies and shirts hanging over backs of kitchen chairs, the worn Persian rug with its frayed tassels, and the little space heater Cam brought home without asking, saying, you're shaking, man, I can hear it from here. Not everything is changed, he thinks, dummied with gratitude for this fixed map of shared possessions he can reshelve, fit into their proper place.

Cam brings him tea that he has somehow—miraculously—infused with pot. He watches nervously as Beau takes it, like he's not used to having another body around. Like they don't know each other, or just met. Little globules of shimmering THC-rich fat collect near the cup's rim. Beau leans over the mug and breathes in the pungent steam. "*Medicinal*," he intones approvingly, pressing his palms to its sides, allowing the heat to penetrate deep into his hands. "How did you get it in there?"

"Proprietary method," Cam says, obviously pleased.

He disappears, returning to the kitchen where he likes to work at the tiny folding table. Beau can hear him sharpening pencils, flipping pages in drawn-out intervals, jiggling his foot against the table's legs. When he comes back he's stoned, visibly so, a sight Beau Larky delights in: Cam all loose and smiling crooked, a lazy smile Beau mirrors back with his splayed body, melting into the couch, his aching spine and general nausea distant concerns.

"Stoned much?"

"Uh huh."

He senses Cam's eyes tracing his body, maybe gauging his thinness, but when he meets them Cam looks away, flushed.

"Hey, come sit down here with me, huh. The fucking, *news* is gonna be on."

"Aw," Cam says, gesturing at his sprawled form. "There's no space."

"No, come on, there's space, there's space. Let me just—" he lifts his legs, motioning for Cam to sit. "There. Come on, sit with me for just a minute, huh. You've been running around all week."

Cam sits like he's never done it before, hesitant and stiff.

"Is this okay?" Beau asks, gingerly laying his feet in Cam's lap.

Cam tenses and then dissolves, taking Beau's feet in his hands, laying his palms flat against the soles and curling his long fingers over the toes. "*Yeah*," he says. "This is great."

Beau arches his feet in delight, closing his eyes. He cannot know that Cam is thinking a series of overwhelming, bliss-laden thoughts about his size nine feet encased in two layers of socks, grey on white, his loosened body stretched on the sofa, his smooth placid face. He can't know that Cam finds these debilitating, or that he's becoming increasingly self-conscious about the proximity of Beau's feet to his lap where he is getting, despite wishing desperately not to, very, very hard.

"Hey," Beau says. "Did we get a new mirror? In the bathroom."

Cam shifts, visibly pained, folding his knees to sit cross-legged. "You really don't know?"

He shakes his head, tipping it back. The weed gives the oxy an edge, and he wonders if he could even put a sentence together, the way he is now.

"The mirror is new," Cam says, "because the other one got broken."

This sets off a series of recollections. Broken, yeah, tiny slivers of glass missed in the original cleanup turning up when they burrowed into bare feet, the difficulty of mounting anything on drywall. "Broken how?"

Cam shakes his head.

"Cam, you gotta tell me, man. I'm in the fucking, Twilight Zone over here."

"The mirror got broken," he says, taking a breath, "because I put my hand through it."

"Oh," Beau says, and now the scene is clear to him, sand shifting to expose this complexly structured thing as it had always been: coming through the door and Cam with his hand all wrecked, violent red seeping through bunched layers of toilet paper, the blood just everywhere—spattered on the tile, smeared between its ridges, running in diluted pink lines down the sink, pooling in a ring around the drain. The mirror missing from its frame, fragments of jagged glass still hanging stubbornly near its edges. And Cam's face so blank, like there was nothing left inside him.

Like he'd fucking, burned it all.

And his own panic, heart going fast, thumping up against his dry throat like, how could he *do* that to himself? Seeing Cam's recklessness for the first time in its full intensity, unmasked. Frightened that Cam, with his methodical notes and underlined theory and perfect grade point average, was capable of something so rash. How could he? His poor fucking, hand. Selfishly afraid that Cam would destroy himself, would let this thing eat him when he was so badly needed on the home front. Thinking, I need him to be okay for this, I'm not okay and I need him to be fine. One of us has to be fine.

Seven years bad luck.

"I'm sorry," Cam says. "I was having a hard time."

He looks at Cam's knuckles on his socked feet and sees the thin white lines etched into them, the unnatural way the middle one sticks up from its neighbours. Never set right, always crooked now. "Your hand," he says, simply. "You shouldn't have done that."

"It was like it just happened. I just got so upset. I don't even really—remember. Doing it."

"I hate that it happened that way."

"I know."

The shape of Cam's folded body, its length made compact, loosens something in his chest. "It scares me sometimes, Cam. The way you get about this stuff. Really."

Cam flushes a little, colour coming to his face, and runs a hand back through his hair. "I mean, you've been so sick," he says. "I worry a lot. It kind of kills me."

There's something you're not telling me, Beau wants to say, even within all this. He doesn't want it to sound like an accusation, because it's not. He doesn't want to put Cam on the spot, to make him blush like that. They're having a hard time, he realizes, he and Cam. They're learning something difficult about negotiation and change, boundaries and limits, seeing and not seeing.

About unspoken knowledge between people, its parameters and reluctant flow.

"I feel like I'm seeing you differently," he tells Cam. "Like I'm seeing you all over again."

Five

That Sunday Beau sits in the laundromat's aquamarine plastic swivel chairs, watching the two bags of clothes he's convinced Cam he's okay to carry so his roommate can stay home and finish his big theory paper, a strange document full of mysterious references from that dense book he's been carrying around. *Virtual, actual, potential.* Words as good as spells.

The dull ache in his spine makes it hard to move or bend, so he does everything slowly, afraid of sudden motion, continually fingering the pill bottle stowed in the pocket of his jeans. He is very stoned, lending his movements a stilted, dreamy quality. Beau makes change, the single five-dollar bill disappearing into the antique machine's slot to reappear as twenty shiny quarters, all noise. It's transfiguration, alchemy, magic. Substitution. He holds them in his palm and smiles to see there isn't a single loonie in the silver pile. The washing machines eat loonies at random.

All quarters, he thinks. Lucky day.

He sorts through the clothes, stacking colours and whites in haphazard piles on the cerulean countertop. Adds detergent, blue and viscous, to the machines, inevitably getting a bunch on his fingers and having to rinse them under cold water at the big low sink in the back. Slams down the machines' lids with all the self-satisfaction he imagines Cam misses in him, feeding quarters into their slots to hear them clank into a vast pile of coins somewhere far below. These tasks are small and ordinary and feel good after so much time spent in bed, but they tire him out, whoa, fill him with a new kind of heaviness he's only beginning to understand. His body is a locus of refusals and protests, always threatening to shut down the show.

Beau loves the laundromat, its dry warmth, the quiet rumble and click-clack of machines running, the smell of soap and dryer sheets. After the frozen damp of the street that settles in his joints and makes him feel about two hundred years old he could sit in this long narrow room for days, soaking in bored phone conversations, the flip of newspaper pages, harried mothers watching their children stumbling between aisles or climbing up on chairs, the rattle of cart wheels on sticky linoleum and the huge decorative roses painted gaudily on the walls. He sits on the ground with his back to a warm buzzing machine, breathing deep and staring out into the dusk. The streetlights have begun to come on, bathing the sidewalk orange. People pass by pushing carts heaped with wet clothes, glancing down at him sitting inexplicably on the floor when there are so many empty chairs, but he doesn't care. He feels insulated, somnolent, relaxed by the vibration of the spin cycle against his protesting back. It's embryonic, the whole thing. A dissolution into simpler, more corporeal states.

A woman about his age watches him from across the room, half hidden behind the pile of clothes she's been folding on the countertop. She bites at the skin around her thumb and stares at him levelly over her hand. He's seen her in here before, pressing overloads of white billowy gauze-like garments into machines and pulling them out smaller, wetter, their fabric all twisted up by the spin. Her long dark hair frizzes in the laundromat's humidity, the strap of her leather purse bouncing on her surprisingly small hips (boy hips, he thinks) as she moves between the counter and dryers. She worries at the frayed ends of her hair, her big faded v-neck, the tassels on her moccasins. She sees him looking and straightens, walking over.

"I've seen you in here before," she says, leaning with her hip on the machine he's sitting against.

"Yeah, I've seen you too."

"You and your tall companion."

He nods.

"How come you're sitting on the ground?" she says, gesturing behind her. "There are lots of chairs." Her tone is serious, like she's seeking straight-up information, and Beau can't tell if it's supposed to be flirtatious or what. Because he looks like he's been in a fucking, car wreck, he reasons, this can't possibly be the case.

"If you're sitting in one of those," he says, following her hand, "you're missing out on some serious therapeutic back action."

She laughs and lowers herself to sit against a dryer across from him, copying the way his knees are drawn up to his chest. "I better get in on that, then," she says. She wears huge feather earrings that tangle with her nest of hair. "I'm Stacey. Nice to meet you."

"Beau. Nice to meet you too."

"*Beau*? What kind of name is that?"

He laughs.

"Is it short for something?"

"Absolutely."

She hunches forward, weirdly intent. Like Cam, he thinks. "For what?"

Beau smiles. "That's restricted information," he says. The pleasure of flirting is routine, easy, irresistible.

She laughs more freely and the sound is surprising, high and stilted. Beau tries to decide whether he finds her attractive and can't, torn between her chipped, possibly bitten-down nails and the blatant lack of bra beneath her shirt. "By which you mean you're embarrassed to say, *or*—" looking at him sideways, trying to keep her lips flat even as they pull up at the corners, all strangled amusement "—you want me to guess."

This is familiar territory for Beau Larky, who understands, not without some vanity, that what he didn't get in height, he got amply reimbursed for in looks. "Pfft," he says. "Good luck."

The corners of her lips flicker. "Beaumont."

"Nope."

"Beaufort."

He shakes his head.

"Beau—*champ*."

"Good guess."

"So it's a big name."

"Very big," he says, enjoying himself, having forgotten how good this feels.

She cups her chin and furrows her brow, miming deep thought. "Well, then it must be Beauregard."

"Whoa," he says, taken aback, "impressive."

Stacey shrugs, pleased.

"How do you know all these Beau names?"

She tugs at the split ends near her chin. "I'm a grad student in English, American lit. American lit is jam-packed with Beau variations. You know, like *Gone with the Wind*."

He eyes her ripped jeans, the stack of silver bracelets piling up on her wrist.

"And your boyfriend is a grad student too, right? I see him on campus all the time."

"Cam's not my boyfriend," he says automatically.

She smiles. "Your roommate."

"Yeah, and let me guess, you already know what he studies."

"Critical theory."

He shakes his head. "You're good. Stacey."

She winds a stray strand of hair around her index finger until it's pulled tight. "I always see him in here with those huge readers. Foucault, Adorno. Derrida. Pretty serious stuff."

"Cam is very serious," he says, not without affection. "You live around here?"

"Right down the street. I'm not from Toronto though, I'm from the States."

"What state?"

"Connecticut."

One of the machines circulating his load clacks to a stop and he stands to open it. The smell of detergent lingers. "How are you liking Toronto?"

"Well, I came here to study. I don't know—I like it enough. It's a different kind of city, I suppose."

"It grows on you."

She smiles, standing to lean on the machine he's unloading. "That's what everyone's been telling me." Regarding him more seriously over her folded hands: "What about you, *Beau*?" In her mouth it is flattened into a caricature, *Bo*, a name in a children's picture book. "Are you a student?"

He finishes throwing the colours into a basket and moves to a dryer. The change in his back pocket is slippery and takes a while to fish out. "No. Not anymore."

"All done?"

"Yeah, all done."

"Let me guess—history? Or languages."

"Photography."

"A *photographer*." She looks him up and down. "Digital?"

"Film."

This delights her. "What do you photograph?"

He pops three quarters into the dryer. "Mostly weddings, family reunions, birthday parties, funerals—"

"Really?"

"No." He laughs. "I shoot whatever. I don't get paid. I worked at like a fucking, meet mall Santa thing one year, but it was a bad scene."

"So what do you do, then?"

Beau can't stand this question, hates it, will go out of his way to avoid it. He's saved from answering when her phone rings and she jogs back to the counter to retrieve it, raising her hands in a *don't go anywhere* gesture. She spends a while laughing and uh-huhing into the receiver, small hips moving back and forth in step with her voice. By the time she's done Beau's getting ready to leave, bags of warm folded clothing lined up on the countertop.

"Beauregard!" she says, intercepting him. "I'll see you again soon."

"Will you?"

"Certainly."

Her face is wide, smooth and self-assured. He's started to think nothing is certain, but this is too serious a response to give, the kind of thing Cam would say with a straight face. "Okay," he says instead.

Outside the slush soaks through his shoes as he walks. What a fucking, weirdo, he thinks, smiling all the way down the block.

Six

When Beau finally gets his clothes on the first thing he wants to do is take them off and go back to bed. It's already eight and Cam will be pissed if they're late again, so he zips up his hoodie and stands. Everything resists.

He tries to look forward to noon, when his session will be finished and he won't have to go to another until the day after tomorrow, which might be Wednesday or Thursday or could even be Friday, he can't say for sure. Time has developed a slippery quality and tends to move mysteriously, without him.

In the kitchen Cam sets toast before him, placing it next to a small cluster of wet red grapes. He looks harried, like he's trying to get a bunch of stuff together and can't. He moves from the kitchen to the living room and back, holding his arms out in perpetual question.

"I really can't," Beau says, looking at the toast.

"You have to eat that or something. You hardly ate yesterday and you definitely won't eat after the session, so." Cam embodies a logic of necessity. He re-emerges with a stack of books and his backpack, trying to fit one into the other. "I need my laptop cord, do you know where it is? Fuck."

"Hey, Foucault. It's under the coffee table."

"And *The Order of Things*?" he yells through the wall.

"The yellow one?"

"Yeah."

"Is here," Beau says, sliding it from beneath the grape bowl. He thinks if he's gonna eat anything it's gonna be the grapes. He pops one back and it's not bad, cool and sweet on his swollen tongue.

Cam returns and stands leaning on the counter, buttoning up the sleeves on his shirt. He's shaved and brushed back his hair and looks fresh, put together. Intensely academic.

"What are you looking so sharp for?"

He flushes and looks down. "You think? Do you think I need a tie?"

"For what?"

"Johnson wants me to give a lecture, on Foucault. There are gonna be like, two hundred students there."

Beau looks at him differently, rolling a grape between his thumb and forefinger. "When?"

"Today, at noon. I'm gonna be a little late to pick you up, I'm sorry."

"Whoa, Cam, that's fucking, amazing," he says. "That's legit, man. Congratulations." He swells with pride for this strange quiet man who's spent so much time bent over his notes, chewing the skin from his thumb. "I'm so happy you get to do that."

"Me too," he says, but looks like he might pass out.

Beau laughs. "You need to breathe," he says. "It's gonna be so good. I'll be okay to wait, don't worry. And no tie, what you've got on is serious." Before they leave he grabs his camera, slipping it on beneath his coat.

After the session the world swims, objects taking on a new intensity, colours saturated and jarring. Linda's gummy yellow nail polish and the hallway fluorescents turn his stomach and he tries not to think, a trick he's become increasingly good at because in this state it's impossible to tell what will put him over the edge. The smell of teriyaki wafting in from the food court comes dangerously close.

Outside it is raining, the pavement cold and slick. Standing just outside the grand sliding glass doors he imagines sitting down on the curb to feel its solidity and press his palms to the gritty unmoving concrete. Instead he walks, the gentle drizzle calming him, evening out his thoughts. A quiet rush has settled over the street and he tries not to breathe as he passes hotdog stands, salty cooked meat and cigarettes following him at a clip. It's twelve-fifteen, and if he walks quickly he can make it to campus before half-past.

Sometimes just the effort of movement makes him sick, but not today. Beau feels his lungs expand and contract with each inhalation, amazed that these spongy bags of flesh can still take this kind of pace, can accommodate him with all that poison his blood must be filtering through them even now. The late winter air is crisp and wet, mud and slush and yellowing grass and the pulp of long-buried leaves filling his nostrils.

Good solid living smells. The smells of things starting over, however slowly.

He finds the class easily, on his second try, and slips beneath the heavy oak door to take an empty seat in the back row. The room is very quiet, and very full. A few heads turn at the sound of the door clacking shut before returning to the front. Beau tries to catch his breath without sounding ragged, desperate. With all these bodies packed close the room is very warm, and he finds he's sweating down the back of his neck. He slips off his big parka and leans back, camera hanging on its strap to settle against his chest, a familiar weight keeping him anchored.

At the podium Cam is pacing, his fleeting loose confidence fixed and magnified for the benefit of two hundred undergrads. He must be nervous but doesn't seem so, the hours of dense theory condensed in his body shielding it from potential slips. There is something about Cam he doesn't recognize and has to do a double take—it's about interiority, and his roommate's sudden lack of it. There is nothing on his face but the content of the lecture and his full involvement with it. How can layers of substrata be folded away so neatly, condensed into a series of creases and slid out of sight?

In his cords and shirt with the sleeves rolled to his elbows and his clean face Cam looks good, really good, and it occurs to Beau that Cam has a whole other life, a life he never sees and understands only abstractly, as a series of complex magical words and thick books left around the apartment and endless typed essays that somehow (mysteriously, through a process having more to do with the occult than with institutional structures) result in a fat forty thousand dollar funding package delivered in quarterly installments to the mailbox of Cameron Dempster, College Street, Unit 9, Toronto. This is what it looks like when Cam is out in the world by himself and not hunching over hospital beds, sleeping in beanbag chairs, shying away from the evening news. All his awards and grants and published articles and *this* sudden bout of unexpected self-assertion.

Beau Larky can hardly breathe.

Cam is saying: "Foucault wants us to consider what it is impossible to think, or imagine, or see, and why we are faced with this particular impossibility at this time and no other. He invites us to think about an underlying way in which things are ordered, or the order of things, so ubiquitous and structuring of all fields of knowledge that it is all but invisible."

The word for this broad epistemological field, he gathers from a girl in the front with the reddest hair Beau has ever seen, is *episteme*. It sounds floral, precise. Having to do with phyla and plant kingdoms, broad intricately ordered branching systems.

"The episteme of any given time and context configures the space of knowledge and determines its conditions of possibility. In other words, what it is possible to know, how things are ordered and relate to one another. The very fact that something like order even *exists*."

The students in the front seats lean forward, stretching toward the stage, and Beau smiles, melting in his chair. They love him, he thinks. They think he's so sharp. He's relieved for Cam, relieved and overcome with something like gladness, a small shard of pure unrestrained joy lacerating his heart.

"If we were to undertake an archaeology of this underlying order, an archaeology of knowledge, as Foucault explains in a book on this method, we would realize that the existing arrangement is not the only possible one, and not even necessarily the best one. It is just one of many possibilities, most of which we can't see simply because we don't know what to look for, or even that we should be looking at all." Cam pauses, checking his notes. "There are thresholds of invisibility," he says, "not because these underlying, archeological orders are *hidden*, but because of a structure affecting our entire field of conceivable representation. They are, you could say, hidden in plain sight."

Beau's staring so hard he's afraid the weight of his gaze might cause Cam to look up, all the way up to the very back row of this concave lecture hall scooped out of concrete, and see him sitting there in his post-chemo slump. He brings the camera to his eye. Through it he sees Cam lean on the podium, one hand deep in the pocket of his cords. He must be sweating buckets, Beau thinks, and is filled with the internal clamour of a thousand desperate half-born things.

"Even the limited visibility we might grasp at, open ourselves to, is filled with uncertainties, exchanges, and feints." Opening his book, the yellow one that had sat beneath an ordinary bowl of grapes just that morning, he reads: "*Because we can see only the reverse side, we do not know who we are, or what we are doing. Seen or seeing?*" Flipping the page, skipping ahead: "*And just as we are about to apprehend ourselves, transcribed by his hand as though in a mirror, we find that we can in fact apprehend nothing of that mirror but its lustreless back.*"

Beau isn't sure if he wants to put the camera down or not. *We do not know who we are, or what we are doing.* He shivers.

Cam bends the book in such a way that its soft spine wraps around his hand where he holds it, a tool made exclusively for his use. He possesses a sudden and total authority that fills Beau with what has to be, for lack of a better word, *excitement*. "Here we can see," he says, "how Foucault's view of the limited and circumscribed field of visibility inherent in any episteme informs his view of the subject, of subjecthood, and of agency." He looks up and scans the rows of students, only a small number of who, from Beau's vantage point, are taking the time to update their facebooks.

In Cam's half-turned body, book held low and resting against his thigh, everything focused on the speech about to come, on this quality of *being about to speak*, Beau finds his moment. He is arrested, in a state of arrest. The click of the shutter is louder than he imagined, echoing off smooth walls into the enormous open space.

"Consider," Cam begins, and stops, tracing the sound (*which he must know well*, Beau reflects belatedly, too late) all the way back to its source and the camera's owner, sitting in the final row trying to fit the lens cap back on. A number of heads turn to follow his gaze.

"Consider—" but he's tongue-tied, and now several more bodies twist around in their seats to see who has managed to draw their TA's attention in this non-negotiable way. Heat creeps up Beau's neck.

"Consider," he says again, dropping his eyes to the book and turning away in a single move of self-possession that involves his whole body and reconsolidates the room's attention entirely on him, and him alone, "this brief passage: *I should like to know whether subjects are not determined in their situation, their function, their perceptive capacity, and their practical possibilities by conditions that dominate and even overwhelm them.*"

After the lecture Beau hangs around the back rows, waiting for students to trickle out and Cam to finish taking questions from those congregating around the lectern and leaning on the stage. He takes a seat by the aisle and watches them leave in small groups until only Cam and the prof are left. The prof is fucking, old, way older than Beau imagined, and walks slowly, labouring up the stairs. Cam alters his pace to match the professor's, hovering over each step and checking his hunched companion's progress as he goes. He nods deeply at what the prof says, careful not to overtake the struggling man.

They shouldn't even let a guy his age have a class in a room like this, Beau thinks. With a hundred and forty stairs to get up and down twice a week.

"Did you know," the prof says upon reaching Beau, "that it's against university regulations to record or photograph a lecture without explicit permission?"

"Oh," Cam says, flushed again, "Dan, this is my roommate, Beau Larky."

"Delightful," Johnson says, and Beau isn't sure if he's being sarcastic or not. The man has an air of utter seriousness and total command, like he's never laughed in his entire life and wouldn't want to. Like it might be somehow degrading to be the kind of person that laughs. He demands, despite his shrunken aspect, complete respect. "Are you a photographer, Beau Larky?"

"It depends who you ask."

"He's a photographer," Cam says.

Johnson smiles, dry and knowing, and Beau has an uncanny moment of wondering if they haven't already met. "Did you enjoy the lecture, Beau?"

"Very much," Beau says, and watches Cam smile down at his shoes.

Johnson nods, noncommittal, like he has no opinion one way or the other. Like the quality of the lecture doesn't warrant any thought on his part. Beau can't imagine handing in a paper to this man to grade.

"So, Cameron," Johnson says, picking up a previous point, "next week Benjamin, Adorno? And that revised bibliography?"

"Yes," Cam says, "definitely, no problem."

He nods and turns, continuing up the stairs. Cam stares after him like he's had his heart broken.

"And Cameron," he says, pausing.

"Yes?"

"I too enjoyed the lecture—very much. It would seem you have a knack for this."

"Thank you," Cam says, and smiles stupidly, like he's had a crucial part of his brain removed.

Johnson resumes climbing at his pained pace. They stand looking at each other, unable to speak. Cam is incredibly embarrassed.

"Hey," Beau says, "your lecture was so good."

"How did you get here? Are you okay?"

"Yeah, I'm fine. I just walked."

"Your hair is all wet."

"I know, it was raining. I'll towel it out."

"I can't believe you walked in the rain."

"Cam."

"What if you get sick again?"

"Are you fucking, kidding? I wasn't gonna miss your major deal lecture on *Foucault*."

Cam laughs. He can't quite look Beau in the eye. "Well, you saw, so."

"I got a really good shot of you."

"How do you know it's good?"

Beau shrugs. "I just felt it. What's the academic superstar word for that shit? Affect?"

Cam nods. "Affect, yeah."

At home they have joints and ice cream sandwiches.

Seven

There is a great thaw coming over things, the loosening of a grip. Beau feels it in his marrow and its sudden sensitivity to fluctuations in atmospheric pressure. He's tired and sags against the balcony railing, watching Cam watch the storm.

Cam leans hard on his crossed arms, tapping out the seconds between flashes backlighting the swollen sky over the lake. He keeps his back stiff but his neck is bent, hanging between his shoulders like his head is too heavy to support. Beau sees the line of tension just below his skin, a thing that could be coaxed out with some patience.

"You think it'll storm?" he says.

"It's definitely getting closer."

Everything is the colour of bruises. Beau thinks of waking each morning to find more and more purpling splotches blooming across his skin, sitting on his bed staring at them with his door shut. His insides shrink back. Even with a hood up over his toque he shivers, the cold damp creeping in through his pores.

He's spent the last hour bent over the toilet and now wants the fresh air, the cold metal against his palms. Cam rubbed his back all through it and he'd almost sobbed at how good it was, the pressure and friction of touch when everything ached so horribly. A cool hand smoothing down the dampened hair at his nape where it prickled with heat. What he wants to say is a thing halfway between *thank you* and *I love you*, both/and, not either/or, but there is no thing like that.

"How far?"

Cam finishes counting to himself, lips moving without sound. "Maybe half an hour, forty minutes?" He leans over the side and Beau follows his gaze to the street below where passing taillights smudge in the humidity, leaving soft reflections on the slick pavement. The air is a charged mass, all latent energy.

I should just ask him not to do it, he thinks. Not to sit through it with me. I should just tell him I'm okay. But the thing is that he *wants* Cam to do it, and that he isn't okay. That this support system disagreement between himself and Lynch cannot account for or accommodate his own increasingly strong desire to have Cam around. He doesn't want to go to a support group, he wants to smoke joints with Cam. These things are not equivalent and cannot be substituted.

There is no wind, everything sitting close and still. He shifts nearer to Cam and sees his friend's body change in response, adjusting its angle. He sees how Cam welcomes it. Their shoulders almost touch.

When the rain comes he retreats to his darkroom and develops three rolls of film all in one go, working through the steps with the ease of automatic motion. The steps, unlike so many things, are always the same. Mix all the chemicals, measuring out powder in plastic spoonfuls, make sure the developer's sitting at sixty-eight and no less. Turn off the light and pry the tops from the film canisters with a can opener, waiting for the satisfying pop. Fill the trays and slide in the clipped negatives, slowly tilting the containers to evenly coat the film.

Waiting for the rolls to develop, Beau sparks a joint, holding it between his lips while agitating the trays. The room is small, just big enough for him to turn around in, and the air is close with pot and the salt-and-vinegar tang of stopper. The smell settles in his clothes and hair, trailing around the apartment after him. Beau imagines he must smell like that all the time, the way you carry the smell of your house, or car, or dog, a thing so constant it comes to stand for neutral. In the amber safelight the smoke is thick and pastel yellow, a sight Beau loves. It gives the closet a mystical quality, like a dream or carnival tent.

He plucks the film from its tray with one hand and slips it into the stopper with the other, using his fingers. Cam would die, he thinks, if he saw this. Then distilled water and then the fixer, a thing of true alchemy. The fixer fascinates Beau. Washing over film it removes unexposed silver halide, leaving only reduced metallic silver, transfigured and stable. The image is made permanent, all potential for further change erased. He's seen unwashed negatives fog in strange ways, the outlines of objects blurring into vague things (*ghost shapes*).

At the kitchen sink he does his final rinse, gently running water over the celluloid's surface and feeling Cam's eyes on his back the whole time, their weight like a question. He wipes his hands on the rag in his back pocket like he doesn't notice, like there's nothing to notice. What (*what*) would they even say to each other through all this charged space, their bodies always so close in this small apartment, brushing past each other, taking up the same corners, readjusting to make room?

There's definitely something there, he thinks, hanging the wet negatives over the bathtub, checking for splotch marks and spraying them down. *Something he's not telling me.*

Beau Larky wonders if he's paranoid, maybe. If being forgetful doesn't make him so. He's read, late in the night, face lit by the glow of his laptop screen, about chemo fog, chemo brain, chemo cognitive impairment, retrograde amnesia. Memory loss, forgetting shit, how to remember, what to do when you can't remember, how to jog your memory. The internet is full of horrifying information he doesn't dare ask Lynch about.

Though the brain usually recovers over time, the sometimes vague yet distressing mental changes cancer patients notice are real, not imagined. They might last a short time, or they might go on for years. These changes can make people unable to go back to their school, work, or social activities, or make it so that it takes a lot of mental effort to do so. Chemo brain changes affect everyday life for many people, and more research is needed to help prevent and cope with them.

Real, not imagined. This is important to him. He goes down lists and checks himself against them, sees that he does have trouble focusing, that he's spacey and quiet, that his thinking processes are slow and disorganized and everything moves at a pained pace, things not quite coming to him when they're called for. That he has trouble remembering the obvious, like Cam's wrecked hand, the ten-hour ER visit and the sound he made when they finally started moving his bones back into place, all sharp intake even with the anaesthetic. The raw row of black stitching holding the skin over his knuckles closed.

You are not stupid or crazy—you just have a side effect that you must learn to manage. Even though this is not a change that is easy to see, like hair loss or skin changes, your family and friends may have noticed some things and may even have some helpful suggestions. For instance, your partner may notice that when you are rushed, you have more trouble finding things.

May notice that I'm losing it, he thinks, and then: Cam's not your partner, man. Though sometimes it feels like that, like now when they share the kitchen in silence and he hangs over the fridge door, swigging back milk straight from the carton while Cam sits absorbed in his text, pencil in his mouth, hair he's tried to tuck back hanging in his eyes. In the *Relationship* box of his emergency contact information section, the admitting nurse had typed *friend*.

Eight

When he's alone in the middle of the day he calls Stacey and invites her over, eager for the relief of company. He's starting to think he thinks too much, shouldn't spend so much time by himself. With Stacey there's no context and thus no pressure—she doesn't know that he's sick, or nauseous, or worried about his head. She can only know what he tells her, and what she infers. She asks why he only has her over when his roommate (*boyfriend*) isn't home, and he shrugs. Cam's busy, he says. He's a really busy guy.

They chill on the couch and smoke weed, watching endless series of documentaries and going *whoa*, Stacey's acrid comments filling the space between them. She's got a wicked tongue. About Derrida she says: *He's such an asshole.* On sustainable local farming practices: *Yeah, if I had a six-figure income I could also enjoy ethically kosher Whole Foods apples for seven ninety-nine a pound.* On the economic downturn: *Hence the vastly more affordable Canadian graduate degree path.* On men obsessed with lavishly decorating their homes for Halloween: *At least they're channeling their passions productively.* On the War on Drugs: *I am actually so tired of hearing about this shit.*

Cam says, watching a lot of movies, huh, and Beau says, yeah, I guess so. DVD cases litter the carpet.

He shows her his darkroom, intensely organized to maximize space. She takes in the stacks of plastic and metal trays sitting on the shelves, jugs of chemicals under the counter, fan and suspended clothesline and safelight and the tongs he doesn't use, preferring his fingers. Everything is labelled, expiry and mix dates scribbled on white stickers adhered to bottles. She is impressed, touching the equipment, breathing in the almost sharp smell of photo chemicals, a smell Beau has always loved. "Nice set up," she says, "but you've evicted your clothes," and he laughs. The clothes accumulate in his room in piles, spilling from the laundry hamper and carpeting the floor.

Take a photo of me, she says in the living room, posing on the armchair and crossing her legs. He lies back on the couch across from her and does, happy to be asked. Stacey stands and poses against the bookcase, leans on the doorframe, extends her arms and makes a face, arching her eyebrows and pursing her lips. She doesn't blink when the shutter closes. Beau watches her through the lens, invited to stare so openly at her red corduroy skirt, white sleeveless silk blouse, complexly patterned pantyhose. Her body twists, contorting for his benefit.

Later he'll look at the negatives and not bother blowing them up, but even now he knows it's a waste of film. The camera is a mirror and she seeks its attention, knowingly returns its gaze with her secret photo face, the face of every woman he's photographed before, practiced in bathroom mirrors all her life to show off her best side, the planned hand running through her hair, just casual enough. Her collusion makes it pornographic, slipping it into something else, something lewd. I know that you know that I know what you're thinking behind that lens, it says. I know and I like it, do it again. There is no fear of the mirror, of seeing or being seen. It's pure will, the will to be looked at. To submit oneself for viewing through the eyes of another. Beau has never seen it quite like this, her self-consciousness either nonexistent or hidden in a way beyond his ability to see.

Cam isn't like that. The second he knows the lens is on him he chokes up, stiffening into a curl of self-consciousness. He stands outside himself and moves differently, all stilted, like he can see himself in the image in advance of its chemical transformation, its alchemy of becoming real, and invests all his energy into resisting this presence. Stacey throws herself into it but it's Cam he wants to shoot, Cam who can be surprised, in a candid moment, into a truly astonishing photo.

"Do you often photograph women?" she asks, slouching against the wall. She looks petulant, cutting, and Beau thinks this is more real, somehow. More true to whoever she is when she goes home at night.

"What do you think?"

"Well, handsome young photographer like you—it would be hard to assume otherwise."

"That's an interesting assumption."

"You invite interesting assumptions."

He laughs. "How do you mean?"

"I can't quite figure you out," she says, and he lets the shutter go.

"Well, I would hope most people wouldn't be so fucking, obvious."

"You seem so much more serious, with the camera. Like your tall friend at the library."

This takes him aback. "Maybe," he says.

"Dark and mysterious." She smiles, smoothing down her skirt where it's begun to bunch up at her hips.

"Open and out there," he counters, and she laughs, pleased.

"I like when people say what they mean," she says. "But I also like a good puzzle."

As he loads a new roll of film she tells him about growing up stoned in Connecticut, the lilt in her voice giving her words a predictable rhythm. He nods along, winding the spool and feeling the oxy (taken, strategically, just before her arrival) begin to lick at the base of his spine. He closes his eyes with pleasure.

They do a couple more shots and he thinks it's pretty fucking, great, having this hot girl posing for him, the perfect mid-afternoon light getting caught in her big dry tangle of hair. Not serious but fun, fun and reassuring, to be flirted with so blatantly in your own apartment. He lights a joint and passes it to her, following her long exhale through the lens. She tilts her chin up like she's having a cigarette.

Stacey tries to hand it back to him but he shakes his head. "Do it again," he says. "The light is ridiculous." The smoke filters through slanting bars of sun, dissolving in wisps. She plays it up and tries to ghost a hit, the whole thing coming apart when she laughs too soon.

"Man, you gotta inhale quick," he says.

"What, like yours would be so amazing?"

"Pfft," Beau says, "fucking, watch," and takes the joint from her, letting an opaque cloud of near-liquid smoke pool from his mouth before sucking it back, effortless.

"Impressive, *Beauregard*." She snatches the joint back and does it herself, a perfect copy of his, so quick and neat he almost misses it. He is beginning to run out of exposures.

It's only when Cam comes through the door, struggling with a pile of books and two grocery bags, that Beau realizes just how loaded their interaction is. How their bodies have shifted, during his expansive show of inattention, into this sex-soaked tableau. Because to Cam, coming home at what is definitely *not* his usual time, Beau sitting splayed on the couch with the camera pointed at Stacey's fluid golden body, top three buttons of her blouse undone as she pulls on the jay, must definitely look like a scene.

"Hey," Beau says, wishing he hadn't taken the oxy.

Cam stands with the door open behind him, cradling the precarious pile. One of the bags he's holding spills open onto their prodigious heap of shoes. "Hey," he says. "Class was cancelled." He can't stop staring at Stacey, his face doing a strange thing where he's obviously upset and wants to hide it but can't get his features to cohere into a unified whole. The effort is beyond him.

Beau gets up and goes to take the books before they can topple. The top one is called *Theory and Affect*. "This is Stacey," he says. "I met her at the laundromat."

"Oh, hey. Stacey."

"She's a grad student at the U of T."

"Hey!" Stacey gets up and comes over to them, extending her hand.

Cam takes it and says, "I know you. From campus." He's all stiff.

"I see you around all the time! It's nice to meet you in an actual formal sense."

"Yeah, and also from Cliff's, I think. Do you know a guy named Cliff?"

She laughs, unstilted. "He's my dealer."

"Oh, no way," Beau says, thinking, *weird*. Why is this so fucking, *weird*? He wonders if he's supposed to know her, from before (before *what*). He doesn't think they've ever met.

"Small world," Cam says. He bends down and starts picking up the spilled groceries—a bunch of newly bruised apples, jam, two big plastic things of yogurt. "I'm just gonna put this stuff away real quick."

Beau follows him into the kitchen, books held tight against his chest. Cam dumps the bags, leaving them to gape on the counter, and swings open the fridge door with more force than necessary. Beau stands with the books in his arms and watches him, unsure.

"Do you want me to leave?" Cam doesn't look at him.

"What?"

"Like I mean, you've got a girl here, so."

"Oh, it's not like that."

"I mean, you guys are having like, a fucking photo sesh, so."

"Yeah, I was just messing around with the camera a bit."

He jams a bag of bread onto the counter, leaving his hand imprinted into the soft loaf. "It's no big deal, I have to do some more work anyway. I can head back to campus for a bit."

"Really, Cam. I was just having her over for a smoke."

Cam finally looks at him, his intensity throwing itself into the space between them, and Beau sees it's precisely this he's always after, the pureness of the emotion and the impossibility of its containment, marks of natural openness that give this lanky man a photogenic quality unlike any Beau's ever seen.

But now it rattles him, shakes up something deep in his chest.

"Hey, I'm really sorry," he says, "I know you've got a ton of work, I didn't think you'd be back till way later." He follows Cam from the fridge to the counter and back, nearly stepping on his heels.

"Beau, it's okay. I can leave."

"You don't have to leave."

Stacey appears in the doorway, taking them in. She's standing on one foot and pulling a shoe onto her other carelessly, like a dude. "Hey, Beauregard," she says. "I think I'm going to take off and grab some food and finish up with my paper."

"Oh yeah, for sure. What are you writing on?"

"Poe."

"Poe?"

"Edgar Allan," she explains, like it's a citation in a bibliography. "I like Poe very much. He's so *dark* and his language is so *excessive*."

Cam's head is hidden in the fridge where he's taking pains to rearrange the bottom shelf, but Beau is almost certain he's rolling his eyes.

"Here, I'll walk you out," he says.

"Oh," she says, "*wonderful*. It was nice to meet you, Cam."

"You too," Cam says. He's holding an orange, and Beau imagines him squeezing it into pulp.

At the door Beau says, "you know, you don't have to go if you don't want to," watching Stacey try to get her second leather man shoe on.

"No, I'm starving, and besides, I've already put you through two rolls of film. Anyway, what are you going to do with all those books, Beauregard? Read some very serious theory?"

He looks down and realizes he's still holding Cam's books. He loosens his grip on them and laughs. "Not likely."

"Although, you know what, here," she says, digging through her floppy shoulder bag, "I actually have some very serious theory for you."

"What, for me?"

"For you."

He leans against the doorframe, resting his temple on its cool painted surface. "Seriously?"

"Very seriously." She finds the book she wants and takes it out, flipping through the pages to remove stray strips of paper, sticky notes, bookmarks. "It's a little annotated, but it should be readable."

"Do you want me to give it to Cam for you?"

"If I wanted to give something to Cam, I wouldn't be so coy about it. It's for you."

He takes the sleek little blue book from her and turns it over in his hands, Cam's pile forgotten on the floor. "*Reflections on Photography*," he reads, wonderingly. "Wow, thank you." How she's failed to identify him as Cam's obviously under-accomplished stoner roommate is not entirely clear.

"I think you'll really like it. Barthes is my absolute favourite."

"Yeah," he says, still looking at it, "amazing."

She re-shoulders her bag and wraps her scarf around her neck twice, tight, hiding her smooth stretch of throat. "You should tell your tall friend to take it easy."

"Yeah, he's just got a lot going on, you know?"

"Trust me, I know the feeling."

When she leaves he tucks the book into his hanging jacket, nervous. He doesn't want Cam to see it, has a *foreboding* about Cam seeing it. A pit of stomach feeling, like maybe it wasn't something he should have accepted. He knocks on the doorframe twice, quickly, and shivers all over. Come on, man, he thinks. It's a fucking, book.

He picks up Cam's pile and moves to the kitchen, feeling the books' solid weight against his chest. He sets them down on the table and braces himself against a chair, watching Cam take eggs out of their carton and place them on the fridge door one by one. "Hey," he says. "Are you okay?"

"I'm fine." He doesn't turn around.

"You're mad at me," Beau says before he can think, and as he speaks he sees it's true.

"Why would I be?" He slams the fridge shut and sags with his back against it. He looks tired.

"Because you're overworked, you come home and—" the oxy is coming on very strong, liquid waves of warmth flooding whatever unfortunate brain center is responsible for processing linear thought. But it's also not a linear thing, somehow.

"Funny how you're too sick to do anything, but when it comes to photo shoots and fucking around with hipsters you picked up at the laundromat, it's all good."

"Okay, I already told you it wasn't like that."

"Popping oxy all day and maxing out our fucking Queen Video credit, having girls over and shit? Are you *kidding?* How can you even think about that shit right now?"

"Cam, I get lonely, man. It's hard to be alone all day and be sick."

Something in Cam softens, like a rigid cord in his spine has been cut.

"We just hang out, you know. And I think you would really like her, honestly."

"Why didn't you even mention it, then?"

The question puts him in a strange headspace, looking up from the bottom of a well into a blinding vista of which only a fraction can be glimpsed at a time. He knew, he knew he shouldn't mention it, that it would upset Cam because (*what*). That it would make something in Cam flatten.

How come when I come over your boyfriend's never home?

"I can't tell you what to do," Cam says, "but I really think you should focus your energy on getting better instead of getting involved with people *you don't even know.*"

He feels a small lick of anger, an unbelievable thing considering the fluid texture the kitchen has taken on. "Man, I can't believe you, I know you're fucking, tired and everything, but—"

"Yeah, because I do *enough* shit around here. Picking up groceries and shit after ten hours of grad school garbage. Paying your rent and your hospital bills."

Cam has never once mentioned this, ever, and now that he does Beau feels like he's been hit, a sharp unexpected pain right in the center of his chest. "Cam," he says, but Cam just looks at him like they don't know each other, like they've never met, and turns to leave the kitchen. Beau hears his door shut, loudly, at the end of the hall.

He has a strong urge to follow but makes himself sit down, placing his hands on his knees and breathing deep, suddenly nauseous, maybe from the painkillers or maybe from the chemo or maybe from that crippling look.

He closes his eyes and sees Cam as he appears in his mind, leaning on all available surfaces and slouching, neck bent, hair falling in his eyes. Because he's exhausted, you fucking, exhaust him, there's only so much of him to go around and you fucking, spread him thin. There's something up with him, too, he thinks. Not just you, but him also.

He thinks Cam might come back but he doesn't, staying in his room the rest of the night. Beau imagines him sprawled out on the bed, lying on his stomach with his feet in the air, arms crossed as he demolishes a volume of something dense with that furious concentration he can produce when he's just *pissed*. Glasses slipping the whole time, roughly pushed back onto his nose. His impatient flips, fingers pre-emptively working at corners even before he's finished reading the page, like he's taking it out on the book.

Beau feels a great blackness coming on, one of the first since the hospital, and bends over himself. Inside him everything is mangled, out of place, not right. Heartsick, he thinks. The word for it is heartsick. Sick in a way no kind of drug can fix. He thinks of knocking on Cam's door but doesn't know what he would say (*I'm sorry*) and whether it would carry any of the resonance (*no one's more important to me than you*).

And he realizes he's frightened because they're having a real fight, not just giving each other a hard time or feeling stressed but having a legit fight, and really sees for the first time how events are transformative, how he and Cam are different people now than they were just this past summer, and how Lynch is right. In his mind he sees his *Support System*, the full thing Lynch is always talking about, the pictures on the little orange counselling pamphlet with a branching line diagram ending in no less than ten eager smiling faces—parents, siblings, extended family, friends, therapists, other survivors, whatever. Lynch saying, it's important that you don't go through this process by yourself. Lynch telling him, you should really look into joining a support group at the hospital.

And then he sees the really big picture, which is something like: he is twenty-four years old and works (*worked*, he remembers) at Starbucks. He currently holds a full-time position in Being Fucking, Sick, with a specialization in Having Fucking,

Cancer. His major existentially motivated interest is messing around with film in a fucking, closet. He's quickly developing what he knows is probably an addiction to prescription painkillers. He doesn't know what he's doing, or supposed to be doing, contented with the evening joint, the adequate income, the mediocre college degree. He could look for a better job, maybe, when he's not sick anymore (knock on wood). He could take some courses. He could try to get some of his photos out, though it really doesn't matter to him one way or the other. He finds pleasure in the act, not the recognition—a confusion of social priorities that has cost him from day one.

Cam, on the other hand, is twenty-four and well on his way to getting a Ph.D. Beau doesn't know how it works in academia, but he knows that whatever is required Cam has it, and lots of it. He's the cream of the academic-theoretical crop, groomed since Beau can remember to make his way through the institution's various hoops and barriers. Cam has things like published articles in legitimately serious journals where his name appears in italics (*Cameron Dempster*, University of Toronto) above double-columned text the size of sand grains. He has awards and grants and fellowships and an enormous funding package they've both been able to live off, somehow, miraculously, for six whole months without depleting. Cam's degree is a formality—he's off to bigger and better things any day now.

And there will come a day, yeah, when Cam finishes his degree and is offered a job somewhere far away, somewhere crazy like Yale or fucking, Stanford, and moves to take it. And then what? What will he do? Go with him? It's impossible. He'll have to get used to living by himself, not seeing Cam all the time, or at all—not seeing Cam at all. When they were younger it seemed so steady and set, but now Beau sees that it's not ultimately sustainable, this thing. They are actually leading (and have always been leading) wildly different lives that will continue to diverge in enormous, heart-stopping ways. Cam will get a sweet three-storey house and department friends and wear ironed shirts and marry someone who hangs off his arm at dinner parties where he drops terms like *poststructural*, while he'll—what? Beau tries to imagine where he'll be in ten years and draws a colossal blank.

His throat tightens and he thinks: one way or the other I'll lose him. And how did it happen that he's wound up so tied to this one person? After all his precautions. After all his effort not to get attached. Because he knew, had always known that relationships are impermanent, shifting, contingent. He had the foster kid's understanding that it was a mistake to think anyone you stayed with was your family—you would get transferred, you always got transferred. You and your small pile of worldly things.

In the early morning hours the chemo catches up to him, forcing him to his knees and then to the floor where he lies still and presses his cheek to the cold tile, listening to the oceanic rush of water in pipes and of things settling inside him, organs struggling to return to some semblance of stasis. Any movement might trigger another wave of heaving, and he fears this. He can hear the blood in his head and his irregular sick pulse, and then Cam knocking softly before coming in.

Focused on the pattern of the tile and the chipped square closest to his nose, Beau feels rather than sees Cam standing over him, but the effect is the same: he knows Cam is in his boxers and tee, and that his face is vague with sleep. He can say with certainty that Cam, having crawled from his bed, is not wearing glasses, and squints into the light. Cam sits beside him and touches his shoulder and says, "hey, man," and the contact and voice are so welcome he wants to cry.

"You're gonna get cold, huh." There is the weight of a blanket drawn over him, and then of Cam's hand in his hair.

Nine

Beau is searching, re-searching. Doing research.

His shelves of old boxed negatives are an archive unlike any he's imagined, and he feels intuitively that all the answers he needs, has been looking for, are here. Why have memories, he thinks. Why even have them when you've had a camera around your neck the entirety of your adult life. Yet there are key differences between memories and photos, ones he can't describe but feels with the intensity of stifled resonance.

He looks through binders of film sheets, scanning strips from years ago on the lightbox to pick out backlit outlines. He can't believe all these old photos, some of them taken as far back as high school. These he cringes to see, identifying them as the products of someone who didn't know how to frame, what to focus on. Of someone who didn't understand how light worked. But they've got an amateur vibe he likes, an energy and excitement and respect for the medium that can stem only from utter amazement at the fact of its operation. He remembers holding the Nikon and staring at it hard, trying to puzzle out what it was and how it worked. Trying to imagine converging light bending in on itself to come back and form an image, but in reverse, creating a material record of a single moment in time, never to be repeated again.

Whoa, the younger Beau Larky had thought, stoned and awed. Fucking, crazy.

And he feels proud of his past self, little foster kid with the weird name developing the first intense interest of his life.

So many of the old frames are of Cam, his lanky body folded into various spaces: sitting cross-legged on the group home bed, blowing smoke out the single window, laughing, reading, hanging off the porch, back turned as he helps his mom in the kitchen. And skateboarding, lots of skateboarding, because suddenly he sees that Cam skateboarding was his favourite thing in the world to shoot. The looseness of it, his limbs flowing with the board, the kick and flip and satisfying smack of wood on pavement. Saying, how do you do that shit, and Cam going, oh, it's you know, whatever. Practice. And him saying, can you slide the rail like that again, and Cam shrugging, like it didn't please him to death to be asked. Sitting all day in parking lots or on the rim of the skatepark's big bowl, sneakers dangling below as he watched Cam roll back and forth across the concrete. Loving the weight of the camera, the smooth leather part of the strap resting on his sunburnt neck and the solid feel of its body over his heart.

One day they took the ferry over to the island and sat on the rocks, skipping stones and chain smoking while he shot three rolls of film, now here before him, imprinted on celluloid in a hundred shades of grey. With the frames backlit he can almost see the colour the day would have been, sky and water the same blue slate, a congregation of sailboats marking the place where the horizon should've been. You learn to read colour from shades, after a while. It's hidden in the intensities.

Great towering clouds marshalled behind the city skyline, at odds with its erratic shape, peaked like an ECG. A true Toronto day, windy and hot, everything gathering, awaiting culmination. In one shot Cam's hair blows back as he gazes over the water, and just from the exposure he knows it was this golden almost-red, a colour that's faded over time. Now only hints of copper remain, washed out. It seems to him that there was something forward-looking in Cam then, an orientation toward potential—like the whole future would open up for him, if he wanted it to. Like he belonged to the horizon, had something intrinsic in common with it. Like he hadn't yet experienced the notion of limits.

He looks happy, Beau thinks, and only with this forced contrast does it become obvious to him that Cam right now, Cam as he knows him at twenty-four, is not. That he carries within himself some intense unhappiness he refuses or is unable to share.

When Cam picked him up from chemo it was raining, cold needling drops, and as Beau walked to the Jeep he kept his face upturned, wanting to take in the whole of the sky—to inhabit it. Cam sat with a fat volume of Foucault open in his lap, arm raised to cradle his head against the window, staring at nothing in particular somewhere across the street. It's inside that he's always looking, Beau thought then. Staring out over things that can't be seen and aren't shared.

When he saw him coming Cam leaned over to open the passenger door and said *hey* with a tenderness that was total and beyond Beau's capacity to understand. I should have given him an out, he'd thought. I never really gave him an out.

He rested his forehead against the cool window and closed his eyes and it was understood between them that he couldn't talk, was too sick to talk, yet even so he could feel Cam watching him between stoplights and welcomed it, this incredible, complete, undeserved affection.

Looking back over these shots he sees how he's invested them with a tenderness that makes him ache, now, to take in. He traces the line of eighteen-year-old Cam's shoulders hunched over the white ferry railing and feels that in them lies compounded a profound repository of concentrated nostalgia. But is it there, really, or is he only inserting it now, moved as he is by the daily drama of his body's failure to thrive? He couldn't say which, only that it makes him feel internally adrift, unanchored. Lonesome for the thing the image testifies, blankly and with all its mute force, has been and will never be again.

It is what I add to photograph, he'd read, *and what is nonetheless already there.*

The book Stacey's given him is glue, attaching itself to his thoughts. He can't tear himself away, or get the words out of his head. They are spells meant only for him, or someone like him.

Last week he developed the roll with the lecture photo on it and clipped just that one frame, blowing it up at four different exposures. It was charged, saturated, infused with something ineffable radiating from the prints. Something of Cam he'd been able to find through feel alone: that quality of *being about to speak*. But that wasn't quite it, either—it was both less specific and deeper than that, some far-reaching, elusive thing defining the logic of Cam's movements and speech and thoughts and dreams and ultimately of his very character. Trapped electricity. An essence, if there was such a thing.

This desire affects me at a depth and according to roots which I do not know.

It holds his complete and undivided attention, this intangible thing. He chooses the best exposure and pins a copy on the fridge door, allowing himself to feel pleasure at how good it is, how intuitive, how obviously not the work of an amateur. Time and experience have changed him and the way he looks through this lens worn perpetually against his living beating heart.

Beau often thinks that photography is a sort of dark magic, a way of owning something without physically taking it. That's why they call it *capturing*. If someone didn't know him, or Cam, they might have said the photographer had been in love.

"That's a great photo," Cam says, searching the cupboard for sugar. He can't stop looking at it, like he's afraid it might move, come to life. Become animate. "Wow."

Beau senses, at times, that Cam fears the lens, shies away from it. Superstitious, he thinks, and recalls the way some cultures fear, in the click of a shutter, the vanishing of one's soul.

Or is it the revelation, he thinks. They are afraid they will be shown to themselves.

Ten

On Beau's birthday Cam takes him to see a movie, which is about all either of them have the energy for. Cam's been getting hardly any sleep, staying up late finishing papers and grading, waking in the early morning hours with a gasp Beau can hear through the wall, like he's coming up for air.

He's not doing well, Beau thinks, wanting to get up and check on him. In the mornings Cam barely talks, sleeping on his feet at the counter. There are dark circles under his eyes.

They smoke up while cutting through the park, passing a blunt back and forth and coughing into their sleeves. Beau curls his gloved fingers and takes in the monochrome sky, searching for hints that the thaw is coming in earnest. Cam pushes up his glasses and smooths down his toque. His hands stay in his pockets, like he doesn't trust himself, and suddenly, just like that, all at once (and how else do these things come to us?), Beau knows, he knows what it is between them.

No, he thinks. Come on. It can't be like that, it just can't.

In the theatre they buy icy fountain drinks and popcorn he puts too much butter topping on while Cam stands by and shakes his head. "That's disgusting, man," he says.

Beau cuffs his arm. "What, you think I'm done? There's still this excellent salt and vinegar powder." He tears open the pouch and upends the flavouring all over the bag.

Cam makes a face.

"What, aren't you glad I'm fucking, eating?" Though it's a joke he immediately wishes he hadn't said it. "Come on," he says, elbowing Cam, "come on, you know I don't mean it like that."

They sit at the very back and put their feet up on the seats in front of them, talking in low voices as they sink into their chairs. Cushioned in the dim lighting and red plush Beau feels sheltered, insulated from external things. They are here, watching this movie, and this is all they are doing. He breathes deep and appreciates the fact of his slow pulse and the warm flow of blood through his wasted extremities, fingers just now beginning to steal back heat from the April chill.

The soft movie light reflects in Cam's glasses, getting caught in distended squares of white and blue. Beau watches Cam push them up at the corners, the motion still imbued with that self-consciousness reserved for unfamiliar things, and thinks how strange it is to spend so much time with someone and never really *look* at them, never sit close enough to feel out the pattern of their breathing and the restless rhythm of their ankle on their knee.

"Hey," he whispers, stilling the motion with his hand, "you nervous or something? It's not like it's our first date."

But it is like that, somehow, and Beau sees that this is the thing, surfacing in his mind in all its enormity, physical and dazzling. Why did I say that, he thinks, why would I even say that ever, and his palms sweat and he feels huge crushing dread about something just off screen.

Even in the dark he knows he's made Cam all flushed.

3. HIGH SUMMER

I look for signs, but of what? What is the object of my reading? Is it: am I loved (am I loved no longer, am I still loved)? Is it my future that I am trying to read, deciphering in what is inscribed the announcement of what will happen to me, according to a method which combines paleography and manticism? Isn't it rather, all things considered, that I remain suspended on this question, whose answer I tirelessly seek in the other's face: *What am I worth?*

Roland Barthes, *A Lover's Discourse*

One

It didn't surprise me when Stacey began hanging around the apartment, bringing her big bag of books and loose frizzing hipster hair I started finding stuck to our furniture, carpet, floors. I'd come home from campus to Beau sitting with her on the couch, playing the N64, watching a movie, smoking the bong, calling her *Stace* in a way that made me grind my teeth. I said nothing because I couldn't be mad; how could I be mad when he was so sick and this obviously took his mind off it? Plus, he could see whoever he wanted.

He could see whoever—if he wanted to.

But just not this fuzzy-haired woman moving around irreverently with novels in a daze, mixing her colours with her whites at the laundromat, smoking our weed and smiling all pleased, like she knew something nobody else could. Hearing her weird disjointed laugh made me want to shake Beau, like, what are you doing? What are you doing, Beau. Wake the fuck up.

It was a bad jealousy, my worst ever. Hearing them chatting as I came down the hall twisted up my insides, made my skin all hot. Though Beau didn't make it seem like they were doing anything except hanging out I began to fear coming home to the sound of his headboard rubbing up against plaster. When I thought about it my mouth got dry and sour.

I knew she didn't know he was sick, though she must have guessed something was up with how thin he was and how quickly he grew tired. It wasn't impossible that she had opened the medicine cabinet and seen his many pill bottles, read the names of the drugs (take one capsule by mouth two times daily until finished) prescribed to *Larky, Beauregard*. This isn't what you need right now, I wanted to tell him. This opaque woman oozing her confidence all over the apartment, fuck. When she was over at our place I stayed in my room or left, working with furious distraction and not returning until I was sure she had gone.

One Saturday I vacuumed the living room, lifting the corners of the carpet to get all the crumbs underneath. No matter how many times I grated the vacuum's bulky head over the floor I could still feel fine grainy particles on the soles of my feet. Beau emerged from his room fully dressed and came to stand in front of me, hands braced against the small of his back.

I killed the vacuum, leaning on its long plastic body. "Hey," I said.

"Hey. Listen, Stacey's coming over here in a bit and we're gonna go out and grab some lunch."

"Okay."

"Is it?"

"Yeah, of course."

"Cam, I know you don't like her. But she's really sweet, man. I know she comes off intense at first. You should give her a chance."

I sighed and turned the vacuum back on, kicking up the carpet with my foot. I couldn't look at him.

"Hey!"

"Beau, man."

I turned away but he stepped on the cord, yanking it out of the wall, the vacuum's hollow roar cut off with a whine.

"I know you're super worried about me, but trust me, I'm not getting into anything right now," he said. "I'm feeling way too sick, you know? And anyway, it's not like that."

"I'm pretty sure she thinks it's like that."

"Just give her a chance, huh?" He came up behind me and put his hands on my shoulders. "She's not so bad."

I let him rock me back and forth in his easy way, leaning into his touch. "Okay, okay," I said.

There was a knock on the door and Beau sprang to open it. Before turning the lock he looked back at me, cocking his head. "Be *nice*, okay?"

"I will, I will," I said, and plugged the vacuum back in so I wouldn't have to hear her calling him *Beauregard* in that teasing way.

They were almost the same height, she slightly taller. Over the soothing din of the appliance I watched them greet each other, her face lighting up in response to Beau's ever-straightening shoulders. She leaned in to hug him and in it was everything I envied her—the ease, the permission, the openness, the placement of his hands on her shoulders, her back. The effortless way her palm settled between his incredible shoulder blades. In this she had already won.

Their bodies fit well together and I couldn't look, had to bite down on the inside of my cheek hard as the gendered unfairness of it all crowded out my vision. Because she could touch him so easily, test the waters and gauge his response while I could never venture this simple thing without consequence, though I longed to. My fingers itched with impatience.

She pulled back and saw me and looked momentarily unsettled, like she was surprised I was there. The vacuum was a blessing that made speech impossible, so she smiled and waved instead. I smiled back in a forced way and gave her a look I hoped said *who the fuck do you think you are*, startling myself with the venom of it, with how extremely ungenerous she made me feel. My insides were all sick and hollow. I had never acted this way toward Beau's various dates before, all those women with slick polished nails and their hair arranged just so and the strange narrow shoes they left on our doormat, but now I couldn't stop myself, didn't care. Not after I had just spent a month without sleep pushing him around in a fucking wheelchair.

With his back turned Beau didn't catch any of this. He gave me a look and said something to Stacey before disappearing into the kitchen. She took a seat on the couch. I turned off the vacuum and started wrapping up the cord, feeling her eyes on my back.

"How are you, Cam?" she said.

I turned, surprised. "I'm good."

"How's the degree treating you?"

"Uh, not bad. I just got some summer teaching work lined up, so."

She put her feet up on the coffee table, crossed her legs. "They gave you a summer position?"

"They gave me two."

"Wow, that's pretty good. Those are hard to get."

"Yeah, they are."

"You must have worked pretty hard for that."

"Yeah, I did." I meant it to sound flat but it slipped into coldness, registering in her narrowing features. I can be such a dick, I thought, startled. These things have changed me in ways I don't understand.

"Well, how nice," she said.

In the kitchen Beau was hitting the bong, and we listened to its bubbling followed by his low exhalation. She flexed her toes while I finished wrapping up the cord, cleared my throat.

"Okay," Beau said, coming into the living room. "Good to go." He was still holding the bong. "Are you ready?"

"Absolutely," she said, but kept sitting.

"Here," I said, taking the bong from him. He seemed vague, distant. I didn't know how he was going to eat anything, let alone lunch. He began to put on his jacket over his t-shirt, fumbling with the sleeves.

"You can't go out like that," I said.

Beau laughed, colouring a little. "Yeah, you're right, you're right," he said, backtracking into the kitchen to get his sweater.

Stacey stared at me hard, like she couldn't believe I was a real person. "So, Cam," she said. "Are you Beau's boyfriend, or what? In this impressive domestic situation."

I stopped and stood, taking in this strange assertive woman stretched out on our couch, her feet on the coffee table like she owned the place. That I was putting away the vacuum wasn't helping. I might as well have been wearing an apron.

Beau laughed from the kitchen. "Yeah, something like that."

I blushed so hard I had to lower my head, but Stacey had already caught the heat on my skin. She chewed her lip, eyes shifting between me and the wall dividing us from Beau. "Hm," she said.

After they'd finally left, Beau holding the door for her while she stumbled into her big leather dude shoes, I lay down on the couch and folded my hands over my stomach, watching the grey spring light filtering in through the windows. "Something like that," I said out loud, savouring the feel of the words, the weight of them in the empty apartment.

The next day was a chemo day, which meant there was no way Beau could see anyone, let alone Stacey. I drove him home from Princess Margaret as he sat in the passenger seat groaning, pressing his face to the window and curling his knees tight against his chest. "Fuck," he said, "Fuck this fucking, cancer shit, man."

The new chemo left him sagging in elevator corners like he had no skeleton, a scarecrow or a puppet of a man with all his different ways of being sick. Long silences in the Jeep followed by hours spent lying very still on the couch with a hand over his eyes, brimming with the snappy edginess (*would you fucking, ease off for a sec*) he got when he was really nauseous, his sentences short and punctuated by profanity as if this abruptness could somehow ward off the unease. But also an intense, unpredictable desire for proximity manifest in the way he'd come into my room and lie on my bed while I worked, hands folded over his chest and eyes closed, listening to my typing tapering off and starting up or flipping through the books on my nightstand and reading my annotations, a thing that left me nervous and thrilled.

Some sessions he went straight to bed and slept through the afternoon into the night, hoping sleep would dissolve the worst of the coming illness. The drugs shut him down, flipped his switch so completely I got into the habit of meeting him right inside the clinic because he looked gutted, looked like he might not make it back down the hallways with whatever chemicals had been mixed into his blood. *Hold on, hold on*, he said, *I just need a sec*, reaching out to steady himself against my shoulder, the wall. Closing his eyes against the ocean within while I stood by with my hands in my pockets and my heart in my mouth.

Other times he wanted company, wanted to sit and chill and smoke and chat at his slow, pained pace, every word an effort as if any movement of his throat might bring on some spasmic muscular reaction. He wanted these things badly though he'd never ask, and I learned to do them all, intuiting them from the angle of his shoulders and neck, the amount of conviction in his laugh.

But he split my attention, splintered my focus. I was tired but couldn't sleep, yet sleep always found me in strange places. It curled me around the photocopier at the library, cheek to the glass, bent my head to the kitchen table when I tried to read, defied the coffee Beau set out for me, snuck up when I was driving so I'd have to bite down on the inside of my cheek, mouth increasingly mangled as I navigated College through half-closed lids. At night I thought obsessively of his cell counts, his wrists. He had a gravity that sucked in all my thoughts and I could do nothing, I was immobilized.

I tried to spend more time in the library, books open around me in an ascetic spread under the adjustable fluorescent lamps. I buried myself in the density of Derrida until my eyes stung but then I'd have to *go*, leaving behind the sprawling grey carpet and rows of hunched backs at tables to make sure Beau had eaten, that he wasn't running some crazy fever or twisting in on himself in bed. And I wanted to see him so bad, my body pulling me from the library toward his distant center, his strange new uncertainty and the way he greeted me now, coming to the door to hold it open or take my books, the groceries, my bag, following me into the kitchen to sit in the far chair ask and how I was—*are you good, Cam?* Sometimes he made me dinner, extra cheesy lasagne and huge ham omelettes and Greek salads dripping with oil.

Do you know what you're doing, I wanted to ask. Do you have any idea what your hand on the back of my neck does to me when I'm reading and suddenly there's your warm palm cupping my spine? How can you not feel it through my skin, Beau Larky? As I sit here and burn up whole.

And each night, late in the night, I woke with a horrible feeling congealing in the deepest pit of my chest, a throbbing livid pulsing thing, and knew I'd just had an awful dream but could never remember what it was. And I thought, each time with great clarity: *you're worried about Beau.* Heavy with dread, withdrawing into the covers, disintegrating strands of the dream clinging to my skin. Though I was shaken in the deep way you are when you wake alone and afraid in the middle of the night, this thought would help me go back to sleep: it is only my mind, it is only my mind. I thought of all the Lacan and Freud I'd read and it calmed me—so many men rationalizing themselves to themselves and in comparison this was nothing, this was not even a thing. I knew what I'd dreamt had no shape. I knew it was only a feeling.

There was a sudden warm snap, winter bleeding away overnight to expose yellowed grass and white bleached sidewalks, gravel and trash everywhere. People gathered like lizards on decks, benches, warm campus steps, shedding their heavy clothes like so many layers of skin. Bright tops and floral skirts and sandals appeared, beach bags and sunglasses in the spring sun that was really a July glare, the confident light of high summer.

The temperature strayed into the high twenties, large bugs flying in through our windows from the sticky heaving street below. We put away the space heater, turned on the fan. Had a big argument about whether we should get an AC.

"You know what really sucks?" Beau said. "Worrying about fucking, money. It's really stupid, and it really sucks."

The next week he was hunched over an ironing board in the living room, trying to follow the steps of an instructional Youtube video getting rapidly ahead of him. Toggling it back to the beginning, he stood holding the iron skeptically over his shirt, mouth twisted up in concentration. "Like, how is he doing that?" he said as the man on the screen produced a perfectly pressed sleeve for the fourth consecutive time.

"What are you doing?" I asked.

"Going back to Starbucks. Gonna take some pressure off your funding package."

"You're going back?"

"Tomorrow morning."

And he did, a week before the end of his chemo sessions, coming home in the late afternoons smelling like coffee, stretching out on the couch and falling asleep to the TV. He brought pastries and snacks I ate while I studied, high and anxious and full of icing. When the chemo ended I allowed myself to take a deep psychic breath.

When I worked on campus I stopped in to see him, having late lunches that turned into day-enders when the weather acted magnetically, pulling us out into the ripe afternoon heat and the lure of sun on bare skin. We strolled down the sidewalk in t-shirts, our faces turned to the sun and its promise of a long hot summer to come. He smiled, closing his eyes against the light. We took the long way through campus to the park, past lazy students stretched out on the grass in groups or pairs brought together by the smell of newly warmed earth, reading, gossiping, smoking.

The park was all green and gold, bikes breezing by with bell chimes like afterthoughts, joggers labouring in skin-tight shorts, office types walking their panting dogs on extended lunch breaks. We sat on a hill with our backs to a big oak, its gnarled bark pressing into my spine through the fabric of my shirt, and lit a joint, and didn't talk, watching people walking past and squirrels quarrelling and cars honking in slow traffic, all their windows rolled down, drivers leaning out in irritation, envious of the day's heat.

Beau looked calm, steady. He didn't say anything about when he would get the chemo results back. "We're really young," he said, as if in response to some ongoing debate. "Still."

It was an overcast day, gusts of warm wind carrying the metal smell of coming precipitation up from the lake, when Stacey stopped me on the sidewalk outside the library.

"Hey!" she said, coming up behind me with what was almost a jog. "Hey, Cam. Wait up." Her hair was everywhere, lifting and twisting, floating around her head.

I'd been rounding the block to find the Jeep, doing a superstitious Beau-thing of mentally knocking on wood each time I considered the likelihood of a parking ticket. "Uh, hey," I said. "Stacey."

"Listen, I feel like we got off on the wrong foot."

I shifted my bag on my shoulders. A book I hadn't positioned well jutted into my back. "That's probably true," I said.

She wore floppy turquoise rain boots with wool socks coming out of their tops over complex, lacy pantyhose. These made her look whimsical, an impression undermined by her brisk serious demeanor. An old shoulder bag rested on her hip in an easy, loose way.

"I feel that I was really rude," she said. "I can be standoffish sometimes, snarky. Anyway, you're not exactly the easiest person to get along with."

"Yeah, well. I'm just that kind of guy, so."

"*So.*"

"Yeah, so."

"Do you always use *so* as a proposition clincher?"

"Are you always so aggressive when you talk to people?"

She laughed in her weird stilted way. "We're not so different, you and I."

Stacey, I knew, was fluent in subtext. I worked out the manifold meanings of this assessment and decided I didn't like any of them.

"You don't even know me," I said, which obviously wasn't the right thing, but what the fuck.

"I know enough *about* you."

"What?"

"Beau talks about you in-*cessantly*."

This pleased me deeply, to my core. She caught the effect of her words travelling across my face and smiled inwardly, in her own secret way.

"What does he say?"

She watched me carefully. "That you're a quiet guy. That you like to keep to yourself. That you're stressed out, and that you don't handle stress well. That you're ridiculously intelligent."

I flushed and stifled it by turning away and starting to walk, my pace indicating she was welcome to follow. "That's what he told you?"

"Directly, indirectly. There are many ways of saying things, don't you think?"

By now the Jeep was fully visible, a yellow ticket trapped under one of the windshield wipers, flapping around in the wind.

"Fuck," I said. "What the hell."

"Do you often get tickets?" she asked.

"All the fucking time," I said, pulling the long yellow strip from under the wiper and leaning against the Jeep to read it. "Forty dollars! Fuck. There isn't even a sign here or anything."

"Why don't you just streetcar to campus?"

"I would," I said. "I do, but today I had to drive Beau to—today I had to drive Beau."

"What, can't he drive himself?"

"No," I said, swinging open the door and crumpling the yellow plastic into my back pocket. "He doesn't have a license."

"Really?"

I threw my backpack onto the back seat. "Yeah, really. He never learned." *Get out, come on, you're not fucking driving, we're gonna get pulled over in a second*, I'd said when he tried to take my keys, telling me *you're not driving yourself to the hospital with a fucking, broken hand, are you fucking, insane*, almost yelling, and me, shortened by the first waves of pain puncturing their way through the shock, snapping, *just call a fucking cab, Jesus.*

"Where are you going?" I asked.

"Home."

"Do you want a ride?"

"Really?" she asked, drawing her head back.

"Yeah, really. We're going the same way, so."

"Definitely," she said, "I'd definitely like a ride," and ran around to the passenger side. She placed her bag between her feet and buckled her seatbelt. "I haven't been in a car in so long," she said, immensely pleased. She peered around, checking out the contents of the side pockets (crumpled napkins, Tim Hortons bags) and the sticky cup holders (the dregs of some watery iced coffee, coins, a pack of Zig-Zags). On the dashboard was a badly creased pamphlet called *Managing the Side Effects of Chemotherapy: A Focus on You*, parts of which Beau had read aloud to me after a session, mock-serious, and which I'd later read with great care in its entirety in case it contained any information I hadn't been able to pry from late-night googling.

Stacey picked it up and turned it over. "Some light reading?"

"Yeah," I said, a little bit horrified. I'd forgotten the Jeep was packed with shit from four straight months of hospital trips. "Titillating stuff."

And pulled out of the parking spot in one fluid move, all displaced intensity.

"I can almost see what Beau likes about you," she said as we drove. "Almost."

In the closed proximity of the car I could smell her perfume, something like orange and spice, or maybe incense. For a moment I saw her very clearly, sitting straight-backed and cross-legged on a yoga mat, eyes closed, deep breaths precipitating the rise and fall of her collarbone, her clavicle. The fine bones moving directly beneath the skin, itself a gleaming tanned thing the colour of almonds, like she had just spent four months in Rio walking sundrenched streets. Sweat drying frizzing hair to her temples during intense positions held for long periods of unbroken focus. Someone in tune with their body, I thought. Someone deeply embodied.

And her sweat, too, just barely detectable—the student sweat of rushing around all day and always having your neck damp, moisture clinging to the small of your back. It was tangy and sweet, a woman's sweat, and sitting there in such sudden proximity to this girl, this woman Stacey with her weird frock-dress and tangible physical body taking up real space in the Jeep and her breasts flattened under the seatbelt, I realized just how long it had been since I'd been close to any women at all. All her bodily immediacy and I was somehow, unbelievably, aroused.

What the fuck, I thought. I wondered for the hundred and fiftieth time if she and Beau had had sex, and how, and what it had it been like. The two basic questions of metaphysics: what is there, and what is it like?

All the while a bad jealousy burning its way through my system, carving out a track for itself.

At the apartment, which she had made her way into by insisting to help me carry up the books I'd left in the back seat (*I can at least return the favour, right?*), she strolled around the living room at her own pace, uninvited, reading names from the spines of books open facedown on the coffee table, stacked on the floor, wedged into the armchair. She stopped in front of the bookcase, rocking on her heels and clasping her hands behind her back.

"Who's your favourite?" she asked.

"What?"

"Theorist," she said, and laughed all stunted. "Your favourite theorist. Sorry, that wasn't the clearest question ever."

I wanted her to leave before Beau got home. I wanted to be here alone, to read a bit, to meet him at the door with a joint and lean in close enough to inhale the burnt coffee smell clinging to his clothes. Sometimes he came home still wearing the green barista apron, a thing I found almost unbearably erotic.

She must have sensed these desires in some unspoken way, psychically pushing away from them. "Wait, don't tell me," she said, before I could speak. "I'll guess." And pointed, without hesitation, to the pile of Foucault by the couch.

"You seem very sure of your ability to know," I said.

"I have an uncanny way of reading people."

"Don't you think that's presumptuous?"

"No," she said, studying the shelved books. "Not at all. Are these all yours?"

"Beau's not a huge reader."

"You're very blunt, Cam. And you don't like to talk much, do you?"

"No," I said, surprised. "Not really."

"But you've got a lot to say. And you have this nervous energy about you." She rose suddenly and picked up her bag, digging through it. She moved quickly and easily, like a lizard or cat. "I have a book here you'll like."

"You love lending books, huh."

"Definitely," she said. "It's such a joy to share a book. There's nothing else quite like it. It's like sharing ideas with someone. I lend books to pretty much anyone who will take them from me."

"Beau is pretty into the Barthes you gave him." I sat down on the couch as she crouched over her bag, evaluating two different paperbacks, weighing them in her hands.

"*Camera Lucida*, definitely. *Reflections on Photography*. It's the only book Barthes wrote on the subject, and right before his death. It gives the text a strange quality, almost haunting. I just knew he'd like it. He is *devastating* with that camera. Your friend, Beau."

She looked up at me again, the corners of her lips working something out, like whether she should smile or not. "You guys are an unlikely pair."

All these statements like probes, and her listening to their reverberations to determine something about volume, shape, and depth. "Why do you say that?"

"You're so different, you two. He's all small and out there and you never know what he's going to say. He's got this quick sense of humour, like he doesn't even realize he's being funny. I can't get over it." She put one of the books back in her bag and stared at the other, entranced, before snapping back to me. "You're not like that—you're tall and reserved and you love books like they're people. Don't you, Cam?"

"Yeah, I guess so," I said, still trying to decide what she was like—what I thought she was like. And I saw, in her tone and bearing and extreme sharpness, that in spite of myself I kind of liked her, that maybe I really liked her a lot. With all her perceptiveness and that wit you didn't expect because she was wearing those big earrings and a skirt.

I hadn't locked the door and now Beau swung it open, already talking. "Hey," he was saying, "do we have any fucking, brown sugar? Because I was thinking I could make—" and stopped when he nearly tripped over Stacey crouching beside her book bag.

"Oh, hey Stace," he said, laughing. He was wet from walking in the rain, hair sticking to his forehead in strands.

"Beauregard," she said, also cracking up. "How was your shift?"

"Not bad at all," he said. And looked at me like, is this for fucking, real?

I shrugged, as in, I don't fucking, know.

"I was thinking of making some strudel," he said. "Apples, cinnamon and brown sugar, phyllo, you know."

"That sounds really good," she said.

"Yeah, you wanna stick around a bit and have some? I'm gonna roll a big joint."

"No, I have to get going and finish some reading. I was just helping Cam carry some books upstairs."

"Are you sure?" I said.

"Or else I'll never get anything done."

Beau pulled off his shoes, the second one leaving his foot with a reluctant slurp of suction. "Very serious scholarly commitments," he said, with the flippancy of someone who's never had to read four hundred pages in a night and works exclusively with images.

She straightened out and swung her bag over her shoulder in one continuous motion. "You have to stay on top of things," she said, "so they don't get out of hand. Don't you think, Cam?"

"Yeah," I said, unable to stop a spill of meaning from blooming in my mind.

"I'll see you guys later," she said, squeezing her way past Beau to the door. "Oh, wait. I almost forgot." Turning, she handed me the book she was holding, stretching so she wouldn't have to move as much. "Little change of pace for you from all that Foucault. You'll like this one. I just know it."

"Thanks," I said, dry-mouthed.

The second she was out the door Beau started talking a million miles a minute, undoing the strings of his apron. "Are you guys fucking, hitting it off or what? Whoa, huh?"

"I ran into her on campus."

"And gave her a ride, huh." He elbowed me, playful.

"Yeah, it was about to rain."

"Oh, yeah. Obviously." He balled up the wet apron and laughed. "She digs you, Cam," he said, peeling off his socks. "Big time."

"What?"

"Yeah, she's got this weird academic hipster thing for you, I can totally see it."

"But you were only here a few minutes."

"Trust me," he said, finding the wall for balance as he worked at the socks. "She's definitely crushing."

But I'm definitely crushing, I wanted to say. On you, Beau Larky. And can you totally see that? Can you?

"What do you think?"

"About what?"

"Fucking, *Stacey*, obviously. She's not so bad, huh?"

"She's okay," I said. "But I'm definitely not interested." If Beau thought I wanted to get set up with this girl, this woman, I would die.

"Are you sure?"

"Definitely sure, yeah."

"Because she seems like your type."

"No, definitely not." Because you're my type, you. Beau, only you.

He sat down on the couch beside me and I was suddenly toppled by the great unbridgeable chasm between what I said and what I felt, what stirred in my chest and the vague stinted words I used to get some diminished semblance of this pressing force across. How could such profound things, potent with meaning inside my bones, become weighed down by such banality?

"We'll see," Beau said, nudging my knee with his own. He was in an irrepressibly good mood, the sentiment spilling out of him and into everything he touched.

He looks so much better, I thought. He looks almost okay.

"What book did she give you?"

"Uh, I don't know." I turned it over and saw that it was a message, as plain and clear as if she'd typed it out herself in expository detail with its thousand different meanings: *A Lover's Discourse*.

I put the book facedown on the coffee table before he could catch the title, afraid that he would see my embarrassment and misread it. It meant something, but not what Beau thought. It was a cipher only for me. Contained in this book was a wealth of practical information, a guide to the strange relation I'd entered into with this woman without even realizing what I'd done.

"More Barthes," I said.

We smoked a joint and he went to shower, the resonance of water hitting his body immediately obvious, different than the sharp torrent of the stream against tile. It signalled his full absorption. I picked up the book, which felt charged, illicit, and read at random:

But in fact Werther is not perverse, he is in love: he creates meaning, always and everywhere, out of nothing, and it is meaning which thrills him: he is in the crucible of meaning.

And had to put it right back down, scalded, even as webs of significance unfolded before me in all their spontaneous brilliance, begging to be picked up and touched.

Two

June was so easy, all lazy drawn-out trips to the grocery store where Beau coasted on the shopping cart, standing on it and pushing himself around, or walked alongside while I steered down the aisles, his newly regained appetite drawing my attention to salami, chocolate-covered graham cookies, sundried tomatoes. We bought enormous amounts of food, steaks and four different kinds of cheese and bacon and portabella mushrooms and frozen pizzas and huge, head-spinning quantities of junk: refrigerated cookie dough, Zesty Ranch Doritos, greasy half-crushed ketchup and salt and vinegar Lays, sour gummies and cupcakes and cartons of ice cream that melted all the way home, their softening cardboard packages sweating condensation. We ate these during marathon pot sessions, stretched out in front of the TV chain smoking joints and eating runny ice cream straight out of the box with spoons, our palms sticky.

Beau licked chocolate from his fingers and I shifted position on the couch, feeling like a bottle of soda that had been shaken too long by someone careless, someone who had trouble telling the difference between that which is serious and that which is not. Someone who didn't understand the thinness, or absence, of certain boundaries.

In amorous panic, Barthes says, *I am afraid of my own destruction, which I suddenly glimpse, inevitable, clearly formed, in the flash of a word, an image.*

Beau started jogging, returning to the apartment with his shirt stuck to his back, gulping in big satisfied breaths that devolved into self-conscious laughter when he caught me staring. He powered down entire jars of water in the kitchen, Adam's apple rising and falling languidly beneath the exceptionally smooth skin on his neck. Removing my glasses rendered the world soft-edged, and as a vague shape I found him almost manageable.

I sat at the table and bit down on the inside of my cheek, trying not to get so unbearably hard. Pretending I was interested in Barthes while he wiped his wet bangs away from his forehead, flicking sweat from his hair. He was starting to look more muscled, solid taut shapes asserting themselves beneath his skin when he moved. His movements were level and calm, all traces of the odd pitching chemo steps smoothed away. I imagined him pounding down the sidewalk, the impact of his old Nikes on pavement like a rubber ball on a court, his small dense frame cutting easily through the air.

"Fucking, five k today," he said, amazed, like he couldn't believe his body had done that for him. Telling me he was going to shower, leaning on the counter with his hip while he peeled off his shirt and absurd, fantastic thoughts clamoured in my mind. It was cruel for him to stand there like that, I thought, shirt stretched between his elbows, when all I could think was how it would feel to slip my hands underneath to touch his warm damp skin.

I don't know if it was the heat or what, but he made me senseless. I found myself spending a lot of time imagining impossible maddening things, like pushing him up against the counter while he spread jam on toast and how his fingers would be all sticky with it, sticky and sweet, or cupping his face while we smoked and blowing my hit into his mouth, the vapour skunky and moist between us, our tongues thick with it. Thinking about it made me incoherent, brimming with want, a musky taste I couldn't get out of my mouth.

I walked around dazed, stupid with lust. I stammered, couldn't speak, my tongue heavy and foreign. I was not in charge of myself. My body spoke for me, saying what I wouldn't, didn't know how.

My discourse is continuously without reflection, I'd read just that morning, distracted, closing my laptop and disappearing into this book that exerted a nearly gravitational pull on me. *I do not know how to reverse it, organize it, stud it with glances, quotation marks; I always speak* in the first degree.

One afternoon I came home from lecture to Beau eating a twelve-inch sub, hunched over the open paper wrapper on the coffee table. He licked sauce from his fingers, picking up limp shredded lettuce and peppers shiny with oil that had escaped from the bread.

"Hey," he said, mouth full.

"Hey. Are you eating a footlong sub?" Not used to seeing him do anything but shy away from meals all year, Beau's sudden gravitation toward food seemed ostentatious, primal. He ate like he was compensating for lost time, his body crying out for calories, trying desperately to restore its diminished mass.

"Yeah, yeah," he said, and laughed. "I know, it's fucking, shameful. I have like, the worst munchies of life right now."

"I forgot that you can really eat," I said, sitting next to him. "What kind is it?"

"Fucking, spicy Italian." He looked at the sub approvingly, squinting with pleasure. "Oh man, with everything on it, minus red onion. And like, triple servings of mayo and fucking, sub sauce. I don't think the guy making the sandwich was too impressed. Do you want a bite?"

I shook my head and he took one instead, sending a drip of oil into his palm. He licked it away, starting at the heel of his hand. I needed to stand up but wasn't sure if I could, safely. It occurred to me that it had been a very bad idea indeed to sit here with Beau Larky while he ate this enormous sandwich in this totally unguarded way. A shiver shifted through me.

"That looks really good," I said.

"Mm," he said, taking a swig of cola, handsome in his thoughtless, incidental way. There were entire worlds of meaning he didn't seem aware of, like the weight of the day's incredible pressing heat slicking his hair down flat, ironing out its curls. It fell across his forehead at an angle, nearly parted and somehow darker, too. Strangely sensitive to the atmosphere and its fluctuations, Beau's hair had only two real states—this near-wet sleekness, like he had just showered, and his big winter hair, all dry and crackling. His fundamental good looks must be somehow, unbelievably, outside his knowledge. Like he couldn't see the effect he had on people. Like he didn't get it, or something.

"We really need to get that AC, man," he said, wiping sweat from his temples with his palms. The motion tucked a curl of hair behind his left ear and required more than leaving the room and shutting myself in my own, more than pressing my face into the sheets. It required a cold shower.

"Tomorrow," I said, standing, keeping my back to him. My shirt stuck to me, clinging even as I tried to fan it out. "I'll meet you at work and we can pick one up. Okay?"

"Good," he said. "Because I'm getting tired of arguing about it. And you look like you're about to enter a fucking, wet t-shirt contest."

"Yeah, well."

We shared a weird intense look I had trouble breaking, slow and stoned with the heat and his proximity and the moisture beading our bodies. In his features all raised in the pleasure of anticipation, his eyes lit with it, I saw the joy he took in giving me a hard time. It's gonna be a long, strange summer, I thought, seeing for the first time that the AC really was a necessity, though not for the reasons Beau might give.

In the bathroom I ran the shower as cold as it went and stepped in, my shirt still hanging off one arm. It was excruciating, a shock to my skin and something deeper, too, like the very core of my nerves, the little bundle shrinking and shaking against this sudden external violence. I squeezed my eyes shut and gasped, then made myself stand there until it all felt like nothing, flesh numbed under the freezing water.

I ran my hands over my face and under my eyes, through my hair. Obscene glaring thoughts coursed through me, one after another. Even in this chill I felt like a live wire, my skin now cooled and clean and ready to make contact, to find *friction*, that which was always missing, the counterpart to tension that was never there, never allowed.

"Ugh," I said, my forehead finding the cold tile.

And thought of Beau, Beau in here and the two of us slipping around in the wet freeze, the water like pins on my back. I wanted to hold him, feel him hardened and throbbing in my hand, breathing hard. To make him come. I wanted to bite his neck, just shut him up for a minute with all his teasing and careless palm-licking. I wanted friction, the delicious friction of flesh on flesh, no regard now for *feelings* or *what it means* or *why*, just my core need to press Beau Larky to the shower tile and feel him moving against me, to press my fingers into his hips and my face into his hair and have him whole like that, breathless and shivering. I imagined the sound he would make, that low exhalation verging on laughter, threatening to slip into a laugh but catching in this breathless foreshortened way, and had to turn my face to the stream.

Fuck, I thought, so turned on it hurt. My nerve endings hummed. It was my own fault for not having sex, ever. For not working the grad student angle, which I knew a certain kind of woman would flip for. Because I wasn't a bad looking guy. Because I was kind of handsome too, in my own weird lanky way, with my glasses and height and awkward angle preceding me. The last woman I'd slept with had said as much, running her hands over my chest, sneaking them beneath my shirt to detain me in the stairwell as we stumbled up to the apartment. Holding my balls in her hand as I sat on the edge of the bed and she prepared to blow me, heavy with the unbearable anticipation of waiting for her to lower her head because I would have never ever moved it for her, couldn't be assertive like that even in my impatience. And spreading her out, fumbling with a condom (health sciences student, I remembered—health sciences student named Jennah), so wasted I didn't think I'd even be able to do it.

But I did, of course, passing out with my face in a pillow and my hand still on her breast, waking to the sound of Beau having equally wasted sex next door. *Fucking*, waking to the sound of him fucking. Feeling ill and radically, inconsolably unsatisfied.

Well, this is fucking weird, I'd thought. This is definitely some weird frat boy shit.

What I really wanted was to pull him down onto the kitchen linoleum where everything would be rough because he'd made me wait so long, longer than anyone should have to, and now my mouth was so dry with this want. I wanted to stretch myself out and let him do whatever came to mind. Whatever his endless lip biting and straw chewing and fingertip licking suggested, because I certainly knew what they suggested to *me*.

It was Beau, always Beau, but at this point I would take Stacey or whoever just to get the endless aching chafing friction out. We'd had sushi the other day after a long library session, and unlike other girls—other *women* I'd eaten with, she didn't get a bunch of vegetable rolls, skirting the fish in favour of cucumber and sweet potato eaten with enormous quantities of ginger. She ordered a big plate of sashimi and ate it lustily, the fleshy buttery fish disappearing into her mouth, dripping soy sauce down her chin in little streams she dabbed away with her napkin.

"What?" she said, catching me staring. "Is there something on my face?"

"No," I said, embarrassed. "You love to eat, huh."

"Is that some weird gendered put down?"

"No! No. Definitely not."

"Did you want to shame me about the quantity of food on my plate? It *exceeds* yours. We could talk excess all day," she said, narrowing her eyes, "if you wanted."

This had a theoretical meaning and an erotic one, and I couldn't tell where these met. "No, it's nothing like that," I said. "I just haven't seen anyone take so much pleasure in eating in a long time."

"What," she said, stirring up the thick sediment of wasabi in the bottom of her soy sauce dish, "you guys don't eat?"

You guys, meaning me and Beau. I took a big swig of water that nearly went down the wrong way, unable to believe how nervous I was, wishing for something decidedly unavailable in theory: the clarity of third person. "I mean, I've been eating mostly by myself on campus lately," I said. "Like in my office, because I'm busy."

"Like a broke-ass grad student," she said, smiling.

"Yeah, exactly. You know."

She wore a tank top that settled over her smooth tanned shoulders in an excellent way I was finding increasingly difficult to ignore. Her brown arms were laced with hints of muscle. I wondered, vaguely, if she had any tattoos, and almost asked. She would take it the wrong way, I thought. We have such a capacity for misunderstanding, her and I.

She was saying, "since your program's what, fully funded?"

"I mean, I get paid to be there, yeah. I was . . . persuasively recruited."

She whistled in a low way meant to convey she was impressed, though whether she meant it sarcastically or not I couldn't tell. "So you are like, a big academic deal."

I shrugged, flushed all over again, and kept myself from having to speak by shoving two rolls in my mouth one after the other.

She laughed. "I'm sorry," she said. "I'm making you all embarrassed. I keep forgetting you're not much of a talker." Looking at me earnestly, straight on: "Which is nice, for once. Not to be assaulted by a male academic trying to tell me what's what."

"I'm not really that kind of guy," I said, swallowing.

"I know," she said, and it was totally unironic.

We ate for a moment in silence, chewing and watching other lunch hour diners in the restaurant's wide wall-length mirrors. "What about Beau?" she asked.

"What about Beau?"

"What does he do?"

"He works at Starbucks," I said.

"And?"

"He takes photos. He's not really looking for career-type positions right now."

"So I gathered. He seems kind of happy in the moment in this totally unpretentious way. I find him *endlessly* fascinating. Your friend, Beau."

I thought that yeah, Beau did seem incredibly happy sometimes just doing a grocery run, rolling a joint, messing around in the darkroom. Because of the illness, I thought, and its forced perspective.

"Beau is your friend from way back," she said.

"Yeah," I said. "From high school."

"How long have you been roommates?" She had finished the sashimi and was going to work on the bed of rice, shovelling it back between sentences.

"Oh, since undergrad. A long time."

"But Beau's not just your roommate."

I looked at her like, what the fuck is that supposed to mean?

"I mean," she pressed on, "you guys seem to have a more intense connection going on."

I didn't know if this pleased me or not. "More intense than what?"

To my total surprise she lowered her eyes, pretending to focus on the decimated rice bed. "Than friends."

I shrugged, staring down the line of tables. There were times, as now, that I became keenly aware of a very thin barrier separating me from colossal despair, one that could dissolve at any time and without warning. I felt hugely lonely and detached, set adrift among the clatter of plates and clicking of chopsticks and scraping of chairs, floating somewhere overhead while my body, flooded with sadness, remained anchored below.

"Beau's my best friend," I said, and felt her let it go as plainly as if we'd each been holding an end of a taut piece of string, her living green eyes flecked through with amber. I couldn't stop looking at her.

"You know what, Cam," she said as we were leaving, our bodies sighing into the humidity that was a balm on skin after the restaurant's chilled air, "I like you tremendously." She placed a hand on my shoulder and let it rest there, smiling opaquely. "You are so strange and high-strung like a telephone wire, but you're all right."

I like you tremendously and yeah, I would show her, have her in her naked hipster entirety bent over a chair, over the arm of the couch, spread wide and wet and willing while I pressed the heel of my hand over her clit and squeezed her breasts, *handled* them. While I forced some surprise from her, the surprise that comes with the confrontation of discrepancies between appearance and reality.

Ugh. What am I thinking, I thought, what am I doing. I jerked off and came quickly, almost as soon as I'd started, standing in the freezing water that now felt nearly warm to me. I felt young and weird and out of place, like I was thirteen and had been caught by my mom with my dick out, mortified. I soaped myself down and rinsed off, which was hard with the water so cold. By the time I came out, new shirt sticking to my damp back as I towelled out my hair, Beau was flipping through TV channels with clean dry fingers, the oily paper wrapper crumpled into a ball and safely out of sight.

"Feeling better?" he asked. Sometimes I wondered if Beau could hear his own tone. If he didn't in some way enjoy the effect he had on me.

"Yeah," I said, "so much better," and thought: I'm going nuts. Are you flirting with me, or what? Because I'm going nuts, Beau Larky, and you have to cut it out. *The other alternates actions of seduction with actions of frustration*, Barthes warns. *The other attempts* to drive me mad.

We got the AC that week, forming a small pocket of coolness against the crazy beating heat that slowed the whole city down, yelling at each other to close the balcony door when we were stoned and forgot and allowed the stored up chill to escape into the street below. Beau grew fond of sitting directly in front of the unit's vents, cranking them to high and tipping his head back as the frigid air dried the sweat on the back of his neck. It seemed to me that he wore an inordinate number of white shirts, some of them old darkroom shirts with the sleeves torn off. He wandered back and forth between the closet and bathroom where long amber strips of film hung drying over the bathtub, sleek and twisted like flypaper, a towel draped around his neck and a joint in his hand, fingers stained with photo chemicals. I tried not to think about the volume of fumes he'd inhaled over ten years of intense darkroom time.

The new flow of cool air helped, externally, a little. I found I could move more freely, unstick my shirt from my back, get high and pull the armchair into the vent's path to read while my skin broke out in goosebumps, pleasantly numb. There was another heat, though, one that had settled in my mind and no change in temperature could ease.

Three

Cliff was waiting for me outside my class when I emerged into the cooling evening, the day's heat still trapped in the sidewalks and rising from them in clouds that could not be seen, only felt. The light was golden and blinding and concentrated in such a way that it appeared to make up the very texture of the air itself. "Hey Cam," he said. "What's good?"

I was only a little surprised to see him. Something about his loose confident pose and the light caught up in his hair made it seem inevitable that he should be there. Natural, routine.

"Hey," I said, shifting my bag on my shoulder. "How did you find my class?"

"I ran into Larky."

"Oh yeah?"

"Yeah, at Starbucks."

"And he knew where it was?"

Cliff pulled out a cigarette and lit it, nodding. "Philosophies of Language, man. He had the time and everything. Beau Larky, eh? He must have an unbelievable memory."

I put this away for later, for when I'd be falling asleep. It sent tendrils of wellbeing down my spine. "Yeah, I guess so."

"Listen," Cliff said, and put his hand on my back. "I have to talk to you, man."

"Okay."

"Do you want a smoke?"

"Sure," I said, because the evening was balmy and the pavement had turned the colour of ripe peaches. "I'll have a smoke, yeah."

He gave me his lighter and we walked through campus, everyone lazy as the last classes let out, shadows deepening into pools across the shaded paths. We cut through University

College and stopped by the field to watch a softball game in progress. I felt young, suddenly and deeply young for the first time in many months. Look at me, I thought, so lucky to be right here, in this velvet end-of-day light, watching this game of symmetry and potential unfolding.

"Beau is sick," Cliff said. "Isn't he?"

I turned to him with my chest full of hurt stunned things crashing around blindly, all of them too stupid to make it out of my mouth and into the golden air.

"Cam, I'm sorry. He is, isn't he."

"Why would you say that?"

"He doesn't look right. He's all thin and worn down. He's fucking pale, hey."

Beau looked so much better to me now with the chemo drugs loosening their hold, awake and more himself, full of good humour. But I'd seen him so sick—I'd seen him all drugged and disoriented with that bandaging on the back of his skull, dozing on the couch like a dead thing. Cliff had no point of comparison but pre-chemo Beau. To him, the change must have seemed obvious and dire.

"Eh, Cam? Is he? Come on, man, this is a serious thing."

The worst thing was that I would tell him, because who else could I tell? He knew all my leverage points, feeling me out the way a vault robber touches all the surfaces of a safe to find the weakest and most pliable before applying pressure in a perfect two-pronged understanding of physics and art.

"Cliff," I said, and it was an effort. "Please."

"If he's sick," Cliff said, very slowly, "you have to tell him."

"No fucking way am I doing that."

"So he's sick, then."

"It wouldn't be fair to him. That's just not what he needs from me right now, and . . . he doesn't really have anyone else."

"And neither do you, hey."

"Neither do I," I agreed. I twined my fingers through the chain-link fence and gazed over the field.

"Don't you think he deserves to know?"

"What difference does it make?"

"It might make a difference to him. But you can't know that, man. You're being so fucking stupid about this."

"It's just actually none of your business," I said, more tired than angry.

"It's—" he reached for the word "—unethical, Cam. Because you're afraid to find out. But wouldn't it be better to know? I would want to know."

"Yeah, well, you're not me, so." Ethics, whether Cliff knew it or not, were never far from my thoughts.

Cliff took out a cigarette but didn't light it, looking at it as if he wasn't sure what it was or how it worked. "How sick is he?"

"Pretty sick."

He exhaled audibly. "How sick? What kind of sickness, huh?"

I thought of Beau's absolute refusal to let anyone know about the whole thing, his stubborn superstitious belief in the power of words that had rubbed off on me, stained my thoughts. To say it out loud seemed like a betrayal of him, of this power. It would bring bad luck, this tempting of fate.

I shook my head.

"Like not shit people die of, right? Hey, it's not like he has fucking cancer." It was a half joke, this move to the extreme, but he was all clarity now, none of that greasy coughed laughter coiling around his sentences. I had to drop my eyes because they were hot, and my vision swam.

"He has fucking cancer? Dude, Beau Larky has fucking cancer and you won't tell him? Are you serious?"

"It's my choice, Cliff. You don't understand. It's been so long anyway, what would be the point? It'll make things so weird and bad between us."

"It's your fault, you waited too long!" He was almost yelling. "And how do you know what he'll say, huh? You don't even fucking know. For all you know he feels the same."

I shivered, taking a few moments to indulge this fantastic, impossible idea. Giving it any serious thought beyond that was dangerous. Beau was opaque to me in this fundamental way and I could not think my way into him though I'd tried, though I'd lost half a lifetime of sleep over it. I would never know him, because I didn't know his desire. And isn't knowing someone precisely that, Barthes asks—knowing his desire?

"You know what, Cam? You know what?" I'd never seen Cliff so riled up. "You know what it is? It's fucking selfish, hey, is what it is, because you're afraid of what he'll say and you don't wanna hear it. It's cowardly and selfish and you're wasting your time, man."

"How would you know? What would you know about it, Cliff? It's just a bad situation. No matter what I do I'm gonna get hurt, or he is, or—"

"And so what if he doesn't love you? Then what, huh?"

Nothing, everything. I opened my mouth and closed it, beaten.

"Hey, I'm sorry," he said, putting a hand on my shoulder. "But you have to fucking think about it." He lit his smoke and dragged deep, holding out the pack.

I shook my head, dizzy. And so what if he doesn't love you, so what.

"If you told him then at least you would know. At least you could get over it and get on with your life, hey. At least then there wouldn't be this thing all the time, hanging over you. Between you and him."

It is between us, I thought. It's always between us, shaping the contours our bodies take when they're in proximity, the way we talk, always around things, feeling out their shapes under some kind of sheet.

"And what if he dies?"

I leaned against the fence, nauseous from the single cigarette I'd had to myself.

"Man, I'm sorry, really. But you have to consider it."

I wanted to yell at him, like, what the fuck do you think I walk around all day thinking? What do you fucking think? "Obviously it's all I think about," I said. "It's all I can ever think."

The softball players were wrapping up their game, leaving the bases empty as they milled in loose groups around the pitching mound. The sky had taken on a brilliant deep mauve and I could feel the evening damp beginning to creep in. I felt colossally, inconsolably lonely, the hugeness of this feeling overtaking me all at once as if I'd stepped into a dark room. Beau would be home now, smoking up on the balcony, gazing out over the purpling city with his arms crossed on the railing, leaning into it so his perfect clean shoulders stood square. The image suffused me with a profound desire to come up behind him and fit my body over his.

Oh. My stupid wasted heart.

"You have to tell him," Cliff said.

"I'm not doing that, Cliff. I can't."

"You can, though. Just open your mouth and tell him, man. It's Beau Larky. Do you really think he's gonna be totally blown away?"

"I don't know, how would I know? If I knew I wouldn't be having this conversation with you."

"Fine," he said, waving his cigarette, distracted. He was getting huffy, short on words. "Fine, man, if you're not going to tell him then I will."

All my blood stopped cold. "Cliff, man. What the fuck. You won't really. You wouldn't, right."

He half laughed, pleased with my immediate reaction. "Watch me."

"Cliff, you said you wouldn't." I wanted to shake him, tackle him down. "When you asked me about it the first time you promised you wouldn't tell him."

"Don't you think this kind of changes things?"

"Jesus, what the fuck." I turned away from him, furious. My face was hot. "You're supposed to be my fucking friend."

"I *am* your friend. I'm trying to help you out. You need it bad, man."

"This is my life you're talking about! It's not a game or a piece of gossip, it's my fucking *life*. You can't just come in and interfere." I turned back, clenching my bad hand so hard it hurt. "Jesus. How can you even talk to me about ethics?"

He laughed into a cough, bringing a hand up to his chest. "Look at how mad you are," he managed. "I've never seen you so mad. Over Beau Larky, huh."

I didn't think, just drew back my fist and swung it, as hard as I could, into his face. I was so mad I could hardly see.

Cliff staggered and doubled over, covering his face. "Fuck," he said, checking his fingers for blood. "What the fuck, Cam!"

"What do you think?" I said, yelling now, not caring who saw. "I can't believe you!"

He straightened, wincing, and I saw that his cheek was swollen and red. My knuckles throbbed.

"I'm sorry, man, but you didn't have to fucking hit me, eh."

"You're such an asshole."

He spat, rubbing his face. "I really will tell him, whether you want me to or not."

"Cliff, I'll kill you, I really fucking will."

He stepped back, cautious now. "Or you could just do it. You do it, and I won't."

I saw this was an elaborate mode of applying leverage, that he understood it perfectly, and that I deserved this for ever telling him the contents of my heart. "I can't believe you," I said, shaking my head. "I can't believe you'd do that."

"Well, I will," he said. "Or you will. It's up to you, hey. I just think he should know, given the situation."

I leaned on the fence, pressing my body into the mesh. "You're making this so hard for me."

"Cam," he said, clapping his hand over my back. "Come on, man. At least think about it. At least consider it."

He talked me into going for a drink and bought us two pitchers at Red Room, the cheap soapy beer half warm before it even hit the glass. "I'm sorry, man," he said after the second, tucking his hair behind his ears. He seemed much more relaxed now, less serious. "I didn't mean to put you on the spot like that, eh."

"Are you really going to tell him?"

He peered into his glass to make sure it was, indeed, empty. "If I feel I have to, yeah."

"I hate you," I said, groaning. "I wish I'd never told you anything."

"I know," he said. "You have a mean right hook, eh." His face was discoloured, the red spot darkening into a spidery splotch. I wished, fervently, that I'd hit him at least twice more while I had the chance because he deserved it and I'd been right not to trust him, with his strange intrusive motives I didn't understand.

"I should have broken some of your teeth."

"You'll thank me for this later," he said, touching the bruised part of his cheek with his fingertips. "Have a fucking smoke, hey."

I took one from the depleted pack that had collapsed in on itself and let him light it for me as he ordered four shots, all gin. They arrived on a little tray, overfull, spilling from the tops of the glasses. "Ugh," I said, looking at them. "I have class tomorrow, man."

"Crazy idea: don't go!" He downed a shot, chasing it with a prodigious drag from his smoke. "Stay home and tell Beau Larky you're in love with him. Shit's so deadly romantic, man."

I tipped back one of my shots, twisting up my face at the shock. "It's not romantic, man. It's awful. It's absolutely unbearable. You don't understand."

"It wouldn't be so awful if you told him. You know what you underestimate, my friend? Closure. Some nice, unam— unambig—"

"Unambiguous."

"*Unambiguous* closure."

I took a drag, feeling empty and warm. I was getting very drunk.

"You know what they say," he continued, "good things come to those who—"

"Fuck off, Cliff." I leaned across the table to punch his arm but he ducked, laughing.

"Will you at least consider telling him?"

"If it'll keep you from doing it. Ah, Cliff, I can't believe you." I wanted to collapse onto the table or pace around, I couldn't tell which.

"Hey," he said, raising his second shot. "Just think about it, okay? Give it some thought."

I picked up my shot and clinked it to his, thinking that I would have to figure this out, figure out how to get Cliff to rid himself of this fucked up, audacious, invasive idea that had somehow taken root in his brain upon seeing Beau Larky working the espresso machine with his wrists too thin. At least he'll warn me, I thought, and knew it wasn't true. He could do any number of things and choose to tell me about them, or not. This was what he wanted me to think, because he knew the last thing I wanted was for Beau to find out from someone else. If it was going to happen, it should at least come from me. So I could at least explain myself (as if there was an explanation). So I could at least see his face.

I panicked all the way home, stamping down an impulse to whip out my phone and call Cliff to plead with him, and if that didn't work, to yell, as if this could accomplish anything the past two hours hadn't and somehow change his mind. I wished, for the seven-hundredth time, that I'd never told him anything at all.

It was Thursday and College was packed with young people walking in throngs, raucously making their way to bars, made-up and bare-armed and loud in the prematurely warm night. Everyone was smoking or laughing or hollering after someone, running for the streetcar or walking a bike down the sidewalk, purposefully weaving through the crowd. I walked slowly, amazed at the excitement circulating on the street, a sense of charged anticipation palpable in the spaces between bodies. Going out and who knew what would happen, where everyone would end up on this soft May night charged with potential.

Anything could happen, in theory. Anything at all. But was the sensation of unfolding worth that of coming to its end?

When I got home Beau was on the couch reading, a blanket draped over his feet though the room was warm. The balcony door stood open, letting in the fragrant night air and its distant street sounds. I came in quietly and he didn't look up right away, creating a moment during which I saw him as he was, as he'd been here alone, in this silence, before my arrival—the way Beau Larky was when he kept company with only himself.

He was reading one of my books, I couldn't tell which. It didn't make me angry as it had in the winter. There was something he, too, wanted to know about me, and that was good. I watched his toes curl beneath the blanket. With the door still partly open behind me I stood motionless, studying his body, trying hard to understand what it was about him that possessed me in this non-negotiable way. I took in his small frame and broad shoulders, the clean line of his jaw, everything proportional, measured just right. He wore a white tee and plaid pajama pants and his slack reading face, by no means remarkable, just another tired stoner, the city full of them. I leaned on the wall, intent, as if by examining his physical features I could somehow locate that elusive thing: the cause of my desire. Nothing about him could explain it.

So I accede, fitfully, to a language without adjectives. I love the other, not according to his (accountable) qualities, but according to his existence; by a movement one might well call mystical, I love, not what he is, but that he is.

"What?" he said, looking up. He was sleepy, calm, stoned, emerging from the book like a large surfacing fish. Then, smiling: "Hey."

"Hey." I took in a bottomless breath, a breath with no threshold but my desire. Then, speaking slowly, as in a dream: "What are you reading?"

"Just flipping through your affect reader," he said. "It's fucking, magical."

I smiled, melting a little. "Yeah," I said. "It is."

"But it's stupid hard to read, man."

"Yeah, it's theory," I said, and laughed. "It's supposed to be time consuming."

He made space for me on the couch and I sat with him, putting my feet up on the coffee table and folding my hands over my stomach.

"Are you gonna write your thesis like that?" he asked.

"No," I said, "I'm gonna write it as simply and straightforwardly as I can, so that no one can possibly misread what I'm saying."

"There will always be misreading," he said.

"Do you think so?"

"How can you guarantee something you say won't be taken up in a way you can't expect?"

"I guess I can't," I said, suddenly heavy. "I can only minimize the likelihood of it happening. I'm always wishing things were more straightforward."

He laughed. "Good luck with that Ph.D. in critical theory."

I groaned, placing my head in my hands.

"Hey, are you okay?"

"I'm okay."

"Aw, Cam. What's wrong, huh? Did something happen?"

"I've just been doing," I sighed, "too much thinking."

"Hey," he said, sitting up. "Are you drunk?"

"Yeah."

"You went out with Cliff, huh."

I nodded.

"He really wanted to talk to you. I haven't seen him in forever, but *man*, was he in a fucking, rush." He stopped, looking at me closely. "Cam?"

"Have you ever wanted to tell someone something," I said, swallowing, "so bad you can't even find the words?"

He looked at me like, what is this all about? And put down the book, leaning in.

"So bad," I said, aching all over, "you're afraid there are no words for what you want to say?"

"Is it a theoretical question?"

"No," I said, and laughed, my eyes wet. "No, it's personal."

"I think everyone has, you know? At some point."

"Have you?"

"Yeah," he said, nodding. He looked down and I thought oh, he's gonna leave it at that. There was a sadness I carried concerning all the things I would never know, couldn't know about Beau Larky, which sometimes, as now, rose to the surface. A sadness about his fundamental unknowability, though we lived in the same apartment, though we'd grown up together.

But then he said: "When I found out I was sick, I didn't know what to do, man. With the chemo happening, I knew you'd have to pick up all the slack. I just wanted to die, you know? I was so afraid to tell you. I didn't know how."

"But why? What could I possibly say?"

"I don't know. It's a lot to ask of someone. It's a fucking, awful thing."

"But I would do it for you, Beau."

"I know, Cam," he said. "I didn't want to put you through it. I knew you'd take it hard." He sat silent, bent over himself in thought. "And I felt like saying it would make it real, somehow. I'm so superstitious about that shit. And waiting to hear about these results is just fucking—ugh."

"Hey," I said, sleepy, suddenly aware I reeked of gin. "It'll be okay."

"You think so?"

"Yeah." Because it has to be.

I dozed off and came to with the abrupt move to consciousness characteristic of unplanned sleep, like being yanked from a bog and set upright, heavy and calcified and dripping. My mouth tasted fuzzy and stale.

"Hey," Beau was saying, "you're all fucking, passing out here, you wanna go to bed?"

"Yeah," I said, groggy, eyelids already slipping back to their default position. "I'll go, I'll go."

"Here," he said, helping me up. "You were snoring so hard."

I laughed.

"I haven't seen you drunk in so long. You're so fucking, funny."

I stumbled into my room, not bothering to turn on the light, and sat on the edge of the bed to take off my socks. He followed me and stood in the doorway, his body sagging against the frame. With the light coming in behind him I couldn't read his face.

"If the tests are all clear I'm gonna get so wasted," he said. "Just slammered. You're gonna have to fucking, peel me off the floor, man."

"We'll get trashed, I promise." I removed my pants with only minor difficulty, one of the legs becoming bunched up and stuck around my ankle. "I'll peel you off whatever floor you want." I rolled beneath my sour filmy sheets, struggling against the many irregularities that existed because I never, ever made the bed, leaving its various components to form knots among themselves. The room was too warm for sleeping, and the sheets needed a wash.

Beau left the doorframe, coming in all the way. He opened my window and leaned on the sill, craning his head out into the fresh air. The night outside was alive with coming summer, laughter and heel clicks and idling cars and the distinct chime of the streetcar rushing past.

I looked at him hunched there, his shoulders as square as I'd imagined while staring over the field with Cliff, and thought: He would understand. No one could understand better than him, who has seen me worrying about him, sitting in the beanbag by his bed, driving him to chemo, following him around, watching him so carefully. Having seen me in that shitty plastic hospital chair every single day without any sleep, he would have to understand.

"You make me feel like it's gonna be okay," he said.

"Because it is," I told him, mumbling, already passing out. Sleep worked on me like a magnet, seeking out the alcohol and exhaustion in my limbs to pull me into the mattress. "It's gonna be okay, Beau Larky. You'll see."

I closed my eyes and felt the mattress displaced under his weight as he sat on the edge of the bed beside my curled body. I sensed his heat through the sheet and wanted to press myself against him. I was drunk enough that this didn't seem absurd.

Maybe I did, because he placed a hand on my arm and let it drift down to my back, slowly rubbing the spot between my shoulders, just below my neck. "Hmm," I said, a small sound of contentment escaping from that twilit region before the totality of sleep.

"What is it that you're so afraid to tell me, huh," I thought he said, but couldn't be sure.

For the first time in weeks I slept incredibly well. When I awoke I had the panicky sensation of not remembering where I'd put my glasses, or if I'd even come home with them, only to find them folded neatly beside my phone where Beau must have placed them after taking them from my face.

Gently enough to keep from waking me, I thought.

Four

I came into Starbucks in a post-library daze, stoned with fluorescent lighting and small single-spaced text in poorly differentiated columns. When I closed my eyes I could see the words printed across the backs of my eyelids in brilliant red, tattooed into my retinas. This is why I need glasses, I thought. I imagined myself blind by thirty-five, an age that seemed distant, impossible. My mind was one-tracked, still running through things I'd read in various combinations, the words ceasing to make sense but refusing to let go.

Beau was at the cash register taking someone's order in a distracted way, looking over his shoulder and yelling it out piecemeal to the other barista. When I saw him I immediately settled down, all thoughts dissipating, clearing out to make space for his excellent solid body, rolled sleeves, lick of hair refusing to settle in its proper place over his brow. *Beau*, I thought, knocked out of myself a bit, unable to believe he could get this reaction from me, still.

Beau, I have to tell you.

I sat on one of the bar stools and left my bag on the floor, settling in to watch him with my elbows on the counter and my head propped on my hand. He moved away from the cash to mix a frappuccino, powders and syrups and skim milk going into the clear pitcher in some complex, pre-ordained order, his loosely tied apron strings beginning to unravel and droop near his back pockets, swinging. He worked quickly, with focus, and I could see how the motions bled directly into his darkroom manner of shaking film canisters, pouring chemicals. All my cells stretched toward him, aching.

He didn't see me until he turned and then his whole face changed, losing its sharpness. He smiled, openly and obviously pleased beyond all hiding. "Cam," he said, and I was floored by his enormous warmth. "How are you, huh? Been studying? Are you hungry at all?" All the while working the latte machine, the blender going behind him with its efficient whine.

"I'm good," I said. "I've been doing a lit review. Shit's really mind-numbing."

"Are you hungry? Have you eaten yet?"

"I could probably eat."

"You want a sandwich? I'll get you a sandwich, what kind do you want?"

The shirt he wore was black and made his hair darker, his eyes contrasting in an incredible, stomach-hitting, knee-weakening way. I don't know what my face was doing, but I'm sure it wasn't neutral. "I could go for a breakfast sandwich," I said.

Beau laughed, leaning on the counter. "It's like, two o'clock in the fucking, afternoon."

"Yeah, well."

"You want the sausage one?"

"One grande green tea latte no foam, one tall iced coffee with milk, one tall vanilla bean frappuccino, half sweet, no whip." The girl on cash was giving Beau a look like, *hello*.

"Absolutely, coming right up," Beau said, only slightly facetious, like he couldn't help it. He started making the drinks, shooting me coy looks over the syrup pumps. He'd obviously had a lot of coffee and was in an exceptionally good mood. "Hey, Del," he called.

"Yeah?"

"I want to get out of here in ten, okay?"

"Well where's Mike?"

"I don't know, but my shift was done five minutes ago."

"Okay well, is that your cash-out or what?" She turned, motioning at the sandwich Beau was popping into the oven like everything was no big deal. I guessed she must be the shift supervisor.

"I'll cash it out in a sec," he said, and looked at me. *No fucking, way*, he mouthed, silently forming the words.

Beau brought me the sandwich with an iced coffee and stood there with a cloth in his hand, like he was maybe thinking about potentially wiping down the sink area and not just standing around. He seemed placid, all immense elated calm. "You gonna eat that?"

"Yeah," I said. Taking a bite brought back my hunger, though I didn't see how I could eat with my mouth so dry.

"Hey, do you want to walk to the park when I get off?"

"Definitely," I said, overcome by the deep giddy pleasure I still sometimes felt when Beau asked for my company, like when we'd first started hanging out and I couldn't believe he actually wanted to spend time with me, thinking he'd made some kind of mistake that only I had clued in on, and that if he detected this in my behaviour it would tip him off and break the spell.

"I need to talk to you," he said.

My stomach flipped and sank while my heart moved to my throat, beating there like something I hadn't swallowed right.

"Grande passionfruit iced tea, light ice!" Del called. She radiated stress.

"Lots of ice?"

"*Light* ice."

"What do you want light ice for? It's hot as hell."

Del looked like the kind of person who knew and understood the Green Apron Book—which Beau especially liked to show off when high, reading out the little encouraging notecards managers had given him (*Beau, thanks for being so receptive to feedback this week!*), the attainment of which must have involved enormous quantities of well-managed sarcasm—the way another kind of person might know and understand a twelve-step manual. She turned from the cash, deathly in her lack of humour.

Beau shot her a look that could have ended an international arms race.

"Make that drink *light ice*," she said, "and then get out of here," pointing a thumb over her shoulder.

"Thanks, Del," he said.

I watched him making the drink and couldn't think, sucking down my coffee too quickly, wondering what Cliff had told him and when. I had a strong urge to text him for reassurance, or leave the store and go for a long jog, or something. I thought I might be sick, with the way my gut had tightened and my palms sweated, leaving wet marks on the counter.

If Cliff had told him, that was it. That was it, then, and what could I do anyway? The simplicity of it stunned me. It was the beauty of Cliff's leverage: its finality. Things that had been spoken could not be unsaid.

"Hey Foucault, ready to go?" Beau came up behind me and put his hand on my shoulder, making me jump. I turned to see him standing by my chair, apronless and collected, the top two buttons of his shirt undone. "Whoa, tense much? You okay?"

"Yeah," I said. "I've been—"

"Doing too much thinking?"

"Yeah."

"Come on," he said, cupping the back of my neck to move me from my seat.

We walked through campus in the high sun. I shifted my backpack on my shoulders as he talked about his shift, and how he liked Del and sympathized with her stress levels from whatever crazy responsibilities Starbs had hoisted on her, but could she fucking, maybe cool it for about three seconds so he could fucking, breathe? I was largely silent, nodding, looking up at the shifting emerald foliage. There was hardly any breeze, only the stir of unseasonably warm air smelling of cut grass. As we waited at the light Beau grew quiet, looking up at me. I saw that his mood had changed.

We made our way through the park, stepping off the paths to make room for cyclists or slow walkers, and came to rest against a tree on a slight rise near its eastern edge. Beau sat down and I lowered myself beside him. From our vantage point on the hill we could see the park's center, the mounted statue of King Edward and the paths meeting around it, like spokes coming into a wheel. I closed my eyes and willed myself to breathe, to be calm, to contain myself for once in my whole life.

Beau shifted closer and put his arm over my shoulders. He smelled overwhelmingly of coffee. "Listen," he said. "I wanted to talk to you."

My heart was going a million miles a minute. "About what?"

"I uh, had an appointment with Lynch this morning, before I went to work."

Oh, I thought, the organ in my chest skipping steps. No, no. "What did she say?"

"She said congratulations, you're all clear. She fucking, congratulated me. Can you believe that?"

"All clear like—"

"Like serious remission action. She said it should be all downhill from here. That it looks like I'm getting better." He closed his eyes and knocked on the tree and laughed.

If you've ever felt serious, bone-deep relief, you'll know that it floods into you like a drug, liquid warmth loosening your limbs. I let my head fall back and cracked it on the oak with an audible thud. "Oh," I said, groaning and hanging my head over my knees, too relieved to feel any pain. "Oh, Beau, that's such good news."

He rubbed the back of my skull in slow circles, stroking away the throbbing sensation. "I know, I know. Don't go cracking your head open over it, huh."

"So no more chemo?"

"Not fucking, ever," he said, and rapped his free knuckles against the trunk once more. "Knock on wood."

"Oh." I felt so loose I thought I might have to lie down.

"Hey, are you okay?"

"I'm good, I'm good. I'm just so happy you're okay. Beau Larky."

"Hey, come here, huh. Cam." He pulled me right up against his side, putting his head to mine. "I love you to death, man. You need to know."

I closed my eyes, overwhelmed.

"You're the kindest, bravest, most patient, most selfless person I know, and I love you. You have a huge heart, you know that? You think it's your head that's the strongest, with all your theory"—he knuckled my skull, roughing up my hair—"but actually it's your heart."

The bright boundless thing inside me swelled, aching with bliss that could have lit the stars.

"I don't even know how—" he stopped, reining in his wobbling voice. "I couldn't have done it without you. There's no fucking, way."

I breathed him in, stunned by his proximity. "Beau, I know. It's okay."

He sniffled wildly, unable to get himself under control, and held me so close I could feel his breath on my neck, and that his cheek was wet. I'd never seen him like that before. I looked out over the grass toward the hill where people in various stages of undress were lying back to absorb the sun beneath the bronze horse, some of them sprawled on blankets with folded foil screens for catching rays, and held my palm over the back of his neck like I'd often wanted to, gently kneading just below his hairline. I knew where his scar would be and longed to touch it, to trace my fingers along its twisted ridge.

"You know what Lynch said? She said I had to go tell you right away, because no one would be happier than you."

"It's true," I said.

"Cam. You're my whole family in the world, you know?"

"Beau."

"Cam, really," sniffing profoundly. "You're all I've got."

"Beau, hey. I know." I twined my fingers through his hair, finding the scar and its delicate crest. I thought that if there was ever a moment to tell him it was now, but sat there instead, dummied by the warmth of relief in my heavy limbs and his solid weight against me. I could have slept for days, stunned with pleasure and a profound lack of concern, my head an empty expanse of oceanic calm. "Let's just have the best summer," I said, stroking his head. "You're twenty-five years old, and you're gonna live to see the end of the year. To see the new year."

"To see twenty-six."

"Yeah. It's a big deal, Beau." The mottled shade spread out around us, broken by shifting coins of brilliant afternoon sun filtering through the leaves to give everything a submerged quality, like the bottom of a lake. "It's a huge deal to me."

Beau helped me up and we went for tacos, sitting silent across from each other in the blue glow of stringed patio lights. We hardly said two words except to order, exhausted and emptied. We had only a beer each, but the way Beau looked at me made me feel drunk, glad for the table and its steady surface. I don't know what he was thinking then, looking at me like that. Like I'd done something impossible for him. Like he couldn't get enough of the sight of me. Like he hadn't really seen me before.

At that moment it almost didn't matter to me whether he knew or not, or whether I would tell him, or what he might say. I'd never been so content to just sit with someone and share their space. Beau ate enormously, famished, but I could only watch, basking in the extraordinary amount of goodwill radiating from him. I was dissolved by his vast warmth and his undivided attention, by my own relief. All my theory and I couldn't even think. *The naked stupidity,* Barthes marvels, *of an intellectual in love.*

It's almost enough, all this, I thought. It's almost enough to go on, to sustain. Because there were other ways to love than how he'd first made me feel, as a kid, sweaty and nervous and greedy and never having the right things to say, always breathless, always thrilled. Because there had been a cool-off, once, a time when I almost (almost) understood what it would be like to have him as just my friend—my best friend—as if this could be enough, all warmth and deep pure regard and the ease of having him around that way, without glaring crushing expectations always gripping me cold.

And wouldn't that be the most ethical thing? To just let it go? To just let go of this thing that's possessed me and twisted me up before my selfishness could kill this friendship, knowing everything that hinged on *almost* and the worlds it could contain.

To know all this and make peace with it. The most ethical act.

"Cam, wake up," Beau was saying. "It's like noon already and I've made you a fucking, unbelievable breakfast."

I sat up to Beau perched on the edge of my bed and almost jumped out of my skin. "Breakfast?"

"Like, incredible breakfast, man."

I rubbed my eyes, sleep heavy, unable to believe he was there. Beau stood and pulled up my shades, letting thick June light into the room. Everything outside buzzed as if living, cicadas and traffic and barking dogs. "Man, you sleep like the dead," he said, crossing his arms. "You slept through two fucking, alarms. You're tired, huh."

"Oh shit," I said, "what day is it? Fuck, is it Tuesday?"

"Tuesday, yeah."

"Oh, my fucking *class*," I said, falling back into the sheets. Critical Methodologies had ended at eleven.

"Yeah, I think that ship has sailed. Bon fucking, voyage."

"Why didn't you wake me? What the fuck, man."

He flopped onto the bed, rolling onto his stomach and crossing his arms to look up at me. I could tell he was in one of his less serious moods. "I'm sure it was the end of the world," he said. "Someone call the press—" spreading out his hands expansively "—doctoral candidate absent from lecture! University under closure until further notice."

"Beau, man."

"Anyway, you work too hard. I think you can take a day off on your fucking, birthday, huh?"

My *birthday*. I had to think about this for a moment.

He laughed, pleased. "What, you don't even remember your fucking, birthday? Happy two-five, man. A quarter of a century down and three more to go."

"Beau, you kill me," I said. "I don't even know what I'm doing with you."

"You fucking, love me," Beau said. He pulled an enormous cigarillo joint from behind his ear and splayed out his fingers, framing another headline: "Roommate rolls massive birthday blunt—doctoral candidate immobilized. You don't even have to get out of bed or anything. How great is that shit?"

I wanted to tell him it was amazing but had somehow gotten all choked up. I was twenty-five years old and Beau Larky was lying on my bed, cancer-free, wishing me a happy birthday.

"You know what I made you?" Beau said, lighting the joint. "Waffles, with fruit and whip. And bacon and fucking, hash, man."

"We have a waffle iron?"

"Yeah, I bought one. I'm gonna pour the batter fresh. Hey, Foucault. You doing okay?" He nudged my thigh, elbowing me.

"Yeah, I'm good," I said, running a hand over my eyes. "You just—you choked me up a bit. With all this."

"What's gonna choke you up is when you miss the rest of this week's dire scholarly commitments, because we're going up to Cliff's fucking, *cottage*." He made a little fist-pump motion, scattering ash over my covers.

Cliff's fucking, *cottage*. "Really? When?"

"Today. Till Sunday, man. Better start packing."

"Cliff has a cottage?"

Beau laughed. "I think it's his family cottage, or something. Like, his grandparents' cottage."

I tried to imagine Cliff having grandparents, or a family, or even being a kid, ever, and couldn't. And then felt a number of things between joy and panic brought on by a sudden clear image of Beau and Cliff throwing jokes across the counter at Starbucks before ambling out for a smoke, Cliff's right hand on Beau's shoulder while his left searched his pockets for a lighter, a cigarette already hanging from the corner of his mouth. "Have you and Cliff been in talks or something?"

"Oh yeah, big talks. *Discourses*. Planning shit for your fucking, *twenty-fifth birthday*. Are you okay, Cam? You look a little green."

"I'm fine, I'm good," I said, hitting the joint and thinking, *big talks*. Discourses.

Beau sat up and drew his knees to his chin. "Cliff knows I was sick," he said. "I told him. I said we should do something really awesome for Cam, who's just had the worst year of his life. Worst year of mine, too, and that's saying something."

"Beau . . ."

He cupped the back of my neck. "Come on, man. I've got coffee on, and these waffles are actually going to fucking, flatten you. *Oh*, and you know who else is coming? Fucking, *Stacey*." He looked me right in the eye, and of course I blushed. "Come on," he said again, and I forced myself from the bed, unsteady with too much sleep, following him into the kitchen's dense summer light.

Five

On the drive up there was a brief confusion over riding shotgun and who had called shotgun first, resulting in Cliff jumping into the passenger seat and laughing hysterically as Stacey physically pulled him back out for a high-intensity round of rock paper scissors, best two out of three. She was strong, Stacey. She and Cliff had a physical ease that could only have come from having slept together on multiple occasions, or from having absolutely no desire to—I couldn't tell which. Beau leaned over me with his arms crossed on the open driver's window and watched them shoving each other around, amused and distant. The things he'd lived through ensured he could not be fazed.

I was still getting used to this new Beau and his sudden periods of immense brimming calm. At times like that I couldn't read him, thinking he looked removed, impenetrable, far away—thinking exactly what he'd said to me at Christmas, driving home from my mom's place in the black frozen night: *You get so distant and I just feel like, how can I even*—approach *you. When you're far away like that.*

The strange symmetry of things coming full circle. You can approach me, Beau, I should have said then. Seeing how it was me who had put up all the fences, kept him at arm's length because I was afraid of his heat, afraid to get burned. Afraid of what he might say, scared of speech, of simple words. Because I was yellow, a quality that had stunted my entire life. A fundamental fear of action and consequence, of confronting what is not known.

Stacey won, even after Cliff insisted on going best three out of five. The Jeep's AC was broken and I drove with the windows down, dry highway heat blasting through the car and sanding down my skin, tossing around my hair. She put on a Paul Simon CD, Beau's absolute favourite, and Cliff miraculously rolled a joint without most of the weed getting caught in the wind tunnel whipping through the car. I kept checking the rear-view to assess how much he'd lost and making accidental eye contact with Beau instead, submerged in that deep blue while Stacey talked at me and I had to keep saying, what?

When we stopped for gas I let Cliff fill the tank, leaving the car to walk slowly across the shimmering tarmac, feeling its concentrated heat on my ankles and rising around me, a thousand tiny particles of dust and pollen and insects and spider webs swimming in the thick light. There were fields stretching out as far as I could see, sun-soaked and hazy with distance. Everything but the road and buzz-saw whine of cicadas was quiet, heat dampening the world down, urging it to sleep.

I closed my eyes and felt the heat on my body, thinking helplessly of the grate of skateboard wheels on pavement and warm air on bare shins as I pushed along languidly beside Beau Larky, who was almost my height when he walked on the curb. I remembered skateboarding everywhere, Beau thinking it was impressive that I could do something small like grind a curb. But it was just balance, and quick execution, and letting the board work with you, trusting it would all come together in a perfect equation of physics and faith. And most of all, committing to a decision once it was made, once you had set the whole thing in motion. Just having the courage to let it happen as it would. Following through.

Back in the Jeep everyone was very stoned, Stacey staring out the window and Beau eating pretzels he'd bought, passing me handfuls over the seatback. I wanted badly to sit beside him. Cliff rolled another joint and kept meeting my eyes in the mirror, glancing up from the weed with self-satisfaction and something else, too.

Cliff's cottage was on the Gatineau River, just beyond Ottawa and the Quebec border. His grandmother, a Québécoise woman, was inordinately fond of him, he said, and offered him use of her cottage year-round. She called him all the time to ask when he was thinking of settling down, now that he was twenty-seven years old, finding a nice girl and a respectable nine-to-five. Lighting the joint, he explained that when he was young his grandma did the bulk of caring for him so his parents could both work. His mother was a lawyer and worked probably ninety-eight percent of her waking hours. He remembered his grandmother's outdoor smell, the peculiar stale warmth of subway and wet wind, the fading hint of perfume woven permanently into her overcoat. I imagined her wearing a green trench with a slight sheen and big silver buckle. Dangerous heels, a propensity to ruffle hair.

The cottage was small and built entirely of wood, the exterior of pine boards fit neatly together with a deck that came around the east side. Some of the rooms had plywood floors, uncarpeted, others uneven hardwood planks smoothed down by years of foot traffic, knots bubbling up softly from the wood. It had the look of something either unfinished or quickly slapped together, left off halfway through construction to be completed by someone without any experience in carpentry.

Inside there were no straight lines, only the illusion of them, everything out of proportion like an acid trip or fun house. Doorframes stood on just-discernible angles, uncanny for no apparent reason until you saw that the top of the frame only met both sides because one beam rose a few inches higher than the other to join it. Ceilings ran crooked where they merged with walls, wavering or curving up in unexpected places. This asymmetry was striking not because it was radical, or because it made the place seem structurally unsound, but because it was so widespread, seeping into each board and line so that the whole thing together, on sight, appeared somehow soft, off kilter. The walls were lined with framed pictures and kitschy oil paintings, none of them hanging entirely straight. It smelled of pine board and dry heat, dust and mildew, like a barn locked up in the high sun. The late afternoon light came in slanted and golden where Cliff had thrown back the curtains.

"There are two bedrooms, and the couch in here folds out," he said. "Stace, you probably want to take a bedroom, eh."

"I can sleep wherever," she said.

"And then you guys can share," he said, looking at me and Beau, and then back at me. "Unless you want to sleep out here."

"You don't want a bed, Cliff?" I asked.

He dumped his backpack on the couch and stretched. "I actually like the foldout. You can see the sun come up in the morning."

Beau put his hand on my neck, tousling my hair at its base. "Just you and me, Foucault," he said, disappearing into the room where I heard him throw himself on the bed. It squeaked and resisted, the springs straining. "It's gonna be a fucking, party in here."

"Steamy," Cliff said, and I elbowed him hard.

While everyone was looking around and bringing stuff in I stepped out on the porch and let the old screen door clap shut behind me, loud against its frame. All was deadened by the heat as I looked out over the black river, taking in its lazy glittering flow. Down a steep bank there was a small dock and a boathouse, crooked as the house itself. I could make out a neighbouring cottage just around the river's bend and a few scattered on the far shore, standing out white against the woods with shining boats bobbing gently at their feet. The air here was moist, carrying the living smell of silt and river weeds. I breathed it in and leaned on the deck's railing, hanging my head to feel the sun on my neck. The wood was bleached white as bone.

The spring screamed and Beau leaned out, squinting into the light. "Hey," he said, "what are you doing?"

"Just taking in the river."

He came out to stand beside me, letting the door snap into place with a bang. "It's pretty sweet, huh."

I nodded.

"You tired, man? You look a little drained."

I straightened and felt the stiffness in my shoulders. I was sun-drained, my eyes aching from staring at miles of bright two-lane highway. Cliff had noticed after a while and passed me his shades, which I couldn't wear anyway because I'd have to take off my actual glasses, and without them I couldn't see shit. On the skin over my nose I could feel the vague lingering heat I knew meant I'd definitely gotten a sunburn from driving with the windows down. "I'm tired, yeah," I said. "I could maybe use a nap, or something."

"Why don't you take one? It's pretty cool in the back room, there's a bunch of screen windows I opened up. Did you see it? That part of the cottage is pretty much in the woods. Lots of shade."

Where the gleam of sun didn't skim its surface the river seemed not black, but composed of many complex shifting shades, brown and green and violet. I imagined it to be cool and deep and full of small living things. "I think I'll go down to the dock and put my feet in, maybe wake up a bit. I'm all sun-stoned, man."

Beau put his hand on my shoulder. "Yeah, do it. I'll come get you when we're ready to eat, huh."

"You don't want help bringing stuff in?"

"Are you kidding, there's like three of us. Anyway, I think Cliff has that situation on fucking, lockdown."

"Okay," I said, and gave Beau the car keys before making my way down the slope. I could feel him watching me from the porch, but when I turned to look he'd already gone, the screen door shaking in its frame behind him.

There was a set of wooden steps where the bank became steep and slippery, its wet soil turning to damp slick clay not even the day's enormous heat could fully dry out. I made my way down them and reached the dock, whose boards were new and freshly cut, fitting together with a linear precision that seemed out of place after the cottage's wavering angles.

I kicked off my loafers and sat to dip my feet into the brown water, which was as cool as I'd imagined and infinitely more refreshing. Between my feet, pale and distorted beneath the water's surface, I could see sun-dappled silt, the few weeds poking through becoming thick and dark as the river deepened, its bottom falling suddenly away. It was almost disturbing, the abrupt black depth. Without giving it much thought I pulled my shirt over my head and slid in, coming to stand and feel fine cold sediment between my toes. I folded my glasses and placed them on the dock, almost forgetting.

And then I put my head under, and then I swam out. I moved through the water slowly, feeling it stir against my skin. It was cool and delicious and filled my skull with the primordial sound of tiny organisms moving through liquid space, the dull roar of submersion. I spread out my limbs and thought: I need to calm down, to be still. I need to give up interpretation, to stop trying to read meaning into everything he does like it's some kind of reliable text. To stop believing I can somehow understand his real motives or feelings if I look closely enough. To give this thing up, let it go. But how could I, with the weight of his gaze on my back so fresh?

He's Beau Larky, I thought, coming up for air. If there was anything he wanted to do, he'd do it, and that was the difference between me and him.

I swam back slowly, dipping my head under to feel the river's coolness taking me in and releasing me.

And how do you know what he'll say, huh? You don't even fucking know. For all you know he feels the same.

So, Cam, are you Beau's boyfriend or what? In this impressive domestic situation.

Don't be mad, but is it Beau? It's that you're in love with Beau. You make yourself sick, like with the mirror.

Cam, you're my whole family in the world, you know?

Cam, really. You're all I've got.

Than friends, more intense than friends.

What are you fucking, doing, fucking up your hand over this?

Stay home and tell Beau Larky you're in love with him. Shit's so deadly romantic, man.

It's unethical, Cam, because you're afraid to find out.

Beau is your friend from way back.

But Beau's not just your roommate.

I feel like I'm seeing you differently. Like I'm seeing you all over again.

And so what if he doesn't love you, so what.

And so what. I pulled myself up onto the dock, water streaming from my body, dripping from my shorts. The sun was warm and soothing on my wet skin. I felt calmed, my head clear for the first time in weeks, maybe months. I was sick, too, I saw. I was sick in my own way.

I love you to death, man, he'd said, pressing his head to mine. *You really need to know.* Telling me I had a huge heart, that I was brave and patient. And wasn't that enough? What kind of person was I, that this couldn't be enough?

I stretched out on the hot wood, facedown, and stared out over the river, the black sun-stained water and perfect cerulean sky, big puffy flat-bottomed clouds moving across it in a procession, their regularity and spacing suggesting something larger, like the ceaseless rotation of the earth. I felt my love for him in my stomach, this intense boundless thing I wanted to curl myself around, protect. This kernel of warmth within me that just wouldn't die, though I'd wished it.

I knew he'd stared after me, watched me walk across the lawn and down the stairs, his eyes on my shoulders. I tried to imagine his face. What I wouldn't have given to see it, to see whether he was tender or focused or worried or what before he could turn away, leaving only the door rattling behind him in its frame.

I closed my eyes, resting my face on my arm. Up on the rise I could hear Stacey and Cliff arguing over how to work the barbeque, Cliff saying, you just have to light it here, eh, while you pull the thing, and Stacey saying, it's not a fucking joint, Clifford. I imagined Beau inside, intent on seasoning whatever the three of them had decided we were going to grill. In my mind he wore an apron.

I should do nothing, I thought. Become an ascetic, wake early to study some obscure thing. Lock myself away, see no one. Wait for this all to leak away, give in to the indelible flow of time. Devote myself to the study of some serious and abstract branch of learning, like Barthes. *I shall get up early and work while it is still dark outside, like a monk*, he says. *I shall be very patient, a little sad, in a word,* worthy, *as suits a man of resentment.*

The sun was still strong and stamped brilliant red splotches onto the undersides of my eyelids. Resentment, jealousy, uncertainty—I was tired of them all. I was tired of not being able to control my reactions to things. I found my shirt and drew it over my wet head, encasing myself in the strange embryonic half-dark of blocked out sun, its white-hot light trying to press through the seams.

Everything signifies: *by this proposition, I entrap myself, I bind myself in calculations, I keep myself from enjoyment.*

I didn't remember falling asleep. When I awoke the quality of the light was different, its brightness intensified but its force weakened. The heat had diffused into a full evening glow that permeated all things, giving the world a slow golden quality, as in a dream. Beau Larky crouched down beside me saying, "hey, you catching some z's here? Passing out? What's up, sleepyhead?" The sun was red and low behind him, wavering over the trees as it prepared for its nightly descent.

My head was heavy and sick with sun. "How long was I asleep?"

"Like, two hours?" He touched my shoulder with his fingertips. "You look a little burned."

My skin, wet and cool when I'd fallen asleep, felt tight and hot. "Ah," I said, sitting up. "Shit."

"Man, I'm so sorry. I should have come to check on you."

I pulled the shirt over my head, the skin on my shoulders stiff and protesting. The fabric felt like sandpaper on my raw back. "I thought you couldn't even get a burn after like, four in the afternoon."

"Right?"

"Did it look super bad?"

"Not yet, but I think it might look not the best by tonight."

I stood, wincing.

"Oh man. Cam. You know what, I bet Stace has some fucking, aloe or something. For your skin."

We walked up the bank, the river silent behind us. I felt groggy and ill. The inside of the cottage was warm with the day's trapped heat, dust stirring up in the rich light. Beau didn't take off his Birks and they slapped on the smooth wood, loose on his feet from years of wear.

It was very quiet.

"Where did everyone go?" I said.

"They went into town to get more beer before the store closed."

"You haven't eaten yet?"

"Not yet, we were waiting for you."

I could see him through the door of Stacey's room, rummaging through her open duffle. She'd left some of its contents trailing across the floor in a flourish of colourful fabrics and small exotic bottles. "I bet she has it. Girls always think of that kind of thing."

"Cliff is driving the Jeep?"

Beau laughed. "It'll be okay, it'll be okay. I didn't wanna bother you, you know? You looked so drained earlier."

"I'm trying to still my heart," I said, only half joking. I imagined Cliff driving with one hand on the wheel and a fat joint in the other, spraying gravel behind him as he screeched around country corners, bubbles flying from his mouth like a Ralph Steadman cartoon while Stacey covered her eyes and yelled directions.

"I found it," Beau said, holding up a green squeeze bottle. "Fucking, hundred percent aloe with vitamin E."

"Is she going to kill me for using half that thing? It looks majorly expensive."

"Are you kidding? She won't care, she has the biggest thing for you. She probably fucking, fantasizes about you using it." He sat down on the couch away from the windows and squeezed a bunch of gel into his palm. "Come here," he said. "Get your shirt off."

Beau talking to me like that made all the hair on my arms stand up. Though the room was dry and hot, I shivered. I wasn't going to argue. I would do anything he told me. I sat on the couch and crossed my legs, facing away from him and lowering my head to leave my back smooth and exposed. I closed my eyes.

He spread the cool gel gently, with his whole palm. It was icy on my hot skin and I winced, feeling the sting as it started to seep in. "Ah," I said.

"Is it okay?"

"Yeah, yeah. It's good."

"You're more burned than you thought, huh."

"I guess so."

I could feel him behind me, his fingers light on my back and his focused presence beyond. I pressed my feet between my palms and made myself breathe. "Beau," I said.

"Yeah?"

I turned to face him, flushed. "I just—"

"Oh, I fucking, missed a spot," he said, smearing a glob of aloe over my nose.

I gave him a shove and wiped at my face, sputtering. He fell over and lay flat on the couch, laughing hard. "What the fuck," I said.

"Cam," he said, catching his breath, "Cam, I'm huh—huh—help—" he tried to say, devolving into laughter. "I'm helping you out. Your nose is going to crisp without immediate aloe. That's the fucking, truth."

"But let me help *you* out," I said, snatching the tube away from him. I squeezed a glob onto my hand and wiped it over his face, cracking up. His energy was contagious.

Beau sprang up and tackled me, pinning me to the couch with his weight. He held my wrists and lowered himself over me until we were face to face, his eyes full of living mischief. "No, I fucking, insist. Let me help you out for once," he said, rubbing his face on mine to transfer the aloe. We bumped noses.

"Ah," I said, trying not breathe so heavily, "fuck you." The length of his body was pressed to mine and I was definitely hard against his thigh or something, though he seemed not to notice.

He stopped laughing and rubbed his nose on mine again, but gently, touching just the very tip, then pulled back and studied my face, intent, like there was something he needed to see. He looked feverish. The couch was rough and nubby and bit into my stinging back, though I hardly noticed. Oh my god, I thought. Oh my god. Through his hands on my wrists I could feel my own pulse, and through his shirt against my bare chest his heart going fast. What are you doing, I wanted to say, but was afraid of the answer.

Beau had eyes like no one I'd ever met and they seemed to me now like oceans, absorbing me entirely. I couldn't think. My breath caught and he opened his mouth like he was going to say something, do something to dispel the ten thousand volts of concentrated static energy that had accumulated between us. Outside there was the crunch of tires on gravel and the slam of the Jeep's door, Cliff's wild laugh in response to something Stacey had said.

Beau shifted gears like he'd been snapped out of a trance and sat up, visibly sobered. There was aloe all over his face, glistening on his cheeks and the tip of his nose. He looked at me hard, the layered shards of blue glass making up his irises startling in their clarity.

I peeled myself from the couch, my skin coming away painfully from the polyester as my heart beat out of time. My whole body throbbed with throttled anticipation, stifled half-formed questions.

On the porch we could hear the clinking of bottles and then there was Cliff himself, pushing through the door with a case of Blanche de Chambly, holding it open for Stacey behind him. "Whoa-ho," he said, taking us in. I imagined how we must look sitting there, me shirtless and flushed and our faces smeared with gel. "What were you guys doing in here? Making out?"

Stacey laughed in her stilted way. She held her two-four like it was a stack of books.

"Wouldn't *you* fucking, like to know," Beau said, all quick and collected, but I could see he was dishevelled, distracted. Not himself.

I wasn't a good liar. Cliff looked at me and I said the only thing that came to my head: "Worst timing ever, man."

Stacey sank against the wall as if weighed down by the case of beer, chewing on her lip. She was obviously deflated, thinking hard. I could almost see the cogs turning in her head, whirring away. She looked at me like she didn't know who I was. "Is that my aloe?" she said.

We went to sleep early and without comment, Beau rolling over and drifting off in his sudden way. I lay beside him in the dark, listening to his breathing grow shallow and fighting down the urge to shake him, to say something that couldn't be unsaid. Something like, what the fuck was that shit earlier, and how can you just leave me like this? My shirt stuck to my aloe-salved back and I stayed on my side, watching his ribs rise and fall beneath the thin white sheet. Outside the forest rustled and churned with ten million crickets, fragrant night air drifting through the window screens.

I thought I wouldn't be able to sleep but did, waking alone to hot morning sun pooling on my face. Beau had already gone, the sheets on his side of the bed cool and dry. I ran my hand over where his body had been, closing my eyes. I wanted him with every fibre in me. I wanted to go back to the other evening, when Beau Larky had pinned me to the couch and looked at me like he was hungry and would have done who knows what if it hadn't been for the slam of car doors in the driveway. I knew instinctively, in my gut, that this was one of those things we'd never talk about again.

In the kitchen everyone was in a great mood, even Stacey coming to sit beside me, though when she spoke it was guarded and somehow distant. Beau dished out scrambled eggs from the pan and roughed up my hair but didn't meet my eyes. Cliff woke up late, swaggering in with his swim shorts on as we cleared the table, already holding an open beer.

"Starting early?" Stacey said, her eyebrows rising.

"Breakfast of champions," Cliff said. "What you got there, Larky? Eggs?"

"And bacon, man."

"Hook me up, hey." He popped open the fridge and leaned on its door hard in a way that couldn't have been good for the hinges. "Beers, guys?" He didn't wait for an answer, passing us bottles before opening Stacey's with his teeth.

"Clif-*ford* don't *do* that, ah! You're going to break your teeth. They're already all chipped."

"They are not," he said, showing off the bent cap clenched between them.

She pressed the cold bottle to his neck, startling him into a laugh. "Fuck, eh," he said, dancing away.

We spent the day in the sun. It was as hot as the day before and even more humid, the dock being the only half-bearable place to sit. Stacey stretched out on a towel, looking exceptionally Burtonian in her one-piece polka dot bathing suit and big floppy striped sunhat, all black and white. She wore black sunglasses with round frames she lowered to peer over when she talked. "Did you put on adequate sunscreen today, Cam?" she said.

"I hope so." I was wearing a t-shirt over my tender back, lying flat on my stomach with *A Lover's Discourse* open in front of me.

"You love that book, don't you."

I nodded, squinting over the river. Cliff and Beau had swum out far and I could see their heads bobbing just above the surface. They talked in low tones that carried over the water as gentle undulations, their laughter sudden and clear.

"Yeah, he's amazing—Barthes," I said. To see Beau swimming, his ribs no longer pressed tight against his skin in a neat row, was a balm for my mind. I felt Stacey watch my watching and looked down, closing the book.

"You always look at him with such longing," she said.

"At who?"

"At Beau. You look at him like . . ." she shook her head and took off her sunglasses, folding them on the dock beside her.

I'm just not going to talk about this, I thought. I am so fucking tired of talking to people about this. I felt her curiosity as an intensity, nebulous and pressing.

"Can I ask you a theoretical question?"

I closed my eyes, struck by a sudden conviction that if she pushed hard enough she'd make her way through whatever protective membrane separated my mind from everything outside it. Psychic osmosis. She could do it, I was sure. "Sure," I said. "Sure, go ahead."

"You know how in critical theory everyone goes on about being dependent on terms we didn't choose? Being subject to power in ways we can't understand or control? Or refute?"

"Yeah, definitely. That we become subjects through subjectivation—subjection to power."

"Do you think it's true?" she said. "That we're always subject to power's terms?"

"Yeah, definitely. It's a trade-off, right. It's better to exist and be subject to something external than to not exist at all. Because there's no such thing—I don't think there can be such a thing as existing without being subject to power in some way. From the moment you're born you're dependent on other people—on your parents, I mean—totally helpless."

Cliff and Beau had climbed onto the floating dock moored near the middle of the little bay formed by the river's bend. They sat on its edge with their feet in the water, their combined weight tilting the platform so its other end was barely submerged.

"And it all devolves from there," I said. "School, norms, beliefs, friends, getting a job, the way you look, who you marry, politics, culture—*fuck*. Everyday life is just this constant violence of like, *imposition*. It's like, can you catch a break ever, or what?"

She laughed, chasing the crooked sound with a mouthful of what I imagined must be very warm Blanche. I saw that I'd already downed three beers, the bottles lined up in an almost-row by my book.

"The idea that you can go through life as some kind of independent self-contained body is just ridiculous," I said. "There are terms, and we definitely take them, whether we know it or not."

"The conundrum of agency."

"Mm."

"But do you think, then, that there are some things that can exceed power?"

I thought of Beau's heart going fast against my chest, only his shirt between us. *What is nonetheless already there*. "Yeah," I said. "I believe that very strongly."

"Things like love," she said.

"Yeah."

She sat up on her towel and leaned back on her elbows, tipping her head toward the sun. Her hair spilled out behind her, nearly brushing the dock. "But love can also be a discourse of power. One of its many forms."

"Yeah, that's what Bourdieu says. Symbolic violence."

"Just think of gendered happiness scripts. Get married and buy a house! Have some kids! This is what love is!" She gestured widely, rolling her eyes. "Whereas the whole time you're doing this totally restrictive hegemonic thing that is structuring your entire life and making you subject to so many things: normative gender roles, capitalism, the nuclear family, to this other person you live with and clean and cook for and *love*, and you actually *love them*, which is the worst thing of all."

"None of that love stuff for you, huh."

She shook her head, slipping her sunglasses back on. "You're such a romantic, Cam. You really are. You don't buy any of that for even a second."

"I just think—" There was an enormous splash, and then unhinged laughter and a bunch of sputtered *fuck you*s as Cliff's head emerged from the water. Beau crouched on the dock, laughing. He looked put together, happy, balanced. Whole and entirely himself. "I just think that as much as that's true, love can also go beyond power. Exceed power, confuse its aims. Even within a script like that."

Stacey popped open her sunscreen and let it pool in her palm, warm and near-liquid, before beginning to spread it over her shoulders. It smelled of coconut oil, rich and sweet and edible. "It's because you're a guy," she said. "You would never be on the receiving end of a relationship like that, so of course you think love and power have nothing to do with each other."

"You don't think so? You don't think that could ever feasibly happen?"

She reached into the water to pull a beer from the bucket Cliff had submerged and passed it to me before taking one for herself. The bottle was cool and wet and hard to open, and I chipped the dock a bit before managing to get the cap off.

"You should try Cliff's teeth trick," she said, trying to leverage her cap against a lighter.

"Or we could just go wild and get a real bottle opener from you know, the cottage."

Stacey laughed. "Cam," she said, "you're actually right."

"What, about the bottle opener?"

"No, about men in love. You know what Barthes says? There is something feminized in a man who's in love, because he's forced to *wait*. And to suffer from his waiting."

"Yeah, well."

"Are you mad?"

"Why would I be, Stacey?"

"Because I hurt your feelings, obviously."

"So then maybe you should cut that shit out."

She looked out across the river, lips thin. Her swimsuit was shiny, its fabric sleek with newness and lack of use. I couldn't believe her body, this curved smooth thing open to the sun and its rays, stretching toward them like they contained some nourishment specific to her.

"Isn't it naïve, Cam," she said, voice hard, "to think that love can be some totally pure thing somehow outside of power and all its complications?"

"First of all," I said, pissed now, afraid I might say something horrible, "I don't think that at all, and second of all, how can you even *live*?" My anger carried me, its own livid acid thing with its power to surprise me, still. "How can you even go through life at all, thinking that there's nothing to love but some veiled expression of power, the will to dominate? How can you even wake up in the morning? It's so *cynical*."

Stacey looked at me like she was adding up a bunch of figures that didn't quite make sense. "Do you think that because you have to?"

"What do you mean?"

"You know what I mean."

"I'm going for a swim," I said, which took unbelievable self-restraint. I felt that if I raised my voice even a bit I'd lose it.

"You don't have to do that."

I pulled off my shirt, stretching it too much at the neck. I wanted to throw something. "Honestly, Stacey, I am so done talking to you about this."

"You don't have to get so mad about it," she said. "We're just disagreeing about theory."

"Are we?" I said, loud enough for Cliff and Beau to turn in our direction for a moment. "Is that what you fucking think?"

"I think it would be *incredibly* interesting if everyone just said exactly what they meant," she said. "That's what I think."

"*Endlessly* fascinating," I said, dipping into her up-down speech pattern. "Just *tremendously* absorbing."

She might have sworn at me but I couldn't be sure. The water closing over my head was deafening. When I reached the floating dock I was out of breath and tempered, pulse beating in my ears. I pulled myself up enough to fold my elbows and rest my head on my arms. Cool river water dripped from my hair.

"Domestic dispute, eh?" Cliff said. Beau looked majorly nonplussed.

"We got into a theoretical argument," I said, wiping at my nose. Back on shore I could see Stacey lying down, her sleek black shape pressed against the dock. Her sunhat covered her face.

Cliff whistled in mock amazement. "A *theoretical argument*, hey."

"Whoa, take it easy, Foucault," Beau said, and I knew he'd meant it to come off as a joke but somehow it fell flat, his voice pitching just off center.

After a while Cliff swam back to get more beer, promising he'd float some over to us if he didn't drown on route. I could see it, Cliff valiantly pushing a bucket of bottles ahead of him as his head slipped beneath the surface, his sloppy drunken dog paddle too weak to keep him afloat. Beau and I lay on the dock, facing away from shore. I rested my chin on my crossed arms and he dragged his fingers through the water, dipping them in and out in a lazy way. I watched his hand moving and felt his great distance, miles and miles though he was hardly a foot away. I knew he didn't want to talk.

The sky was a perfect azure, not a single cloud, the heat a physical thing pressing against my skin. I was nearly dry now, the last of the moisture prickling at the back of my neck as it evaporated.

If I was Stacey I would have said, you wanted to kiss me last night, didn't you, Beau.

If I was Cliff I would have said, what was that deadly romantic shit you pulled last night, hey?

Because I was Cam I said nothing, preferring to share his silence and its perfect agreement. There were long periods we could spend together not saying anything at all, the calm between us a medium of understanding I couldn't stand to break. Through this medium I sensed his distraction, but also his desire for company as plainly as if it'd been spoken. If I stood to let him be he'd ask me not to go—I felt this in my gut.

A sailboat went by, stately and white. Someone in a baseball cap sat cross-legged on the bow, shielding their eyes from the sun with an upraised hand. We watched its leisurely progress across the bay and down the river, out of sight. The current pulls it along, I thought. The sails are for—what? For the way back upstream.

We were quiet for a time. I pressed my ear to the weathered boards to listen to the soft lapping of water beneath, amplified and hollow through the fibre of the wood.

"Cam," he said. "How's your back, huh?"

I could feel his eyes on the back of my head as if he'd put his hand there. "It's okay," I said. "I put on a ton of sunscreen."

"Did you reapply it? It washes off."

"Oh yeah, with Stacey's thorough assistance."

"Before you guys got into a theory conflict."

"Yeah."

"What were you fighting about?"

"I'm not sure," I said, glad to be facing away from him. "I'm not sure about Stacey. I feel like she's always trying to be hostile in a roundabout way, indirectly aggressive. I feel like theory is a front for her. An excuse."

"An excuse?"

"Yeah, a way of being confrontational without having to own up to it. Of talking about things without actually saying them."

He was so close I could almost hear him thinking. It could be like this, I thought, always like this.

"You can be like that too," he said. "Saying one thing and meaning another. You just count on people being able to read you, to understand what you actually mean."

It is frightening to see how well someone you keep so much from can know you. I felt pierced, stripped down. He must already know, I thought. The things he knows would flatten me, destroy me. And thought again of what could be done with words, consonants and vowels put together in the flow of speech. Words and their tremendous power.

I turned my head back but didn't look at him, staring out over the river instead. In the dead heat nothing stirred. "There are things I want to say badly, but can't, Beau. Things I don't know how to say. I'm afraid the meaning won't come across, or I'll be misunderstood. But for her it's a game."

"I understand, Cam. Really."

"Yeah?"

"Yeah. I don't really mind. I mean, how you are, you know? I don't mind it. You're a quiet guy. And I think you communicate more than you think you do, it just takes a while to figure out how to read you. It takes time, and patience, and I think Stace would love a shortcut." He dipped his hand back in the water, skimming its surface with the tips of his fingers. "But that's lazy," he said, "and people are not puzzles, or theoretical problems."

I turned to see the light caught in his hair and skirting the tip of his nose, the rest of his profile hidden in the crook of his elbow where he rested, eyes downcast to watch his fingers tracing patterns in the water. He appeared deep in thought. "It was about last night, wasn't it," he said. "And the aloe."

"What was?"

"Your argument."

"Why do you think that?" I said, glad for the dock's gentle rocking motion.

"Because she seemed upset, and I felt like there was something—" he stopped. "I felt like there was so much tension, and it was because of me. I think she thought that—ugh." He stretched out his arms, shaking water from his fingers like he was trying to purge himself of something. "Cam," he said.

"Yeah?"

"Listen," still not looking at me, "I'm so sorry if I made things weird between you and Stacey."

"Beau, I told you. It's not like that."

"I think it is, at least for her, and maybe for you. And I know I just said I feel amazing, and I do, but sometimes I think I'm still not totally myself, you know? Since I fucked up my head. I feel unsure about things, I get strange feelings, I just—" he pressed the heels of his hands to his forehead, rubbing his eyes. "I don't think before I act."

I sat up to keep my heart from sinking too quickly, so quickly I thought maybe I should've stayed flat, lying prone and sharing his space, sharing at least this one thing with him. I had a bad moment where I thought for sure I'd be sick, first crossing my legs to bend over myself and then hanging them over the edge to sit with my feet in the water, feeling its grounding coolness. The river here was too deep to really warm up in any substantial way.

How can you do this to me? I wanted to say. How can you lead me on like that? I felt like he'd hit me, dizzy and ill. I should just tell him, I thought. I really should. I should say: But I'm in love with you, Beau Larky, and you can't, you just can't—what? Pull me around like that. Look at me like there's something you need to *do*. Hold down my wrists and rub your nose on mine and look at me that way, oh.

That's what I should say, instead of talking around this thing in circles.

"Cam?"

"It's okay, Beau," I said, though I could hardly speak. My throat was thick and contracted without my permission. "It's not a big deal, whether Stacey was mad or not. Let's swim back, huh? I don't think Cliff is coming back anytime soon."

We swam back slowly. I felt weak and hurt, bruised somewhere deep and soft within me. I stayed low in the water and tried to focus on its resistance to my strokes, its stubborn density pushing against me, pushing back. I needed to be tempered and I would not cry over this, I would not. *I get strange feelings, I don't think before I act. Sometimes I think I'm still not totally myself.*

He'd made a mistake, and now he meant to say: Don't make anything of it, don't get ahead of yourself. Don't get your hopes up.

My throat hitched.

Beau climbed up onto the dock and I followed. Stacey was gone, her towel and sun lotion abandoned. Several empty beer bottles stood in crooked groups—mine and hers, and some of Cliff's, who was nowhere in sight. I wrapped my towel around my shoulders and sat down, emptied.

Beau stood over me, dripping water everywhere. It streamed from his hair and ran down his neck, beading on his collarbone and chest, liquid gold in the impossible blinding sun. The skin on his arms had broken out in goosebumps all the way to his shoulders. He ran a towel over them, stretching it over his perfect back. His hair was thick and so wet it appeared much darker, nearly black. He shook it out like a dog, spraying me, and towelled it down in a rough way, closing his eyes. Parts of it plastered themselves to his forehead. A single drop of river water stuck to the tip of his nose and I longed to wipe it away for him, to feel his cool, wet skin against my own.

"What?" he said, and I looked away, my face hot. His eternal question. This is just never going to happen for me, I thought, crippled by the idea. This is never going to happen for me in a hundred million years.

"You're soaking wet," I said, lost. In the astounding midday sun everything seemed blackened, overexposed. And how will I live? I wondered. How will I even get up, now?

Beau flicked his towel at me. "So are you, Foucault," he said, voice spilling over with affection. "In theory, if you get in the water, you'll find that in practice, you get fucking, wet. Do you wanna come up, or should I bring you a beer?"

"I'll stay," I said. "And dry off." I needed desperately to be alone and to breathe, to even out my breathing. I didn't have my glasses on, and this made it almost bearable to look at him directly.

I watched him move up the stairs and thought: He must really not know. He either doesn't know, still, or he knows and doesn't reciprocate, and I can't even tell which is worse anymore. But what was that shit yesterday? That he *apologized* for, as if I could ever be interested in Stacey or what she thought. Apologized for getting between me and Stacey. I felt tossed around and crushed, bruised all over.

But what was he *doing*, acting that way with me in the first place? What was he doing that he felt he had to explain, apologize for? I felt desperate and didn't know how to shake it, wasn't sure if I could. It had been something and he'd taken it back. He knew what I did with ambiguity.

And then I thought: What the fuck am *I* doing? Getting all cut up like this when he *doesn't even know*, he doesn't even fucking know how I feel and I'm not even close to telling him. It's absurd, a fucking lifelong waste of time. Like, what am I *doing*, agonizing over him like this, spending months and months thinking of nothing but him, *only him*, taking care of him better than I care for myself, giving up all my time and energy just willing him to get better, never sleeping and breaking my back and rearranging my life. It's a huge fucking waste of time, a stupid half-baked wish that, what—that somehow he'll, what—that somehow he'll come to love me. But he'll never love me, not in the way I need him to. I'm setting myself up. I'm kidding myself.

But I can't help it, I thought. It's not something I control or understand.

The broad river glittered black and gold, liquid ore. I closed my eyes and knew I would live the rest of my life, the entirety of it, without ever having had this one thing, this only thing I wanted. The stupid blank unfairness of it, the sheer bad luck, appeared before me as a monolith, vacant and unmoving, colossal in size. And then for the first time, not the first time ever but the first time in a long while, I felt deeply sorry for myself. I wished, not for the first time, that I'd never met him, never seen his small solid frame and felt this undeniable thing so deep in my body. Arbitrary, that I should have had to meet him. Such a fucking waste of life. I could have been somewhere, anywhere else, living my life, loving someone, anyone else.

But I didn't want anyone else. I wanted him. I wanted him and I would have done anything.

I can't help it, I thought. It's a violence because I can't help it, and Stacey is right. There are no choices here and this is not my fault, and this is the greatest violence I know.

Cliff and I drove into town, going five under the limit because we'd been drinking all day. Goal: get a fresh case of beer without getting pulled over by Gatineau's finest all over our Ontario plates. Cliff lit a joint and I rolled down every single window, sending a rush of air through the car and forcing him to readjust his sweatband, tucking his hair behind his ears.

"Real chill like," he said, reclining in the passenger seat till he sat with his knees up.

"We're actually going to jail," I said. "Quebec jail."

He passed me the joint and cocked his head. "Say goodbye to your academic career, hey."

"Goodbye, tenure," I said, taking a big haul that threw me into a coughing fit. Cliff clapped my back. "Yup, we're definitely getting arrested," I said, eyes watering. "That shit is happening *tonight*."

"Criminal record, here we come."

I laughed, feeling unusually reckless. "Cliff, you're a fucking drug dealer." The world outside rushed by, green and gold. Beau's CD was on, Paul Simon telling us he was a rock, he was an island.

"It's never too late to start on your path to a Starbucks career. There are many perks: minimum wage, standing for hours, getting bitchy complaints from entitled fools, *and*—" here he elbowed me, grinning "—working right next to Larky all day long."

I couldn't think about Beau. There was something bruised within me radiating a massive imbalance of feeling I could hardly bear. I'd volunteered to get beer with Cliff because I couldn't stand it, sitting beside Beau and feeling such great blackness sweep over the day, putting on a face like I was fine when I felt stretched out and weak. My insides ached in time with my thoughts.

"Eh, Cam?"

"Ah, I dunno."

"What were you guys doing in there last night, huh?" He was playful, drunk. I felt hugely heavy, as I had all the time in the winter when the light was brief and cold and Beau was always in the hospital, when I'd helped him into his coat each afternoon so gingerly, careful not to pull on his IV. I hadn't cried in forever, not since he'd gotten sick, but now I felt like wailing.

"Nothing," I said, "it was nothing."

Broken-hearted. The adjective appeared to me objectively, in the third person. As in, he was broken-hearted, his heart was broken. Him being me.

"I don't know man, it definitely looked like *something*."

"Trust me, it was nothing."

Cliff blew smoke out the window, delighted. "Did you guys make out?"

I shook my head.

"You did! You totally did." He tried to whistle but couldn't, the sound getting lost in the current of wind streaming through the Jeep.

"Cliff, it really didn't happen like that. He did kind of, I don't know. Really surprise me there for a second. I thought—ah, I don't know. I thought so many things."

"Did you think he was going to make a move?"

I nodded, waving the joint away. "I really did."

"Because I don't know what you did, but he's totally into you. He like, can't even get it through his head, man."

"What?"

"Yeah, he's all like, what's going on with me?"

I guided the Jeep around a long turn, our bodies leaning into it. "What? Cliff, have you been taking to him?"

"Yeah, been talking to Larky a bit for sure," he said.

"About *this*?"

"Chill, chill. Calm down, hey. Not directly. I've just been scoping out the situation a bit, feeling it out."

"Like today?" I pictured Cliff's head bobbing just beside Beau's, their voices low and secretive and punctuated by laughter. They'd been in the water at least two hours.

"Yeah, but also the past few weeks. Just general inquiries. Don't be mad, don't be mad."

"I'm not," I said, and saw all at once that tonight I would either go to bed right away or get horribly wasted, one or the other. It couldn't go down any other way. "Unless you told him, and then I'm gonna pull over and leave your body in the woods. Don't laugh, man."

Cliff was cracking up hard, coughing in his wet way. "I didn't, I didn't. I swear. But you fucking should, friend. I'm telling you, he's game."

I shook my head. "How can you know that? He just told me he wasn't feeling himself and he wasn't thinking. He *apologized* for getting between me and Stacey."

Cliff howled, slapping his thigh. "You and *Stacey*? Not in a million years, my friend."

"That's what I said, and he said he didn't think so." I looked in the rear-view and saw that in my excitement I'd driven past the liquor store, its purple SAQ sign receding behind us. I checked my blind spot and turned the car around, kicking up gravel on the shoulder.

"Cam, he is backpedalling *so hard*. Oh man. He does something he feels nervous about, right, and he wants to go back on it before anything can happen. Before it can get to be a risk. Because it fucking sucks, eh, to put yourself out there."

I shook my head, wishing I could clear it. "Beau's not like that, he doesn't do shit and then try to backpedal. If there was something he wanted to do, he'd just do it."

"Cam," Cliff said, throwing the roach out the window. I'd only had three hits. "People act all sorts of ways when they're stressed. You oughtta know. You know what he said to me? *I don't know what came over me.* Well, I do, hey, and sitting around watching you guys being all cute with each other like nothing's up is tension central."

"You're setting me up," I said, parking. The lot was nearly empty and my approach into the outlined space was less than neat. "You want me to tell him so you're giving me incentive." This was a new tack, I saw. The tack that comes into play after if-you-don't-tell-him-I-will fails to show results, though for all I knew that tack might still be in effect.

We got out of the car, the firm thud of slamming doors pleasing in the evening lull. A couple teenagers chased each other to the SAQ entrance, trying to snatch away each other's baseball caps. Their sandals slapped on the pavement, a single pink flip-flop left behind and retrieved in a one-footed hop. I leaned on the Jeep's hood, enjoying the warm metal on my arms, and took in Cliff across from me, his green headband and reflective shades and sleeveless shirt. He looked like a rock star.

"Cam, I'm your friend. I care about you. You know that, man."

The Informer, I thought, affectionately, who busies himself and *tells everyone everything. The man of Ethics, the unpersuadable science of behaviour that is actually a kind of logic: either this or else that; if I choose (if I determine) this, then once again, this or that: and so on, until, from this cascade of alternatives, appears at last a pure action—pure of all regret, all vacillation.*

Parts under the hood clinked and ticked, cooling down. The world was irradiated with burnt light, the pavement turning the colour of brass.

The logic goes: *either you have some hope, and then you will act; or else you have none, in which case you will renounce.* That is the discourse of the "healthy" subject: *either/or.*

"I can see you're all pained and Larky there is just losing his shit watching you like he does, biting his lip. Have you seen him do that?"

"What? No."

"Yeah, hey, get this: this afternoon when we were chilling on the dock he watched you reading *the whole time*, man. *The whole fucking time*. And just, going to town on his lip, Cam. Why would he be doing that, huh?"

We made our way across the pavement, ambling. "I don't know, there could be many reasons. He could be worried about anything. Beau is really hard to read, you can't just make assumptions." But I already was, imagining him looking at me that way. *Going to town on his lip the whole fucking time*. Cliff could be right, or not. There were infinite ways to put together discrete pieces of information, some more costly than others. He could have been nervous about having to explain himself, or about the tension with Stacey. Or, most likely of all, about hurting my feelings, since I was the glass object waiting to get dropped.

Because I hadn't minded. He must have seen it in me, then, my unchecked desire.

"How can you know, Cam, if you don't just talk to him about it? He was already all over you, man."

The liquor store had the dry coolness of open refrigerated shelves and the echo of clinking bottles on tiled floor. We went straight for the Blanche, grabbing a case each.

"Maybe also some hhh-whisky, hey?" Cliff said, exaggerating the American pronunciation.

"Oh yeah," I said. "Hhh-whisky." Definitely a wasted night, then. I was definitely going to get completely trashed.

"Like uh, our Silver Dollar night, eh?"

"Was it whisky?"

"It was all sorts of things," Cliff said, and laughed loud enough for the cashier to give us a look.

The air back in the Jeep was stifling though I'd left the windows down. "You're gonna tell him, Cam. You are, man, you have to," Cliff said, getting in beside me. He didn't bother with the formality of seatbelts. "He wants you to. Just give him what he wants."

I shook my head, smiling. If I could know what Beau wanted, oh. "Or you will?"

"I will too, hey." He elbowed me and I cuffed the back of his head. I could see he meant well.

But the amorous subject replies: I am trying to slip between two members of the alternative: i.e., I have no hope, but all the same . . . *Or else: I stubbornly choose not to choose; I choose drifting:* I continue.

Cliff reached over to turn the CD back on, Paul waxing poetic about the virtues of emotional detachment, which had always struck me as hopelessly paranoid, and impossible in any case. It was Beau's darkroom music, what he hummed as he moved around with wet strips of negatives held up high to keep them from brushing the floor. Paul's a bit of a dick, he told me once, wiping developer from his hands, but he knows what's up.

Six

We were all very drunk. With the humid night air pressing against black glass and seeping into the cottage through opened screens there was some talk of going out to make a fire that died down as Cliff continued topping off our glasses, whisky neat all around. He was a shockingly good host, appearing at my side with the bottle before I could even finish my glass. The whisky was pricey, no JD or Canadian Club but some stiff local Québécois sour mash that went down smooth and put a heat in my stomach and an ease in my limbs. I swished it around like mouthwash, feeling the alcohol bite my gums. He'd pulled out all the stops and I saw this was how he showed his affection, imbuing it into his ever-widening range of substances and sharing them freely, transferring his strange brand of twisted good will.

It was ritual or magic, or something like it. Talismans and potions and enchantments, brews and powders and herbs. Voodoo from this strange man who'd neglected to remove his aviators from his head though he sat beside a kerosene lamp, his weed spilling across the glossy cover of Stacey's *Vogue*.

With liquor sitting on top of five cold beers I stretched out next to Stacey on the couch, my feet up on the coffee table while she sat cross-legged. Rolling the whisky over my tongue I listened to her talk quietly and lay back, heavy with alcohol and heartbreak. She didn't mention the afternoon or start anything theoretical, and I thought she must be sorry—sorry but too proud to say so—and felt warmth for her, this woman I would never get along with.

Beau was glued to his camera, doing that thing where he partied through the lens, talking at Cliff with it still pressed to his eye. The camera was safe, I saw. It created distance. I resented this, though it was really no different than hiding behind a book, or an idea. All this willed opacity all the time and I just wanted to shake him, get him to say something final to me. Do me this one favour, Beau Larky, this one thing: ease my mind, oh. *If I could constrain the sign, submit it to some sanction, I could find rest at last. If only we could put our minds in plaster casts, like our legs!*

Stacey saw me watching and I looked away, but she said nothing. I imagined she had developed many new ideas on the subject.

"Hokay," Cliff said, standing suddenly, "it's ten PM and high time for some serious lines, hey."

"*Lines*," Beau said, putting the camera down on the card table. Seeing it there, away from his face, not in any sort of physical contact with his body, relieved me. "Sit tight guys, but I think Cliff might be producing some fucking, coke."

Powders, I thought, and other enchantments. Produced from the magician's sleeve.

"Oh Clifford," Stacey said, sitting up straight. "Spectacular."

"Just tremendous," I said, and she slapped at my elbow. Her eyes glittered.

"I mean, Cam here is just falling asleep, eh."

Beau laughed. "You talking his ear off, Stace? Tiring him out?"

"If anyone tired him out today it was you," she said, and he looked down at the deck of cards in his lap, snapping their edges against his palm.

"Nothing a couple lines and shots won't fix," he said, beginning to shuffle. The cards were greasy and curved and moved nimbly between his fingers in a mechanical way. He stared past them at an unfixed point on the floor.

I wanted badly to sleep, to be alone. To know what he was thinking. I felt old and stiff, company weighing on me like a wet coat.

"Okay Cam," Cliff said, motioning for me to come to the table. "It's all you, friend. Belated birthday coke. How old are you now?"

"Twenty-five," Beau said, pushing back his chair without standing. He'd picked up the camera again and was fishing in his pocket for film, spilling three plastic canisters onto the tabletop in a clatter of sound. The contents of his pockets seemed like an intimate reproach, my knowledge of them painful and bright: yellow spools of Kodak and his torn leather wallet folded in on itself and his keys on that ancient plastic coil keychain starting to lose its colour and loose change that jangled against his thigh when he walked.

"Twenty-five," Cliff said, whistling. He'd pulled out his coke bag, the white powder sticking together in hard clumps he began to break up with his credit card on Stacey's *Vogue*. Sociological and aesthetic interest, she'd said, flipping through the fat volume as we lay on the dock, *primarily*. "That's like half of a half of a hundred years."

"Half of a half is dealer math, Clifford."

He laughed, tapping powder from the card's edge. "The only math I ever learned. And a half of a half is a quarter."

"And a half of a quarter?" she asked, coming to sit across from Beau. He was winding the film into the camera with its series of mechanized clicks.

"Is not worth selling," he said, and laughed in his sudden wild way. "How about this nice fat one here, eh Cam?"

He slid the *Vogue* over, gesturing to the neat row of lines led by a doubly thick one positioned closest to me, partly obscuring a feature called *The 108$ party dress*. The model on the cover wore sticky green eye shadow and big frizzing hair, like Stacey but without the smirk.

"This big one?"

"That big one, friend." He passed me a neatly rolled bill.

I bent over the magazine, a move made awkward by the table's lowness and my extreme height, and hesitated over the line. The bill felt distant. There were times, as now, when I felt overwhelmed by the small elaborate rituals of drugs, as if even bending down to inhale this coke in one swift motion would require a gargantuan expenditure of energy.

"Come on, Foucault," Beau said, finished with the film. I felt him clap my back and nudge me forward. "You don't need to theorize about it."

With Beau Larky's hand between my shoulder blades I snorted the line and came up laughing, wiping at my nose. He had the camera and I heard it click, the sound delayed as if travelling from a great distance.

Washing away bitter chemical aftertaste with beer, we sat hunched around the table talking at each other, everyone bold and sloppy and congratulatory. Beau kept fingering the greasy old deck like he was nervous, suddenly I wondered if he wasn't nervous about—what? Nothing, everything. Cliff brought out shot glasses and filled them too high, whisky spilling over onto the plastic tabletop each time they were replenished. There was a profusion of howling and backslapping and table grabbing, glasses tipped back to the meaty chop chop chop of Cliff cutting new lines with the Joker and wiping it clean against the magazine's spine.

Beau put on music and stood by the table, dancing a bit in a precarious, shuffling way that involved hanging his head and moving his shoulders, leaving his perfect smooth neck exposed. Cliff kept tapping his back and passing him the *Vogue*, Beau balancing the magazine flat on his palm and hunching over it to snort with the bill rolled between his fingers, not bothering to sit down.

"Do you really like this stuff?" Cliff asked.

"What, coke?" Beau said, laughing.

"No, Paul Simon."

"I fucking, *looove* him. To fucking, death, man. Rhymin' Simon." He closed his eyes and wiped his nose on his arm. "Kodachroo-woah-*ome*," he sang, in his low off-key way.

"Driving Cam fucking nuts playing that shit all day, huh."

Beau laughed and came up behind my chair, wrapping his arms around me. "Cam fucking, loves it. Don't you, Cam."

"When your door's closed," I said, enjoying his weight and warmth against me. He smelled of sunscreen and river water.

Beau rested his chin on top of my head. "Aw, come on," he said, rocking me back and forth. I wanted to sit him down and tell him everything before the mood passed, before this powder that made me want to talk about whatever (anything and everything, anything and everything) wore its way out of our systems. Beau Larky, you know I love you, right. You know you know you know, don't you. Beau, don't you.

Stacey locked me into a conversation with what felt like a near-audible click, that of tracks changing, of wheels following new grooves. She was telling me about high school in Connecticut, and how boring everything always was, and me saying yeah, yeah, waiting for my turn to talk and wanting to share everything, the entire history of my limited twenty-five-year life, thinking: This is really not the right drug for someone full of things they're trying not to say.

The conversation widened and broadened and narrowed again, Cliff and Beau drifting in and out, Beau explaining to Cliff somewhere behind me why exactly Paul Simon was one of the finest songwriters of all time, and Cliff saying, okay, okay, I see how you would say that, but what about Gordon fucking *Lightfoot*, and Beau going, *pfft* Gordon Lightfoot *whatever*, how about 'Late in the fucking, Evening,' how about fucking, *Graceland?* All the while his camera clicking and whirring as he wound the film back, like, how could he even focus through that thing with the amount of coke he'd done?

Somehow we got to talking about first loves, or how first love is different, or whether it is at all. "I think," Stacey said, "the first time you fall in love it's like, you're just *learning*, still, how to do it. You get all roughed up and you're all *vul*-nerable, you just don't really know what to do yet, or how to do it. You forget to protect yourself, to think of yourself, too."

"You get caught up and too involved," Cliff said, using the broad windowsill as a perch.

"I thought you didn't believe in that love stuff," I said, teasing.

"Doesn't mean it hasn't happened," she said. "It can happen to anyone."

Burned, I thought, there was someone who could burn even her, with how cold she is. Or maybe she wasn't, always. Maybe she didn't used to be.

"I think the first time I was in love was in middle school," Cliff said.

"Starting early, huh," Beau said, pulling up a chair beside me. He had quieted down and was intent on the conversation, listening heavily, with his entire body.

"With who, Cliff?" Stacey said.

"My fucking teacher," Cliff said, and laughed. "Ms. Matilda Crawford. Oh *man*, Ms. Crawford. You have no idea."

Stacey burst out laughing and cuffed his arm. "You are *so bad*. You are *so much worse* than I thought."

He shook his head, smiling all sneaky like he did, long hair swinging free and sticking to his temples. I wondered who he had loved, and when. What it looked like when Cliff cared for someone. When he did something tenderly, other than rolling a joint.

"Cam?" Stacey said.

"Yeah?"

"What about you? What about the hopeless romantic over here?"

Beau laughed, clapping his hand over my shoulder. "What? *Naaah*. Cam would never do something like *that*."

"Oh come on," she said, "then why is he blushing?"

"You're blushing," Cliff said.

Beau looked at me hard, his eyes widening. "You're all flushed!"

I waved my hand in their general direction, vaguely, like, aw, come on guys, but my throat felt stopped up, like I might choke, like I was already choking.

"Oh my god," Stacey said, "look at you getting all embarrassed."

"Cam? You've been in love?" Beau had his hands on the table and now put them in his lap, fingers intertwined. I met his eyes and wished I hadn't, because he was definitely searching me, looking for something through all that raucous coke glitter.

I nodded. "Yeah."

He blinked and shook his head, incredulous. "What? With *who?*"

I looked at Cliff beseechingly, with desperation. Please, please. Help me out here, out of this hole I've dug for myself.

The fucking Informer in on this with me and now what, come on.

But it was Stacey who spoke, suddenly and with conviction. "What, you think Cam is too rational for that?"

"Cam is too careful. He'll think about something a hundred times before doing anything."

"Are you kidding? He's idealistic, it makes him soft. And anyway, these things happen even to careful people."

In my jittery coke clarity the subtext was hardly bearable, or maybe not at all there.

Beau ignored her and leaned in, speaking to me, only to me. "Cam, who were you in love with?"

I looked at him and then at the table and then at Cliff again, and finally at Stacey, who looked like she'd swallowed something the wrong way and now had it stuck in her throat. I saw he'd entered into that all-encompassing singlemindedness he got sometimes, like when he couldn't let a photo go and had to take it again, and then again, just in case. There would be no dissuading him.

"Aw, let him be, Larky. He's all flustered and shit, hey."

Stacey laughed. "*Beau*," she said, slapping her thigh. "You can't *stand* not knowing." She shook her head, unbelieving. "You can't *stand it*."

He turned from me to look at her and a dark thing passed over his face, and then all at once I was afraid they might stand and start to hit each other, or something. Jesus, I thought. Oh my god.

"It's not a theoretical issue, Stace," he said, finally. "It's not fucking, epistemology or some shit." He crackled with suppressed energy. I couldn't remember the last time I'd seen him that way. Maybe in the car, when I broke my hand. Maybe then. "If he doesn't want to talk about it he doesn't fucking, have to."

"Could have fooled me, the way you're pressing him."

I saw his jaw tighten, all the complex muscles and sinews holding his skull together drawing taut, contracting. "Beau," I said.

He turned to me and loosened a bit, something in his bearing going slack. "She's right," he said, "I'm sorry."

I shook my head. "No, you guys go ahead and swap first love stories, I'm just not up to it right now. I'm gonna go out and have a joint. And calm my coke jitters." I was feeling them, too, the tension in my grinding jaw and that extreme parchedness all through my sinuses, like the moisture in the membranes had been entirely siphoned out. The tips of my fingers tingled.

"Yeah man," Cliff said, visibly relieved. He'd leaned so far back in his chair it looked like he might tip onto the floor. "Here, use my weed, hey." He tossed me the bag and I put it in my pocket, already standing.

"Thanks man," I said. The spring door screamed at me and then I was sighing into the humid night, Cliff saying to no one in particular, did he take papers? He doesn't even have papers, hey, and Beau saying, he just needs a minute.

The deck was illuminated by a single bulb, its glass casing broken, only a broad rusted socket remaining to hint at some presence long gone. Big moths battered themselves against the bulb with a dull meaty sound, dusting the air and leaving traces of shimmer on the hot glass. There was the reedy trill of insects, millions of them drunk on warm wet river air. A swollen moon, almost fully round, turned the water silver where its light met the surface, a narrow white triangle broadening out as it reached the shore.

I leaned on the deck's railing, the wood soft and damp on my arms. In the circle of light emanating from the single bulb I felt encased, sheltered from the dark lawn beyond. Somewhere over the water a loon called out twice, the sound lonely and haunted. The weed was in my pocket and I knew I'd forgotten papers but didn't really want it bad enough to go back in, needing only to step out of the close cottage heat and its accumulated tension.

Needing to breathe.

First love, I thought, midsummer and wet, just like this. He wanted to know so bad. He was, what? Consumed. Consumed by the need to know. But didn't he, already? I rubbed my humming fingers together, encouraging blood to circulate. It was not sustainable, this thing. It had gathered too much intensity too quickly, suddenly accelerating after lying dormant for years and years and now I felt it moving beyond me and into everything I touched. Into the atmosphere between Stacey and Beau and into her laughter, harsh, like she wanted to cut him with it. There was something about it all I didn't understand, a key piece of information that would change everything if only I could acquire it, fit it into the picture to find I'd been assembling the whole thing upside down all along.

And that dark thing passing over his features, changing his face.

I sagged against the wood, exhaling slow, thinking yeah, first love, just like this, midsummer and wet, the whole world steaming after a downpour that had left the porch and trees slick and glistening. Puddles settling on the smooth wood, lining grassy hollows, the air misty and alive with the sound of invigorated insects trying to make themselves heard over the din of the party inside, forty drunk teenagers screaming at each other over the thump of a bass. After the clutter of the house, plastic cups in various stages of fullness lining every available surface intermingling with beer bottles and greasy remnants of pizza, pop cans, lighters, crumpled napkins, and scattered chip bags, the porch had seemed open and fresh, a space in which many things—anything—could happen.

And I'd leaned on the wooden rail though it was wet, just like this, like now, the wood soft and cool after the hazy heat of the party where many people had obviously ignored the injunction to not smoke inside. The air living earth and the musk of something blossoming, sleek waxy buds exploding into pale green flowers on the tree hanging over the yard. Swirling around the mess of ginger ale and liquor lining the bottom of my plastic cup, it was long before I'd read anything about potentiality in the theoretical sense, but even then, even being sixteen (barely, barely just sixteen and trying not to look it) I knew what it was, feeling it empirically, in my bones, at the tips of my ever-lengthening fingers. A sense of pure vitality—oh, I can go anywhere from here, I'd thought. Go anywhere and do anything at all. Because I am wasted and young, and because I feel so deeply.

I wondered, now, if I hadn't summoned it. As if, surreally, my desire had made it so, conjuring from among the assorted kids in this packed house none other than Beau Larky, spilling onto the porch in a confusion of sloppy wasted excitement, his laugh like moving water. Like potential, if it were a phonetic thing. The sound was all vitality and did something to my insides that was pleasant or violent, or maybe both. Smoking my joint with me and then, when his very cool much older group home friends came out to fetch him for a game of flip cup, choosing to stay on the deck to share another. That he could prefer to stay out here, with me, *alone*, over going inside with these guys—one hulking and cut, straight-fitted Celtics cap barely fitting over his meaty skull, the other thin in a painful muscular skeletal way, like an anatomy model, and this senior girl whose fluorescent orange bra pushed through her overstretched tank top—filled me with panicked elation.

They went in and the door slammed, a final sliver of stray party noise escaping into the night air. It quieted to a murmur, a dull roar, and then it was like we were underwater or on the deck of a ship, gazing out over the dark wet yard with its thick pools of shadow. A strange space, one in which anything could happen. One in which you could drown.

I took a deep breath of humid living air.

It's like you're on the water, I'd said, and felt immensely stupid, felt it strongly even now, berating myself: That was such a transparently, desperately stupid thing to say.

But he'd said, yeah, that's why they call it a deck. Like on a ship, you know.

When he smiled I couldn't breathe. I was only sixteen (barely) and had never been in love before, so all I knew was that my stomach felt tight and that he was like no one I'd ever met. That it was absolutely imperative I impress him, if this was even possible.

Work with me on this, he said as he leaned in with the joint and I clicked the lighter, leaning away, dipping in and out of his delicious gravitational pull. Scared to come too close, afraid to breathe him in. It was almost erotic, the way he said it, flipped my stomach. Holding the lighter with my palm cupped so intimately over the flame, so near his face, I already felt chosen, singled out, part of something larger. I imagined that doing anything with Beau Larky, having him want to do it with you, would feel like an accomplishment, a validation.

He smelled strongly of liquor and locker-room deodorant, the kind that comes in cans and doubles as cologne. I wondered how I smelled. I must have been nearly a head taller than him.

Nearly.

My teenage heart beating erratically in my frightened chest, the world sparking with the energy of this sudden dire unknown thing.

You know what, Cam? His eyes living and impossibly blue, and something noticeably wrong with my throat. It's Cam, right?

Yeah, I'd said, like I wasn't sure. Yeah, definitely.

The door shrieked on its ancient Québécois hinges, drawing me out of it, and there was Beau Larky all over again, no longer so fresh-faced but still young and wasted, past illness betrayed only in the stiff upright way he held himself, as if always bracing against some unseen force. "Hey," he said, "you okay? You've been out here forever."

I turned from the yard to take in his small sure frame that I so loved, still, that could get this reaction from me, still. "Yeah," I said, "I'm good."

"You forgot papers," he said, coming to stand beside me. He was holding a pack and set it down on the railing between us.

"Oh, yeah." I brought out the weed and made a weak attempt at rolling, my numb uncooperative fingers creasing the paper and dampening it with sweat. "Ugh," I said. "Coke fingers."

"Here," he said, taking it from me and rolling it tight, his enormous patience manifest in the smooth practiced motions of his hands. "Cliff told me to check up on you."

Beyond Beau's head was the window, Cliff and Stacey framed at the table in full yellow light, the kerosene lamp between them miraculously upright. They were laughing and cutting more coke, Cliff looking up from the *Vogue* to check the window in small furtive glances between bringing the card down, chop chop chop. To check on me, a strategic order. I knew that from their angle the glass would be opaque, the deck beyond visible only in brief flickers of shadow cast by the lamp's flame.

"I'm okay," I said. "I just really didn't want to talk about it."

"I know, I'm sorry. I don't know what's going on with me."

I don't know what came over me, I'm not feeling myself.

"Coke, man. I feel so coked out. I just wanna—ah." I shook my head and sank down in one of the deck chairs, stretching. The wood was very damp, almost wet. I fished around for a lighter but he had it, sitting beside me and leaning in so I could touch the joint to flame. So much intimacy in smoking, so much unspoken coordination of bodies and motions in this thing we did all the time.

"Do you remember," I said, taking the smoke in deep, to what felt like the very bottom recesses of my lungs, "when we met at that house party, in the summer?"

"Yeah," Beau said, surprised. "On the deck, and the air was so wet. Just like this." I thought he wouldn't go on, but he said, "and you said it was like being on the water."

"Like on a ship, you know. The deck." I passed him the joint.

"Yeah, I knew right away, what you meant. Man, I was so wasted that night. I got so sick." He exhaled a huge amount of smoke and we watched it curl away, disappear. "I think because I didn't really smoke weed, but I smoked so much that night. I just kept smoking and fucking, toking." He laughed quietly. "Do you know why?"

"No," I said, thinking that the pocked surface of the ripe moon with all its craters looked just like a human face, another one of those things you couldn't unsee.

"Because I wanted to stay out there and talk to you, and I couldn't think of any other way to do it."

"Really?"

"Yeah," he said. "I wanted to talk to you so bad."

"Why?" It was hard to speak, with how swollen my throat had become.

"I don't know. I'd just gotten out of a really bad home, and Mike and those guys were so nice to me, but you seemed so calm and interior and put together, and I just thought—I just felt like you had something I needed. I felt it so strongly."

"I hope you got it, that thing," I said. "I hope I could give you that."

And he said, "Cam, who were you in love with?" as if this followed directly from what I'd asked. "You never told me you were in love."

He's asking me, I thought, my heart nearly audible in the thick still air. This is as close as he'll ever come to asking me.

I pulled on the joint and shook my head. No.

"Was it in high school? Was it before I met you?"

"It was after."

"Is it something I should know? Like something I don't remember?" He'd turned in his chair to face me, intent. "Something I've forgotten."

"Beau, nothing like that," I said, seeing for the first time that he really doubted his memory, that maybe he was unsettled by the fall, still, in ways I didn't understand. "Your memory is good."

"Cam, with who?"

"You're giving me such a hard time," I said. "Over this. I really wish you wouldn't."

"Will you really not tell me?" Like he couldn't believe it, that there was anything I wouldn't share.

I shook my head. *You're gonna tell him, Cam, you are man, you have to.*

"You're so fucking, private. There's all this stuff I don't know about you, still."

I could say the same, I thought.

He paused, thinking. Inside Stacey was yelling, *hah*, what did I tell you, what did I tell you, and Cliff was saying huh, what*ever*, beginner's luck. Someone banged on the table.

"Is it someone I know?"

"Twenty questions, huh."

"Is it?"

"Yeah, someone you know, for sure."

"Someone I know well?"

"Yeah, I think so."

"It's Stacey, isn't it? That's why you didn't want to talk about it. You got so embarrassed."

I sighed. "It's not Stacey, Beau. There is nothing between me and Stacey. Nothing."

"Really?"

"Really."

He sat back and put his feet up on the deck's fencing. I could see he was frustrated, damped down as if doused with a bucket of water. I could almost feel him running through things to say, rapidly flipping pages in a catalogue. Don't you think it's you I'm in love with, Beau Larky, I wanted to say into this warm dark space. Isn't that why I can't look at you straight.

"And what about you, Beau?" I said instead, yellow yellow yellow.

"What about me?"

"Have you been in love? Nobody gave you a hard time, in there."

"I don't know," he said, and I saw he was chewing his lip. "I don't think so. How would I know?"

"Trust me," I said, "you would know."

"What, do your palms sweat? Heart beats fast? Can't fucking, breathe?" He said it like it was a joke and I expected him to laugh, but he didn't, growing silent and staring off over the silver-tipped river.

"Pretty much," I said. "Pretty much exactly like that, yeah." I took a deep breath. "Beau, there's something we really need to talk about."

"I know," he said. "There's something on your mind. I've felt it for months."

My heart was going fast and I tried to think straight, to think how I could put it. I could have gone for another line though my palms sweated and my fingers buzzed. I breathed again, collecting myself to speak, when he said, quickly, out of breath though we were sitting so still, "Isn't it that—" and then Cliff spilled onto the porch, stumbling over the raised step and stretching the rusted spring, and we looked at him and each other and I saw that Beau was relieved, maybe more relieved than I was, though how anything could unnerve Beau Larky I couldn't say.

We went inside, where Cliff and Beau made short work of finishing off the whisky while Stacey and I switched to beer, cold and refreshing after the bite and drip of so much cocaine. I wanted badly to calm down and still the sick beat of my heart in my chest, each thump a reminder of the late hour and the bad drug eating out my brain. Looking at the clock on the mantle I saw it was three forty-five in the morning and was immediately overcome by the full bodily exhaustion of knowing the night has grown old and things are winding down, ending.

Beau was hugely wasted, kept coherent and upright only by the gargantuan quantity of chemical he'd ingested. He sat in his chair like it was a raft in rough water, spreading out his weight and clinging to the seatback with both arms behind him for support. He didn't look well, and for a moment I had to remind myself it was June and not January, and that he was going to be okay now, really okay, for sure. Cliff upended the bottle over their glasses and they clinked them together and drank, and then Beau made a wobbly line for the bathroom where we could hear him getting sick.

I stood to make sure he was okay. The door was ajar and in the little room's harsh fluorescent I saw that my arms were dotted with dozens of raised red bumps straining against the skin, mosquito bites I hadn't noticed on the porch. The only thing that itched was my nasal passage, newly lined with what felt like sandpaper.

I leaned with my hip on the counter and watched him throw up again, trying hard not to think of before, or even of now, really. All those nights I kept him company on cold tile bleeding into one another, their content not as relevant as the fact that they had been, and that I had, and that he had, too.

"Ugh," he said, wiping his mouth, finished.

I passed him a wad of toilet paper. "Are you okay?"

"Yeah," he said, standing unsteadily to lean on the sink. In the white light he looked trashed, glass-eyed and pale and worn down. "I'm gonna god to bed. Go to bed."

I made him brush his teeth and drink some water, thinking the hangover would just shatter his head if he didn't. In the room he threw himself across the bed, sprawling out, more drunk than I'd seen him since before he'd gotten sick.

"Hey," I said, "you need to sleep on your side, okay?"

"My side," he repeated, closing his eyes.

"Yeah, your side. Here." I turned him over and he slumped into the position, one arm hanging off the bed. "So you don't choke in your sleep, okay? Beau."

"Are you gonna sleep?" he slurred.

"No, I'm too coked out, I gotta stay up a bit." My eyes were wide and dry and I felt I would never sleep again.

"Aw."

"But stay on your side, okay?" I took my pillow and wedged it against his back so it would be hard for him to turn over.

"Will you come later?"

"Beau," I said, smoothing back his hair. "Are you okay?"

"Juss wasted." He made a small hiccupping sound and I brought the wastebasket over, just in case.

"You drank too much. You're a little guy, you know? You'll feel better once you sleep it off."

"Sleep it off," he agreed. "You're not mad, huh Cam?"

"Hey, of course not." With all the endless teasing stripped away by nausea he didn't sound like himself at all, and I wondered for the fortieth time if he was actually okay. He's got stuff he tries to hide, too, I thought. Even he does.

His breathing levelled off and I left him in the bed, coming back to the living room. Cliff was passed out facedown on the couch, snoring. Stacey sat at the table, doing yet one more line from her smudged magazine. I sat down across from her. Beau's camera was there and I replaced its lens cap, wrapping the strap around its blocky black body. It was full of information he'd review later, reading into the images whatever he could, pinning them up around the apartment for me to puzzle over. Film and its blank opacity, I thought. The Beau Larky special.

"Look at him," Stacey said, pointing her thumb over her shoulder at Cliff. "Isn't he cute, once you get over all his drugs and rock star sunglasses?"

I laughed. "He's something else."

"Is Beau okay?" she asked.

"Yeah, he's fine, he'll be fine. He drank too much, for how big he is."

"The little guy. You take really good care of him."

I nodded.

"Are you tired? Do you think you're going to bed?"

"No, I can't sleep," I said. "I'm so fucking hopped up right now." I shook out my hands, as if this could move blood through them more efficiently.

"Do you want to take some beers and a joint down to the boathouse? Let Clifford snore in here?"

I looked at Cliff, his arm stretched out to cradle his head, greasy hair falling over his face. I didn't know how he could sleep—it seemed impossible, with all that coke in him. I felt I would never sleep again, already dreading birdsong, the first flush of pink dawning over the river. "Sure," I said.

I filled the pockets of my shorts with fridge beers, peering into Beau's room across the hall. He was motionless, breathing audibly, still on his side. My best friend in the world, all five feet five inches of him, oh.

We walked barefoot across the grass, unable to find our shoes in the dark. The dew was cold and grounding, reminding me that I still had a body, that I wasn't just a collection of buzzing nerves encased in nebulous flesh. I couldn't see the dawn but sensed it pressing close against the night sky. Somewhere behind us birds whistled to each other, calling shrilly back and forth.

The boathouse smelled of river mud and polished wood, old fishing gear and gasoline. Stacey flicked on the light and I saw there were two boats, all gleaming wooden panelling, rich mahogany dark as chocolate and red cherry wood bordering stitched leather seats the colour of cream. They had big engines and looked like they could really move, designed solely for pleasure and show. Light refracted from the water's surface, trembling in a fragile shifting geometry on their glossy sides. I'd never seen boats like that before.

"Wow," I said.

"Cliff's grandfather's show boats," she said, and tried to whistle.

I stepped into one and felt it rock with my weight as I collapsed into the fragrant upholstered seat. The steering wheel was carved from a single solid piece of wood, the controls and gauges ivory-rimmed. "It's like being in a Rolls."

"All aboard," she said, and hopped in to stretch across one of the benches, her bare legs long and brown against the leather.

There was a classic captain's hat on the dashboard, crisp angular white fabric with a navy bill, an anchor stitched in gold thread gleaming above. I put it on, cocking it at a rakish angle like I was Beau Larky, small and sure.

Stacey laughed. "Where to, captain?"

"The *high* seas," I said, dumping out the entire contents of the weed bag on the shining cherry dash, pleased with my sudden cleverness. I started sticking together papers for the biggest joint I could manage without them coming apart—a *cannon*. My fingers were still damp and numb, and I had to restart twice.

Stacey settled in the seat directly beside mine, reaching over to pull a beer from my pocket. She grasped it by the neck.

"Hey," I said, and she smiled.

"Are these exclusively for your use?"

"No, they're communal."

"*So*," she said, mimicking me, "well then," and stretched across my lap to access the other pocket, brushing the length of her body against my thighs. I shivered, hands incapacitated by the nearly complete joint.

"Stace," I said, more sharply than I intended, and she laughed in her jarring way.

"You called me Stace!"

"Yeah, well."

She opened a beer for me and I took it, relieved to have something other than words in my mouth. The joint was fat, and only a little crooked. We lit it and smoked in silence, leaning back in the expansive seats and listening to the hollow knocking of the boats against their docks. In here there was no birdsong, only the slow lap of water on wood, and I felt the late-night coke stress leave me, draining from my extremities. I wanted to melt into the leather.

Stacey stretched and slumped down with her legs wide open, so wide I could see a curl of dark hair escaping her shorts, lying tucked against her inner thigh. The skin there looked soft and tender where it disappeared beneath stretched denim. I knew I should look away, but there was a gap between this thought and its execution, my eyes autonomous and loosened, all the night's inebriation settling down in my limbs.

"What a monster," she said, and it took me a moment to realize she was referring to the joint.

"Mm," I said. She wasn't wearing a bra and in the boathouse damp her nipples stood out against the thin fabric of her tank top, hardened. Her body approximated an open book, all invitation. Come on in, it said. The water's fine. I surprised myself with how hard I'd gotten, like in the Jeep with her all bodily proximity and scented almond skin.

She met my eyes and smiled the way I'd seen her do at Cliff, like there was some secret only the two of us knew. "Do it," she said, "since you want to. Don't you, Cam."

I said nothing, flushed. I would be lying if I said I didn't. I had never seen a woman look as good as she did then. I remembered my distant desire to surprise her, stun the words out of her. *I'll show you* and yeah, here she was, ready.

She ran her hands down her smooth thighs, over her knees and back. "Do what you want for once in your life."

The truth is that I did want her, but not her exactly—her flesh and its friction, and the brief joy of real human contact. It was like I hadn't felt drunk at all, not the whole night, not until this very moment, all the alcohol conspiring with the weed to sneak up on me at once. I looked away and swallowed, trying to shake the feeling, to shake my excitement at the prospect of real sex with this girl, this woman, this sleek gorgeous woman with all her sureness of self.

Fuck, I thought.

"Or are you going to hold out for someone so careless as Beau Larky?"

I thought this would make me angry but it didn't, not with the amount of THC pressing me into the seat. If not Beau then me, she was thinking. If you can't have him you should forget about it and have me instead.

Careless, and he was, in the end. To want to know so bad when it was all laid out in front of him, plain as a set of directions, obvious in all the silences and hollows and deferences that made up the fabric of our lives. To lead me on that way and act like it was nothing, like it had meant nothing to him. I had a sudden urge to throw him out of bed and scream at him, like, what are you *thinking?* What do you fucking *think?*

She touched my shoulder and, not sensing any resistance, settled into my lap, straddling me. Her breasts pressed tight against my chest. I melted down into the creamy white leather, stunned by her immediacy, her warm smell of coconut sun lotion and concentrated female sweat.

"Do it," she whispered, murmuring into my ear, her breath tickling at my skin, "since you want to." I pulled her shirt over her breasts and looked at them. Her skin was the colour of milky coffee where it had been covered by the swimsuit, hints of vast complex networks of blue veins hidden just below the surface, nipples small and firm and pink. She ran her thumbs over them and pressed herself against me, warm through her tiny shorts. I reminded myself to breathe.

"Look at you," she said, laughing in a soft breathy way, all exhale. "You can hardly take it." Her stomach was flat and golden, a stark contrast to the pale breasts.

"Stacey," I said, and it was a question, and then she put my hands over her breasts and it wasn't. There was the slow fumble of shorts and buttons and zippers, and then only the aquatic dull thump of the boats against their docks and the clink of their tether rings and our breathing growing heavy. She pushed hair from my forehead and I tipped my head back over the seat, captain's hat falling away. I could tell from the tangled motion of her fingers that it had grown long.

Several times I thought for sure I would come, then thought about Beau and didn't. She went first, grinding her hips into mine, pulling at the hair near the base of my neck and groaning freely, low and uncontained. The sensation of her tightening around me, wet velvet insides contracting on my dick, flesh on flesh, put me over the edge.

"Mm," she said, squeezing. She cupped my face and leaned in to kiss me.

I pulled away before I could even think.

Stacey stiffened and stood all in one move, as if she'd just then understood what was happening. Everything was sticky and I thought, suddenly cold: condom, no condom, ugh. The idea of exchanging fluids with Stacey, of having just done this, made me sick.

"What the fuck?" she said, seeing my face. "What the fuck are you even doing?"

"*Me*?" I said. "What about you!"

"What, you can fuck me but you won't kiss me?"

"You're the one," I said, buttoning up my shorts, "coming on to me. Shit."

She pulled her shirt back down, hiding her perfect breasts from view. She looked like I'd hit her. "You are holding out," she said, slowly, with venom, "for someone who does not give a *single fuck*. You think it's virtuous? I know you, Cam." She spat over the side of the boat, disgusted. "I know you better than you think. You think it's some kind of trade-off."

I shook my head. "Fuck you, Stacey, fuck you for starting this and acting like I fucking wronged you."

Trade-off.

"It's not a moral question, Cam! What, you think if you fuck me Beau won't want you? In your mind it's so simple, me or Beau, as if these were two ends of some kind of spectrum. Well, I hate to be the one to break it to you, but he's not going to want you *anyway*, no matter *what* you do."

This hit me hard, in that large bruised hollow taking up space in my chest. I had a gut-wrenching memory of Beau leaning over in tenth-grade math to help me with a problem, writing out the necessary equations in graduated steps with hardly any thought, the clean smell of his anti-dandruff shampoo and the gum he chewed crackling pink between his teeth. I had only passed math because of Beau.

"Cam, he hurts you *incessantly*. How can you love someone like that? Who must know how you feel and doesn't give a *fuck*."

"He doesn't know," I said, desperate. "He doesn't."

She laughed, and it was bitter. "How can he not?"

"What is your problem," I said, dizzy and ill. "Why can't you just leave me alone about this, just let me be, *fuck*." I ran a hand through my hair, trying to soothe down the ache in my skull. "Why would you even want to, if you knew?"

"There was something I had to see."

I laughed. "It's just like you, to be so fucking empirical about it. The scientific method, huh, Stace. Intersubjective verification. *Endlessly* fascinating results."

She got out of the boat with the speed of an animal, her movements feline. It rocked violently against her missing weight. "There are other people in the world," she said, wiping her eyes roughly, with the heel of her hand, "besides Beau Larky."

And then I saw how it was that I'd hurt her feelings, deeply, without thought, and wanted to die. "Stace," I said, but she was already gone, slamming the heavy boathouse door behind her. I imagined her stalking up the stairs and across the lawn, long brown legs scissoring through the grass, and felt like a piece of gum on someone's shoe.

I wanted to tell her I was sorry, but it meant nothing. I was a horrible, cowardly person, and I would be dissatisfied for rest of my natural life, blind to everyone but myself, settling for anything while thinking only of Beau, who slept calmly in the cottage above, wasted.

Empty gratification, I thought, and heaved over the boat's side, listening to the splash of my vomit hitting water. When I let go of the wood panelling my palms were clammy and my knuckles white. The boathouse had grown cold with the encroaching dawn, a sense of shifted time settling over the damp wood though there were no windows.

Soon, I thought, sinking to the boat's carpeted floor, in a matter of days, this golden stretched out week of pause will end, and we'll go back to the city with its incessant pressing heat, that aggressive spiteful Toronto sidewalk heat, and I'll go sit in air-conditioned library corners, tucked away from the world, or loud crowded coffee shops where I will be an island unto myself among all those milling bodies meeting for brief spurts of caffeinated conversation, and I'll write my dissertation, finally start writing it as a physical thing on paper that will outlast me, maybe, sitting dusty and bound on some Robarts shelf full of just these kinds of hopeful, long-forgotten thoughts. *(Barthes 1978, 44)*, I'll cite, and in these names and numbers and dates will be buried the memory of river water on Beau Larky's lip. This is the record that will remain of that golden time, when Beau Larky nearly kissed me. Barthes 1978, 44, emphasis mine.

How our lives and dreams and most fervent desires are channeled into these dry hopeless things.

I lay on my side, pressing my face into the rough red carpeting that smelled of fish and weeds, wet river silt and all its assorted layered decay. All these things soon, and more. Like turning thirty, a frightening distant age I couldn't fathom but which would certainly find me in the very meagre timespan of five years, exposing me to a series of unthinkable, life-ending things: standing tall at Beau Larky's inevitable wedding, smiling, betrayed only by my eyes and their display window distance. Seeing my face become lined and my posture stooped, already, as I crumpled beneath the burden of my height and the difficulty of holding it against the weight and grind of so much accumulated time. The furrow that would crease my forehead from endless inward focus as I became less shy than outright strange, unused to casual conversation, stuntedly academic.

Holding Beau's kids and having them call me something heartbreaking, like *Uncle Cam*.

"Oh," I said, "*oh*," and saw that I was crying, not just crying but breaking into huge, chest-rending, heaving sobs. My heart was sick and cored out.

How can you love someone like that?

I wailed, shaking, allowing myself this grief, tasting tears in my throat.

Who knows how you feel and doesn't give a single fuck.

Happy birthday, happy fucking birthday. I fell asleep with my throat raw and dry, soothed by the boat's gentle rocking drift.

The morning was bad, worse than any in a long while. I woke to a piercing throb splitting my skull and lay still for a few moments, trying not to breathe in the carpet's wet rot while pressing my hands to my head, as if this could contain the hangover. Breathing deep, I made myself stand, bending over and squeezing my eyes shut as broken glass rolled from one end of my skull to the other with no regard for the soft organ sitting between. The boat pitched and I held onto its side, coaching myself through the wobble in my stomach. It was empty and tight, and nothing came up when I heaved.

Outside it was impossibly bright, a full morning sun already climbing over the far treeline, inundating the world with golden red light. The sky was cloudless and deeply blue. Unlimited ceiling, I thought, stupidly, shutting my eyes and leaning for a moment against the boathouse's side.

"Ugh," I said, stumbling up the stairs, each motion painful and forced. Cold coke sweat beaded on my neck and lower back. I checked my watch and realized I didn't have it, that I must have taken it off at some point in the course of the wild sloppy fucked up night. The cold dew was baptismal on my bare feet and I swallowed a brief desire to lay in it, to absorb the cool night earth on my back and brilliant hot sun on my face.

The cottage was quiet and filled with light. Cliff lay facedown on the couch, snoring over the incessant muffled tick of the mantle clock. Whisky glasses in various stages of fullness littered the coffee table, dispersed among scattered creased playing cards and Stacey's

Vogue, its cover smeared and cloudy. Beau's camera lay beside it, strap still neatly wrapped around its hard shell.

I looked away.

I made myself coffee, trying not to clatter around too much, clumsy on the balls of my feet. Stacey's door was closed and I stood looking at it for a long time, leaning on the counter while chugging down two glasses of tepid tap water that tasted like it had come straight from the river. I felt off-kilter, fundamentally unbalanced, out of sync. I didn't look into Beau's room, though the door stood ajar, and took the kettle off the heat before it could make any real sound. In the absence of its building mutter and the hiss of the gas flame I could hear him breathing, sawing out low whistled snores reserved for deep unconsciousness.

For a moment I imagined leaving the coffee and getting into the bed, folding myself around him as I had that one time at the hospital, when he had, with his complicated system of nonverbal permissions, let me. Instead I poured the thick dark liquid into a mug, grounds collecting near the rim because the filter on the press leaked. I found *A Lover's Discourse* on the coffee table and took it outside, squinting against the light as I made my way down the stairs. On the dock I lowered myself into a Muskoka chair, stiff from sleeping on the boat's hard floor.

The river glittered, serene and timeless. To be a body of water, I thought, was to never be truly fazed. To absorb any shock or perforation with the indifference to minute disturbances of temporal things that sheer vastness affords. The coffee was hot and bitter and I sipped it slowly, washing it over my tongue. Its black smell filled my sinuses, easing the laboured motions of my brain grinding to a start. I could have easily drunk ten cups, sip after relished sip.

I half read, distracted, alternating between gazing at the page and staring into the distance. Through the sun's glare catching in my glasses I both saw everything and didn't.

"Hey," Beau said, and I turned to see he'd come all the way down the stairs, soundless, standing with a mug in each hand. "Want some company?"

I nodded.

"I brought you coffee," he said, settling in the chair beside mine. "But you've already got some, huh."

I flashed him my cup to show it was empty, but didn't trust myself to speak. My voice would be all gravel, or worse.

He set the mug down on my chair's broad arm and we sat in silence, feeling the day's growing heat that had drawn a mist over shadier parts of the river, their depths slow to warm. Beau slipped off his Birks halfway, loosely nestling his heels in their smooth brown hollows, oiled and worn. He rested his bare feet on the sandals' straps.

"Hungover?" I said, and he nodded.

"Oh man. Destroyed." His nose ran and he kept wiping at it with his arm, sniffling. I dug into my pocket and found a balled-up tissue.

"Thanks," he said, blowing hard. He peered in to examine its contents and I saw that the crumpled white surface was speckled with blood. Beau twisted up his face. "Ugh. That's what you get for six fucking, hours of straight coke."

I checked my own nose reflexively, but it was pained and dry.

"I gave you a really hard time last night," he said, quiet. "Harder than usual."

"You did."

"I really put you on the spot."

"Yeah."

"I'm not that nice to you sometimes, huh, Cam. After everything."

I shrugged, as if I wasn't sitting next to the singular source of all my despair. "No one's that nice on coke," I said, but he shook his head, and I could see there was some new understanding between us.

"Did you and Stace get in a fight?"

Stace. The clink of boat tethers and her whispered exhortation to *do it, since you want to.* The weight of her in my lap, straddling, like it was something we'd always done, something that didn't require thought. Sitting here, stretched out in the sun with Beau Larky, head throbbing, taking in the pleasing touch of new heat on skin, I had almost forgotten. "What, the other day?"

"No, last night. After we all went to bed."

"How do you know?"

"She was crying," he said. "When I heard her come in. For a while."

"She was *crying*?" I ran a hand through my hair, diminished and suddenly cold.

"Yeah man."

"Fuck."

Beau looked at me over his cup, holding it with both hands. "What did you do?"

I shook my head. "I was so awful to her, Beau. I didn't think. I didn't realize—"

"That she's in love with you?"

"Yeah."

"She'll be okay," he said, kicking off his shoes entirely. He let his feet rest flat on the dock and leaned back in the chair, closing his eyes.

"No," I said. "She's never gonna look at me again." What I'd done to her I wouldn't wish on anyone. I'd have to apologize. I'd have to at least try.

"People get over these things," he said. "You'll see." In his total stillness he conveyed a knowledge I could only grasp at, an assurance embedded in his very bones.

"How can you know?"

"Cam, people can get over anything. I was trying to get over the idea that I might *die*, and I was almost there."

(Almost.)

Not everything, Beau. There are some things people don't get over.

We sat in silence, him so still he might have been sleeping, face upturned to the strengthening sun, me with the book open in my lap and my gaze far away. A white trail of smoke emerged from one of the distant cottages though it must have been early, still, too early for people on vacation to do anything but sleep. He'd told me about Stacey so many times.

"What are you reading?" he asked. Somehow it seemed a natural corollary of his original questions, a different tack.

I held up the book, still open, so he could see the familiar grey cover, but he said, "No, I mean, specifically. In there."

I looked down at the page where I found all the words perfect in their predestined order, each following the next with a gravity that was cumulative, built with each syllable. With a gravity that was fateful. "*The Last Leaf*," I said.

"Will you read it to me?"

"You want me to read to you?"

He nodded and tipped his head back. "You know I like it. When you read to me."

I drew up my knees and balanced the book on them, stunned. He did, then. He did, because it calmed him, all those measured abstract words and their rhythm drawing him to sleep when he'd been so sick, teetering on the edge of something great and black. I'd seen him through that, nobody but me, and said nothing, and that was love. That was what love was, beyond anything someone sixteen and breathless could imagine, standing on a deck in the wet summer night.

"Here and there," I began, taking a deep breath, "on the trees, some leaves remain. And often I stand deep in thought before them. I contemplate a leaf and attach my hope to it. When the wind plays with the leaf, I tremble in every limb. And if it should fall, alas, my hope falls with it."

I looked at Beau but he was motionless, eyes closed, basking. I went on.

"In order to be able to question fate, there must be an alternative: she loves me / she loves me not; we require an object capable of a simple variation (*will fall / won't fall*) and an external force (divinity, chance, wind) which marks one of the poles of the variation. I always ask the same question (will I be loved?), and this question is an alternative: *all or nothing*."

I swallowed. Exhale, exhale. "I do not suppose that things can develop, be exempted from desire's *a propos*. I am not dialectical. Dialectic would say: the leaf will not fall, and *then* it will fall; but meanwhile you will have changed and you will no longer ask yourself the question."

And you will no longer ask yourself the question.

I wanted to look at him but didn't get a chance, because then Beau Larky did something wholly unexpected, and took my hand in his.

Be quiet, be quiet, be quiet.

He held it for a long time.

Seven

On our last day at the cottage we drove into town and walked on the river, taking in little candy shops and ice cream joints with their bright plastic displays, greasy diners and Adirondack furniture outlets. The grass bordering the river was green and neatly cut, giving off the raw bleeding smell of summer. Here the Gatineau narrowed into a lock, its immense mass channeled into a system of doors and levers, contained by the brute strength of poured concrete. Vague tufts of cloud lined the sky, trailing into wisps near the horizon.

We stopped at an ancient store that sold bait and ice cream and smelled like an old-time cold storage, ice blocks packed with sawdust, cool and dry. The floors were warped pine and creaked with our weight as we studied the white plastic board with four dozen flavour cards slotted into it, some of them scrawled in thick black marker like afterthoughts. The freezers contained huge cardboard cylinders of country-style ice cream in a hundred pastel colours, the more popular flavours scraped down to the bottoms of their drums.

Emerging into the sun as from underground, dry heat rising around our ankles, I watched everyone eating their ice cream: Cliff's marbled black cherry, my plain chocolate, Stacey's vanilla all cream, like the leather seats, and Beau's bright blue bubblegum with hard pink kernels of candy dispersed throughout. He spat them out all along the sidewalk, some landing in the water, little white balls sucked free of all flavour. He had a massive sweet tooth and chose flavours like a kid, selecting for sugar content and brightness of colour. Beau Larky, shameless and stoned.

Down the walk where the river came to a bend there was a canvas tent, purple and indigo hung with heavy velvet curtains. *Fortunes*, the sign said. *Palm and Tarot Readings 20$*.

Cliff smiled and pushed up his shades. "Look at that shit."

"Someone should get their fortune read," Stacey said. She spoke lightly. Behind sunglasses facing into the day's glare her eyes were impossible to read. Since the boathouse she'd acted like nothing had happened, and I was glad.

"Someone like Cam," Beau said. "See what the future has in store, huh." He nudged my shoulder with his.

She looked away, crossing her arms.

I shook my head, stomach suddenly empty. The hand I'd been holding my cone in was sticky and I licked at the skin between my thumb and forefinger. "No way guys."

"Don't you want to know your future?" she said.

"No," I said, "and you don't believe that mystical stuff anyway."

She shrugged, cocking her chin in the direction of the booth. "The woman probably knows more than I do." A shrunken woman in a headwrap had emerged and now stood by the awning, one gnarled hand holding the curtain aside. She regarded us distantly, her skin leather. She wore a hundred beads that clicked together when she moved.

"Get your fortune?" she asked. "Palm and tarot, twenty dollars, *non*?" Her accent was Québécois and heavy and she was thinking: *Anglo tourists*. She smiled at Cliff, who looked like approximately twenty million dollars.

"What, me?" he said, and laughed. "No, no. *Him*." And pushed me forward like an offering.

She smiled again, drawing back her lips. At least three of her teeth were composed of various types of metal, gold and silver and something between. "Handsome young man in love?"

I blushed hugely, down to my neck. "Absolutely not."

"Come on, Cam," Beau said. "Do it up. You might like what you hear." He'd finished the last of his waffle cone and licked his fingers with an air of total satisfaction.

I looked at Stacey and she did the last thing I expected, smiling. "Yeah, come on Cam. I'll pay for it."

"Stace."

"No, really. Come on, get this woman to tell you something profound."

Somehow I found myself in the tent, mouth dry, Cliff and Beau cracking up and high-fiving outside while Stacey shushed them. My weird loud friends always setting me up for shit that made me want to crawl into the floor. "Have a seat," the woman said, and I did, taking a chair across from her, a velvet-covered table between us. The tent was solid canvas and no external light broke in, though its heat was obvious through the fabric. The air hung dead and still, somehow insulated against sound.

"You want palm or tarot?" she said, and I said tarot, because I couldn't bear the idea of her reading my hand, holding it like a phone with a crucial long distance call on the line, divining fates already inscribed in the very structure of my bones.

The idea of absolutely knowing anything made me ill.

She began shuffling the deck, long shiny cards edged with wear changing places. "Does this involve calling up spirits or something?" I said, trying to make a joke.

"Spirits?" she said, and smiled. "No, all the information we need is right here." She tapped the shuffled deck with her long curved nails, making a clicking sound. "But you are, how you say—*nerveux*. Nervous."

And I saw that I was, palms sweating in my lap. Am I so superstitious now, I thought. Am I really so convinced.

"Interesting." She looked at me hard, eyes huge and dark in the tent, the only light coming from a set of lava lamps on the floor. "Because you think much but share little. *Tu as peur d'être vu*—afraid of being seen. That is why your friends chose you, and not another."

I shivered, a wave of energy shifting my shoulders.

"I know you already," she said, looking through the deck. "Here you are." She put down a card in the centre of the table, a young man in a green tunic gazing intently at a pentacle floating just above his raised hands. *The Page of Pentacles*. He looked nothing like me.

"See how he gazes at that which he holds, as if it could tell him something. He walks slowly, insensible of that which is about him. He is focused on inner things, *non?*"

I nodded, stunned.

"This is the card for scholars," she said, matter of fact, sly delight at my surprise creeping over her features. "You are a student?"

"Of theory," I said.

"Responsible, withdrawn, preoccupied with moments of *réflexion*. *Non*? Young of body but old of mind."

"It's true," I said, intrigued now. But it's just a card, I thought. You can get lucky with a card. She saw me all shy out there and got lucky.

"And what is he worried about, since he feels much but says little?" She drew a second card from the deck, this time from the top, without looking. "The Five of Cups," she said, setting it down on top of the first.

It was a dark card, its grey sky a stark contrast to the yellow of the first. The figure in it stood straight and stiff but for the shoulders, which bent in sorrow over the spilled contents of three overturned cups. He was cloaked in black. My heart clenched in recognition.

"You see yourself here, *non*? More than in the other, interesting. It is a dark card—loss, dejection. Hurt and disappointment. In many matters—financial, spiritual. But in your case I think it is obvious that you are most concerned with love. *L'amour non partagé*—how you say. I don't know. Do you know what I mean?"

L'amour non partagé. "Love that's not shared," I said. "Unrequited love."

"You love deeply, without limit. But the one you love—they do not know your true heart, and this causes you great distress. Am I right?"

"Yes." I was suddenly afraid of this old woman with her shining eyes and hidden knowledge, somehow gleaned from the cards and my body, the stoop of my shoulders like those of the cloaked figure. Self-portrait, I thought.

"But see, you are focused on the spilled cups, when two still stand—there is always hope in such matters, as you well know, since you agonize so. And here," she drew another card, crossing the cloaked figure with it, "is a major obstacle, that which crosses you. The High Priestess. A very fine card."

"The High Priestess?" Now she will tell me about the women in my life, I thought, relieved to be off this track.

"See how her cloak covers the scroll she holds? Some things are implied and some spoken, and you fear this. You fear the future as yet unrevealed, and so sit in silence. True?"

I said nothing and she nodded.

"And above," she said, drawing a card, "the Two of Cups—the card of *l'amour réciproque*—you know?"

"Reciprocal love." When I spoke my voice was quiet, more so than I'd intended.

"Shared love, yes. See, the lovers here toast and pledge to one another, both giving. This is what you wish to arrive at, make your own. But it is not yours at present."

The problem of the gift, says Barthes, is such: *and what about me! Haven't I given you everything?* The selfishness of it plaguing me, always.

"You are tired of always giving of yourself," she said, looking at me seriously, abandoning the cards. "You need something, too. It is someone here, no? Someone here with you now."

"Who is?" I said, stupidly.

"The one you love."

I turned to look behind me but the tent was closed, only a small strip of sunlight creeping in between the grass and canvas flap. Of course she would guess it was someone with me. This was an obvious and safe guess.

"May I guess who it is?"

I tensed up, suddenly cold, and almost stood to be farther from her, to increase the distance between myself and this woman who smelled like potpourri and seemed to know my heart. It's just a game, I thought. They get people to come in and play for twenty bucks and it's all a game. She'll guess Stacey anyway, of course she'll guess the only woman there.

"The little fellow with the dark hair, big laugh. It is him, *non? Il est trés beau*—exceedingly handsome."

"How can you know that?" I said, unnerved now. It was like she'd pulled out a cabinet containing the inside of my skull in labelled files.

"The cards tell me," she said, smiling, "and you do, too. Your body speaks for you, always. Now below," producing the next card from the pile as I wondered if she'd go through the whole deck like that, "is what is beneath you—that which you already possess, and have used, and made your own. Strength—a very powerful card."

The image was of a woman against a saffron sky holding shut the mouth of a cowering lion. The lion's tail was tucked between its legs, and the woman's expression betrayed nothing but extreme, catatonic calm. "Wow," I said.

"Yes, wow." She laughed. "Self-control, patience, discipline, inner strength. Compassion, gentleness. The triumph of the mind over the passions. You have done much to restrain yourself in order to aid the one you love, and this is to your advantage. It shows greatness of heart."

Beau Larky hanging onto me and saying, his voice in a wobble, *you're the kindest, bravest, most patient, most selfless person I know*. I could no longer hear them outside and guessed they'd moved into the shade to sit down.

"And behind you, that which is past—great suffering, illness. Not your own, but another's. This I can see in your shoulders, *non*? You cannot straighten them though you try."

You think it's your head that's the strongest with all your theory, but actually it's your heart. Oh, Beau.

"And before you, the influence to come." She produced the next card, brandishing it with a flourish. "*La Roue de la Fortune*—very interesting. The perpetual motion of the universe, and the flux of human life. Also *l'équilibre*—balance."

"Is it a lucky card?" I said. If my advisor could see me here, indulging in cards and fortunes, he would lose it. But she knew, there was definitely something she knew. There was some reason in her reading, deep thought and design of a plane I was not familiar with.

She smiled, flashing her teeth. "It can be. It means change, of a sort. Some kind of influence, a form of *chance*, is coming into your future to affect the course of events in a way you do not foresee. But that," drawing another card, holding it so neither of us could see its face, "is not what will come. Now tell me," setting it facedown on the table, "do you wish to know your future?"

I realized I was chewing at the skin around my thumbnail and stopped, putting both hands on the edge of the velvet table. The whole time Beau held my hand he'd said nothing, not a thing though with his fingers twined through mine he must have felt my pulse quickening to meet his touch. Each time my chest rose and I breathed deep he damped it down, running his thumb over the heel of my hand, through its valley, down the crease.

Don't speak, don't speak. He didn't let me once.

"I don't know," I said. "What are you going to tell me?"

"You fear the future. The cards have their own wisdom, but they cannot predict, only suggest. They show potential variations, not solid outcomes. How we act on them is of utmost importance—but you are not a man of action. Men of action do not have questions about *l'amour non réciproque*. The choice is yours."

"I just don't want you to tell me how he feels, because . . ." I trailed off. Because I couldn't bear it. I didn't speak because I couldn't bear to break it, his skin on mine, his hand so cool, like he'd never sweated in his life.

"You think I can tell you what is in his heart? Nobody can do that. You already know that, as well as you can."

And then he'd stood and said, *let me make you breakfast*, except I knew that wasn't at all what he meant. I sat in the kitchen and watched him frying bacon, chin resting in my hands, staring, as I had so many times, at the outline of his shoulder blades through his shirt, but now unselfconsciously, without thought. For the first time I thought that maybe he wanted me to. *He wants you to, give him what he wants.*

"Show me," I said.

This was obviously what she'd been waiting for. She flipped the card immediately, with relish, leaning in to see it with as much anticipation as myself. "Ah!" she said, clapping her hands together powerfully, just once. "*The Page of Wands.*"

The card showed a figure of a man in a yellow tunic against a brilliant blue background. He held a wooden staff, small bits of greenery sprouting near its tip. "What does it mean?"

"Here," she said, tracing the card with her finger, "a dark young man stands in the act of *déclaration*—proclamation. He is charismatic, energetic, warm, but also impulsive, and sometimes directionless. He brings unexpected news, and his tidings are strange." She smiled, looking at me sideways. "The ends of your questions," she said, "depend mainly on him."

4. The Magician

What I want, deliriously, is to *obtain the word*.
  Roland Barthes, *A Lover's Discourse*

One

He wakes early, earlier than usual though it's Saturday and he doesn't have to work. It's already warm, the day's heat gathering in thick golden bars trying to make their way through the blinds. He gets up and stretches, feeling his bare feet stick to the floor. It's stupid hot and will only get hotter.

He raises the blinds and leans on the windowsill, taking in the alley below, its dumpster and scattered cardboard boxes, a woman in a long flowing skirt and big sunglasses half running over the stained pavement to catch the streetcar at the stop around the corner. The air, humming with potential heat, is full of the city's smells already: fresh bread from the bakery down the street, yeasty and warm, sour-sweet trash, bitter coffee. He breathes it in and lets it go, allowing his lungs to expand.

These are the first days of summer.

His body feels full and solid, his stomach steady, his head clear. It's been almost a month and a half since his last session, and it shows—his hair's lost its dull dryness and developed a new sleekness to it, a shine. When he looks in the bathroom mirror he sees his skin is more pink, as if the blood beneath, having been purged of poison, is somehow better oxygenated. He brushes his teeth and doesn't worry about their enamel for the first time in weeks.

He dresses without showering and grabs his camera, swinging it over his neck. The apartment is still, Cam sleeping down the hall with his door closed, and he moves quietly to avoid waking him. Cam's been sleeping so well lately, going to bed at normal times and making it through to the morning without interruption, no more stifled drowning gasps leaking through the shared wall.

He takes a swig of orange juice straight from the carton and then another, unable to believe he's awake and upright and moving around, fully dressed. He slips on his shoes and locks the door gingerly, gently jiggling the key past the point where it sticks.

The building is old and retains moisture, trapping it in the walls. They are damp and waxy to the touch through layers of oil paint, breathing humidity into the hallways and leaving everything smelling of plaster, wet basement. The stairs creak as he takes them two at a time, running his hand over their old wooden railings with missing rungs, the wood polished by years of use. These ancient things fill him with joy. It is of late his primary emotion, springing up in his chest at the sight of the sun in the street, the palette of colours composing the corner fruit stand, snapping up from him unbidden to meet Cam coming through the door with his stack of books. The world is a living thing and he unfolds within it, within himself.

He walks to the pool and swims its length beneath the water, coming up for air only twice. Underwater he listens to his pulse beating in his ears, the rush of blood moving through his head, the aquatic echo of vibrations travelling enormous molecular distances. When he emerges his eyes are red with chlorine, but his heart beats strong and his lungs fill easy. Beau sits on the pool's edge with his feet in the water, watching the play of early morning sun on its rippled surface, glittering and broken only by the powerful breaststroke of a lean woman with a swim cap on. All is well within and without.

When he showers he laughs to himself without meaning to, the stunned emission of pleasure escaping as he closes his eyes and feels the hot water washing over his head as nothing short of a caress. Such plain ordinary things incapacitate him.

Beau walks home with his towel draped over his neck, skin fresh and cooled and all his pores open to the strengthening heat that will crest at midday, baking the sidewalks and making the distant pavement waver in the sun. Now the air is still balmy, and it seems to him that everyone passing by in the street is smiling, walking at a leisurely pace in shorts and sundresses and light suits.

The sky is a lovely pale blue that will fill out and deepen as the day stretches on.

He snaps a bunch of guys loading guitars and amps into a panel van at the curb, some of them trying to smoke while lifting. The old Vietnamese man who runs the fruit stand washes his windows with a squeegee, a roll of paper towels tucked under his arm, and Beau snaps this, too. Inside the shop he walks slowly, savouring the size of the melons, the shiny quality of the apples and oranges, the brightness of peppers and bananas sitting in bunches. Sometimes, as now, he sees the point of colour photography—there is something about the vitality of these objects that in monochrome would be drowned out, lost. Beau takes in the stacked metal shelves of potted herbs crowded next to bursting flower bouquets, vibrant and lush in the small space, the displays of lucky china cats and phone cards and cigarettes. He buys mushrooms, green peppers, fresh vine tomatoes, huge oranges that barely fit in the palm of his hand. From the butcher across the street he picks up ham, salami, a big block of cheese.

Climbing the stairs to the apartment he feels new muscles in his calves tensing on each step, leveraging the weight of his body. Upstairs he sits out on the balcony and smokes, pleased with the simple task of rolling, all the while listening for Cam's footsteps in the hallway, the slow sounds of him getting up.

He can't wait. He actually can't. What (*what*) is with you, he thinks, but knows, and almost doesn't care, now that it's been so long. He brims with the feeling and isn't sure he could shake it now, even if he wanted to, even if he tried. Mostly he doesn't want to. Mostly he wants to surprise Cam, because there is nothing more pleasing in the whole world than Cam caught off his guard. Beau takes his time cubing up the fresh produce, grating cheese, whisking eggs, putting on water for the coffee he'll pour right as he hears Cam stumbling around.

I am a new person, he thinks, after this thing. This thing has changed me in so many ways.

Cam gets up well past ten. Beau reheats the kettle and listens to him running water, brushing his teeth, making the old floorboards in the hallway creak with his lanky weight before arriving in the kitchen in his boxers, hair plastered down on one side and sticking up on the other. He is sleep-heavy and vague, lazy with the fact of the weekend, and Beau likes him this way. He stretches and Beau hears his spine pop, decompressing from the night's stress.

"Sleep well?" he asks, and Cam nods *yeah*, the whole thing luxurious, like he can't even be bothered with words. Cam has been less careful lately, loosened by the weather, dressing all sloppy in shorts and stretched-out old tees when he heads to campus, his worn Birks slapping around on the tile, shedding cork from their sides.

He has in his mind a proposition, half formed, he thinks Cam might not be averse to. That Cam might even welcome, since he often looks at him too long and with too much feeling. He sees this and doesn't know how to read it, or if it even should be read.

"Cam loves you," Stacey said one night as they sat on the balcony smoking, her feet up on the railing, ankles crossed.

"Yeah," he said, sealing a joint. "He loves me a ton."

"No, I mean, Cam is *in love*. With you."

He had heard this before, many times, but it sent a brief flicker of thrill through him, even so. "Stace, no. It's not like that."

"Is that really what you think?" she said, with a strange intensity.

He laughed. "What else would I think?"

She gave him an incredulous look, like, *okay*, and suddenly he was so mad all he could think to say was, *what the hell, Stace*, and so said nothing, because the silence between them was awkward enough. Feeling heady and strange, unsettled because she'd named his desire, expressed it so plainly in a way he could not.

Cam is in love with you.

"Stace, wait," he said when she was leaving, catching her at the door as she shouldered her bag.

"Beauregard." She let the door close and leaned against it, mouth pressed tight and twisted with curiosity. "What's up?"

"Why did you say that thing earlier, about Cam? Why do you think that?"

She smiled. "Why *don't* you think that?"

"I wish you'd just be straight with me."

Something about his tone and its sudden shift must have pushed her, because she stopped smiling and straightened. "You're a good guy, Beau," she said, coolly, "but you don't notice shit. Don't you see the way he looks at you?"

The way he looks at you and yeah, now he does see it, sees it all the time, can't unsee it. He feels, strongly, that he can't let this happen between them. This feeling is too new, too impulsive on his part. He's been thinking lately about the porch, about his reaction to this tall quiet person, the desire to be around him stronger than the pull toward Mescini and all these older guys who would make social life in this new Toronto suburb bearable for him, maybe even fun. Thinking that this feeling has a history he doesn't understand. He feels like, if this is so obvious and so mutual, then why has it never happened? Which makes him think, maybe it has. Maybe there's a very good reason for all the careful distance between them, one that's been lost in the shakedown of his mind.

He stays up late on the couch and hunches over his laptop, searching: *love, in love, signs of being in love, in love with best friend? how to tell if you're in love.*

But he's already asking the question.

Questions contain more information than answers, Cam once said, dealing with a student on the phone, tracing a pattern on the fogged glass of the balcony door. How you ask a question is key.

Two

The night they return to the city there is a party. A party of *epic proportions*, Cliff keeps saying, enamoured with the grandiosity of the phrase. In the Jeep there is much speculation about the coming night's plans, and then a lot of teasing about what the old French woman had told Cam, who sits flushed and shakes his head and when pressed on this point says, simply: *she told me I would get strange news.*

Cliff turns his whole body around in the passenger seat and cranes his neck over the headrest, giving Beau a look that is nothing short of loaded, like this should mean something particular to him and him alone.

Beau is still wildly hungover in a deep psychic way he's sure has something to do with the amount of coke and whisky he ingested just over twenty-four hours before. His head aches, and though he jokes incessantly and takes pains to steal Cliff's aviators and hand them to Stacey for inspection he can feel something dark creeping in at the edges of things. He's hit repeatedly with a cringe-inducing image of himself going, *Cam, who were you in love with*, dragging it out, unable to let the question go though he could see it made Cam recoil. And it was *because* of this recoil, precisely because of this drawing back that he couldn't drop it, and because of this that he now sees himself as he must have been, forcing down the last of the whisky and choking back the gag reflex that began as soon as the amber liquid hit his throat. As if he needed that, as if he hadn't spent enough of the past ten months throwing up.

Will you really not tell me?

He endures a wave of intense, pulse-quickening shame. You are not a good drunk, he thinks. You forget boundaries. You get out of hand and say whatever. Fuck, man. You're twenty-fuck-ing, four, and get a hold of yourself.

Twenty-five now, he reminds himself. As if it matters.

He feels Cam's pained silence and evasive answers physically, as a reproach.

Beau, there's something we really need to talk about.

What (what), he'd wanted to say, because he almost already knew and Stacey was right, she was absolutely right that what he couldn't stand was *not knowing*, that limbo state of being almost there but not quite. *Isn't it that*—but if asked what he might have suggested to Cam at that moment he couldn't have said. He took in Cam's fantastic long body and the way it supported his clothes in the sticky night air and felt deeply afraid.

His desire to know why Cam had refused to answer and his fear of this knowledge reside in almost perfect balance. The coke, which had almost tipped this balance from its delicate state, remains in him as a vague heaviness and gradually increasing distance between his body and thoughts. He imagines trace amounts of the drug clinging to his nerve endings, slowing his movements and blocking receptors necessary for smooth cognitive functioning. *Serotonin,* he thinks abstractly. Shit, man.

He doesn't quite allow himself to cling to the fact that Cam, though given ample opportunity, hadn't once withdrawn his hand.

The party is supposed to be at a house rented by Cliff's friend, or friends, the number of which isn't entirely clear, and is to contain such incentives as three floors, a fantastic deck, and a generous quantity of free alcohol for those early enough to take advantage of it. You guys better be there, Cliff says, looking at them with special emphasis as they idle at the curb in front of his apartment, Stacey pulling her bags from the Jeep's trunk in the luxurious end-of-day glow. Beau has moved to the front seat and now hangs out the open window, nodding. Yeah, yeah, he says, don't worry man, but Cliff folds his sunglasses and says, *I mean it, hey*, in a way that is not at all jokey but betrays knowledge of some deep intangible weariness that has begun to settle over the group.

With just him and Cam in the Jeep the silence hangs heavy and unobscured, and Beau understands it's been masked only by the presence of others. He feels keenly aware of some unspoken friction between them, a thing more exhausted than tense.

At home they smoke a joint on Cam's bed and don't look at each other or talk. When it gets too dark to see Beau reaches over to turn on the lamp, bathing a small fraction of the sheets in yellow reading light.

"So," he says, tracing Cam's stretched body. Cam's hopelessly dirty feet rest on the pillow with his head way down at the other end of the bed, facing the doorway. He's got his chin propped on his folded arms, and Beau can't see his face. "What do you wanna do?"

"Oh," Cam says, the word expanded into one long sigh, an exhalation of pure resignation, "I don't know."

"You wanna go to this thing? Meet up with Cliff?"

Cam turns onto his back, letting his head hang over the bed's edge, hair falling away to expose his forehead. His eyes are closed. "I could go either way. I'm kind of beat, man." From his tone Beau can tell he's sensuously imagining getting under the covers with a book of theory the size of a briefcase.

"Yeah. I'm deadly hungover."

"Still?"

"Still."

"You gonna go?"

"I don't know, we should probably go."

"Cliff won't care. He and Stacey are going to be on like ten different drugs before you even get there."

"I think he really wanted us to go."

"Yeah, well. He didn't drive everyone back to the city through seven hours of traffic, so."

Beau studies Cam's bare feet, their undersides calloused and grimy from weeks of not wearing socks. Cam's toes are long and have wide knobbly knuckles he keeps spreading in a rhythmic, lazy way. Beau is filled with a strong urge to reach out and place his hands over the arches, an impossible heart-quickening thing.

If anyone tired him out today it was you.

He adjusts the pillow behind him and sinks down, drained.

Cam sighs. "You really wanna go, huh."

"I just really feel like we should," he says. "I have a—feeling about it." And he does, all at once he sees that this is exactly the thing—an omen communicated through Cliff's fixed look, a physical dread that grows as the light fades from the window and Cam's spine becomes increasingly limp. He hasn't been entirely successful in shaking his superstitious streak.

Their phones go off at the same time, precipitating a moment of reaching into pants and searching between sheets. It's Cliff saying, *where are you guys??*

And then: *Stacey says hurry up man*

"See," Beau says. "He's shitting bricks."

Cam groans. "What time is it?"

"Almost ten."

"Man. Where is this thing?"

"Like, Roncesvalles."

"Seriously? Fuck."

"Come on, Cam. House party. Haven't done a house party in fucking, forever."

Cam's phone buzzes and Beau leans in to read the message over his shoulder:

you guys wimping out in bed or what hey

He laughs. "Come on, it'll be fun. Let's go give him a hard time."

"You know," Cam says, tossing his phone out of reach, "why don't you just go? You obviously want to go. I think I'm just gonna stay in and sleep it off. I need a vacation from that vacation."

Beau is silent, thinking. The point, he feels strongly, is to go together. Somehow, everything hinges on this.

"What you're not gonna go now?"

"Come with me," he says, allowing himself to touch Cam's foot, cupping his hand over the heel. "It'll be fun, you'll see." And though his superstitious self blanches at the undefined quality of the promise that finally gets Cam up and out of bed, he adds: "I'll make it worth your while."

Three

The house isn't hard to find, the noise of a dozen front yard smokers and porch drinkers drawing them down the street to a three-storey Victorian lit up from wall to wall, the vague thump of a bass spilling from somewhere upstairs. There is the delicate crash of a glass breaking followed by a shriek from the corner of the yard, then everyone making a long, drawn-out sound of mock disapproval.

The stairs are narrow and packed with bodies, everything warm and close. They push through and on the second-floor landing are intercepted by Stacey, who grabs Cam's wrist and pulls him off into the hallway. Beau follows with some effort, squeezing past a group of girls holding something boozy-sweet in red plastic cups. One with a lip piercing turns to address him before realizing he's only passing through.

"Whoa, Cliff wasn't kidding, huh," he says, leaning against the wall. The top of his head bumps against a framed picture of a multi-limbed Hindu god Cam steadies before it can fall.

"A party of *epic proportions*, hey," Stacey says, miming Cliff's expansive hand gesture, and bursts out laughing, sloshing foaming beer onto her hand. Her eyes are the size of saucers. "I'm so glad you guys came."

"Almost didn't, thanks to Grandma Bedtime over here." He elbows Cam, who shoves him right back. "You look like you're having a fucking, blast, Stace."

"You have no idea." She laughs again, and it's not at all stilted or jarring, but full of capacious good will.

"Where's Cliff?"

"Clifford is just about *writhing* with impatience for your *imminent* arrival." She slings her arm around Cam's neck and pulls him close. "Come on, I'll get you guys some beers."

Beau finds himself trailing behind them, keeping his eyes locked on the back of Cam's head where the hair is matted from contact with the driver's seat headrest and curling in the humidity, and then just like that they're gone. He feels slow, weighed down with the psychic aftertaste of dirty drugs, and all at once wishes he hadn't come. Why the urgency? Stupid fucking, superstitious hunch, man. Everyone in the hall shouts to be heard, lips pressed to ears over the rising din.

He passes a doorframe through which he can see there are about twenty bodies packed into a space the size of his bedroom, reclining on the bed and carpet and cushions and perching on the windowsill, indiscriminately leaning into one another. He can hardly make out the walls.

"Larky!" Cliff spins him around, hands clamped to his shoulders. He reeks of cigarettes. "I nearly died of old age twice waiting for you and your fucking roomie to get here, hey."

"Cliff," he says, laughing. "This is a serious fucking, housing code violation situation."

"And rapidly escalating, eeeh. *Man* am I happy to see *you*." His eyes widen with delight and Beau sees he's high, Stacey's high, everyone at this party is fucking, sky high.

"Is Cam here?"

"Yeah man."

"*Excellent.*" Cliff presses a small baggie into his hand, giving his shoulder an enormous squeeze. "I saved those for you."

Beau looks at the baggie wonderingly, thumbing the two gel capsules filled with coarse crystals of what might be dirty road salt. "What are they?"

"M, man."

"M?"

"MDMA."

"Ecstasy? You guys are all on E?"

Cliff nods, grinning. There is a thin sheen of sweat slicking his forehead, dampening the hair near his temples. Beau endures a tremor of palpable excitement and its high voltage taste in the back of his throat. He's only had E once, and it wasn't even good. He's sure what Cliff has is good.

"One for you, and one for Cam, okay? Make sure Cam takes one."

"Doctor's orders, huh."

Cliff slaps his back harder than necessary. "You know it, Larky. Let's get you some booze, hey. You want beers or what?"

He follows Cliff upstairs, tossing back the pill with the mechanical ease of someone used to popping meds four times a day. The third floor is oddly laid out, the staircase leading up to an open kitchen, all can-strewn countertops and boxes of empties. The sink overflows with glasses and mugs no one has bothered to wash. There is a long island-type counter serving as a rough boundary line between kitchen and living space, where the entire west wall is lined with wide old-Toronto windows with panes of thin warped glass. There are less people up here, but the room is still packed. A deck just beyond the kitchen is identifiable only by backs of smokers pressed against the windows, giving the uncanny impression that they are floating unsupported three storeys above the ground.

The fridge is absolutely out of fucking, control. When Cliff opens it four cans of assorted beer tumble out, hitting the cheap linoleum in a clatter. Beau catches one before it can sustain a dent while Cliff collects the rest, laughing uncontrollably. "Fuck, eh," he says. "Ho-*ly*."

The shelves are jammed to capacity with liquor of all sorts, the whole thing an exercise in geometric imagination. Cliff replaces two of the cans with some difficulty, removing other bottles at random while trying to fit them back in. By the time he's opening his second beer with the bottom of a lighter Beau can feel the drug creeping into the tips of his fingers, warming them with a restlessness that makes him want to jump around. He slouches against the counter. It's made of granite, cool and solid against the small of his back.

"Hey Larky, how you feeling man?" Cliff is talking nonstop, avidly greeting everyone who crosses between them, which in a narrow space like this one directly beside the fridge is a fucking, *lot* of people. Beau thinks he must have been introduced to everyone in the house by now, and remembers the names of exactly no one.

"I'm feeling fucking, *great*," he says, buoyed by the words and their irrepressible cadence. What a delight, to form words. A thing he's never noticed before.

"Are you sure Cam didn't leave?"

Cam. The single syllable fills his head with a resonance that blanks out all other thought. "Naw, he was with Stace."

"Man, you better go find him before you melt into the floor, friend."

He realizes how much he's slouching and shakes it off, straightening. The warmth is no longer limited to his fingers, but localized in what must be his living beating heart pumping it into every last extremity.

He wanders around the house, drifting in and out of conversations that feel like different worlds, totally singular, self-contained things unto themselves. He wants to talk to everyone at once because everything happening is new, irresistible, these various centers of discussion drawing him in like planets with their gravitational pull. On the stairs he's coaxed by people coming back from a smoke to head out onto the porch with them and have another, and on his way back inside he somehow comes to rest on a couch where he's told an elaborate story by a group of women about a mutual friend they all happen to secretly hate. There's a bag of Lays on the table, but nobody's eating it. All their mouths make clicking chewing motions that mirror his own.

His insides feel like a basket of warm laundry.

Scanning the second-floor hallway, he runs into a college friend and winds up smoking no less than four joints heavily cut with tobacco. Conversation is contagious, springing up boundlessly between bodies passing in narrow spaces where it's impossible not to make eye contact with everyone, stop and chat and tell them how much he likes their shirt or get into a heated discussion about the downsides of living so far west (in the *deep* fucking, west end, okay). He is on an adventure through the house, vaguely reaching toward some not yet known point where he will come, inevitably, to the place he feels he should be. Organically, in a way having nothing to do with goals or plans.

Alive, he is alive. The fact of his aliveness floods him with incredible good will. He's heady with it, this fact of him, of *Beau Larky* and his very own body in a state of wellness identical to that of all the other bodies in this hot loud space, this realization a great rush that crests at the peak of his skull and turns his limbs liquid with pleasure. He imagines all these disparate bodies functioning properly, moving together yet existing as self-sufficient organisms. *Autonomous*, like Cam would say—*Cam*.

He has totally forgotten that he is supposed to be looking for Cam and now has a sudden, profound, all-consuming urge to go stand by him, be in his space, the space that always opens up to him without prompting. With the M this seems obvious—the way Cam always angles himself toward Beau, like everything he's saying is vital though it's not, though Beau talks mainly in vague sentences interspersed with fucking, unpolished verbal punctuation.

Though I talk like a stoner, he thinks, and is embarrassed, ashamed.

Upstairs he comes to rest against a radiator and spots Cam across the room, back turned, unmistakable in his red plaid shirt with the sleeves rolled clumsily to his elbows in a loose way that just won't stay up. He's talking with one of Cliff's annoying hipster friends, Jeremy or Jeffrey, who even over the din of eighties hits and shouted exchanges Beau can hear explaining that if people are going to dance to fucking Blondie, they could at least do it with *a sense of irony, man.* He wears an intensely groomed handlebar mustache and a real Stetson with an ostentatiously wide brim turned way up at the sides. Easy there, cowboy, Beau thinks, and almost laughs. Cam tends to attract this kind of company, amateur critics, part-time intellectuals, the fashionably hip, drawn to his serious bearing and academic status (*that's Cliff's friend doing the Ph.D., right*) with the transparent desire to offload curated opinions and loudly discuss their book purchases and argue with the best of them, yee fucking, haw.

Cam nods, worrying at his sleeve with his left hand while his right holds a beer bottle down by his thigh, sloppily, gripped by just the neck. He says something Jeremy/Jeffrey either doesn't agree with or doesn't understand, or both, judging by Cam's expression. As Beau approaches Cam is saying, *I'm not sure there's anything inherently valuable in adopting an ironic worldview*, and Jeremy/Jeffrey is all, *the value is having a critical stance, man*, and Cam says, *that kind of stance can get pretty totalizing and circular pretty quickly*, and Jeremy/Jeffrey's like, *well otherwise you're just a pawn to like, your feelings*, at which Cam slouches dramatically, deflated. He seems tired and somehow sad, exhausted by some enormous towering thing, and Beau wonders if he isn't drunk, or maybe sun-sick from the long westward drive into the increasing end-of-day glare.

And now, brimming with the pleasure of what he already knows will be Cam's reaction when he comes up behind him, Beau sees that the point here, right now, right in this well-timed instant, is to rescue Cam from a conversation he's gotten himself into and doesn't want to be having, sweeping in with the effortless manner of those who have always had to shoulder the labour of constantly, in each new setting, *establishing* themselves. Beau has always affected social ease out of necessity, having never had anyone to do this for him, and knows that in this regard Cam defers to him, always. He'd had, even as a kid, the understanding that Cam would follow his lead, look to him for direction. It was in his silences, his whole body stillness as he watched Beau drawing trig figures for him in his notebook, rapt. A whole other kind of deference, contingent and shaped by—(what?)

"It's so much easier to be critical, and tear something down," Cam says, "than to create something new," and Jeremy/Jeffrey says, face twisted with scorn, "man, that is some sentimental bleeding heart *bull*shit," and Beau's M-quickened heart goes out to Cam, who will never, in his extreme sincerity, find it easy to live under the conditions most people take for granted, always hoping for something better, and more.

"Or maybe," Beau says, coming up behind Cam, hands on his tall friend's shoulders, squeezing before he can help himself, "it's that you can't see the value of something if you aren't fucking, open to looking."

Cam visibly jumps and turns, flushed all over. "*Beau*," he says.

He looks so disoriented Beau laughs without meaning to, unable to hold back. The sound has its own volition, a living thing he's been keeping in his throat that's just now managed to push its way out. A healthy, vibrating, feathered thing.

Cam loses all interest in Jeremy/Jeffrey. "What are you *on*?" he says.

Beau's pupils are the size of quarters, a fact he's ascertained from his reflection in a mirror mounted at the head of the second flight of narrow, carpeted, body-clogged stairs. With some difficulty he finds the baggie with its remaining pill and presses it into Cam's hand, covering it with both his own. The skin-on-skin contact is almost unbearable. He's filled with a sudden irrational urge to go swimming, the visceral memory of cool crisp water on warm skin. "Courtesy of Clifford," he says.

"Cliff gave you M?"

Beau laughs again. "He insisted you take one. Go ahead, don't fucking, disappoint him, huh."

Cam's face does a strange thing, like he might be really, really upset but hasn't yet decided if this is the case. He's in a funny mood, Beau thinks, the kind of desperate borderline half-mood he can get into when he's tired, or had a bad day teaching, or gets drunk too quick. With Cam it's impossible to tell where this kind of mood will go, and Beau will usually ease off and leave him alone to think it through, but now he feels a compulsion to force the issue. He's confident he can pull Cam through it, wants badly for Cam to join him on what he sees is the *other side* of some vast psychic divide. He's already gotten his roommate out of the house and into the city's distant west end. To get this drug into him, comparatively, should be effortless. Beau sometimes feels he can make Cam do anything at all, and thrills at the thought.

Not anything, he reminds himself. Come on, man.

"How do you feel?" Cam asks.

"I feel fucking, *amazing*," he says. "I feel like a fucking, brand new roll of fucking, Kodak Tri-X. Jesus, man. You have *no idea*."

Cam turns the baggie over in his hand, examining the pill. He looks so comically apprehensive Beau can't help but laugh. "Come on, Foucault," he says, placing his hand on Cam's neck, "don't be so fucking, serious about it, with those *excellent* glasses on. Whatever happened to empiricism, huh? You're not gonna leave me all *high* by my fucking, *self*, are you?"

Cam flushes hard, all the way down his neck, and Beau catches himself in the relentless teasing note his voice has begun to acquire. Are we fucking, *flirting*? I am absolutely not flirting with Cam. And then, surreally: Maybe *this* is what makes him so tense—that I flirt with him *all the fucking, time*. That I fucking, *flirt with Cam and I don't even know it*, whoa.

He shakes his head, trying to dispel the thought. "That guy really upset you, huh," he says. "What a dirty hipster." Jeremy/Jeffrey is long gone, presumably sneaking off to *have a sense of irony* somewhere else.

"That kind of cynicism just . . . kills me," Cam says, and pops back the gel cap, washing it down with a swig of beer. "Anyway, fuck it. Fuck that guy."

"You were so mad at him," Beau says, finding the wall for support. He leans back and looks at Cam, smiling in a stupid way he can't quite get a handle on. His body is making decisions for him, running the show. Beau hasn't yet decided what exactly the show is supposed to be about, only that it's happening, happening quick, and taking him along.

"Because he doesn't even know what he's talking about," Cam says, "only that it sounds smart and makes him feel good to be so knowingly dismissive. And he thinks it's lame that *I* care so much. It's like, why even live."

"Fucking, brighten up, Foucault. It's his loss." Beau sinks further into the wall, enjoying the way this slight motion draws Cam into his space as he leans in to compensate, decreasing the distance between them. There is no thought in these motions, he sees. These are the motions of people who spend enormous, habit-defining amounts of casual time together. "What sentimental bleeding heart bullshit were you telling him?"

"Come on man," Cam says. "I wish you wouldn't fuck with me like that. You know it's important to me."

"I know," he says, "I'm not," and sees this is true, that he wants nothing more than for Cam to share this information with him in this close space formed by the natural boundaries of the hastily painted wall, the bookcase, and their slouched bodies. "You know I always want to hear what you think. Even if seventy-five percent of it goes over my fucking, head."

Cam laughs, loosening. "Okay, okay." He closes his eyes, thinking. "I would have just said that sometimes you have to make an effort to be open to things, you know? To make an effort to see them differently, because some really tired, boring, ordinary thing you're ready to ironize and dismiss might actually be really strange, and brimming with potential, and—it's what you said, Beau. That you can't see it because you're just not open to looking."

Beau bristles with pleasure.

"I just think," Cam says, polishing off his beer, "that you don't have to engage in high-level cultural critique to find something profound—that the profound thing is already in the world itself, waiting just within reach, like if you tilt your head just right, you know?"

"Like a really amazing photo," Beau says, falling through the stunning geometry of a great internal ever-unfolding space, "that makes you see something you see everyday in a way you never saw it before," and Cam says, "yeah, just like that," and their eyes lock and Beau forgets a series of really important things, like that he's holding a drink that probably needs to stay upright.

"Hey," Cam says, tone softened, "where have you been, huh?"

"Just around the whole house like, forty-seven times, which took forever because I am really fucking, high."

"Doing what?"

"Looking for you," he says, "to give you this crazy drug."

Beau hasn't yet allowed himself to fully feel the magnitude of Cam sitting in a beanbag by his bed late into the night, soothing down his thoughts with long strings of abstract words, but now the drug delivers it to him all wrapped up and concentrated. He sees Cam driving him to chemo, coaxing him into swallowing toast, staying up with him in the early morning hours under bathroom fluorescents to rub his shoulders and smooth down his hair while he puked and wonders what (*what*) was he thinking, giving himself over to this all the time, ignoring his work, forgetting his sleep? Cam pulls at an unravelling sleeve, his intensity all split up for once, and Beau thinks: Here is the only person who has ever stuck it out with me, *taken care of me*. And never called it that, once. And never taken an out.

He doesn't know if it's the drug or what, but suddenly he's hyperaware of this field of warmth between them, his head brimming with it. *Cam and Beau*, this must be what Cliff means when he says *Cam and Beau*, like they're a unit or something, a tag name for a single cohesive thing. Like how it was in high school—are *Cam and Beau* coming? What do *Cam and Beau* think?

You're falling in love with him because he takes care of you, he loves you. He's the only person you really see, he thinks, and all at once fears what Cliff called *word vomit*, sees how this would be something he could fall into with ease. Since he's always fucking, talking, and not ever fucking, thinking. He wants to put his hands over his mouth but knows the gesture is cartoonish, absurd.

Cam says, "you okay, Beau?" and Beau says, "yeah, just high," and feels a wicked smile twisting up his face and knows he has to jettison the situation before he says something he can't take back. As in, *think* man, use your fucking, *head*.

"You want another drink?" he says. "I'm gonna get us beers." He doesn't wait for an answer, feeling the question on his back as he crosses the room, Cam's intensity amplified to a near-audible crackle, a live wire tensing before it jumps and snaps. By the fridge he bumps into a bunch of guys he hasn't seen since before he got sick, which is now almost a whole year ago, and doesn't really make it back with the promised beers.

The next time Beau sees Cam he's dancing with Stacey, their bodies never quite touching, hovering just inches apart. He doesn't look like he's not enjoying himself. Stacey wears a shirt/dress that is too long to be one and too short to be the other over a pair of dark patterned tights, doing this twist-shimmy thing that involves tossing her head back every few moves. Her hair frizzes in the room's wet air, curling tendrils sticking to her temples where he can just make out the damp shimmer of sweat. Cam is looking good, really good, and Beau is suddenly aware of his body, its height and angle and the easy way his clothes sit on his lean frame, limbs all loosened with the M. He doesn't think he's seen Cam so loose, ever. His neck bends (*slopes*) toward Stace, who is nearly a head shorter and stretches out to meet him, her whole body involved in the motion. They crack up and yell at each other over the music, which is Blondie, the one about love being so confusing, and Cam's sleeve has made its way down his arm once more where Stace fixes it for him, neither of them stopping the complimentary back-and-forth, give-and-take motion of which their bodily interaction is composed.

That's a lot of tension, Beau thinks, for a situation where there's supposed to be *nothing between me and Stacey, Beau, nothing*. And wonders again if he wasn't right, if there isn't something going on after all that Cam just doesn't want to talk about with him because—what? Because he knows. Because of how you were at the cottage, and now he has seen your true heart.

Will you really not tell me?

He leans into the granite countertop, turned away from all conversation and the whooping behind him, absorbed by Cam, and his glasses, and how they slip down his nose, and the way his watch hangs off his wrist as he reaches up to fix them in a move he must not even notice as his knees bend slightly, just so. Beau bites at the skin around his thumb and thinks, it's true, so then it's true. That you walk around and don't even know your own desire.

"Stare any harder and your eyes are gonna fall out of your skull, bud." Cliff is beside him, arms crossed on the counter to support his weight, one elbow resting in a spill of what smells like raspberry Smirnoff. He seems not to notice.

"Cliff," he says, and feels like there might be more, but there isn't.

"They look good together, hey."

"Yeah. They should date."

"Oh yeah?"

"They could talk about biopolitics and Nietzsche's sign chain and affect and Foucault and the empty signifier and whatever fucking, else."

"Oh, *hey. Hey*, are you *jealous?*" Cliff looks at him incredulously, tucking long strands of increasingly greasy hair behind his ears. "I *knew it!*" He makes a frenzied gesture that is something between a fist pump and a series of intense pointing jabs. "Oh, I fucking *knew it!* Larky is *jealous.*"

Beau flushes deep, which is not something he's used to doing and with the drug heating the blood in his face feels incredibly dire. "What do you mean, you *knew it?*"

"I was so right about you."

"About me what?"

"About you and Cam."

"Me and Cam what?"

"You fucking *know* what. *Larky.* Come *on*, man." He notices the vodka spill and cringes, pushing Beau over to a drier section of countertop where he pops open a gel cap, emptying it into a perfect pile of crumbly brown crystals. "It's M time, my friend. You want a line?"

"Sure," Beau says. "I'll have a line, yeah, fuck."

Cliff pulls out what looks like Cam's actual fucking, business card (B.A., M.A., Ph.D. Candidate, Department of Critical Theory) complete with the University's crest, using it to divide the pile into two fat lines. Only some of the finer crystals become smudged into the counter's surface.

"This is gonna be so gross."

"You know it," Cliff says, and vacuums up his portion. "Mm-*mm.*" He sniffles, tipping his head back and wincing. "Disgusting."

Beau takes the bill from him and inhales, the burn exploding behind his eyes. "*Jesus*, man. Ugh." The rush is immediate, lighting up sparks in his head.

"Whatta you think of these drugs?"

"I think they're wonderful."

"My thought exactly." Cliff swigs back his beer, wreathed in a fuzz of contentment. He puts it down on the counter and lets one hand stray to the lanyard in his pocket, pulling on it to jingle his keys. "So," he says. "What are you going to do?"

"About what?"

"You know what."

"Just be straight with me, man."

"Well don't just *stand* there, hey."

"What can I do, Cliff? Really."

"Go tell him what you're thinking."

They look at each other, stand and trace each other's faces in a way too focused for ordinary interaction, and Beau realizes he kind of loves Cliff, sees the two of them chilling on the dock and talking, feet wrinkled from too much time in the water, remembers them playing badminton, wasted, the whole thing made difficult without the formality of a net, and canoeing, which between him and Cliff and all the alcohol had them going in circles. There is a great deal of warmth spreading through his limbs and he suddenly feels that if he's going to say this to anyone, it's going to be Cliff, that somehow Cliff will understand—Cliff, who didn't ask weird questions or give him a hard time about the illness and his year-long disappearance and about not being told.

"It's just been the worst year of my life, man," he says. "And I grew up in fucking, foster homes, you know?"

Cliff nods.

"I was just so sick all the time, and he took such good care of me, and he was always there, and I just—I don't know. He put his whole life on hold for me. I'd never seen anything like that." He looks down at his shoes, overwhelmed. Heat flushes the back of his neck. "But I mean, my head's not been right, since February. I can't really trust myself, how I feel."

"What do you mean?"

"I feel like I'm not remembering things right. Or just not remembering, at all. Since I fucked up my head."

Cliff cocks his head and sniffs, riveted. "Like what?"

"Like—this is going to sound weird, but I want you to be real with me. Did Cam and I ever have like—a thing?"

His eyebrows go up so high Beau almost laughs. "A thing?"

"Man, you know what I mean. Did we ever fucking, you know, like—" he can't say this, how can he say this? Cliff will make fun of him for the rest of his life. Larky, you got a *thing*? How's that *thing* going? I think Cam forgot his *thing* at my place, you might wanna come pick it up, hey. He drops his hands. "Ugh. Forget it."

"Hey, Larky, hold on. I know what you're asking."

"Yeah?"

"Yeah. I don't think so. I think he would have definitely mentioned it."

"Why would he mention it?"

"Because, man, this is Cam's like," he reaches for the word, snapping his fingers, "*structuring* preoccupation."

Beau feels his heart thump in a sickening, arrhythmic way. *Don't you see the way he looks at you.*

"Isn't it obvious?"

"That what?" (*what*). The conversation has become its own thing, something other than he intended. He's not sure if he wants Cliff to go on.

Cliff breathes out all at once in a quick, exasperated way. "Beau, Cam is so in love with you he doesn't know which way is up. Wake up and smell the coffee, hey."

He wants to sit down but there is nowhere to do this, so he leans on the counter instead, shaking his head. "That's not true. People have been telling me that since fucking, forever. Look at him with Stace."

"Man, Cam is not into Stacey, he's on emm-dee-emm-*eh*." He laughs wildly, without reservation, like he might be unable to stop. A few members of the group squished in directly behind them turn around. "Dude, there really is something wrong with your head."

Beau's mouth is incredibly dry, like at the hospital, and he clicks his tongue against its roof. He's full of sick excitement. "How can you know that?"

"Because he told me."

He runs his hands over his face, trying to make sure it's still there. His pulse is all out of time, like it's unsure if it should keep pace or speed up, deliberating between the two. Or slow down, maybe. Maybe he would like it to slow down.

"You okay, Larky?"

"I'm good, I'm good. Fuck." He knocks back the remainder of his beer, all warm foam, and nearly gags. Across the room Cam shakes down a near-finished joint like a sugar packet, Stacey's hand resting on his shoulder in an assertion of obvious interest. Beau looks at him and cannot reconcile this fact, shared with him now by two separate people, with Cam's lanky frame slumped against a bookcase, his satisfaction with the quality of the roll, Stacey's hand moving to his chest.

"You better not be fucking with me," he says.

"Of course not, hey." Cliff is wearing a loose tank top imprinted with some kind of tarot card imagery Beau can't identify but which seems to him, in his intense highness, impossibly elaborate and beautiful. It involves a robed figure against a stunning yellow background, one hand raised to the sky and the other pointing to the earth, a horizontal eight (*the symbol for infinity*, he thinks, awed) suspended over his head. Floral growth in brilliant greens and reds crowds the frame, glowing with otherworldly warmth, an aura not of this place and all its own. It's only when Cliff stops talking that Beau realizes he's been zoning out, distracted, lost in the density of detail before him.

"Sorry, what?"

"Seriously man, are you okay?"

"It's just a lot," he says, "to take in." And then: "Are you sure?"

"Beau, I'm sure. Don't you see it?"

"I see it and I don't. I feel like I'm only seeing it because I want to. And why do I want to?"

"Because you love him, isn't it obvious you love him? Like what were you guys doing, at the cottage? You told me, '*I don't know what came over me*,' but you *do*. You're beside him all the time, touching him all the time, making him nuts. You're driving him crazy, Beau. Watching him like you do, like you did on the fucking dock for *hours*, man, *hours*. Asking him *who he was in love with* like you don't fucking know. Do you want him to say it to you? He's never gonna do that, man, and you're kidding yourself if you think you don't know what's going on. Watching you guys together is like, an exercise in fucking *self-restraint*, and I'm on way too many fucking drugs for that right now."

Beau laughs, a single stunned sound, all stilted astonishment. "Oh my god," he says.

Cliff slaps his back. "Here," he says, pulling a mostly depleted mickey from his back pocket. "Time for shots." It occurs to Beau that Cliff runs mainly on drug time rather than in relation to any real temporal system. He sees now that the figure on Cliff's shirt is holding a wand, definitely a wand raised to the limitless expanse of saffron sky. In its features he reads authority, self-possession. Confidence.

Cliff takes a swig straight from the bottle and hands it off to Beau, who discovers, empirically, that it's full of gin. With his palms sweating and the drug flooding his brain he can hardly taste the liquor. He pushes his hair back from his forehead where it's so damp it almost stays back by itself, like he's gelled it. He wants badly to be beside Cam, to displace Stacey and her possessive hand, like she owns him, like he's an object that can be picked up and put in someone's bag. But isn't that what you want, he thinks. Deep down. You're afraid of him going away. You want him to yourself. He shakes the thought and downs another swig, grimacing.

"Larky, you seriously have to capitalize on that shit. It's so deadly romantic, it fucking melts me right down, hey. People go their whole lives looking to find something like that. It's a total fucking waste."

They've both turned to the room to watch Cam, who leans in for Stacey to light his joint. They look intimate, conspiratory, the flame illuminating their faces for a brief moment of focused pause. He puffs several times and exhales a cloud of smoke that appears, from their vantage point, tremendous, collecting near the ceiling and refusing to dissipate. "That's my best friend in the whole world," Beau says. "My absolute best friend."

"I know, man."

"That's an entire lifetime of friendship, right there. Standing there."

"Larky, I know."

"So you better be one hundred and forty fucking, percent sure about what you're saying to me."

"Two hundred, hey."

Cam feels them looking and turns, his eyes meeting Beau's in a sudden and direct way that is the affective equivalent of a high voltage current, not pleasant but jarring, like an unexpected kick to the stomach. Beau's insides shrink in a grip of intense cold and he understands that he is, above all, afraid. Stacey follows his gaze and they begin making their way over, weaving through the tightly packed space.

"Oh-*ho*," Cliff says, grinning wide, "speak of the devil, hey."

"I'm gonna go," Beau says, tipping back the mickey harder than necessary and garnering only a small gulp. He has somehow managed to finish the bottle by himself.

"Go *where*? You can't go *home*, man."

"Not home, I just gotta—" he places the bottle on the counter, double-checking to see if it really is, unbelievably, empty. "I just need a minute. I can't—Cliff, I can't."

"Larky, come on!"

He shakes his head. "I'll come back, but I fucking, can't. I can't be here right now."

"All right, all right. Fuck, eh."

He feels Cliff squeeze his shoulder but he's already intent on the hall and getting into its darkened, crowded corridor where he will be sheltered from the rapidly developing situation by dozens of unfamiliar bodies and their mundane, inconsequential, passing talk. As he turns the corner he catches Cam saying, *is he okay?* and Cliff going, *he's fucking high, man, give him a break*, and Cam going, *I can't believe you gave him M*, to which Cliff responds, *he's a big boy, he can handle it*. There is laughter and what must be his hand clapping Cam's back.

Cam's voice is overwhelming, a fantastic tender thing with its gravelly edge sharpened by years and years of smoking culminating in this moment of forming words while holding back a lungful of high-grade pot. Beau leans against the wall and closes his eyes, heart beating too quickly. Fuck, he thinks, what the *fuck*. He runs his hand over the back of his neck and slicks away sweat. He is wet and nervous and elated all at once, so turned on he can hardly take it in his suddenly tight black Levi's with all these people around. Indecently, uncontrollably, teeth-grindingly aroused. Charged to the degree that even contact with the wall seems erotic. Stifled, warm all over, the entire surface of his body suddenly open, tense, ready to go. Hungry, unable to think of anything else though he tries, is trying so hard. Pent up, swollen, a sick heat gathering in his gut.

He zeroes in on the memory of cold pool water closing over him as he breaks its surface, shocked to attention.

The bathroom line is its own party, a thing stretching nearly all the way down the hall. Topics of conversation include how long the current user has been inside, whether they're going to hurry the fuck up, and who's got a bill or card ready. It's mostly a fucking, coke line, Beau thinks, joining in and pressing himself to the wall, knowing this could take a while. A girl in front of him complains to her friend that she has to fucking pee. People push past on the right side of the corridor, impatient with the scattered, wandering quality of the queue. Every couple minutes the door swings open, groups of chattering people spilling out, touching each other's arms. *Could they fucking do that somewhere else*, the girl in front of him says, turning to him, and he shrugs. He takes in the size of her pupils and imagines his own must be dilated to their physical limit.

If Beau had to describe the effect of the M, he would say that it makes everything feel really fucking, intense. He knows he should be wasted but feels alert instead, the liquor warming his gut in a distant, unimportant way, the sensation paling in comparison with his whole-body reaction to Cam's smoke-hardened voice, a thing he wants to wrap himself in. The thought of Cam's lips closed around the joint induces a head-to-toe rush he shuts his eyes against, leaning hard on the wall. He stares up at the ceiling, biting his lip, and when he looks back down finds he's next in line and the door is swinging, mercifully, open.

"Hey!" the girl says, emerging. "Did *you* wanna join me for a quick line?"

Beau shakes his head, floored with the drug he can still feel deep in his nose, on what must be the outer surface of his brain, and pulls the door shut behind him. He slides the lock and leans hard on the sink, making himself breathe. Breathe, man, breathe. With the noise outside muffled and the thump of the bass reduced to vibrations travelling from the sink into his forearms he feels calmed, this closed-off space with only his lone body to occupy it constituting a physical moment of pause.

There are smeared grainy lines of coke all over the sink's flat surfaces, and the mirror is speckled with what look like the remnants of someone sneezing, hard. Parts of its silver backing have rusted away near the edges of the frame. Beau turns on the tap and splashes lukewarm water on his face, rubbing his eyes. He looks flushed, alive, disoriented. Really fucking, high. He never thought his eyes were so blue but now sees how bright they are, how vivid and pure. It is startling, like looking at someone else.

He thinks of Cam again, involuntarily, of his rolled sleeves coming loose, his long relaxed body, the way he holds his drink down low and only by the neck when he laughs, other hand buried deep in his pocket. There must be holes in his pockets from how much he keeps his hands in there.

Cam, oh—he thinks of these things and wants to scream. There is a weird energy in him, and he can't think of any way to get it out. He turns on the tap all the way, hoping the water will get colder as it runs. You need to calm down, he tells himself. Fucking, cut it out. He cups his palm under the stream and swallows a few mouthfuls of almost-cold water, realizing how thirsty he is only with the feel of liquid in his parched mouth.

Beau tries to imagine what he will do when he sees Cam and can't, staring down a complete blank. The drug makes him feel reckless, outside of himself, and he is afraid. His heart beats quickly, fluttering at his throat, threatening to make its way out.

Because you love him, isn't obvious you love him? Beside him all the time, touching him all the time, making him nuts. Driving him crazy, Beau. He sees Cliff's wide shining eyes and motor mouth and wild impatient gestures and isn't sure if he wants to kill him or kiss him.

Someone outside is hammering on the door with their palm, saying, *fuck, hurry up in there huh* to a lot of laughter. "Hold on, hold on," he says, palming another few sips before turning off the tap. He wipes his face on his sleeve and unbolts the door, pulling it open to find Cam leaning on the doorframe, sagging with radical impatience. Beau's pulse skips as he feels his face change, mirroring Cam's in mutual recognition.

"*Beau.*" Cam puts his hands on his shoulders and steps inside. Beau reaches behind him to swing the door shut, bolting it without thought. They burst into laughter, bending over themselves as people outside groan in complaint, rapping on the wood in a chorus of *hey, come on*s and *what the hell*s.

"Oh my god, I was looking for you. Are you okay? You didn't look so good, earlier. Shit, I gotta piss so bad, hold on." He turns and Beau listens to the stream hitting water, watching Cam's head tip back in release. He thinks Cam must be incredibly wasted, to be so uninhibited. He leans into the wall as he stands over the toilet, supporting himself with one long arm pressed to the tile above his head.

"How can you even think about doing that right now," Beau says, understanding for the first time how it might be that people die of dehydration on amphetamines. He's glad Cam has his back turned because he's all out of hand, flushed and overwhelmed by his roommate's presence in this tiny bathroom, the warmth between them palpable, transmitted through the air like static and thick as glue.

"Because I just drank a fucking keg of dirty hipster beer washed down with about a litre of our good friend Jack Daniels. Fucking jay-*dee*," he says, and bursts out laughing, steadying himself against the wall. He's in an incredible mood, good humour throwing itself from him and into everything he touches.

"Holy shit, Cam," Beau says, collapsing against the sink in a fit of giggles. "What the *fuck*."

"I know," Cam says, "I'm actually gonna die. Like, actually." He flushes the toilet and turns, doing up his fly. "This drug is so *nuts*."

"Fucking, unbelievable. You can hardly feel yourself drinking."

Cam turns on the sink with a single move of his wrist and stares at the stream for a moment, mesmerized. "Oh, I can feel it all right. I feel it *aaall* in my *body*." He shivers visibly and shakes his head fast, like he's trying to rid himself of something sticky.

The bathroom is small, and with Cam washing his hands Beau has no choice but to press himself into the door, doing his best to avoid any actual physical contact, a thing he feels, from the heat of Cam's thigh almost brushing his, might be irrevocable, life-ending. Like stepping into a ditch whose bottom you can't see and realizing it is actually far deeper than you initially thought. His heart is going so loud he's sure Cam must be able to hear it, even with the water on.

"Hey," Cam says, flicking off the tap, "how are you doing? It didn't make you feel sick, did it?"

The intensity of Cam's full attention on him is like nothing else under the sun. Cam's face is placid, his eyes eager, deep, warm, liquid chestnut flecked with gold. "No," he says, dry mouth clicking, "no, I feel fine. I've never been so high, ever."

"How much did he give you?"

"A hit and a line."

"And a *line?*"

"Cam," he says, laughing, "don't worry, don't worry so much about me, huh." He places his hand on Cam's arm, just above the elbow, meaning for the contact to be brief, reflexive, casual. The thrill is beyond anything he's ever felt, physically, with another person, and he finds he can't remove himself, doesn't want to. "What you need to worry about are your fucking, sleeves."

"Oh yeah?" He sounds like he's been running and doesn't want to show it. They are so close Beau can smell the whisky and pot on Cam's breath, rugged sweet. Someone outside pounds on the door and they both ignore the sound, a vague removed thing travelling from twenty-five thousand miles away.

"This is a serious situation," Beau says, finding the edges of the unravelled sleeve, the plaid material all scrunched and crumpled and damp from being re-rolled several times, "and obviously not something they cover extensively in the Ph.D."

"Not really, no."

"Here." He folds the sleeve over several times, careful, drawing it out, unhinged by the feel of his fingers on Cam's flushed bare skin. Cam holds deathly still, like he's afraid to breathe, watching in awe, reverence, total deferral. He seems to be shaking, though this might Beau's perception of his own hum, a thing originating deep within and spreading through his limbs unwilled. He tucks in the sleeve's corners and gives the whole thing a tug, demonstrating its new stability. His hand lingers, reluctant to break contact.

"I guess I better do a line then, huh," Cam says, pulling his arm away to dig through his pocket. "Since you're all high." It is like shorting a circuit or hitting a switch.

"Yeah, do it," Beau says, gathering himself, relieved and not. He watches Cam crush the leftover crystals through the bag, pressing them between his thumb and forefinger with a satisfying crackle as he surveys the mottled surface of the sink. Hairs and small particles of things Beau doesn't want to know the exact composition of litter the porcelain, encrusted within dried coke smears and pools of soap residue.

Cam makes a face. "That's disgusting, man," he says, and Beau holds out his hand automatically, in a move requiring no planning or forethought. There is no discussion as Cam empties the bag onto the skin just above his knuckles and they work at arranging the mess into a rough line. The banging on the other side of the door grows more persistent and Beau bangs back, yelling, "fucking, hold on a sec," which inspires a series of profanities from whoever has been waiting for what is now, he realizes, quite a while.

"Jesus," Cam says, rolling up a bill, "I feel like I have no sense of time," and Beau nods, lost in the curve of Cam's nose and resonance of his voice, now low and raspy, like he's preparing to share a secret between just them, just the two of them, Cam and Beau. The friction in his jeans has become nearly unbearable. He holds up his hand and Cam leans over it, steadying Beau's wrist between his palms before inhaling as much of the M as he can manage in one go. He tips his head back, sniffing. A few crystals remain grouped in clumps on Beau's skin, and he offers these to Cam, questioning.

"No, no," Cam says, "you," and so he does, gathering them up in a single lick. The powder is bitter and makes him gag, and for a bad moment, hunched low over the sink, he thinks he might actually vomit. Cam's hand is on his back, planted solid between his shoulder blades as it has been so many times these past months. "Beau," he says, and no more, though the silence that follows is laden with all things unsaid.

Beau turns and they look at each other, eyes becoming tangled, impossible to separate. Cam is totally present, in it, plugged in, his intensity and openness channeled into the quality Beau immediately recognizes as *being about to speak*. Like in the photo, the one he couldn't stop studying, keeping it pinned in the darkroom to look at as he developed film the past few months, blowing smoke over its surface and thinking, always, *but what does it mean*. "Just tell me," he says, before he can stop himself. "You can tell me."

Cam lowers his gaze but doesn't blush. "Beau, I—"

The hammering grows louder and more determined, shaking the door in its frame. "Fucking, *wait*," Beau yells, "*fuck*." He turns back to Cam, feverish. "Say it, say the thing you're always trying to say."

Cam shakes his head. "Don't ask me that. It can't be unsaid."

"Say it. I want you to say it to me."

"Don't you already know?"

"Why are you so afraid to tell me?" He takes Cam's hand in his own and presses it to his chest, laying it flat over his rapidly beating heart. Cam shivers, visibly taken aback, reaching with his free hand to steady himself against the sink where he knocks over the loose-lidded soap dispenser, sending viscous pink ribbons of

Dial down the basin's sides. He seems not to notice. "Tell me, Cam. I'm asking you, this is me asking you."

Now Cam flushes, deeply and thoroughly, and Beau sees it in him, the whole enormous dizzying thing in its duration and gravity and scope. "Are you sure?" he says. "Beau, you need to be sure, because I'm on drugs and I will, I'll say it and then I won't be able to take it back."

"I'm sure."

"Jesus, Beau." He looks like he might pass out. "How can I say this to you?"

"Cam, I'm asking you. I'm sure." Someone outside is jiggling the doorknob and cursing. Beau slams his hand against the door, just once, hard, and the motion stops. He keeps his other hand over Cam's, where he can just make out the warm palpitation of its frenzied pulse. "Remember at the cottage, you said there was something we had to talk about, that had been on your mind for months. You said you would tell me. And I kept asking you," swallowing down the memory, "who you were in love with."

"Beau," Cam says, as if it pained him. "It's you I'm in love with. It's all I think about. It's all I can ever think."

Something vital clenches in his chest, giving way to overpowering sadness of a kind he's never in all his life's haunted nights known. So it's true, then, so then it's true.

"Can't you tell?" Cam says, and though he speaks softly it's anguished, the root of that broken hand recklessness seeping through, its magnitude total and frightening. All at once Beau sees that he really would do anything, anything at all, and not think twice, and that somewhere in this is a profound loss of self. He tightens his grip on Cam's hand and realizes Cam is shaking, trembling all over like he's cold.

"Hey," he says, "hey, come on. Cam. I feel it too, don't you know I feel it too?"

He's not entirely sure what happens—it has something to do with the crest of liquid warmth breaking at the peak of his skull and their proximity in the tight space and the change in Cam's features, like huge internal pieces are falling into place somewhere far within—but somehow Cam's mouth is on his and his hands are in Cam's hair and he finds himself backing Cam into the wall, pressing hard against his cords. The friction is incredible, unlike anything he could have imagined. Cam makes a small sound in his throat, stiffens, dissolves. His mouth is firm and tastes of Jack Daniels, pot, long-stifled anticipation.

"Do it again," Cam says, and Beau does, this time slower, holding Cam's face in his hands, stroking his temples. Cam slouches down against the tile to meet him, spreading his legs out, and Beau presses into him, overwhelmed by their proximity. It's hard for him to pace himself.

The door jumps in its frame, ricocheting from a series of rapid knocks. "Holy fuck, eh, hurry it up in there! Other people have drugs they need to do too!"

They pull apart, jarred by the sound, breathing hard. "Oh my god," Cam says, running a hand back through his hair. His glasses sit crooked, fogging in the corners. He makes no move to fix them.

Beau steadies himself against the wall and is glad it is there, isn't sure he could stay standing without its assistance. His mouth is wet and mashed up and he wipes at it with his arm, dizzy. His legs feel distant and weak, no longer a part of him. He buzzes all over. "Shit, Cam," he says. "Jesus Christ."

Cam meets his eyes and bursts out laughing loudly, crazily, bending over himself. He leans on the sink for support and howls, holding his sides, barely able to stand.

"What?" Beau says, stunned.

"I can't," he tries to look at Beau but cracks up again, wild, "I can't believe that just ha—ha—ha—" stopping to catch his breath, "happened." He wipes at his eyes under his glasses, pressing his fingers into them, and Beau sees he's relieved, so relieved it's debilitating.

"We should probably get out of here," Beau says, so matter of fact it sets him off and gets Cam going again and now they're both laughing, unable to stop, hanging onto the sink and each other's shoulders. "I mean, it's only been like an hour," he manages, unbolting the door. As soon as the bolt is off it flies open, the person on the other side nearly falling into them, driven by the full force of his weight.

"What the *fuck*," he says, and they see it's Cliff, green headband slicking his hair down flat except where it's begun to curl up at the ends in the suck of humidity enveloping the hall. He takes them in and his face changes, blooming with surprise. "Whoa-ho, look at Cam and Beau all high making out in the fucking bathroom, hey!"

They all laugh, losing it, sagging on the doorframe. The three girls standing behind Cliff push past them, sighing theatrically and flipping their hair. The door slams shut.

"You were, weren't you! You were seriously making out. I fucking told you!" Cliff says, and it's not clear which of them he's talking to.

Beau ignores this, grinning stupidly, and takes Cam, who is limp and stoned and willing, by the hand, leading him down the stairs. Their trainwrecked faces say it all.

"You're welcome!" Cliff yells after them. "You hear? Thank me later, hey!"

Outside it is raining, the porch packed with milling bodies but the yard nearly deserted, populated with only a few hardcore stragglers holding shirts over their heads or pulling on hoods against the steady drizzle. They squeeze their way past to sit on the steps, watching people stumbling by on their way in and out of the house. Beau finds the sound of the rain soothing, water pattering on wood in a rhythm old as time. His heart beats in his throat, and he thinks couldn't speak if he wanted to. He hasn't let go of Cam's warm pulsing hand.

"How long?" he manages.

"Always. Since I can remember."

"Shit, Cam." That huge sadness rounds the corner, soaking him. Of course. How else? "We never did anything like that before?"

"Anything like what."

"Like that, in there."

"No," Cam says, and Beau can tell from the click in his throat that his mouth is very dry. "Never."

"Why didn't you tell me? You should have said something."

"How could I? You were so sick. I was scared. I was starting to think I'd rather not know."

Have you ever wanted to tell someone something so bad you can't even find the words?

The whole thing is a kaleidoscope, pieces rearranging into stunning new formations, disparate fragments taking on new meaning by virtue of juxtaposition:

Feeling Cam sitting at the kitchen table watching him cook and turning from the stove to find he looked hungry, but not in any ordinary way. Like he was somehow starved internally, in his soul. Perpetually flushed and reluctant to make any kind of contact, like he wasn't sure if it was okay. Getting so angry about Stacey before it was obvious Stacey wasn't interested in what he thought she was. And even before all that, the younger Cam holding so still to watch with complete awe as Beau leaned in, close enough to touch heads, manipulating equations and checking his speed so Cam could follow along in the heavy math book balanced on their knees. Saying, but with the negative exponent you have to invert the fraction first, right, while Cam nodded and chewed the inside of his cheek, lost.

So bad you're afraid there are no words for what you want to say.

It's a stereogram he's been staring at for ages and only now sees, the obviousness of the image stupefying, blinding. How could he not have seen it, before? In his constant inwardness. In his stubborn refusal to speak.

You're a good guy, Beau, but you don't notice shit.

It occurs to him that on some level he did know, did and willed himself not to, and is sickened. Because he was ill, and had no one. Because he was afraid. He stares down at his knees, fighting off the dark crackle on the horizon of things. You'll never live this down, he tells himself. Not if you live to be a hundred.

"I'm so sorry, Cam. I'm so, so sorry. For everything. I've been so awful to you. Taking you for granted, leading you on all the time."

"Beau, you couldn't have known. I tried so hard to hide it."

"You gave up so much for me," he says, suddenly anguished, "you put your whole life on hold and I just—I'll never live it down, Cam. After trying so hard not to be selfish, I've put you through so much. Without even realizing, without even thinking."

There is a pause, a velvet night silence bookended by the quiet rush of rain and roar of the party spilling from the confines of the house. Someone on the deck is making a big deal about losing their last cigarette.

"Listen," Cam says, taking Beau's face in his hands, "I would have done those things for you anyway, no matter what. Because I love you like I can't even say. Do you understand?"

Beau nods, overwhelmed.

"Hey, don't cry. Beau."

He wipes at his eyes, trying to get a hold of himself. He doesn't know if it's the drug or what. "I'm gonna make it up to you. You need to know."

"I know." Cam stands, pulling Beau with him. "Things are going to be so great for us, Beau Larky. You'll see."

They walk home in the late night that is almost morning, the world around them steaming. The sidewalks are wet and the leaves glossy, everything blooming in the fragrant air. Beau can't stop thinking about the deck, so long ago now, and of his strange, undeniable desire to stay and talk to this lanky stranger while his friends played flip cup inside. There is a perfect symmetry in this, the inherent balance of the world's primordial machinery grinding just beneath the surface of things.

Cam walks with his hands in his pockets, staring up at the gauzy halos shrouding the streetlamps, avoiding puddles instinctually, by feel. He seems taller, his shoulders somehow straightened. Beau links his arm through Cam's and sees how this small gesture makes his friend happy in a simple, total way, though he is silent and doesn't break his stride. And how he himself likes it, walking arm in arm with Cam through the slicked-down July night, taking in the settling city, only the occasional weaving cyclist splashing past. Everything is painfully alive, and his chest aches with gladness.

It is late, but not so late that birds can be heard from the trees or the rose tint of dawn seen over rooftops in the distant east. Not late enough to be sickened by the hour or cowed by the ominous threat of impending sun. With the M slowing its surge through his system Beau is euphoric but calm, coming down into a state of pure placid gratitude, a complete thankfulness for the fact of being and the miracle of existing in this moment. Of getting to see Cam like this, silent and steady, vast stretches of contentment unfolding in the space between them, punctuated by the rhythm of their steps on wet pavement. The drug's fervent edge has dissolved, leaving him languid and full, at one with time and its ceaseless blank flow. He feels his concord with larger things in the easy fluid throb of his pulse in his fingertips.

At home the only light left on is the small reading lamp in Cam's room, and he keeps it that way, stilling Cam's reach for the hallway switch with his hand. They splay out on Cam's bed, unrushed, all the heat and friction of the tight bathroom and its fervid exchange diminished, transformed. Cam takes off his glasses and rolls a joint, grinding the weed with his fingers and spreading it out in the spine of that little grey book with the soft cover he loves so much. When he's finished he lies back on the pillows, folding his hands behind his head. Beau stretches out on top of him, propped on his chest, and they take turns smoking, passing the moist hits back and forth directly between their mouths. Beau follows Cam's heartbeat through his shirt and smooths back his humidity-curled hair. They hardly talk.

There is something sacred about this, and they feel it instinctively between them. It is as if moving too quickly would break the scene, jarring it into something other and less. When Beau finally presses him into the sheets Cam stiffens, searching. Are you sure, he says, because you need to be sure. Beau's hands are under his shirt, held flat to Cam's chest where he can feel his roommate trembling in a great internal way.

He's waited so long for this, Beau thinks, and now he's afraid.

Hey, he says, let me do it. I'm sure.

Beau.

Let me do it for you. I want to.

Cam lies back and exhales and closes his eyes and Beau says, hey, hey, look at me, huh. You gotta relax. Stroking his hands over Cam's stomach, down to his belt and just beneath the elastic of his boxers until he loosens, saying, all the while, work with me on this, huh, help me out. He savours the way Cam looks at him—captivated, reverent, in total deferral. He would let me do anything, he thinks, anything at all, and endures a thrill of boundless anticipation.

5. The Letter

I-love-you is active. It affirms itself as force—against other forces. Which ones? The thousand forces of the world, which are, all of them, disparaging forces (science, *doxa*, reality, reason, etc.). Or again: against language.

Roland Barthes, *A Lover's Discourse*

All is well. The days flow by in an endless melding procession of work and pot and sex. Beau can't get enough of the look on Cam's face when he surprises him in the shower, slipping in to interrupt the meditative morning act of lathering shampoo into hair. In the mornings Cam is slow and syrupy with sleep, half unconscious even as he stands. Beau loves his long body curled up in the stored warmth of the sheets, its length dense and immobile. He wraps himself around Cam and nestles into his back, resting his face in the hollow of his neck. Cam's hair is damp and thick and he makes small contented sounds in his throat, reaching to silence his alarm.

Beau cooks every chance he gets, standing at the counter stoned and absorbed in the process of transforming ingredients into elaborate meals he's worked out in his head during the monotony of ten-hour shifts. He grows confident and makes dishes that are more and more complex, experimenting with techniques he's never tried—julienning, parboiling, deglazing. On the balcony he plants an herb garden, basil and parsley and oregano and cilantro sitting in their planters in a neat row. After work he walks through the market, cutting down the bright sun-drenched streets to pick up ingredients, octopus and limes and chilies and heads of garlic the size of baseballs. Sometimes Cam meets him on campus and they go together, enjoying the simple symmetry of walking side by side with their bags on, Cam bracing his hands on the shoulder straps of his backpack and Beau's messenger bag bouncing on his hip. They sort through enormous stands of fruit and buy spices by weight from shops where the owners know them by name.

Beau takes more photos than he has in his entire life, savouring the feel of the old Nikon around his neck, its worn strap and boxy shape and firm weight on his chest. He works it purely by feel, muscle memory deposited in his fingers telling him how much focus he needs, whether to go down an f-stop or stay, contented, right where he is. Rolls of film collect in his pockets, little spools of potential waiting to be transformed. If he is in the right kind of mood, and the light of the evening turns just so, Beau will take Cam's hand in his, holding it as they cut through Trinity-Bellwoods' rolling green expanse on their way home.

In the evenings they get high and touch each other in all the ways they can think of for as long as they can stand, thrilled with the newness of the arrangement and its sprawling possibility. Beau can't get over the look on Cam's face, all gratitude and surprise and total abandon. It intoxicates him to bring his friend such pleasure. He eases Cam back onto the couch with his body, pressing into him and giving instructions: lie down, don't move. He kisses Cam's hands and undoes his fly and when Cam's exhale verges on a whimper says, don't make a fucking, sound.

Cam does everything exactly as instructed.

They start having actual sex, the full deal, coaching each other through it. Neither has ever done anything like this before. Relax, Beau says, it's not gonna work if you don't relax, and Cam says, slow, okay, go slow. It is more intense than he could have imagined, and this injunction is difficult to follow. At times he rushes, losing himself in the transaction and coming to breathing hard, face pressed to the shower wall or Cam's sweating back, heartbeat echoing in his ears. He can't pace himself though he tries.

Cam, on the other hand, moves slowly, carefully, every movement planned out and thought through with what Beau imagines must be incredible restraint, for this man who has waited so long. The drawn-out rhythm of it drives Beau nuts, makes him greedy, insatiable. It's like being fourteen all over again. "Ugh," he says, "come on," and feels Cam shake his head against his neck where he will wake, tomorrow, with a ripe red mark left by his roommate's teeth. When he comes it's debilitating, earth-ending, and he lies there emptied, his capacity for thought erased. He's never had sex like that before. He now sees the difference it makes when the other person is focused and careful and as desperate as you; how it changes the feel of the thing into an interaction as intricate and complex as a conversation. How it matters when someone knows your body—when your best friend who has seen your body so many times works to learn its layout by feel.

Near the end of August he starts to get incredible blinding headaches, debilitating tides of liquid static that turn the whole world to light and noise. He stops in the kitchen and sits at the table, bowing his head to its cool plastic surface where he rests his temple and breathes, trying to absorb some of the material's mute solid quality into himself. He is strangely light sensitive, the bright rectangle of his laptop screen burning through his retinas into what feels like the very surface of his brain. He lies facedown in his bedroom in the dark and fights nausea brought on by enormous pulsing stabs behind his eyes, imagining electric signals ricocheting around the inside of his skull, sticking in the depressions made when his head got knocked around and all that soft tissue bruised on contact with bone. In his mind these areas are permanently blackened, dead.

The episodes (and they do feel to him like full-blown episodes, periods distinctly separate from and to the exclusion of daily life) overtake him unexpectedly, forcing him to brace against streetlamp posts, walls, benches. At moments like these, the world continuing, unbelievably, its roar and motion around him, as if everything was the same as ever, he feels that his head will split, cracking in two like a dropped melon. Beau presses a hand to his forehead, palm flat, as if this could keep the needling swelling sensation contained.

When Cam isn't around he allows himself to take four Percocets and pour a bath he doesn't move from for hours, afraid to agitate and stir up the sleeping feeling. Tilting his head in any direction is agony. In the tub he submerges himself entirely, retreating beneath the water and its lack of concrete sound. Distant wavering acoustics soothe his thoughts into simple movements void of form and definite content. He closes his eyes and marvels at the red splashes painting the undersides of his lids, afterimages that shift and bleed before fading from view. Silent explosions go off behind his retinas.

He comes up from his acoustic oblivion to Cam knocking, that old familiar sound, and knows he's been underwater too long, though with the percs units of time don't mean very much, or else stretch in unpredictable ways. *Beau, you good*, Cam says, and he calls back *yeah I'm fine*, recoiling from his own voice resounding in his head like fine pieces of tin skimming the inside of a steel drum.

In the episodes' deepest grip objects develop a bright fuzzy outline, doubling outside of themselves into spills of colour fragmenting his field of vision. He gets nauseous, the old feeling overwhelming not in its strength but in its force of corporeal memory, immediately casting him into a web of buried associations: waxed hospital floors, starched sheets, changing light, hollow suppressed hunger, the burn in the back of his throat, January, Cam's cool hands.

It's probably nothing, he tells himself, but when he goes to see Lynch her face says otherwise, crinkling around the edges as she prods him into more detail. She wants to know when the spells come on, how long they last, what the pain feels like and whether it's localized. She's interested in triggers and anything that exacerbates them—light, noise, motion. Beau answers mechanically, in clinical terms. He doesn't swear or joke.

He leaves her office with a handful of intake sheets stamped with set dates for full bloodwork, x-rays, an MRI, and sits outside in the leafy island parkette, palms pressed to warm pebbled concrete, trying to empty his head. The street is covered in enormous solid blocks of imposing rectangular shadow from the buildings above, broken by narrow bars of sun marking the spaces between. It's regal, this place, he thinks, finally understanding what is meant by the lovely word *avenue*, a great tree-lined boulevard of late summer light and shade. Lately he can't get a single coherent thought together, everything inside him torn up. He hopes in the deepest part of his complex tangled heart that it's nothing but stress, an excess of noise and burnt coffee absorbed during overtime shifts.

He doesn't tell Cam anything, taking an extra hour on his lunch break to be put into a hospital gown and injected with dye that makes him flushed all over while he lies still in the cylindrical machine and closes his eyes, trying to sleep through the electric drilling boring itself into his brain even with the noise-cancelling headphones on. The machine goes off like a foghorn, reverberating in his teeth between lulled periods of rhythmic shuffled wheezing, like air escaping a struggling respirator or weak bicycle pump. When the radiologist asked him if he wanted music he said no, and now regrets it. There is an episode waiting for him just around the corner, and the percs and oxys are inconveniently at home where he makes a point of leaving them. He knows he takes too many too often, and is afraid.

The neurologist asks him a series of questions, memory tricks and basic math, and all he can think of is February, the layers of gauze taped over his split scalp and the young intern (*doctor*) leaning over his bed with that endless tapping of pen on corkboard and Cam all sleep-deprived with blood caked into his cords. He shines a light in Beau's eyes and tests his reflexes, asks him to balance on one foot and walk on a line of dirty masking tape stuck across the floor. Everything looks fine, he says, scribbling responses on the form that will go back to Lynch's desk and into his growing file, the thing an organism with a life of its own—his life, in numbers and dates and graphed cell counts, everything important happening between the lines.

We'll just have to wait on the tests and see, he says. And then, like it's just occurred to him, taking in Beau in his black coffee shop shirt with the rolled sleeves: "Were you prescribed painkillers during cancer treatment?"

"Yeah," he says. "Oxycodone, Percocet. Tylenol 4, I think."

"And do you still take them?"

"Sometimes. For the headaches."

"You should be careful," the neurologist says, taking off his glasses and laying them on the table. "If you take them too often they can actually make the migraines chronic, and worse. Not to mention the potential for dependency."

Too late, he thinks, leaving the hospital to step into the brilliant blinding sun, birdsong and traffic flooding the avenue as he searches pockets he knows are empty. Back on shift he finds he can't finish out the day, telling Del he's feeling sick and has to go, cutting through the park to escape the roar of the place and the bitter coffee smell woven into the fabric of his clothes.

The news is not what he'd hoped. It doesn't hit him the way he thought it would, and he wonders if maybe his immense, immovable, glacial calm isn't really a lack of reaction at all, but a deeper, more keen response gathering, taking shape somewhere within. A thing that will come out in its own time and on its own terms, flattening him. For this reason he thinks it best not to go home, and to wait, and to show patience, the kind of patience only those who have spent weeks watching light changing on yellow walls understand.

He folds the stapled charts into his back pocket and walks down University to the harbourfront, numb to the late August sun, his inner landscape vast and spectacularly empty. At the lake he sits, letting his feet hang over the concrete drop while watching ducks diving and sifting for breadcrumbs, bits of moist hotdog bun thrown by an old man in a windbreaker and chinos, an outfit excessive for the warm day and light wind carrying the smell of seaweed and wet sand from the island. Beau leans back and closes his eyes. With his face upturned to the sun he remembers taking the ferry with Cam, young and stoned and not yet familiar with University Health Network intake protocols. It doesn't feel like his memory, but a thing from a distant time—historical, almost. In his mind it is rendered in sepia, as a photograph.

The mind is a faulty camera, he thinks, whirring ever on.

He thinks about timing and luck, the only frames available to him with which to make sense of this experience, this chain of events that has been his strange life over the past year. If he was Cam he might have been able to corral the whole thing, shuffle it into a coherent theory, a self-contained universe with its own logic in which it is possible to make decisions and consider objects requiring solid reference points and fixed sets of rules: ethics, epistemology, metaphysics. What he will do is opaque to him, but if he reaches he can feel out its shape, a huge sleeping thing in the back of his mind. Already forming, without his direction or involvement, is a plan.

He calls Cliff and meets him on a back patio where they get so wasted that by five they have to stumble back to the cool shaded interior of Cliff's apartment and sprawl on the couch, talking in half sentences to keep each other from falling asleep. When he gets home he's still drunk enough that fitting the key into the door is a struggle, its slippery edges never quite lining up with the slot. It takes him several tries, and when he finally pushes his way inside he feels defeated, stretched out by the thousand forces of the world, none of which, when it comes right down to it, he really understands. You could live a hundred years, he thinks, and not even begin to scrape the bottom of it all.

"Hey," Cam says, "you're all wasted."

Beau sags against the wall and makes like he might kick off his shoes, but finds he can't summon the effort or coordination necessary for the task. Cam is sitting on the couch in his boxers with a volume of Barthes and a pencil, the latter removed from his mouth to act as a placeholder as he sets the book aside. Beau tries to imagine what it might be like to be Cam, to inhabit a space where it is possible to glean meaning from printed words on a page, to pick up volume after volume of dense text and carefully work his way through it with the simple faith that, with patience, something of value will emerge. He's trying to get at it, he thinks, whatever it is. He'll never stop trying to figure it out.

He wasn't going to tell Cam anything, meaning to sit on the knowledge and let it develop a flavour until he understood exactly what it meant for him, but now, faced with Cam so pleased to see him, Cam as he appears in his mind's eye lining up with Cam in the flesh, the real Cam with his bare feet and unlit joint balanced on the edge of the ashtray in one of those rare moments of symmetry between real and imagined, he decides he can't. Cam doesn't have his glasses on and this makes him seem vulnerable, somehow naked.

"I have really bad news," he says, all at once, no planning. It's a kind of unrestraint he's unused to, having spent his whole life carefully calculating what other people should know, or not know. People talk too much, in his experience. They'll say anything at the least prompting and are surprised when consequences and complications arise. Six foster homes have instilled in him a strong sense of boundaries, and of the necessity of keeping important things to oneself. Lest they get out into the world. Lest they cause unforeseen damage. To say this dire thing so openly, without thought, leaves him giddy and frightened, as if waiting for a sudden blow.

Cam's face hardens, a thing his eyes are unable to do. "Beau," he says.

Beau is overcome, suddenly and completely, with a great heaviness. How can I do this to him again, he thinks. How can I ask him. He sinks down to the floor and sits with his back to the wall, facing Cam across the room.

"The cancer," Cam says, and Beau says, "yeah."

They sit in silence, each withdrawn into the bleak space of their own processing. Beau endures a deadening wave of blackness, sticky and thick. "I wasn't going to tell you," he says. "Because I don't want to do it again, this thing. I can't even . . . imagine it. But I trust you, I trust only you. Do you understand?"

"Your shoes," Cam says, simply, as if this is a direct answer. "You should at least take off your shoes."

"So I'm giving you an out."

"Beau, I don't want—"

"No, fucking, listen to me, okay. Cameron." The use of his full name stills Cam to attention. "It wasn't fair, what I did to you last time. I was afraid of what you might say if I gave you the option, so I just didn't. And that was wrong."

He wonders if it had ever occurred to Cam to simply jettison the situation, wash his hands of it (only once, in fact, on a crisp bright October day as he stood on the curb overwhelmed by the enormous contingency of things), and cringes inwardly at the colossal amount of hidden leverage he's held over his friend all this time. How could he say no? He would have never said no. He sees now that Cam could have never refused him.

Because I can make him, he thinks, and shivers. His face is numb.

Cam stands and crosses the room, kneeling before Beau where he proceeds, calmly and with searing gentleness, to untie his shoes. Beau watches Cam pulling at the laces of his worn red sneakers and says: "So you don't have to do this for me again. No strings, man. I won't hold it against you. Really." And then, before he can stop himself: "So take it, I want you to take it."

Cam shakes his head, removing first one sneaker and then the other before sitting down, crossing his long legs. He is totally still, but Beau knows he is devastated from the quality of energy radiating from him, a wounded, violent signal originating somewhere deep within, the kind of thing that broke the mirror and maimed his hand. "I don't want it," he says, cradling Beau's foot. "It's not even a question."

And then, somehow, without having wished it or even really noticed, he descends into the greatest blackness he has ever known. Lynch asks him how he's feeling and he says fine, but a profound sense of apathy dogs him throughout the day, shrouding his motions. His main emotional response consists of heaviness, and a subdued ache in his chest he does his best to ignore.

He takes so many painkillers he can hardly think, moving as in a fog. Everything is more manageable this way, parcelled out in brief neutral fragments that pass by and fade quickly from view. Beau imagines time as a set field with definite boundaries he must move through one way or another, and feels it would be best for everyone if he registered as little of it as possible. Just get through it, he thinks, gritting his teeth as he closes his eyes against the streetcar's sway, a smooth pitching motion like that of the sea. Vast slices of time disappear from his consciousness, missing and unaccounted for.

When the chemo starts he has all his prescriptions refilled. The pharmacist places them on the counter, scans his Rx, and doesn't even blink. That it's possible to obtain so many heavy-duty narcotics with so little hassle amazes him. Cancer, he thinks. Passport to whatever. He sees, from a great distance, Cam's anguish, and decides this is not something he can presently deal with. The less he feels for Cam, the better.

He hides from Cam, scheduling the sessions to fall on days he knows Cam will be at the university, holding things like office hours and meetings and writing his *dissertation*, a thing Beau understands will culminate years and years of intense solitary labour he will never quite be able to grasp. Cam doesn't talk about what he's writing, and Beau doesn't ask. His curiosity about external things is at an all-time low. He lets Cam drive him once a week and walks the other three, stopping in the park to smoke a joint that makes the way home almost bearable. It takes the nausea a while to catch up, and if he paces himself he can get back before it gets out of hand.

It's a fucking, race, he thinks, absurdly. Consciousness has taken on a surreal quality, everything inflated and decontextualized. It's so much harder to do things than he recalls. He lets the stop bath remain in its tray for days before remembering to rinse it out, at which point the liquid has evaporated and left deep crusts of white salt residue around the edges. The darkroom stands closed and the camera lies untouched on the nightstand, gathering dust. He doesn't bother with Paul Simon.

And sometimes, in the evenings, as he stands on the balcony smoking and watches the progress of the gathering dusk, he wonders if maybe he needed the pills after all, if there wasn't some absolutely legitimate reason he'd been prescribed the antidepressants that followed him around in his case file and were made available to each set of foster parents at their local pharmacy to be doled out if they found any aspect of his behaviour irritating. What (*what*) was it, he thinks, shaken by the visceral memory of holding pills under his tongue, the bitter powder tang of them dissolving between his cheek and gums before he could covertly spit them out after dutifully opening his mouth for a swallow check. So many crushed pills flushed down toilets and sinks, so many tabs stashed in his pockets and shoes until, inevitably, *difficulty taking medication* had been inscribed into his file as well.

The meds made him feel slow and not himself, unsure if he even remembered what he was like, and he fought them as hard as he could. But maybe I needed them, he thinks now, cowed by how easily this weariness overtakes him, this sense of the overexposure of all things. Like a bad print. Like the sloppy work of someone who doesn't know what the fuck they're doing and can't pay attention to the fucking, timer.

Leaning hard on the railing and holding his hit, he remembers how impressed Cathy was by the smallest things, like that he washed his dishes as soon as he was done eating from them, dried them and put them away, took his shoes off and lined them up neatly on the doormat, asked politely before assuming anything, would never help himself unless prompted, and insisted on helping with dinner, all without being asked. Not understanding that this was behaviour developed not out of politeness, or any sense of obligation, but from years of habit calculated to pre-empt, minimize, and dilute any potential problems with the various sets of strangers who were paid thirty dollars a day to put a roof over his head. There are different ways of dealing with living in systematized care, and Beau Larky had seen them all. He'd shared homes with kids who acted out, talked back, refused to listen, snuck out at night, did all kinds of drugs, and treated the other (the real) kids in the family with a degree of venom he didn't feel capable of producing, physically fighting against the crippling unfairness of somehow ending up in the system *through no fault of one's own*. But he didn't want to take the drugs, so he behaved immaculately. The last thing he needed was to give anyone a reason to single him out.

Except Cam, who read the prescription labels with academic interest, running his fingers over the type. "Beauregard," he said, sitting on the narrow group home bed, hunched over the bottle. "That's your name." And Beau nodded, embarrassed and thrilled to attain this level of candidness.

But now he can't, withdrawing from Cam instinctively, in a move having more to do with self-preservation than anything else. In the night he shrinks from Cam's touch, turning over to roll out from under his roommate's arm and curl up by himself near the edge of the bed, and in the evenings he retreats from the living room to sleep alone, leaving Cam at the kitchen table with his open books, staring far away. Cam says nothing, allowing Beau this space. Sometimes, when he thinks no one is watching him, Cam's face takes on a desolate, hollow aspect, like he might crumple in on himself and never get back up. If Beau thinks about it too much he feels like he might cry, and so doesn't. Something damaged and sore has taken up residence in his chest.

The oxy disappears from its bottle at an astonishing rate.

"Hey," Cam says one morning as Beau comes into the kitchen, not yet stoned and still soft with the night's sleep. "Come here, huh."

Cam is in his going-to-campus getup, collared shirt and cords and bare feet he will slide into the jarring contrast of Birks on the way out the door. There has been some talk of Cam looking for jobs in September, resulting in his increased attention to things like *professionalism*, not a state that comes naturally to someone who caps off their day with a succession of joints. Beau stands in the doorway and hesitates, a blank dire thing tightening his throat.

"Really, Beau. Come here for just a second, huh." He's leaning on the counter and opens his arms so tentatively Beau can't say no, not to this request from Cam who loves him beyond understanding. I've been so awful, he thinks, and shrinks inwardly as he crosses the kitchen to let Cam enfold him. He rests his head against Cam's chest and listens, limbs loosening, to the steady beat of his roommate's solid healthy heart.

"Beau Larky," Cam says, voice wavering, "what's going on?"

Beau shakes his head. He feels that if he speaks his heart might spill out of his mouth.

"You're so stoned all the time," Cam says, stroking his hair. "You're hardly there. You take too many of those pills, you know? But just tell me, tell me what's going on."

"Nothing," he says into Cam's shirt. "I'm sick, man. I'm sick and depressed."

"Is it bad? You can tell me, Beau."

He shakes his head.

"You haven't told me anything. I know you get more chemo than you tell me about. I know you don't want to talk about it, that you feel worse than you let on. I've given you space, but I want to be there for you, if you'll just let me. It's killing me, Beau. To watch you like this."

"I can't put you through that again," Beau says, tucking his hands under Cam's shirt to feel his warm back.

"You're putting me through worse. I'm worried sick. We hardly talk, some days."

"I know," he says, chest clenching. "I don't know what to do."

"At least tell me what Lynch said. Let me know if it's bad, I can handle it. I'll be okay, I swear, but I can't deal with this distance from you."

"I just thought it would be fine, now. You know? After that fucking, awful year. But it isn't. And to ask you to do this again is just—fucked, Cam. It's fucked."

"It's not a transaction," Cam says, his voice travelling enormous inner distances over landscapes twisted and vast. "I want—I need to do it for you. You can trust yourself with me. You're my family."

The effect this word has on him is total and unexpected, loosening a small injured sound that has been crouching, suppressed, in his throat. He wishes he'd taken the time to pop the oxy before showing up in the kitchen like this, sober and open and unrestrained. Cam rubs his back, silent and firm.

"How am I supposed to make decisions," Cam says, finally, "if I don't know what's going on? How am I supposed to wake up in the morning like everything's okay?"

"I don't know," Beau says. "There are so many things I don't know."

"But you could at least tell me this."

"I can't, Cam," he says, succeeding in getting his inner turmoil under control. "I can't even think about it myself."

"Is it bad?"

He shakes his head.

"Please, Beau. You have to let me know. It's important."

"I'm not going to involve you in this right now, okay. I need you to let it go."

"What are you even saying?"

"Exactly what I mean. Let it go, man, please."

Cam untangles himself and steps back, crossing his arms over his chest. He looks like he's been hit. "I can't believe you," he says, "after everything. How can you be so cold? I've always been there for you, no questions asked, no matter what, and that's all you can say to me? And you think you're doing me some kind of favour?"

"I made the decision to let this thing happen with you without all the relevant information, okay. I might have made it differently, if I'd known I had to go through all this shit again."

"That's what life is, Beau! Making fucking decisions without all the information on hand. But you have to accept that and trust it will be okay. Or else what the fuck are we even doing here." He finds his glasses on the table and puts them on before beginning to pack his bag in rough stilted motions, mangling the cover on one of his books.

Beau stands with his back to the counter, watching. Now I've done it, he thinks, amazed at this turn of events. Now I've really hurt him. The situation feels drastically beyond his control. "Why does it matter?" he says. "What do you want to know, exactly? Fucking, percentages? Fucking, treatment success rates? So you can what, rationalize it, hedge bets? *Theorize* about it?"

Cam tucks in his shirt like he's strangling someone. "So I can sleep at night," he says, picking up his backpack to sling it over his shoulder. He trips into his Birks and slams the door hard enough to rattle the cupboards. Beau tips his head back and breathes, listening to the rhythmic thump of Cam making his way down the stairs, the noise echoing through the hallway until it's cut off by a second, distant slam, that of the front door. If he stepped onto the balcony he would have been able to watch Cam's progress down the sidewalk, seeing him stop at the corner to fix his glasses and wipe his eyes.

Instead he focusses on breathing, processing the full significance of their exchange. His heart is beating quickly and his throat is tight. This is what it's like to be vulnerable to someone, he thinks, and hates it. All your life you work on avoiding this shit, staying clear of it, only to end up here, neck deep in this thing with fucking, Cam Dempster. He can't tell Cam what Lynch has told him, can't deal with it, doesn't want to. To admit he's even sick again is enough, too much. He runs a hand though his hair, pushing it back, reeling in shock at the unexpected pleasure of harnessing that swelling blank static accumulating in his body and taking it out on this person who has never done anything but care for him, put him first.

There is something truly fucked up in you, he thinks. Something truly fucking, dark.

Making fucking decisions without all the information on hand.

Beau has never had a true psychic intuition, but feels it now, feels it as strongly as if an external voice were projected into his head. Cam has told him, conveyed hidden information with nothing but the angle of his shoulders and the strain in his voice.

That's what life is, Beau.

He walks over to the garbage bin and places his foot on its pedal to peer in, a heightening of superstitious tension gathering in his throat. Under a scattering of orange peels is a crumpled envelope, not an uncommon sight in their apartment, but its unfamiliar red letterhead draws him automatically, no questions asked. A whole other type of knowing.

Its paper is stained with soy sauce and transparent with grease near one corner. The seal is not the regular blue of the university but cardinal red, serious, crisp, and regal. *Stanford University*, it reads. *California.*

Stanford, he thinks, silently forming the word, mouthing it to himself. Seeing if this is a real thing. *Wow.*

The envelope is empty and he puts it aside, kneeling to really reach into the garbage, pushing past the morning's cold coffee grounds and what is definitely an old roach. Finding the letter's bottom corner, he understands that Cam has torn it up. The energy he feels is frenzied, like if he doesn't find the rest now, right this instant, it will disappear, its text obscured with concentrated Starbucks brew. He tips the bin on its side and starts scooping out entire handfuls of trash until he has what are three quarters of a coffee-saturated letter on very, very good stationery, heavy cream paper he can tell has been embossed even with the moisture soaking it through.

Beau gingerly wipes coffee grounds from the fragments and lays them flat on the table, smoothing them out, the trash spilling onto the floor behind him forgotten. It's like someone else has taken up residence in his body. Though the morning is steaming, his feet are cold.

Dear Cameron Dempster,

In response to your application and recent interview, it is my pleasure to officially offer you the post of Assistant Professor within the Stanford University Department of English and Critical Theory, conditional upon successful defense of your dissertation in the coming fall. Should you wish to accept this post

Beau can't read the rest because his eyes are swimming. The date on the letter is September 6—nearly a week ago, now, and just two weeks after the dated bloodwork results on Princess Margaret letterhead. He imagines Cam carrying this carefully folded letter in his pocket, or tucked into a book of Foucault, looking at it furtively, running his fingers over the words to assure himself of their reality. Reading them silently to himself several times a day, tearing away at the skin around his nails, willing himself to sustain. And then, calmly, with much the same blankness that must have preceded his encounter with the mirror, tearing it into quarters and depositing it, crumpled envelope and all, into the kitchen garbage. And then having breakfast like nothing had happened.

He wants to scream. He wants to take Cam and shake him, really fucking, shake him like with the hand, like when he'd only stopped because he realized the motion must be jerking the damaged appendage around something awful, jolting the dislocated bones.

What were you *thinking?*
What the *fuck.*
What the *fuck!*

He's so mad he's afraid he might do something rash, and so sits at the table and places his hands on either side of the letter, palms flat on the plastic top, breathing.

What do you think, are you fucking, stupid? How could you, how could you do that shit, *fuck*. He wants to kill him. If he sees Cam he's one hundred and forty percent sure he'll kill him, strangle him with his bare hands. How can someone be so fucking, smart, he wonders, and not fucking, *think*. He hates himself. He hates the cancer and he hates himself, wants to reach into his core and tear it out, this fucking, awful black thing taking up residence and running his life, running Cam's life, making Cam's decisions, making this whole thing impossible.

"Ah, *fuck*," he says, slamming his fist down on the table so the whole thing rattles and the bong tips over. He catches it before it can roll to the floor. The mirror is bad luck, but a broken bong is a whole other category of misfortune. He stalks to the bedroom and starts pulling on his jeans, jumping into them, exclaiming in frustration when he sees one of the legs is inside out. He feels out of control, like he's not sure what he might do, like he might do something final, irrevocable. He forces his feet into his shoes, tearing at them, and slams the door behind him.

Beau takes the stairs three at a time and walks at a clip, not a single coherent thought in his head. He has no conscious plan and no idea where he's going, realizing he's been making his way to campus only when he enters it, led entirely by spatial memory, his body's instinctual ingrained knowledge of the route formed through having walked it so many times. He is blinded, so angry he can hardly see, wiping at his eyes as he walks. He resents this, he resents everything. His cheeks are raw.

Cam is in his office with the door open, laptop out in front of him though he's obviously unfocussed and staring out the window, chin propped in his hand. He's a fucking, space case in his own way, Beau thinks absurdly, with a pang of affection strong enough to make him sick.

At the sound of footsteps in the hall Cam turns, clearly surprised. "Beau, hey," he says. "What's going on?"

"What the fuck are you *thinking?*"

"What? Calm down, calm down. Jesus."

"*Me* calm down? *You* calm down. What the *fuck*." He tears the fragments of letter from his back pocket and holds them up, shaking. His whole body is shaking.

All the blood drains from Cam's face. "Beau," he says. "Fuck."

"Yeah, fuck is right, man. Fuck is all I can fucking, *think* right now. What are you *thinking?* What's *wrong* with you? How can you be so fucking, *stupid?*"

"You weren't supposed to see it, I didn't mean—"

"You could have at least used your fucking, department shredder! What the *fuck*." He throws his hands up in the air, feeling like his skull might pop open. A number of heads have emerged to peer out from doorways down the hall. "How could you do that to me, to yourself? How could you put that kind of responsibility on me? Of knowing this, of being responsible for *this*." He shakes the pieces of paper that have devolved into a ball in his hand.

"What am I supposed to do?" Cam says, standing. "What do you expect me to do, when you don't tell me anything, when I have no idea what's going on with you, when for all I know you could be fucking *dying?* What do you think, Beau? How do you think I'm going to act? How am I supposed to make decisions without any fucking information?"

"Exactly! This is exactly why I don't give you information! Because you'll go breaking your fucking, hand, or worse. You have no sense of self-preservation, man." He stares at the crumple of paper in his hand, unable to comprehend that it has travelled thousands of miles from some prestigious desk on the sun-soaked west coast only to end up here, torn and stained and stuffed into a garbage bin in a Toronto kitchen. Cam's future, he thinks. This was the beginning of Cam's fucking, future. "Is it even worth it?" he says, dropping the scraps on the desk. "Do you think it's worth it, Cam?"

"It's just a job," Cam says. "I can always get another job."

"*Stanford University*. Admit it, admit you wanted to take it."

"Of course I wanted to take it! What do you think? But this is more important to me. If anything happens to you, I—" he shakes his head and wipes his eyes under his glasses, smearing away moisture. "Please, man, you have to calm down. It'll be okay."

"How can it be okay? Are you out of your fucking, mind? You turned down a job offer from *Stanford University*. I can't *believe* you."

A small crowd has begun to gather just outside the door, lingering uncertainly around its periphery. Cam looks at them, pained. "Beau," he says, "come on. Let's go outside, at least. I can't do this in here."

Beau turns around to take in the developing scene, understands he *is* the developing scene, and doesn't give a single fuck. His anger carries him elsewhere, beyond the confines of his physical body, this imperfect ailing structure that has let him down so much. "You could have at least told me," he says, all measured venom, and turns to stalk down the hall, taking the stairs two at a time. He is afraid that if he looks at Cam too long he might hit him, that they might get into an actual physical fight. He's halfway down before he hears Cam slamming the office door and running up behind him, long legs working on the stairs in complex rhythm.

"Beau, wait," Cam says. He sounds demolished.

Beau keeps walking, taking broad fast steps, not even slightly out of breath, understanding for the first time how athletic he's become, how finely he's managed to tune his body in the brief break its been allowed. He pushes through the heavy front doors and into the late summer sun where the air tastes high and crisp and somehow autumnal, already carrying a threat of the chill to come. He makes it all the way to the sidewalk before Cam stops him with a hand on his shoulder, jogging up behind.

"Beau," he says. "I'm sorry. It was never my intention to hurt you. You know that."

He spins around, shaking off Cam's grip, hands clenched and pressed to his sides. His heart is beating in a way that makes it hard to believe he is sick, has ever been sick enough to seriously fear dying. "It's like, I was always fine, I was always fine around you, and then suddenly now I'm not, and it's like—you should have been honest with me, you should have just been honest with me the first time around." He can see Cam wants to touch him and steps back, smoldering.

"You weren't honest with me either, so."

"Like it would have made a difference!"

"I don't know, I don't know shit. You don't tell me anything, you just walk around stoned and act like everything's okay. Fuck, Beau."

"This wouldn't even be an issue if you had just told me the first time around, how you felt. It wasn't right for you to fucking, put your life on hold like that and not tell me. I might have acted differently, if I'd known you were—if I'd known you were in fucking, love with me. Jesus, Cam."

Cam runs a hand back through his hair. "What, driven yourself to chemo? Gone to outpatient counselling?"

"You know what, fuck *you*."

"If I'd told you how I felt," Cam says, "before you knew you were sick, what would you have said? If one day we were just chilling and smoking up and everything was normal, and I told you that. Be honest."

Beau exhales audibly. "No, I would have said no. I would have said I don't feel that way."

Cam nods. He turns and stares down the sidewalk, southward where the streetcar tracks run and the cityscape opens up, hands braced against the small of his back.

"But you know what?" Beau says. "It's not something that can be told. It's something that has to be shown, and you fucking, win. You really got me, you got me hard. I don't know how you did that." He shakes his head. "I can't fucking, *believe* I'm doing this thing with you. If you told me six months ago this is what we would be doing I would have fucking, laughed."

"Hah," Cam says. "Ha-ha."

"I wish you'd never stirred this up in me. I can't fucking, stand it. I look at you and I can't, Cam."

Cam turns back to him, face twisted with something just beneath its surface. "You think you can get close to someone and still keep boundaries when it suits you, but you can't have it both ways, Beau. It doesn't fucking work like that."

"You're gonna go, you have to go."

"Go where?"

"Stanford."

"Man, I'm not going *anywhere*. You must be out of your mind. That fall must have actually fucked up your head."

Beau laughs hard, like he might not be able to stop. "This coming from *you*."

"Listen, I know you had a fucked up childhood, and you don't open up to people, and you're used to relying on yourself, and you get into *dark* fucking moods so deep it's like pulling you from the bottom of a pool, but I have always been there for you, *always*, and nothing you can say will dissuade me from this."

Cam's ardour disables him, weakening his resolve with this sudden declaration of perfect understanding. *You get into dark fucking moods* and yeah, this is a dark mood, the darkest yet, one he doesn't feel he'll ever shake though this must not be true, though the spells never last indefinitely, waning just as he comes to feel he can't bear any more. Or maybe it's one long spell, he thinks, flooding over him and retreating like a tide in some ceaseless biological rhythm he will never get his head around.

"I can't be responsible for you making this decision," he says, suddenly tired, that full-body ache returning as the adrenaline wears off in a reminder that it's been less than twenty-four hours since his system was last flooded with hospital-grade chemicals. Moving into this awareness of limited physicality is like coming down from a drug. "I can't do that to you. You've already given up so much for me. You're fucked up in your own way, Cam, because you have no sense of limits. Look at you, putting your hand through mirrors, throwing out job offers from Stanford. You'll fucking, destroy yourself."

Cam shrugs. "Maybe," he says. "Maybe that's true. But you have a serious fucking issue with getting attached to people, so you freeze everyone out. You're afraid to get close, dependent. But we're already close, Beau. It's too late for that."

Beau hasn't eaten anything yet, and now, standing in the high noon sun, he feels dizzy and faint, overwhelmed by the day, the situation, this lanky man who has somehow succeeded in stifling his anger. "You have to take it, Cam. Call them and tell them you've changed your mind. They obviously want you there."

"I'm not taking it, Beau. I'm not."

"You're not even out of school and they're offering you a tenure-track job. At *Stanford*. You're twenty-five years old, man. I can't accept that. I fucking, can't."

"Well, you should start processing, because I'm not taking it, so."

"You're being so fucking, stupid about this."

"This is more important to me, Beau. You know that."

"I can't even listen to you right now. I can't, man. Do you even hear yourself talking?" Small licks of anger return, gathering at what must be the sphincter in his chest as he thinks that he could really hurt Cam, that at this point it wouldn't be outside the realm of possibility. As in, what are you *thinking*, what the *fuck*. He looks around for somewhere to sit but there is only grass, the lush department lawn stretching away from the sidewalk on a slight rise. His vision swims with small black dots colonizing its periphery.

"Hey," Cam says, "are you feeling okay?" and Beau says, "yeah, yeah." He decides he will absolutely not pass out, that passing out is not a viable option, not here in front of Cam who he must, at all costs, convince. Where Spadina meets Bloor there is a small parkette bordered with flat, backless stone benches that mark the beginning of campus, and Beau makes his way to the nearest of these before his body can catch him off guard. He will need all his energy, he sees now—all this and more. Cam follows him wordlessly, hovering behind.

There is a great incessant rustle in the leaves and a slanting quality to the light, which viewed from Beau's low vantage splinters into a million different colours, a fragmented prism of all the varied beautiful things not immediately available to the naked eye. He sits and hangs his head and doesn't look at Cam, who stands over him with his hands on his hips and his face turned to the sky.

"Listen," Beau says, "I'm not asking you, I'm telling you. You have to go."

"I'm not going, Beau. You can't make me."

"But that's the thing, Cam, that's exactly it. I *can* make you. I can make you do anything I want, and you'll fucking, *let me*." Without the aid of mind-dulling opioids Beau Larky's superstitious imagination is unusually sharp, and as he says this he knows, in the pit of his gut, that he shouldn't have, that he should have never voiced it, not so bluntly and not in the daylight and not the way it appears in his head, straightforward and clear-cut.

It's like the disclosure of some unsaid spell. Cam seems to sense this, and shivers. *Don't ask me that*, he'd said in the bathroom, breathing so hard. *It can't be unsaid.* "Do it, then," he says now, "if you're so sure."

Beau hesitates, but only for a moment, tossing his head back as if seeking a sign from the patches of blue visible beyond the tangle of branches above. Hesitation is a major flaw—one has only to look at Cam to see this. Even so, it takes all he has, everything hard and internal, all the shored up and carefully stored reserves of strength and conviction, all the resources he's packed within himself during long winter months spent staring at blank hospital walls, sitting hunched over his knees grinding weed slowly, placidly, as if it were a necessary labour to get out of the way before the relief of loading up a one-hitter, of gritting his teeth against pain he didn't dare make a sound to acknowledge, to look up at Cam and make this final, most complete gesture of unshakeable self-containment.

"If you don't go," he says, "we're done. You can do what you want, but if you don't take the job and you stay here then I won't ever see you again. Do you understand? No matter what. Because we're done here, you and I."

The words are surreal, leaving his mouth to hang in the space between them in a cloud of bad energy he feels he could almost see, if he looked harder, or differently. Cam's face collapses and then hardens as he struggles to get himself together, to muster some kind of coherent front.

Stricken, Beau thinks, amazed. The word for how he looks right now is *stricken*. He feels distant and hugely detached.

"You're not serious," Cam says. "You don't mean that."

"Do I fucking, look like I'm not serious? Jesus, Cam. Come on, work with me here."

"Beau, you're *sick*. You can't be sick by yourself."

"Sure I can, I've been by myself most of my fucking, life, and I can definitely be alone again. I'll be fine, man. It's you who will have a hard time, but you'll get over it, trust me. People can get over anything."

"You're so fucking stubborn! You think you can handle everything by yourself, but you're wrong, Beau!" Cam takes a few stiff steps, like he wants to pace but isn't sure what he should do. "Who will drive you to the hospital? Who will put you to bed? Who will make sure you eat? Who's gonna sit up with you and rub your back when you're throwing up at three in the morning? Huh? Who's gonna worry about you and keep you company and read to you and, and—and love you? Who will love you when you need it? Because you will."

Beau shakes his head, stifling the pang growing in his chest. "I'll take care of myself, Cam. I'm good at it. I can't have you stretching yourself out like that, running all over the place, putting yourself in bad situations. You'll do anything and not think twice."

"Because I love you! I'm only human. I try to do what's best and sometimes it's hard to say what that is, when you're deep in a thing. But I can't do this, Beau, leave you like this. Take it back, please."

"I'm not taking it back," Beau says, controlling his voice, seeing that Cam is on the verge of going over some high internal ledge. "This is the best thing, you'll see. I'm gonna pack up my stuff and find a smaller place and figure it out, and you'll pack yours and ship it down to California and go do what's best for you for once in your whole life. I fucking, mean it."

"How can it be the best thing? If you're sick and we're four thousand kilometers apart, man. If I can't ever see you. If I can't be with the person I love most."

"Jesus, Cam. This is so hard for me. Don't make it harder."

Cam wipes his eyes under his glasses, looking away. When he speaks his voice wavers, running off without him. "I can't believe you, Beau. You're killing me. You're breaking my fucking heart."

The effect his words have had is so much worse than Beau could have imagined. It's just for now, Cam, he wants to say, seeing the anguish in Cam's limp hands and heavy shoulders, but knows this isn't true. If you give him up now, he thinks, you give him up forever, because things will never be the same between you. Not after you've hurt him like this.

"Man, don't cry," he says. "Please." He wants to stand and reach out and hold Cam's face, but knows this would be an irrevocable and risky course of action. He's not sure if he can trust himself, if he's as firm as Cam thinks. If maybe his foremost desire isn't to take the whole thing back and go home and smoke joints in bed, repeating how sorry he is as if any amount of apology could compensate for what he's done. "I can't stand it, but this is the right thing."

Beau watches from a great height as Cam gets on his knees, right there in the street, and takes his hands between his own, pressing his forehead to them. People passing by on the sidewalk glance back curiously to see what he's doing, this tall academic down on the pavement before a noticeably handsome, if pale and unrested, young man. And then Beau sees how desperate Cam must be, how it doesn't matter to him, or maybe never even entered his mind which members of his department might be watching from their windows at this very moment as he kneels with his head bowed in front of this slumped little guy in Levi's at the corner of Spadina and Bloor while the traffic flows endlessly by.

"Won't you miss it?" Cam says, quietly, in a whisper.

"Miss what, Cam."

"This, me. The whole thing."

"Of course I will, Cam. Of course I'll miss you." He allows himself to stroke Cam's hair, flattening down the thick unruly mass with his hands.

Cam lets out a single strained sob, the sound escaping before he can choke it back.

"Hey," Beau says, invoking the simple string of words his roommate has calmed him with so many times, "hey. It will be okay. You'll see."

"How can it be okay? It'll kill me. I'll die."

"You won't die, Cam," he says, seeing, without wanting to, fat drops of the deepest red dotting the bathroom tile, smeared into the grout in a way they couldn't fully wash out, not even afterward with repeated attempts, remaining still in the bathroom that had been theirs but would soon be someone else's and endowed with a whole new series of associations, as if all this had never been. "You'll be okay. Trust me."

"What can I do, Beau, to change your mind? What can I say?"

"You can't," he says, fighting down the overwhelming tightness rising in his throat.

"Just tell me, tell me and I'll do it. Please, Beau, please."

"No, this is just what it's going to be."

"Oh, Beau. No. No, no, no. How can you say that to me? Please don't say that." Cam is sobbing in a scary way, like he might break open or pass out. His whole frame shakes though he doesn't make a sound, face pressed to Beau's lap in a fit of grief exceeding the potential for vocalization.

Like a cut so deep it doesn't bleed, Beau thinks, and I did that. I just did that to him a moment ago, nobody but me, and that's fucking, it. He thinks it's amazing how easily you can destroy someone you know well, marveling abstractly at the efficiency with which this can be done.

"Beau, you'll change your mind. You're just upset, but it will look different to you in the morning, and—you'll change your mind, won't you? Beau, won't you? Won't you, Beau. Because I'll die, I'll die, I'll die . . ."

"Shh," he says, bending over Cam to press his face into his hair and breathe in his smell, pencil shavings and libraries and stale coffee. There is an ache in him unlike any yet. "You know I love you, right. You have to know this. Even when it doesn't feel like it. Okay? Okay, Cam? Because it's true."

Cam nods and sobs and lets Beau remove his glasses, the lenses smeared and as wet as his face. Beau folds them and sets them aside and smooths down his roommate's hair, watching the spectacular kaleidoscope of variegated light caught in the shifting foliage. His foremost wish is to feel nothing at all.

The following weeks remain in Beau Larky's mind as a time of bad fights, the kind he has seen on television and sometimes between members of his various foster families but never participated in himself. The type of confrontation where the main objective consists of hurting the other person in the most cutting, exacting, efficient way possible. He challenges himself to use as few words as he can think of putting together to solicit the maximum imaginable effect. With Cam, this is not a difficult goal to attain. He watches, amazed, as his words induce Cam to pace and break plates and slam doors, paint chipping away from their frames in large pieces to reveal layers of light blue primer beneath.

You'll make him crazy, he thinks, recalling Cliff's warning. You really fucking, will. The thought leaves him giddy and sick with the desire to test the threshold of his influence. There must be limits, though it's difficult to see where these might be. Cam is like a marionette on long, well-anchored strings, a piece of finely sensitive litmus paper, a goal post left wide open.

I trusted you, I trusted only you and you eviscerated *me.*

The smallest, most ordinary conversations spiral out of control, derailing into snapped exchanges of grief. Any topic or situation is precarious ground. They argue incessantly, unable to share the space, yelling and clenching fists and storming from the apartment in clouds of violent energy that can only be walked off. Beau gets so mad he can hardly see, needing to stand out on the balcony to cool down and prevent himself from doing something stupid, something he really won't be able to take back.

You did it to yourself.

Thick black tension accumulates in the living room until Cam stops coming home at predictable times, staying long hours at the library or in his office where he types, between fits of distraction, the final chapters of his dissertation. Once he begins the process the whole thing takes hardly any time to write, emerging organically and with ease. Because he knew, already, all along, what he wanted to say. It was the getting around to it he found difficult.

Just admit it! Admit that you need me here, that you want me here.

This is such an easy out.

Yeah, well. It's a little late for that, so.

There are things Cam says to him that stay with Beau long after the whole thing is over, after the boxes have been packed and stacked and taken away in the old Cherokee it eats him alive to imagine Cam driving alone across the flat snow-blown Midwest, pushing his glasses up and leaning forward to see through the gusts of white drifting over the windshield. He replays these to himself when he's trying to fall asleep at night, or pressing his face to cold bathroom tile, or curled in on himself, half dead with painkillers. They are things he will never get out of his head. He's sure Cam feels the same.

Will you stop playing that fucking song.

How's it going, Cam, he says one evening after his roommate returns from a library session. The dissertation.

I'm almost done, Cam says, not looking at him, dropping his backpack in a careless, *fuck it all* kind of way. Just sorting out references, at this point. He hits the bong hard enough to suck the bowl's contents straight through into the murky brown water, and laughs. Stanford will be thrilled, he says, if that's what you're losing sleep over.

Some deep venom has seeped beneath the surface of things, corroding all they say or do, loading the simplest statements with suspicion. No action is pure of it. Sometimes Beau wants to stop and say, *we were both wrong, okay, can we admit that we were both wrong and this can't keep going the way it's been,* but can't, because Cam hid the letter from him and because he's already made up his mind to go it alone, to spare Cam the coming spring. More than anything, he wants to go back to being solid and self-contained.

Sitting limp and lead-brained on the couch (*you can have it*, Cam said as they divided up their stuff), chewing oxy to bypass its time-release function, Beau Larky thinks hard on Paul Simon's warning about the boundary between negotiations and love songs being slippery, and difficult to draw. The photo and its trapped electrical energy hang on the fridge till the very last, an approximation of the apology he can't bring himself to give.

6. A Stranger Comes to Town

Neither knows the other yet. Hence they must tell each other: "This is what I am." This is narrative bliss, the kind which both fulfills and delays knowledge, in a word, *restarts* it. In the amorous encounter, I keep rebounding—I am *light*.

Roland Barthes, *A Lover's Discourse*

It's strange, the things you remember coming back to a place after a long time. The humidity and its sticky wet mass smudging the streetlights into halos, the whole world softened in contrast with the Valley's perpetual even sun. How temperate the summers get here, slick grey concrete collecting heat before exuding it all in a great release spanning the night. The pleasure of waiting, lingering on the threshold of things. The certainty of being about to be asked.

I thought it would hit me harder, being back. After how homesick I'd been. But I was okay, other than the initial weak moment of seeing the vantage over the lake from the plane, the little green and grey peninsula stretching below striking something familiar deep within. I've been less emotional lately, or trying to be, trying to get myself in check. To get a hold of myself and find some fixed aspect to things that might somehow remedy this unshakeable sensation of seasickness and drift induced by living.

After the keynote I walked down University in the gathering dusk and thought about the number of times I'd traced this same route, across the avenue into Princess Margaret and back to Toronto General, stopping to gaze at the greying mid-winter sky in perpetual question. My whole life then this series of endless, impossible questions, and no visible record of these or my steps remaining. Thousands of people walk this same way every single day and carry their own psychic impressions, so that the visceral memory of this time and motion is available only to me. And when I go, to no one.

The last winter I walked here a massive ice storm had knocked out the city's electricity, tearing down power lines laden with frozen weight. In the dark apartment I'd packed my bag with books, weed, my toothbrush, and a change of clothes, and walked through the sleet to Princess Margaret, slipping around on the several inches of clear ice lining sidewalks the city had not yet salted. They were running their emergency generator, weak lights flickering at the ends of hallways, everything illuminated at minimal capacity. I sat with him in the odd half-light, listening to someone's respirator working close by and the wail of sirens just outside. The window was frozen solid, a thick pane of twisted ice distorting the world beyond. We didn't talk much, lost in ourselves in the deepening gloom.

In the morning, a week before Christmas, I walked back to the apartment, picked up the Jeep, and took Beau Larky home. It was the last time I did that for him.

Standing on the doorstep now, taking in the mist steaming from the trees and the living green of high summer, the full apex of the planet's year, I almost didn't want to knock, or go inside. It's like: you try to explain to someone what it is you love about Toronto so much, and since it's not a particularly large city, or one with radical pioneering cultural movements, and since people there can be so pretentious and the transit so slow and the weather incredibly variable, inevitably they don't understand what you mean. Because it's really not about any of those things, or anything you can name, but about the way the sun slants off glass at dusk, the early heat gathering at the beginning of the day, the erratic skyline and towering clouds building incessantly behind it, brief violent rains of fat coin-sized drops opening up from the sky. The sun-painted corner fruit stands and street vendors and screech-rattle of ancient streetcars and wet copper smell of the wind off the lake and soft summer nights glowing fluorescent while you sit out on rooftops and talk until dawn. The steadily sloping sprawl of it, its messy mixed urbanism and hundreds of parks tucked away in scattered green pockets opening unexpectedly before you.

In short, it's about the *feel* of the place. And since feelings have to be experienced in order to be understood, there is no way to take that expansive thing unfurling in your chest and convey it into the chest of another. Its magnitude, born of the particular alchemy of all that is you reacting with this singular place, will be inevitably lost.

Feeling all this, condensed and palpable, a quality that could be isolated and extracted from the air, I hesitated over the doorbell, knowing once I went inside the spell would be broken and the sensation now so easily named would dissipate. And knowing I was nervous, standing on the porch of these people I used to know, feeling my heart in my mouth, filled with the old fear of actually physically talking to someone you haven't seen in ages but were once close with, knowing tangible conversation will expose the irrevocable difference that has developed over time. Fearing silences, pauses, gaps. Knowing I had changed, but not knowing how.

I let my hand hover over the buzzer, only half serious. It was the sleek kind that doubled as a communication system. The door was solid oak and varnished and had a serious gilt brass knocker that made me pause and step back and sit on the iron porch railing, arms crossed. I looked at the matching pots of chrysanthemums on either side of the door and thought: This is crazy. This is fucking nuts. Maybe, I thought, I had the wrong house. Maybe I had the wrong idea entirely.

It'd been a long while since I'd been back in town.

"Hey, bud!" He swung open the door, and before I could say anything had me crushed up against him, breathing in cigarettes and coffee and a strong women's perfume I didn't recognize.

"Hey," I said into his shoulder. "Jesus, man."

"Jesus is *right*, man. What are you fucking doing, hiding out on the west coast so long, hey?" He slapped my back and roughed up my hair, a whirlwind of insistent proximity.

"Doing serious shit, man."

"Rigorous academic activity, hey."

"Very rigorous."

He let me go and stepped back to appraise my appearance, allowing me to do the same. "You look good, Cam," he said, nodding. "You look well."

Cliff looked like a god. He really did. He hadn't cut his hair and had it tied back in a loose bun, like a European football star or serious swimmer between races. He wore a faded *Wish You Were Here* v-neck and cut-offs, his feet bare on the concrete porch. Even in this casual getup he looked clean and adult, as in the polished ads lining Annex lawns and bus stop benches in which he sported a button-up shirt and vaguely psychedelic paisley tie. To see him so unchanged relieved me. "You look fantastic," I said. "Really, Cliff."

He laughed. "Yeah, I'm doing not too bad for myself lately. Business is good. Is that a fucking briefcase?"

I looked down at it, suddenly self-conscious. "Yeah man. I was giving a keynote, so."

"Because you are a *big* academic deal, hey!" He clapped my shoulder, giving it a squeeze.

I shrugged, hiding my hands in my pockets. "Yeah, well. You know."

"Here, what am I even saying. Come inside, hey." He stepped aside and held the door for me, the wall of cold air behind him leaking out all at once, as an exhalation. The hair on my forearms prickled where I'd rolled the sleeves.

"Some serious AC in here," I said, thinking of the old apartment, the struggling window unit and dripping air.

"Central air, man. Deadly. Once you go serious home improvement, you never go back."

The floor in the entrance hall was solid hardwood, long gleaming planks that felt cool and smooth on my bare feet after standing in loafers all day.

"The floor," Cliff said, following my gaze, "is original and restored. The house was built in nineteen ten."

"Like the year nineteen *hundred* and ten?" I said, amazed at his bougie homeowner's pride, a real showman's attention to detail, this gleaming wide hall so unlike the grow-op apartment where he'd chain smoked cigarettes and sold stimulants in powdered form.

He nodded, pleased with my reaction. "Turn of the fucking century, man."

"Whoa," I said, and wished I hadn't, the word's thousand sticky associations damping me down. "The perks of being a real estate insider, huh."

"Honestly, Cam, I cannot fucking *believe* this market."

He led me into his kitchen, a beautiful room that was all black granite and strategic lighting where his woman stood as if posed, engrossed in the act of pouring expensive whisky into crystal tumblers at the detached island with the nonchalance of a bartender, a lit cigarette smoking in her free hand. She was like no one I'd ever seen, a curvy soft woman with a hard edge squeezed into a sleeveless black dress with a red polka-dotted apron overtop, a plump bow tied high at the small of her back. Cartoony as hell—the kind of thing Minnie Mouse would wear, except on her it didn't look cartoony at all. She had jet black hair pulled away from her face in a bun and severe bangs cut straight across her forehead, as if razored against the edge of a ruler. Ink crept down her arms in sleeves and up her neck like ivy, full colour tattoos leaving me a little dazzled. She radiated enormous warmth in a palpable, bodily way, something you could almost feel on your skin, like sun. She handed me a glass and her hand, which was cool and soft and had smooth glossy nails painted a deep red to match her lips, none of them chipped or uneven or clumpy, as Stacey's so often were, touched mine.

"Cam," Cliff said, "this is Valerie."

I nodded, flushed. "Valerie Laponte."

"Ah," she said, pleased. "You're good with details."

"I can be," I said, self-conscious though she must have been used to talking with overwhelmed men.

"He's an academic, babe. They're good with that kind of thing."

"Your talk was excellent," she said, dragging deep on the cigarette, her lipstick leaving a sticky ring of red around the filter. "Just such a pleasure."

"How did you get my talk?"

"I streamed it. Don't they warn you that your intellectual property is about to be recorded?"

"Oh," I said, "wow," and swigged back a larger portion of my drink than I'd meant to. They did in fact tell us the panels were recorded, though I'd never thought anyone actually sat down and streamed them. That it would matter enough to anyone who wasn't already there. Because who would it matter to?

I imagined Stacey grading essays and gritting her teeth as she listened to my voice digitally transmitted over thousands of miles to her small windowless office, the kind of thick-beige-oil-paint-over-exposed-brick basement office issued to sessional lecturers, her comments growing increasingly acerbic as her generosity leaked away.

If Valerie could find it, anyone could find it. Anyone could stream it, and I would never know.

"I listened to it this afternoon. It made me feel contemplative, and a little sad." She looked at me intently enough for Cliff to fall silent, her dark shadowed eyes open and kind, and I knew, without anyone saying anything, that it was obvious, that even strangers could see it in me, that as hard I'd tried to shake this thing and get better something damaged remained on my surface, hidden in some place I couldn't see. Maybe in my voice, even, in the way I spoke and in the things I said. That it would always be like this now, people exercising caution around me and asking how I'm feeling and taking care to talk around things in my presence, because I was fragile and might get broken, and nobody wanted to see that go down, or be around when it did.

People can sense when you've suffered. They can sense what you can and can't handle. Valerie had the face of someone you could really open up to, tell everything to, and I knew they must have talked about it, at some point. People who live together talk about everything.

Cliff and Valerie had met the previous summer while Cliff travelled between Gatineau and Val-des-Monts, helping his grandmother fix up her cottage after a bad rainstorm sent a tree falling through the roof. He worked shirtless, hoisting buckets of tar from his grandfather's ancient pickup, a bandanna tied around his forehead to keep hair from his eyes. In the evenings he sat on the riverbank and smoked joints, muscles humming, pleased with the day's labour. When he returned to the city he had with him a Québécoise girlfriend, picked up somewhere between shingling the roof in the hot sun and sharing chicken salad sandwiches and games of cards with his grandma in the shade of her screen porch.

"She's clairvoyant," he said, later, after we had a few drinks and stood outside smoking. "She says sometimes she can read people's emotions, or their thoughts if the connection is strong enough. She gets like, little flashes, man. I think it's because she's so—*empathetic*, you know?"

From Cliff's third floor back patio the CN Tower was clearly visible in almost full skyline profile, lit up blue and white. Baseball, I thought. It must be for the ball game. I thought of Valerie's gaze, placid and penetrating but ultimately kind, and had no problem believing this. She had read me in a half a second. She had read me from my voice alone. "Do you really think she can do that?"

"Of course, man. It sounds weird to say, but I would believe anything she fucking told me. I mean, wouldn't you? Coming from the person you love."

I nodded, watching him inhale, holding my own cigarette away from my body, as a prop. I didn't want to smoke it, but I did want the fresh air. The fresh air and his company, a thing I had sincerely missed.

"She makes me crazy," he said. "She keeps me sharp, man. I never know what she's going to say. It's pretty stupid, the way she makes me feel, but hey, right. Am I right?"

"That's what happens, Cliff. You can't fucking think straight for a minute, and before you know it . . . ugh."

"Hey, Cam. Are you okay? I mean, really."

"I'm good, you know. I'm doing better. I try not to think about it too much."

He nodded, dragging. "Because I mean, you and Stacey—she couldn't make it, hey."

"No. She's teaching a course right now. She would have had to pay for the flight."

"You don't have to pay for flights."

"Man, these days I feel like I don't pay for anything. Everyone's always paying me, grants I didn't even apply for coming through the door all the time. Travel expenses, conference fees, fellowships. It's a little surreal, the whole thing." As we talked we didn't look at each other, staring over the city and its beautiful shape wreathed purple and white in twilight haze, incandescent, wet heat shrouding its contours and softening its lines.

"You're up for tenure review," he said, "aren't you."

"Where'd you hear that?"

"I have my sources," he said, smiling. "What, you think I don't keep tabs on you? You worry me sick, friend. You disappear off the radar for months at a time and who fucking knows what's going on down there, know what I'm saying?"

"You're a good friend, Cliff," I said, telling myself that to avoid getting choked up I should just breathe evenly through my nose, as I'd coached myself so many times. Getting through conversations without breaking down, I saw early on, would always be a challenge.

He must have sensed this, because he put a hand on my back and let it rest there, standing close. "When will you know?"

"Oh," I said, "it went through. They gave me tenure."

"Cam! Fuck, eh." I endured an intense wave of him messing with my hair, which didn't matter because the humidity had already caused it to wave and curl in all the wrong places. "That's a big fucking deal, man. That is cause for some serious celebration, hey."

"Yeah, I guess so," I said. On the connection from New York I'd run through vast mental reserves, trying to compile a list of things that made me feel celebratory, or excited, or even anything, and couldn't. If I could name just one thing, I thought, resting my face against the window's plastic pebbled edge and feeling the roar of differential atmospheric pressures meeting, it would be okay.

"I bet Stace was stoked about that."

I shrugged. "I guess."

Stacey was impossible, not something I could think about for extended periods, or at all. When we talked it was always a fight waiting to happen, tense and bitter and forced. I could see her now, running her hands back through her hair, pressing it tight against her scalp with her fingers like she wanted to tear it out. Saying, you have to get over it, Cam, and me saying, I'm trying, obviously, obviously I want nothing more than to just get over it, and her saying, you sure have a funny way of showing it, and me saying, nobody asked you to come down here, to do this, and you're free to go, so.

I knew she was jealous of my accelerated success and resentful when I was out of the house, which was almost always, now. The more I worked the less I had to think, and so I worked insane, gargantuan hours, the night security guys who knew me by name letting me out of the building long after dark. Articles appeared in all kinds of journals, and when I looked at the proofs sent to my desk I could hardly believe I'd written them, had ever had the presence of mind to stick these words together into coherent formations. Absent, always, from myself.

Most nights she waited up for me at the kitchen table in oversized shirts and sweats, marking undergrad papers and drinking acidic black coffee in staggering quantities, her eyes narrowed and bagged. You could at least call, she said. How am I supposed to know what you're doing? How do I know if you're coming back at all?

Cliff emptied a jar of pot onto the wide railing, proceeding to roll it, without asking, into a moist blunt paper. I'd been afraid, coming here, that maybe he didn't smoke anymore, and was now serious, and truly adult, but he was just the same, really, just the same in a new context, and that was all. Maybe we were all like that—the same but different, variations on a theme.

"Serious realtor-grade marijuana, huh," I said, wanting to change the subject.

"What? You think I don't grow weed now that I sell fucking houses?"

"I would be disappointed if you didn't."

"As would I, hey. Come on, Cam. This is fucking chateau chez Clifford." He laughed, standing tall to seal the joint, obviously pleased with the quality of his work. "Do the honours?"

"Yeah," I said, sparking it for us, the first inhale dusky and sweet.

"You know, Cam," he said, "you don't have to do anything that doesn't make you happy."

It was so much worse that Cliff already knew this, a cold blow to my chest. "Yeah."

"You're so unhappy."

I'd never put it this way to myself, though I saw now it must be true. Name one thing, I dared myself, just one thing. I knew the thing I would name. I shook my head, passing the joint. "I don't feel the same way about her as I did about him, if that's what you mean. But I mean, I accept that. I don't think I'll ever feel that way again. I just have to take what I can get and make the best of it, you know? I have to try to be happy."

"But you're not."

"No. I don't know what to do, man. I just hope with time it will pass."

He looked at me hard, peering into my face. "Aren't you going to ask?" he said.

"About what?"

"You know. It's why you came here, from so far."

"I came to see you, see how you are."

"You can ask, Cam. Go ahead."

Inside the doorbell chimed its three calm notes. We looked at each other, everything a hanging question. Though the night was warm, I shivered, the motion shifting my shoulders. "Is someone else coming over?"

"No," Cliff said, edging his way to the sliding door and opening it just a crack, sticking his head inside to listen. "I don't think so."

With the glass open we heard the bell go off again, urgently, like someone impatient had pressed it twice in rapid succession. I watched Cliff at the door but couldn't bring myself closer than that, leaning hard on the deck behind me, sagging into the wood. I was somehow, unbelievably, out of breath. We listened, Cliff absently tightening the bun holding up his hair, as Valerie left the kitchen where she'd been updating her blog (*Wake and Bake, Girl*) and playing what must have been Bjork or the White Stripes or some other vaguely garbled shit, her stockings whispering over the hardwood with each drop of her heel. There was the bolt on the door being opened, and then her rich voice steeped in warmth and the pure delight of honest surprise carrying in from the alcove, her accent transforming the name, expanding it into a luxurious foreign thing: *Beau!*

I blanched, feeling the blood leave my face. My hands were cold and damp.

"Shit," Cliff said, meeting my eyes across the deck. For a bad moment I thought I might throw up.

"You didn't tell me he was going to be here," I said, putting out the joint that had been smoking, untouched, in my hand. It sputtered against the wet wood.

"I didn't know! Cam, really, I didn't."

"Cliff, I can't—you should have told me."

Cliff slid the door shut, horrified, and put his back against it as if bracing for an impact from within. "Cam," he said, "he stops by here all the time. He and Val are so tight. I swear I had no idea. I thought he was working tonight."

I put my head in my hands and made a sound like *oh*, feeling suddenly faint. "Are you fucking setting me up? Did you fucking invite him here?"

"Cam, you have to believe me. I would never do that to you. Are you crazy? After what happened? I would never, I swear."

"I can't be here."

"Cam, it's gonna be okay."

"I have to go, man."

"Cam, she's already invited him in."

With the glass closed I couldn't hear them downstairs, and this was good. I found it incredibly difficult to breathe. "Didn't you fucking tell her not to? Doesn't she know?"

He shook his head. "No, she doesn't know, how would she know? What do you think I've told her? I'm sorry, man, I didn't fucking think this through. Listen, it's gonna be okay."

"How can it be okay?" I collapsed over the railing, hanging my head and making a strangled sound into the wood. "I can't see him, Cliff, I can't. I'm so fucked up over this as it is and—"

The sliding door rolled back with the near-hydraulic precision of newly installed equipment not yet warped by cold and moisture and excessive use and Valerie peeked out, her eyes wide with unexpected developments. "Babe," she said, "Beau Larky dropped by. I'm making drinks, you guys want anything?"

"Stiff whiskies, babe," Cliff said. "Like, really stiff, hey," and when she shut the door turned to me, combing his hair back with his fingers. I'd never seen him so panicked. "*Shit*," he said.

"Make him leave," I said, pressing myself to the patio's railing, "make him leave before he knows I'm here."

"She probably already told him you're here. You're probably the reason he's here."

The reason he's here. My heart skipped several beats.

The last time we'd had sex Beau cried the whole time, weeping into the couch while I asked if he was okay and he said yeah, yeah, keep going, I'm just ugh, all over the place. It was Christmas morning, the day bright and crisp and no snow anywhere, colours bleak and washed out by the early sun's stark angle. There was a three-dimensionality about objects, a realness. A return to the plain sense of things. Through the balcony windows the city appeared dusted with dew, ten hundred million droplets of it studding rooftops and lending glitter to streets among long jagged pools of shadow thrown by the light. Afterward I lay beside him and held his face and stroked his temples and said, you know I don't have to go. You know I don't want to.

I didn't even get you a fucking, gift, he said, suddenly affectless in that way he'd developed with the drugs. I didn't know what to get for someone you're sending away.

Leave now, I thought, staring over the city. Sneak through the living room and walk out the door, run down the street and don't look back.

"Cliff, I can't," I said. "I really can't."

"Listen, I fucked up. I fucked this up for you, okay. But I promise I'll fix it."

"What am I supposed to do?"

"Just be chill about it and I'll sort it out. It'll be okay. Trust me."

"Cliff, I'm serious."

He regarded me with helpless sympathy, the kind you give to a person you have to tell that someone they love has died, and I saw that he hadn't know, hadn't set it up, and had no solution I could feasibly use, and understood all at once that it was really going to happen, I was going to come face to face with Beau Larky, have to greet him, say his name. Cliff walked me down the stairs, his hands firm on my shoulders, steering from behind. I was stiff and wooden, moving automatically, as in a dream.

In the kitchen Valerie had poured a full round of tall amber whiskies over those plump-bottomed ice cubes produced by truly exceptional, top-of-the-line refrigerators, and stood smoking another indoor cigarette, arms crossed tight over her no-longer-aproned chest. Three drinks stood lined up on the counter, the fourth held aloft by Beau Larky, who was, unbelievably, smoking, one of Valerie's cigarettes hanging loose between the fingers of the same hand that held the glass.

Though I hadn't seen him in years the sight of him flipped my stomach. He wore a red Hawaiian-print shirt and black jeans and looked, with his clean-shaven jaw, smooth like he'd done it just that morning, or right before he came, like ten million dollars. He was one of those men, I saw, who would only look better with age, filling out and growing pleasingly angular over time, whereas I would stoop and melt and run myself into the ground. But he was different, too, hardened, holding himself tall so that his height didn't appear immediately striking. Or maybe it was standing next to Valerie, who was so petite, that made him seem taller—I couldn't say. His face had developed lines I didn't remember, becoming stark and drawn so he appeared, with his hard eyes, impassive, like nothing could move him. Like if he laughed it would be cutting.

We are adults now, I saw. Now for real.

"Cam," Valerie said, "this is Beau Larky. He's an amazing photographer." She touched his perfect broad shoulder, the motion made without any thought and levelling in its intimacy. "Beau, Cam is a professor of theory at Stanford University. He's in town giving a keynote for a conference."

"I know," Beau said, finding my eyes across the room. "We've met."

"Oh," she said, "no way. Do you know each other through Cliff?"

I shook my head because I couldn't speak, but Beau said, "something like that."

His voice, the sound of it after so long, debilitated me. I stood rooted, torn between wanting to leave and wanting to stay there, right there on that spot, staring at him, taking in this changed person I had so missed, had stifled thoughts of for months and months on end while sitting in air-conditioned California mini-mall coffee shops with sprawling parking lots, watching harried mothers pulling limp, uncooperative toddlers along by the hand or pushing them weakly on swings, resigned and half-asleep in the mid-afternoon heat, the whole time knowing I'd made a colossal, life-altering, irrevocable, can't-ever-take-it-back mistake.

What are you doing, my mother had said, leaving here? What are you doing, moving away from Beau Larky? Is it something he did? Are you guys breaking up? Did you get into a fight? Is it worth it, Cam, for a job? Her torrent of begging questions approximating my own unspoken set.

It's your decision, in the end. In the end you get to decide what you want to do, and I can't tell you otherwise. Looking down at her wine glass, the fourth she'd had since my arrival, tracing the dried ring of red marking its depleted edge. But it saddens me, you know? Because I thought you were different, Cameron. I thought you'd stick it out.

And what had I thought, about myself? A huge, astounding, dizzying quantity of *nothing*. The Valley heat was incredible, unlike anything I could have imagined or prepared myself for, an enormous crushing entity of dry energy baking itself into clay surfaces that continued to cool long into the night. I hoped only that it would transform me, removing these things from my bones.

Cliff elbowed my arm, jarring me back to the cool tobacco-flooded kitchen where Beau was exhaling a hit and ashing his cigarette over the sink. The smoke met with cold air streamed from a ceiling vent and fell, deadened, to the floor. "Sorry, what?"

"I said, how was your flight," Beau told me, touching the rim of the backward Jays cap cocked far back on his head. There was something obnoxious about it, the reversed cap, though it eluded description. I couldn't read his face.

"It was okay," I said, mired in a degree of sick fascination I hadn't known it was possible to feel, pulled and repelled in equal measure. "It was just a connection from New York, so."

"It's a long way," Beau said, expressionless, "from California."

I should go, I thought. I need to get out of here before this escalates into something I can't handle, with how I am, with how long I've been trying to shake this thing. I wanted to sit down but couldn't make the physical motions necessary to initiate this course of action.

Valerie must have actually been a fucking psychic, because she met my eyes dead on and said, firmly but gently, "sit down, Cam," at which point I did, miraculously finding my way to one of the leather-upholstered bar stools clustered around the island. I wondered how I looked, in my radically loosened tie and crisp shirt with the rolled sleeves, to Beau Larky, who had once chilled with me in nothing but boxers and tees, doing bong hits and talking in circles on our battered old couch. The tall stool was not kind to my long frame.

"I bet you're beat," she said, playing with the silver stud in her lower lip, rotating it between her fingers. "You haven't slept in, what?"

"Eighteen hours," I said automatically.

Cliff slid one of the full tumblers across the island's granite surface where I caught it, downing three large gulps all at once. When I set it down the whisky was half gone. As long as I kept the length of the kitchen between us, I thought, it would be okay.

Beau stubbed out his cigarette, dropping the butt into an empty wine glass, and crossed his arms over his chest. He was in incredible shape, the lean muscular structure of his build obvious even through the shirt. It was a ridiculous thing to wear but on him it didn't seem so, sitting naturally, conforming to his solid shoulders as if custom-made. He had the sleeves, though short, rolled a few times, and when he shifted position the right one pulled up enough for me to catch a glimpse of what was definitely a tattoo, complex black lines stenciled on his bicep.

I don't know him anymore, I realized. He is a stranger to me.

"I see you're travelling alone," he said, and I downed the remainder of my whisky.

"Yeah."

"Guess Stace couldn't make it."

"Guess not."

I looked to Cliff for assistance, but he was staring from me to Beau, lost. Valerie moved to replenish my drink, ice tinkling against the glass. "Cliff, babe," she said, leaning in between us, close enough that I could smell her perfume. "I need to talk to you."

"Okay," he said.

"No, like," whispering it through her teeth, into his ear, "I need to talk to you, upstairs. Now."

"Sure babe, no problem, hey."

No, I almost said, looking to Cliff like, are you fucking serious right now?

He stood and shrugged like, *sorry, man*.

"Apologies." Valerie smoothed her hands down her hips where her dress had bunched up. "Me and Cliff just need to get a few crucial things straight. Right now."

She started up the stairs, whisky in hand, doing that pissed-off walk women used when you were about to catch an earful, all legs and hips. I'd seen Stacey stalk across our living room enough times to know. Cliff scrunched up his face like, *fuck*, swigging back the entirety of his drink before trailing along behind. There was the slam of an upstairs door and then her voice, its kindness warped into a low acrid hush rising steadily over his protests.

Beau hadn't moved. He stood by the stove, arms crossed, that jarring bit of ink peeking from beneath his sleeve. "Well," he said, scratching at his jaw. His fingers made a rasping sound, and I realized his shave was not as clean as it seemed. "That's that."

My gut was full of what must have been lead, mouth dry as the fucking Mojave, a thing I had seen for the first time just last year. Vast expanses of cracked dirt, baked earth, and nothing more. That shimmering gasoline-over-tarmac effect truly deadly sun produced.

"Don't tell me you have nothing to say," he said.

The upstairs volume increased, intelligible snatches making it though the din, *are you serious* and *that poor man coming all the way here.*

Beau uncrossed his arms and pulled up a stool across from me, leaning on the counter. I immediately stood, backing away from his sudden proximity and his smell, the smell I hadn't been able to get out of my clothes and blankets even four thousand miles away. Pot and photo chemicals and head & shoulders crisp apple shampoo, fuck.

I wanted to die.

"It's so weird to see you like this, in a tie."

"Yeah, well. I was giving a keynote, so."

"You've changed."

"So have you."

He shrugged, fishing around in his pocket, the motion jangling his keys and what must have been an absurd amount of change, the kind of small change accumulating in the pockets of the distracted, the spacey, and those who can't be bothered. In the pockets of the perpetually stoned. "I don't know why I came here," he said.

"You knew I was in town."

"Yeah, I saw the conference poster. I thought you might be here. I don't know why." He pulled a pack of cigarettes from his shirt pocket and flipped it open, offering them to me.

"You don't really smoke now," I said, taking one, careful not to brush his hand.

"Really."

"Where'd you pick that up from?"

"Fucking, Cliff. Kills time during shoots, you know."

To hear this old placeholder still in use as punctuation weakened me. The moment of pause, an opportunity to collect his thoughts mid-sentence, the rough compositional crutch tossed in the way other people use *like*, or *um*—a thing I'd almost forgotten. It had been so long since I'd last heard his voice.

I watched, mesmerized, as Beau lit his smoke, lowering his head over the flame. He flicked the lighter and held it in my direction, and, seeing my hesitation, slid it across the counter instead. We smoked in silence, listening to the hum of the central air and the crackle of burning paper and Valerie upstairs saying *you must have known he would come*. I wanted to stare at him but restrained myself, gazing at the far wall. I could hardly breathe.

"I heard your talk. I streamed it." He nodded, exhaling an astonishing lungful of cigarette smoke. "*Conditions of possibility*. Incredible fucking, title."

"You shouldn't have come here," I said.

He laughed, the familiar sound muted as if leaking from beneath a layer of glass, contained and not entirely sincere. "I know. Cam," he said, using my name, his tone softening, "don't you think I know?"

Careless, Stacey had called him. Reckless, impulsive, irresponsible. So opaque to himself a mirrored room wouldn't help. I'd never wanted and feared someone so much at the same time.

"I fucking, wish I hadn't," he said, hand straying to his pocket again. A quick dark thing passed over his face. "Hearing your voice like that, after so long, something in me just . . . I don't know. I felt like, I just had to see you. No matter what. It compelled me."

I looked down at the counter where my cigarette had left a trail of ash. *I just had to see you, no matter what*. I knew I should say something but couldn't, didn't know what, or how. Beau Larky telling me my voice had compelled him to show up here and me just eviscerated, husked. Jesus. I was sure he could hear the sick hollow thump of my heart against my ribs.

"Aren't you going to say anything?"

"What do you want me to say? What do you think I would have left to say to you, now?"

I could feel him looking and lifted my head to meet his eyes, immediately wishing I hadn't. Beyond the flat opaque quality of his gaze was a vast emptiness, a desolate desiccated space stretching into distant horizons of need. I thought again of the desert and its endless wasted plain. A hard flicker of something vital and bent and raw moved just beneath—the thing that had made it possible for him to do whatever he'd put himself through. Some special kind of suffering known only to him.

Standing with only the counter between our bodies, I could see that among his dark lush hair some strands near his temples had gone a sort of peppered white. "I'm gonna go," I said, "I have to go."

"Don't go, man."

"No, seriously, I have to fucking go. I can't be here. What do you even think you're doing, coming here? What do you think is going to happen? Jesus. You have no fucking idea what you've put me through." I picked up my briefcase and wedged it under my arm, suddenly angry and hot all over, like I might cry. I would not do this in front of Beau. I would not give him this satisfaction.

Beau stood and made like he might come around the counter but must have thought better, bracing against it instead. "At least hear me out. Before you go. You came all this way, and I won't get another chance."

"What makes you think I want to hear anything you have to say? I didn't come here hoping to see you. I have my own life now, and that's what you wanted, so. I wish you'd just let me be."

He looked at me, biting his lip, and ran a hand back through his hair. "Okay," he said. "That's fair. I can respect that. Okay." Upstairs they'd stopped yelling and calmed down, gentle reconciliatory sounds of preparation for rejoining a group carrying through the ceiling.

"Tell Cliff I'm sorry," I said, "tell him I'll call," and turned before I could think about it too much. Clutching the briefcase I made my way down the hall, heartbeat pulsing loud and arrhythmic in my ears alongside all the desperate fluttering half-baked things his voice had stirred in me. The alcohol loosened my spine and limbs and gave my movements a strange loping quality I could feel as keenly as his eyes on my back, resting on the tender place between my shoulders at the base of my neck. I knew, without looking, that he'd left the kitchen to lean in its doorway, arms crossed over his chest to contain whatever ache resided there.

"Cam," he called, as I opened the door, "I'm sorry too, okay? Just know that I'm sorry."

I stopped for a moment but didn't turn, then made myself close the door behind me. It shut quietly, with the small neat click of custom-fitted hardware falling into place, and then I was alone, outside, breathing Toronto mid-summer humidity deep into my tight aching lungs. The street steamed, the world unbearably verdant and brimming with expectation. A group of students walked by, one of them dancing ahead and saying *come on they're gonna go on in like five man.*

I stared at the stairs, lost, the idea of negotiating these impossible. Oh, I thought. Oh, what am I doing.

The worst thing was that I wanted him even now, that even now after everything I would drop my whole life, everything I had, throw it away for the chance to share his space and smoke morning joints and make sloppy extravagant pancake breakfasts and watch him hanging strips of film to dry and run my hands over his cool smooth skin. To have it the way it had been, before.

I made my way down the stairs but couldn't move further, sitting on the second-to-last step and resting my head in my hands. I could have used the smoke, now. Now I wouldn't have left it there, burning on Cliff's expensive Annex countertop like some vague unfinished thought.

Always so undecided, the thing in me. Always coming or going and never staying in one place.

That final fall I'd packed up all my things, the entirety of my worldly possessions compressed into garbage bags stuffed with clothes and hastily stacked, poorly labelled boxes of books, keeping a cold face though I wanted to cry, to keel over and weep as I removed the traces of my presence in Beau Larky's life from this home we'd shared for years, from this only place I'd ever felt a hundred percent myself. I took no photos, not off the fridge or the walls or any of the framed ones on the bookshelves, leaving them for Beau to deal with. They were, and had always been, his.

Later, trying to find Barthes' *Mourning Diary* among vaguely designated tags scrawled in grief-soaked Sharpie, sitting cross-legged and cutting through packing tape on my first ever salary-funded floor, I saw they'd followed me anyway, dozens of prints folded between pages and little envelopes of negatives used as bookmarks, forgotten about, re-emerging now to tighten my throat and press my weakened body to the carpet. I didn't have the heart to throw them away.

Okay, I'd yelled, the last of the boxes cradled in my arms, *bye, then*, and when he didn't answer went down the stairs into the morning sleet half-dark and loaded it into the back of the Jeep, hands freezing against the wet trunk. Walking around to the driver's side, I looked up at our balcony for what I knew was the last time, thinking I would never step foot in there again, now, never stand out on the deck smoking joints in the velvet dusk or look out those windows as I heated the kettle or watch smoke curling its way through slanted dusty midafternoon light.

I had my hand on the door handle when he came down, pushing through the heavy front entrance, slightly out of breath from the stairs. He stood on the curb watching me, the car's body between us, his drawn pale chemo face stretched with what must have been regret, or pity, or some other thing his enormous distance rendered impossible to read. I watched, limp and gutted, as he came around the Jeep's hood and leaned into my body, putting his arms around my bent frame. I could feel his palms on my back. Bye, he said, stroking my neck. Bye, Cam. Be safe, okay? Hold tight. Be well. And put me in the car and stood on the curb with his arms crossed as I drove away, watching him receding in the rear-view mirror until I turned the corner and all at once, just like that, he was gone.

Sitting here now, head in my hands on Cliff's newly paved entrance steps, I saw I was really no different than the mangled twenty-five-year-old who'd had to keep pulling over on the highway, crying so hard he couldn't see straight, drive straight. By the time I'd hit Nebraska I was raw and silent, watching the white windswept cornfields unfolding before me in their stunning flat expanse, mute wonder at the ceaseless change of human life weighing down my thoughts. That night I pulled into a gas station parking lot and slept in the back seat, waking curled and cold and cramped, a sick wasted thing unfurling in my bruised chest.

I'd gone, I saw now, because I really thought he'd change his mind; that as time passed he would find it hard and realize his mistake. Each day I waited for the call that didn't come as I began to see I'd vastly underestimated his self-reliance, stubbornness, resistance, remembering he'd grown up without anyone to lean on and been fine, and could be fine again, if he so chose. That Beau's greatest motivating desire had never been for parents, or connections, but rather to *make it out of the system*. I sat at my desk and made myself work, stood in the kitchen and forced myself to eat, talked myself out of bed each morning and into the blinding arid sun with a lecture in mind, always fearing I'd get a phone call from someone back home telling me he'd died, or worse.

No one called. No call ever came.

I moved the briefcase from my lap and set it down beside me, thinking, what does it all matter. What does it all mean. I'd spent a decade of my life reading dense texts by articulate people obsessed with these same questions, and felt no closer to any kind of answer. There'd been a time it seemed almost within reach, a thing I could extend myself toward and grasp, if only I tried.

There was a faded weathered skateboard propped against the steps, maybe some neighbourhood kid's or maybe Cliff's. The grip tape was all worn down and near-smooth in places, the edges of the wood rough and chipped. I picked it up and flipped it over between my hands, studying the deck's eroded underside where the paint had been scraped away by an anonymous series of curbs, only small flecks of pink and green remaining in snatches of ghost text.

To feel the familiar, intuitive weight of the deck in my hands calmed me. I set the board down right-side-up on the pavement and put my feet on it, rolling it laterally back and forth while I sat bent over myself and imagined impossible things.

I didn't hear the door open until I saw the sliver of light, its long yellow wedge expanding into a pool before me and casting my shadow down the lawn. "I knew you'd be out here," he said.

I turned and he was behind me, standing at the top of the stairs. He closed the door and sat down, resting his elbows on his knees.

"How did you know," I said.

"Because no way would you leave without hearing me out."

I said nothing, staring ahead into the street.

"And that's what, your fucking, skateboard-plus-briefcase keynote ensemble?"

"Yeah, what you missed out on with the audio was seeing all the post-talk kickflips."

"Do you think you could still do one?"

"Do what."

"A kickflip."

I shrugged. "Probably. It's all muscle memory."

"Do one," he said, propping his head on his hands. "I bet you can. It would be . . . so good to see." It was strange and lonely, the way he said it, lacking any obvious intonation but drenched in feeling all the same.

I shivered. "Really?"

"Yeah."

I found myself standing on the board, balanced over the trucks as I filled my lungs and flexed my knees, feeling out the bolts' looseness and give. I rocked back and forth and without ever really deciding to kicked the deck up, hooking a toe under it to get the right amount of spin. The motion was smooth and instinctive and the board took over for me, working with the force I'd applied to clatter back to the pavement, still firmly under my feet. A brief stunned sound escaped me.

Beau smiled, the expression softening his face into some semblance of its old self. "Your tenure review went through, huh."

That he knew anything about this stunned me. "Word travels fast."

"Congratulations. That was quick, even for you."

"Yeah, well. My progress was accelerated by factors beyond my control, or choosing. I had a lot of time on my hands."

He sat silent, watching me and fingering something in his pocket. There was the distinct hollow click of pills against plastic and I realized he was stoned, enormously mellowed on painkillers or something, and that the strange fragmented quality of his speech was a direct result of the meds he carried around. That maybe he was stoned all the time, halfhearted and vague and leaving his sentences trailing, waiting for others to fill in the implied blanks. My heart clenched.

"And how's that Starbucks managerial gig going for you," I said, aware of the cruelty but unable to stop myself.

"I don't work there," he said, "anymore." And pulled out the bottle, standard orange prescription with the white child-proof top, its transparent plastic chalky with pill residue.

"You do photography, now."

"Yeah," he said, popping the bottle and tossing back a pill. Though the night hummed with insects and cars the crunch of it against his back teeth carried, sounding loud and clear. "Weddings. I shoot weddings." He looked at me pointedly, pocketing the pill bottle.

"What?"

"Congratulations. If you need a photographer, you know who to call."

"I'm not married," I said, quickly, all at once, shaking my head.

"You will be," he said. "You're engaged."

"I don't know where you could have heard that."

"Good news travels fucking, fast, Cam. When's the big day?"

When Stacey told her family they'd thrown her a big celebratory barbeque at her grandfather's Texas home, a sprawling ranch-style bungalow with its own pool and wrap-around deck and smokehouse. I'd stood by and held out my hand to be crushed by an endless stream of meaty relatives whose names I couldn't remember, feeling the blackest thing I'd ever known crouching somewhere just out of sight. I hadn't told anyone.

"She asked me, Beau. What am I supposed to say? She's been there for me through some really bad times, and—" I shook my head, turning away. "I'm just doing my best to be happy with what I have. With the resources available to me."

"And does she make you happy?"

"How can you even ask me that."

"Does she?"

"Sometimes. We're teaching a course together in the fall, so."

He laughed, a horrible hollow sound wrung from a deep withered place. Layers upon layers to Beau Larky, all of them composed of sheer cutting edges. I wanted to lie down and never get back up. "What, Theory of Marital Bliss three-seventeen? Happy Homemaking Methodologies two eighty-nine?"

"Like it would have been my first choice, Beau!" My voice was all over the place and I couldn't rein it back. "Like I wouldn't have done anything to stay with you instead! Like I didn't beg you for months to change your mind while you broke me into tiny fucking bits. Man, fuck you."

"Cam, I'm sorry. It's just, seeing you is . . . I don't know. It's a lot. To see you like this." He folded his hands together where they hung between his thighs, staring at a fixed point just beyond my briefcase.

I kicked up the skateboard from the upside-down position it had assumed during my outburst. I felt like I'd run a great distance, dry-mouthed and breathless and full of a weird frantic energy, like when I'd sat beside him in tenth grade math, palms leaving sweat prints on the desk while I tried to look normal, to look cool as if sitting beside this self-assured kid whose way of slouching back in his chair as he penciled in answers without pause didn't render my whole self flustered and weak, made of thin cardboard exposed to a sudden strong wind. Because I couldn't stop looking, didn't want him to see I was looking at the stacks of numbers piling up on his graph-lined paper, at the curl of dark hair tucked behind his ear. How badly I'd wanted him to like me. How I'd never been so enamoured with someone in my whole life.

Him saying, you don't really get math, do you, and leaning over my notebook to identify the exact points at which my answers had begun to stray. And me floating home, ecstatic and confused.

To do an ollie is easy: apply direct force to the board's tail end and allow the front to snap up, sliding your foot along its length, feeling the grip tape's rasp and resistance against the side of your shoe. I was going to wreck my loafers, and I didn't care. I kicked into it, getting only a few inches off the ground, and landed solid enough to try another, this time clearing a whole deck of air, taking out my frustration on the board.

Beau pulled the smokes from his pocket and lit one, exhaling with his head turned to one side, the gesture conspiratory, like he was about to share crucial information and had to check if anyone might be listening in. "Cam," he said.

"Yeah."

"Do you want to know the reason I'm here?"

I shook my head though I did, though I wanted nothing more, because to hope for this was ridiculous, absurd, and a waste of everyone's time.

"You do."

"No."

He looked up at me, grave, the cigarette sitting loose between his fingers. "How've you been?"

"I've been okay."

"I heard you tried to kill yourself."

I stiffened, stepping from the board, suddenly cold all over. "Who told you that?"

"Twice."

I should go, I thought, I need to go, that he knows this is already too much and I need to leave, get some sleep, take a flight home and figure my life out. I was overcome with a visceral, full-body, almost-like-you're-back-there-again-and-can't-quite-tell-the-difference memory of feeling heavy in my whole self and all my aching cells, sick and hollow and for the first time ever literally eviscerated after they'd pumped my stomach empty of its contents, and then some. To use an expression so much and then forcibly experience its actual meaning is a humbling, life-changing thing.

"Well, obviously it didn't work, so."

"Cam."

I shrugged, overwhelmed.

"Twice?"

"The first time was an accident."

I hadn't meant to, the first time, toying with the idea earlier in the day as I swallowed, numb and unthinking, eighteen Xanax, feeling drowsy and pleasantly distant but not fucked up, not like I was going to lie down and give up the ghost once and for all. Thinking, not without bitterness, that it would have been useful to have some of those serious terminal illness pain-management-grade oxys Beau Larky took so many of. And then forgetting about it, wiping it from my mind, and meeting up with Cliff, who was visiting, and smoking joints, and then downing some beers, and then all the coke, and then whiskies on ice, and then snorting some more coke and the next thing I knew I was on the carpet, Cliff slapping at my face saying what did you take hey come on you need to tell me right now hey Cam come on, and me saying, with some effort, *Xanax*, and him saying how many huh, shaking me when I didn't respond, the world slow and gelatinous and sounds dragged out, distorted and delayed.

Cliff was shockingly calm, more so than anyone had any right to expect him to be, like this was just par for the course and something he'd done a hundred times before. Like I hadn't just overdosed on benzos and cocaine and alcohol. You're going to throw it up, he said, a statement not a question. Right fucking now. Take your fingers (here bringing my hand to my face for me, gripping my still-crooked wrist tight) and stick them down your throat. Fucking do it or I'll do it for you, and don't think I fucking won't, hey. And me saying: *but it's been all day,* all the intonation gone from my speech, and him saying, you are so fucking stupid for someone with a fucking Ph.D.

You know they're gonna pump your stomach anyway, hey, he told me on the way over, the world outside the cab's window sliding by distant and blurred. You fucked up, Cam! You fucked up so bad. And me shaking my head against his sleeve, stubborn and mute, wishing I'd tried harder, the first weak shades of an unshakeable idea beginning to colour the edges of my mind.

Later, in the hospital, where they'd emptied my stomach and flooded my protesting brain with beta blockers, I was put on suicide watch, which meant someone sat by my bed the whole three days, bored young psych interns in mint blue scrubs reclining in a chair in the far corner, reading magazines with earbuds on or flicking through shit on their phones, present to make sure I didn't try to hang myself, or jump out the window, or slit my wrists open with a jagged piece of meal tray plastic, or otherwise remove myself from this life. Check myself out.

Do you want me to call Beau, Cliff said, blowing steam from the top of his seventh caramel macchiato, and I said no, not under any circumstance can Beau know about this, and him saying, isn't that why you did it? I just feel like he should know, and me shaking my head, vehement, cheeks wet with tears I couldn't feel or help producing.

"But the second time you meant it," Beau said.

"Yeah." I couldn't look at him. "The second time I tried."

The second time I really had, severely miscalculating Stacey's return-from-campus time in relation to the amount of time the pills needed to work. Not counting on her obsessive and minute attunement to my psychic state. She'd taken Cliff's place by my bed when he had to head back after the first time, staying to sign me out of the emergency psych ward and never quite leaving, returning a few weeks later to catch part of a lecture series, a pretext for visiting, and then finding a job and getting a place and taking the thing upon herself like I was some damaged object that could, with the right approach, be mended. Like I was a project in severe need of management.

When I awoke I was in a bed not my own and the light was low and grey. Natural light, I saw, filtering into this monochrome room with its plastic-encased machines. A hospital room—I had been in enough of them to know. I tried to flex my hand but it was stiff and bruised, an IV stuck in the back of it and another in my aching wrist. Cliff was there, in a chair by the window, calm and expressionless, absorbing the weak light. He stared into space, hair pulled back in a ponytail and getting truly long. He wouldn't cut it, I saw. He was really letting it out.

When he saw I was awake he smiled and pulled the chair close, careful not to make too much noise. Hey bud, he said, how do you feel, and when I shook my head he said: I bet you feel awful. I bet you wish you were dead.

My mom had always wanted to do stuff for me, and for the first time in my life, I let her. You have to get away from that place for a while, she said, picking me up in her blue Corolla from Toronto Pearson, crushing me to her perfumed chest. You just need to come home and have someone take care of you for a bit. Obviously frightened by my distance and blank display window face.

She drove me to her place, taking the highway in a long blur I hardly registered as I sat stricken, a rapidly cooling cup of coffee pressed tight between my palms. She fed me tea and soup and other things I barely touched as I lay curled on the couch with the TV on or slept all day in the guestroom, covers pulled over my head.

Come on, Cam, she said, at least come sit in the garden, and I did, listless and unresponsive, unmoved by anything external, the spring sun on my skin not a sensation, but a registered fact. In the evenings she sat with me and stroked my head, smoothing back my hair like she used to when I was little and home from school with a bug. Telling me, I know you miss him. I know it feels like it will never get better, and me saying, mom, I just want to die.

Cliff came often, reverent and shy in my mother's home, removing his shoes and hiding his smokes and avoiding profanity as much as he could, making her laugh when he forgot. *Mrs. Dempster*, he called her, and she said, oh no, just Cathy, Cliff, Cathy is fine. Stacey had come too, stilted and awkward in the space until my mom began pulling her aside for kitchen conversations that lasted hours and encouraged her, somehow, pushing her to try. It calmed me, the sound of them making tea or pouring wine and talking in their low maternal voices about me, and how I was, and whether I would improve.

Cam, baby, she said one night, tucking hair behind my ear, a useless self-defeating gesture built of habit and a hard, steadfast, truly adult love. There are people who really care about you, and you can't hurt them like that again, no matter what. You have to pick up and move on, okay, baby? You know Stacey is a wonderful girl. You know you've got things you have to do.

"Cam," he said, "listen, I know, I know I have no fucking, right to be here talking to you right now, but I have to tell you. I was so fucked up by everything that was happening. I needed you to take the job and I knew you wouldn't and I didn't know what else to do. I think I went a little nuts." He dragged deep and tossed the smoke, crushing it beneath his sneaker, hugging his arms and bending over himself. "I couldn't let you turn down that opportunity on my behalf. Do you understand? I knew it would fuck you up, but I never thought . . . I never thought it would be like this."

I shook my head.

"I was so upset, man. Cliff called me and I thought, I have to go see you, I have to go and explain myself and apologize and . . . fuck, Cam. I bought a Greyhound ticket and I was gonna come down, I got on the bus and everything and I rode it for three fucking, days."

"Why didn't you, then?" I said, voice cracking. "I missed you *so much*. I wanted to see you *so bad*. I waited for you to call every single day."

"I don't know. I thought about so many things, Cam. On the bus ride. It had been so long, and I knew Stacey was already down there, and I just thought . . . I don't know. I thought like, what if I come and you don't want to see me, or it makes you worse, or just stretches the whole thing out, or what if you're so different it's scary, or what do I even say to you, now." He shook his head. "And when we hit the Sacramento bus depot I realized I couldn't, I just . . . I couldn't do it. And I cashed in my return ticket early and rode all the way back to fucking, Toronto. I'm sorry, Cam. I don't know why."

"You *don't know why?* You went all the way to Sacramento and then pussied out and you *don't know why?*" Furious because I had always been there for him, always, no matter what, and he'd known I needed him and hadn't come, and had this fucking bullshit excuse of *I don't know why*, like there was anything he even needed to know other than *Cam is in the fucking hospital, hey.*

Charismatic, energetic, warm, she'd said, *but also impulsive, and sometimes directionless.*

There had been times, lying in the grey daylight in a bed not my own, my throat so raw it hurt to swallow and feeling like someone had scraped it down with a scalpel, I'd allowed myself to hope, though Stacey had explicitly warned me not to, that he might come. I imagined, from my strange reversed position, having always been the one sitting by the bedside and not in the bed, on the giving rather than the receiving end, that he would come and take my IV-taped hand and tell me—what? That he was sorry, that he'd made a mistake. That he missed me. Lying there, after the second and infinitely more serious time, listening for familiar footfalls in the hallway, I'd almost certainly thought he would, and when he didn't I allowed myself to drift into a blank haze, losing strings of hours to sleep, or something like it.

You asked for him repeatedly, Stacey told me afterward. Over and over.

"I was scared, Cam," he said. "I didn't know what to do."

"You knew I needed you and you *left me.* I almost *died.*" The effect his presence, his actual real physical immediacy less than three feet away had on me was beyond anything I could have prepared myself for, even if I had known. My chest brimmed with ten thousand words, all the words I'd choked down and repeated internally for months and months while I dragged myself around and tried to approximate wellbeing, stability, balance. "You could have at least called," I said. "The way I worried about you was just—ugh. It just wasted me. I can only take so much."

"I'm sorry, Cam. You have to know I'm so sorry. It wasn't right, what I did to you." He put his head in his hands and pressed his palms to his cheeks, as if trying to ascertain they were still there. Numb-faced, I thought. Numb-faced and stoned.

And then just like that I was so mad, like I'd been when he shut himself up in the darkroom those last few weeks, sentimental Paul Simon garbage leaking from under his door at all hours, "Something So Right" and fucking "Hearts and Bones," an unbearably sad song that just gutted me which he must have put on repeat and played like, thirty-five times in a row, stoned out of his mind on oxy and whatever the fuck else they'd prescribed him, because it was easier that way, and me hammering on his door after some extended crying jag, saying, *will you stop playing that fucking song, please, would you just fucking stop it.*

"I can't believe you," I said, "coming here and saying this shit to me. Stoned off your face."

"I know, I know."

"Five *years*, Beau."

"I know. There's really nothing I can say. Except that I've missed you, Cam, I've missed you like . . ." he shook his head.

How long I'd waited for him to say that.

He looked up at me, no longer distant but shaken, like great internal plates were moving within, a shifting geology I no longer knew, and stood, and did the last thing I could have imagined, getting down on his knees before me and taking my hands in his.

"Beau," I said, recoiling, and almost toppled back over the skateboard.

"Listen, listen. You know why I'm here."

"No."

"You do, though."

His hands were cool and firm and dry, and he smelled like he always had, darkroom and pot and now cigarettes, and some cologne I didn't recognize. "Beau, come on."

"I've come here to convince you to take me back, at any cost. Okay. To forgive me. I made a huge, huge mistake, and I understand if I can't take it back, but I have to at least try."

"Beau," I said, "come on. Get up."

"No, Cam, this is serious. I'm serious, I've never been so serious."

"This is crazy," I said, dry-mouthed and weak. "I don't even know you. You're a stranger to me."

"I don't know you either, anymore, but seeing you I just— I fucking, know you feel it too, I know you do. Don't you, Cam. Be honest."

"Am I so obvious?"

"I miss your obviousness. I miss how you can't hide shit. I miss all your books lying around and how fucking, quiet and far away you get, and smoking joints, and marathon movie sessions, and cooking for you, and waking up in the morning with your fucking—" he looked away, shutting his eyes, and I saw this was hard for him, that he must have practiced saying this but still found it challenging, and that his grip on my hands had tightened, like he was afraid I'd pull them away, "your fucking, long warm body in the bed. And your glasses, fuck. I miss all of it."

"Beau, come on. You have to stop. I can't."

"Because you want me, don't you. Still."

"How can you say that to me."

"Because you do, I know it."

I shook my head, flushed, the whole thing like meeting him all over again, being sixteen and off-kilter and wordless.

"Don't leave, Cam. Come back to my place and we'll smoke bowls, play some Scrabble. For old time's sake."

Come back to my place. I swallowed, staring at him openly, knowing he could see my unchecked desire. Reckless, I thought, that he would ask me this, knowing fully well my inability to say no. I hadn't played Scrabble in years but remembered our old board, the special fiftieth-anniversary edition with its expanse of green felt, like a pool table or lawn, made more pleasant to play on than cardboard by the lush muffled sound the wooden letters made when laid down. The board he must have, still, because I'd left it and almost everything else, understanding for the first time the power of objects, their muteness actually a kind of absorption, carrying energies long forgotten and temporally displaced.

Within the set bounds of this board, fifteen by fifteen squares, anything could happen. A perfect representation of the nature of potential—within these limits, infinite possibilities. Never the same game twice.

It's some stoner game you used to play with him, Stacey said when I refused to join her and a friend in an impromptu San Francisco Sunday café session, *isn't it*.

"I fucking suck at Scrabble," I said, "and you always win."

"Not always."

"Almost always."

He laughed, the sound shaky and provisional. He was nervous, I realized. Though his hands stayed so still. "It's because," he said, "you have no sense of strategy. You just try to make the most interesting words. Objectively, you should be a way better player than me."

"Because I forget that it's a competition."

"You get caught up in the shape of the word. And its feel."

"Things that don't matter."

"But they do, Cam, I see now that they do. It's like what you said, at the party, about potential. Do you remember? About changing your angle, and the profound thing being right there, in front of you."

I had chewed down, without thinking, the whole inner lining of my left cheek, and now ran my tongue over its raw mangled surface.

"Or your talk, that I—that compelled me. About what makes things possible, or impossible."

"Beau," I said, tracing his set adult face, its new severity and old playfulness in direct contrast yet forged in the same place, shaped by the same fissures and upheavals and mediating calms lying like seas between. "You have to get up."

"Say you'll come."

"I can't, you know I can't. How can I do that."

"Please. This is me asking you. Just come."

His hair had straightened in the humidity, falling over his forehead and the tips of his ears, flattened down by the hat's rim. Up close the white strands stood out in jarring contrast, stirring some dormant quickening thing in my ever-clenching chest.

Pity, I realized. It had been hard for him, too, in ways I didn't understand.

"No one's ever hurt me like that," I said.

"Cam. I admit that I needed you and didn't let myself. I couldn't let myself go with you, I don't know why. I couldn't bring myself to ask you to stay. I admit it now."

"I'm just so mad at you. I can't see how I'd ever be less mad."

"I'll make it up to you, Cam. Just say you'll come."

"That's what you said last time, and look."

"I know. But I have to convince you. Please just fucking, come."

I would be lying if I said that having Beau on his knees like this, begging me, visibly frightened that I would refuse him, didn't satisfy some deep lonely desire for symmetry I'd carried within since I'd first seen him on that rain-slicked porch. "And what?"

"And I'll show you my insane darkroom. And I have beers and joints and Scrabble. And we can talk. Please, Cam. Just grant me this one fucking, thing."

"And you'll, what, sell me on a wedding package?"

"You'll come, then?"

"Yeah, I'll come."

He pressed his brow to my knuckles, exhaling audibly. "Thank you."

"Now come on, get up."

He stood and took off the baseball cap, tipping his head back and turning his face upward, eyes closed. I was flattened by a gut-level memory of walking with him in the market, the July sky white with heat and the atmosphere a vacuum, soundless and still as it is right before a summer downpour. And when it started raining, the water coming down heavy and all at once in a great silent curtain with its attendant hush, Beau saying, *shit*, and curling over himself to shield the Nikon with his body, and when we couldn't find an overhang running and stretching the neck of his t-shirt to hide the camera beneath, laughing like he might not stop.

"You have to cool it," I said, taking a deep shaky breath, "because I'm pretty overwhelmed. Seeing you after so long."

"I know, I know. I'm sorry. So am I."

I kicked up the skateboard and placed it by the steps, then picked up my briefcase, breathless and nervous and stoned. I felt myself suspended at the edge of some unfolding tentative thing, wavering on its threshold and fearing its undefined shape.

"We'll just take it easy," Beau said, seeing that I really did mean to follow him down the sodium-lit street, hands in my pockets and briefcase under my arm. "We've only really just met."

ACKNOWLEDGEMENTS

This book was written under enormous financial stress in Recession-era Toronto without assistance from any public arts funding body, MFA program, or patron. Despite this, it is the product of one of the happiest times of my life, and a record of the kind of existential magic everyone should get to feel at least once.

Thanks to the wild and beautiful group of friends who shared my joy and formed the fabric of my days—you know who you are. I'm particularly grateful to the following people: Bailey Gardner, my Ideal Reader, who read and re-read multiple drafts of this novel with a genuine and undiminished enthusiasm that is every author's wet dream—thanks for always believing in this project, and for enjoying it so much. Tory Hetherington, who I'm lucky to have known, and who has always been way too kind to me—thanks for your love, support, and guidance, and all those aimless days and raucous nights. Chris Needham at NON, for taking a chance on this book and being so very cool about the process—I'm grateful for the opportunity. Angie Fey at Speakeasy Tattoo, for designing such a dope cover. Mylène Gamache, who generously took the time to fix my mediocre French—*merci beaucoup, mon amie*. And most of all, Jason Smith, my best friend and constant companion, who showed me that real love is a process, and that sometimes it's hard. That shit was deadly romantic.

Finally, thanks to you, the reader, for taking time out of your day to spend a few hours with Cam and Beau. If you enjoyed their adventures even half as much as I do, please tell your friends about this novel, and take a moment to post a review on Goodreads or Amazon (or both). To a small press author, your support makes all the difference.

Curious about what happens next? Check out camandbeau.ca for updates on a sequel, *Middlemen*, coming soon.